Mercy brought forth the leather bag containing her mother's diamond bracelet. She held the pouch at arm's length, as though the highwayman were something unclean. "Here," she said. "Take it and be gone." She threw the pouch at him as hard as she could, but he caught it neatly.

"Contempt makes you even prettier," he declared softly. "Two favors before I go."

He reached out and caught hold of the thin gold chain of a small, heart-shaped locket that encircled Mercy's neck. He tugged, the chain broke and the locket fell into his hand. "Please," Mercy said, "there's little value in my trinket. You can't get more than a few shillings for it."

"I have no intention of selling it," the Gentleman replied. "I shall keep it as a memento of our first meeting. In return permit me to bestow a small gift on you, Mistress Mercy. This is a little out of my line, but I must demonstrate to your young friend down the road that I take orders from no one."

He stood directly in front of her now, though he kept the pistol trained on Peter Staples and the coachman. Bending toward the girl, he lifted his mask part way up his face, to a point just above his lips. He kissed her hard, full on the lips, then leaped away. In a moment he disappeared into the screen of trees. "Thank you," he called happily, "we'll both remember that!"

Long after the highwayman had gone, Mercy could still feel the strong yet surprisingly tender touch of his lips against hers. And she wondered if his motive had been to defy Peter and teach him a lesson rather than because he found her irresistably attractive.

Other titles in the Ace Hall of Fame series:

DAUGHTER OF EVE

THE SCIMITAR

The Highwayman

NOEL B. GERSON

ace books

A Division of Charter Communications Inc.
A GROSSET & DUNLAP COMPANY
360 Park Avenue South
New York, New York 10010

THE HIGHWAYMAN

Copyright © 1955 by Noel B. Gerson

An ACE Book

Published by arrangement with
Hall of Fame Romantic-Historical Novels Inc.,
Produced by Lyle Engel

First Ace printing: March 1979

Printed in U.S.A.

FOR CYNTHIA

The [Louisburg] expedition was one of the wildest undertakings ever projected by sane people

—BENJAMIN FRANKLIN

Contents

Mercy

BOOK ONE

ONE

A TRIP down to Boston was always exciting, particularly this year, when life in the Maine District had been so quiet. Margery Mercy Pepperrell leaned back against the thinly padded cushions of the coach and smiled to herself in anticipation of the days to come. She knew that her parents wanted to return home to seashore Kittery in time for the forthcoming holiday season, but there was always the chance that her father's business with Governor Shirley would keep them in the capital of the Massachusetts Bay Colony longer than they expected. And that would mean spending Christmas in the city.

Each of her nineteen Christmases, Mercy reflected, had been spent in the huge mansion at Kittery, and each of them had been alike. Neighbors had come from miles around, even from the town of Portsmouth directly across the Pascataqua River in the new colony of New Hampshire, to pay their respects to New England's leading merchant and his lady. And Mercy, bored with the talk of her elders, had spent hours alone in her room, staring out at the gray-green waves of the Atlantic as they had rolled onto the beach that fronted the family property.

3

Although she suspected that she was the envy of every young woman who had ever heard of her, Mercy thought that there were distinct drawbacks to being the daughter of so wealthy and influential a person as William Pepperrell. She could never relax; she had to remember at all times who she was and she needed to exercise constant care in what she said. As if echoing her thoughts, her mother, sitting opposite her, coughed sharply in warning.

"Sit up, Mercy!" she said in a voice that had once been musical. "A lady never slouches."

"Yes, Mamma." Mercy responded automatically, unthinkingly, then caught her father's eye.

William Pepperrell lowered his left eyelid slowly and grinned surreptitiously before transferring his attention back to the thick pile of papers he was studying. A feeling of gratitude stole over the girl, and she thought that all the things New England said and felt about her father were true. There was no one in all of the New World who was his equal.

He did not look his distinguished role, however. Despite his height, he was certainly overweight, and the benign expression on his face, the mild look in his pale blue eyes belied his reputation as an Indian fighter, diplomat, and trader whose name commanded as much respect in London as it did in Boston, Philadelphia, and New York. It was somehow typical of him, Mercy thought, that he, who had done more than any other man to pacify and civilize this seventy-mile strip from Kittery Point to Boston, should pay as little heed to his surroundings as if he were riding across his own estate.

Even while she admired her father, Mercy resented his preoccupation with business matters. It seemed wrong—and disturbing—that he should fail to share her enthusiasm and sense of anticipation. She looked out at the thick forests of oak and blue pines that lined this stretch of the rutted road between Salem and Lynn, then shifted restlessly, but discreetly, on the seat. An almost limitless sea of trees, with settlers' farms scattered here and there in clearings, was nothing new to her.

What was far more important were the styles currently in fashion in Boston. She had tried to discuss this vital topic with her sister, Elizabeth, but that young matron was too busy preparing a nursery for the expected arrival of Master Pepperrell's first grandchild to fret herself over the dip of a neckline or the length of a hem. It would be useless to ask her mother's opinion, Mercy was sure, positive that her only reply would be a long lecture on modesty and decorum.

And it was small comfort to know that Peter Staples, her father's principal aide, who rode a gelding just within eyesight outside her carriage window, was beaming at her. No matter what she wore, Peter would be delighted; no matter what she said, Peter would be enchanted; no matter what she did, Peter would think it perfect. Feeling his glance on her, she allowed her eyes to meet his for an instant and smiled. He was so pleased that she felt guilty over taking his attention for granted.

There was something wrong with her, she told herself sternly, for not responding more enthusiastically to Peter's open adoration. For a young man not yet thirty he had come far in the world; her father said he was as sharp and shrewd a trader as could be found in all of York County. He had fought bravely against the Penobscot Indians on many occasions and was highly regarded everywhere. And only recently he had been appointed secretary of the inter-colonial war council, a high honor. Surely Peter would be a good match for any girl, and there were many, Mercy knew, who considered him handsome. His blond hair was crisp and wavy, his eyes were as blue as her father's, and his shoulders were strong and broad. She was more than a little unfair when she ignored him, yet she was not looking forward to being caught by him under the mistletoe on the eve of the New Year. She was convinced that 1745 would be a very special year, for her friend

Amanda Timkins had told her as much when they had secretly read tea leaves together. But Peter would hardly be one to make the year particularly significant; although he was constantly under foot and was accepted by the entire family as her suitor, he was not her idea of an exciting man. He could not sweep her off her feet in 1745 or any other year.

Mistress Pepperrell touched her husband on the arm, and Mercy looked at her parents curiously. It was an unspoken family rule that her father must never be interrupted or disturbed in his work. "Will, dear—I'm still upset."

Annoyed, but controlled as always, Pepperrell sighed and patted his wife's hand. "There's nothing in this world to fear, Mary. I've told you as much a score of times."

"All the same, my bracelet is valuable." Her double strand of diamonds was famous throughout the colonies, and Mercy thought it typical of her mother to describe it merely as valuable. The stones were matched, and no other gems owned by any lady in the New World could compare with them. What was more, they had been a personal gift from the King when William Pepperrell had concluded a complicated deal with a group of French fur traders that had added appreciably to the wealth of George II.

"Very well, my dear." Mercy believed that her father was the most patient man alive. "You know I can refuse you nothing, not even your whims." He leaned forward and rapped on the ceiling of the carriage. "Murchison!" he called to the driver, his normally quiet voice loud and penetrating, "pull over to the side of the road and halt."

In a few moments the team of blooded geldings was drawn to a stop so expertly that the occupants of the carriage suffered a minimum of jolts and bumps. Peter had already reined in his mount, and he opened the carriage door before the driver could step down from his box. He glanced inquiringly at his employer, and Pepperrell, indicating with a faint nod that he wanted no discussion in front of Mercy, climbed out.

The girl pretended complete indifference and studied the stitching on the gloves she had sewn for herself just last week, but she listened intently, and, as she knew her father's voice so well, she was able to hear most of what was said. She missed his first remark and Peter's reply, but then the men warmed to their topic and became a little less cautious.

"There will be no need for firearms, Peter." William Pepperrell was crisp and firm. "I permit no shooting in the presence of women. What's more, you're far too important to me and to Massachusetts Bay to risk your life unnecessarily. And I certainly don't trust Murchison's aim at close quarters with that ancient horse pistol he carries."

Peter protested vehemently, and his disappointment was clear to Mercy, though his words were mumbled. But there was no mistaking her father's emphatic answer. "We're wasting time. If we expect our dinner in Lynn at noon we'll need to keep on the move. Can't you understand, Peter? There will be no unpleasantness, I'm sure. I'm merely catering to my lady's mood."

Accustomed to being obeyed without argument, he terminated the conversation by turning back to the carriage and looking up at his wife. She smiled at him with the complete trust of a woman who has accepted her husband's judgment as final for a quarter of a century. He was taking action in her behalf, and she felt at peace.

"I'll take those beads, Mary," he said. "I'll put them in my safekeeping until we reach Boston."

Without question she slipped the diamonds from her left wrist and handed them to him. He quickly dropped them into his deerskin workbag, handling them as though they were bits of glass like those he manufactured in a small plant at Portsmouth for trade with the Indians. Then he slipped the documents he had been reading into the bag, and these he fingered so carefully, making certain they were neither folded nor crushed, that Mercy could not restrain a smile.

She was tired of sitting, and if the men could stretch their legs, so could she. Her mother might object, but she could remain in the cramped carriage no longer, and she jumped to the ground. The woods were very still, the countryside seemed deserted, and suddenly she understood the meaning of the others' actions, the significance of what they were taking such pains to conceal from her. She laughed aloud, triumphantly.

"I know!" she said happily. "It's the Gentleman."

Peter was at her side in a moment. "Who told you about the Gentleman?" he demanded.

"Andy!" Merriment bubbled up in her anew. "I thought he was teasing me, but he meant every word."

"I shall have words with Andrew when we return to Kittery," Pepperrell said quietly, "for filling the mind of his sister with nonsense. He should know better than to frighten a child."

Peter Staples thought that never had the word "child" been less applicable. Mercy was an adult woman, as ripe as any man could want, and Peter wanted her badly. Her long, red curls sparkled even in the weak sunshine of early December, her lips were full and provocative, and her mischievously lovely green eyes showed both maturity and intelligence. Not even her long, beaver-lined cloak could hide her high breasts, her tiny waist, or the long line of thigh and leg. Mercy was very much a woman, and only in the eyes of her parents could she still be considered a "child."

Unabashed by her father's stern tone, she grinned cheerily at him. "Just imagine!" she teased. "William Pepperrell afraid! I never thought I'd see the day, Papa! And particularly when your opponent is neither a regiment of troops nor the royal treasurer of His French Majesty, but merely a seedy and disreputable cutpurse."

New England's most prominent citizen became very

busy rearranging papers with meticulous care inside the leather bag, which was resting on the floor of the carriage. He examined sheet after sheet, then folded it, and it was some minutes before he replied. "There have been rumors," he said with a casual indifference, intended to soothe his wife, to whom his words were actually addressed, "about a highwayman who has allegedly been very active in these parts of late. You know how these stories start. Each little tidbit is embroidered and enlarged until it bears no resemblance to the truth. This particular devil is supposed to treat his victims with gentlemanly respect. And so some incurable little romantic," he added, frowning faintly in Mercy's direction, "has given him the name of 'the Gentleman.' "

The girl seemed so interested that Peter felt compelled to contribute his bit to the subject. "There's more to this fellow, the Gentleman, than meets the eye, Mercy," he said. "Some claim he's a baronet who left England after a particularly nasty scandal. But others say he was born right here in New England. That doesn't quite fit, as his manners are a little fancy. You know how folk hereabouts have a pretty plain upbringing."

"Peter," William Pepperrell interjected heavily, "you've made great progress in the past few years. But you still have two lessons to learn. Never repeat information other than facts that you yourself know to be true. And never under any circumstances gossip with women."

"Yes, sir."

Mercy gigled suddenly and threw her arms around her father's neck. "If Peter hadn't told me, I'd have pestered you until I learned every bit as much from you. So you should be grateful to him instead of annoyed, Papa."

The great man contented himself with an unintelligible grunt, but his lips twitched suspiciously. Then, with care, he removed a floor board from the carriage, just inside the entrance, and revealed an area approximately three feet square and eight inches deep that was carved out of the solid oak of the chassis. He placed his deerskin bag inside, replaced the board, and stepped to the ground. Picking up a few pinches of frozen dirt, he smeared the earth over the cracks until there was no visible sign that the board concealed a hiding place.

Then he handed his daughter into the carriage and followed her in. Peter remounted his gelding as Murchison slammed the door shut and climbed up onto his box. Mercy was not content to let the subject drop, and after a moment or two she raised her head. "It seems to me," she said, speaking loudly over the creaking of the wheels, "that the Gentleman must be marvelously brave."

"What an unladylike observation." Mary Pepperrell was shocked.

But the head of the family maintained his unruffled demeanor. "What's so all-fired brave about him, Mercy?" he asked. "Only a coward wears a mask and attacks helpless travelers."

"I wouldn't say that they're so helpless," the girl responded spiritedly, tossing her red curls. "I'd say a man had to be something more than a coward to take Colonel Storer's papers from his wallet, especially as the colonel had an escort of eight armed militiamen at the time. And what about Moses Butler? I've often heard you say there's no fiercer man in Maine than Captain Butler—"

"He's a crude ruffian," her mother murmured.

"He's more than that," Mercy said. "He has the strength of—of a bear. All you need to do is take one look at him to know that the brute has great power in his hands and arms. But do you know what the Gentleman did, Mamma? After he took Moses Butler's moneybag, and Butler jeered at him for hiding behind the protection of his pistol, he offered to fight the captain with his bare fists."

"I take it that Andrew is the source of your information?" A bleak look came into William Pepperrell's eyes, and his whole appearance changed. He became grim and hard, and was the jovial overweight merchant no longer.

Mercy knew this mood well, but her loyalty to her brother prompted her to come to his defense. "Andy only repeats what he hears around Kittery, Papa. He means no harm, and I encourage him, you know. I love to hear the stories he brings home."

"You've allowed the boy too much freedom, Will." Mary set her mouth in a prim line. "Some day he'll be in real trouble, wandering like he does into ordinaries and taverns. A Pepperrell shouldn't associate with drovers and common seamen and fisherfolk."

"A boy is brought up different than a girl," her husband said doggedly, instantly reviving an old argument. "But I promise you I'll have a long talk with Andrew when we go home, and I'll lecture him on what's proper to be repeated to a lady."

It was difficult for Mercy to hold back a flippant retort, but she knew all too well that both she and her younger brother would be punished all the more severely if she made an issue of the matter. If she said nothing, perhaps the incident would be forgotten during the course of the busy visit to Boston. If Andy were forbidden to repeat gossip to her, life would become even more dull than it already was, and she vowed to exercise greater caution in what she repeated in the presence of her parents hereafter. Unless she took positive steps to prevent every avenue of fun and excitement from being cut off, she would assuredly become a perfect model of propriety, but she would surely die of boredom, too.

And she had no intention of using her sister Elizabeth's method of escape. Both she and Andy thought that Elizabeth had made the mistake of her life when she had married Nathaniel Sparhawk, now a junior partner in William Pepperrell's many ventures. There was no more sober, virtuous or hard-working man anywhere than Nathaniel, but Elizabeth rarely laughed any more, and she who had once been as gay and mischievous as any girl in the entire Kittery-Portsmouth area was now as gravely, primly decorous as her mother.

Mercy averted her eyes when she saw Peter Staples staring discreetly and intently through the window at her as he held his horse to an easy canter, and she wondered whether he would grow to be as stiff and unbending as Nathaniel if he became a member of the family. Sudden wealth did strange things to some people, as her mother was so fond of pointing out to her, and she had to admit to herself that she didn't actually know Peter well enough to judge him correctly.

He was unquestionably competent, or William Pepperrell would not have loaded him with responsibilities; already he was in charge of the family's shipping interests, which were vast and complex. The settlers obviously liked him and respected his abilities as a soldier, otherwise he would not have been elected captain of a militia company at such an early age. But Mercy thought as she studied him that she had yet to learn whether he possessed a sense of humor. And she could not decide whether the carefulness of the court he paid her was due to fear of her father or a lack of real ardor. Before the visit to Boston was completed, she told herself, she intended to discover a great many things about Master Staples.

The carriage jolted to a sudden stop, and Mercy's reveries came to a halt. Her father, impatient as always at delays, slid back the aperture in the carriage roof and peered up at his driver. "What's wrong, Murchison?" he barked.

"Sorry, sir," The man tugged respectfully at the broad brim of his soft hat. "But there be a tree fallen acrost the path up yonder, just this side o' the crick."

The merchant opened the carriage door and jumped to the ground. Surveying the situation ahead, he smiled thinly; a stout oak sapling blocked the road on the near side of a little creek, which the team and carriage would have to ford, and a heavy growth of trees on both sides of the path made a detour around the obstruction impossible. Walking with a nimble step surprising for a man of his bulk, Pepperrell examined the offending tree trunk, then kicked it experimentally with the toe of his expensive boot. It had been cut down very recently, and the gashed end was still sticky with sap.

Peter, who had dismounted, joined him, and Murchison stood a few feet behind them, not daring to express an opinion until he was asked for one. "The three of us," Pepperrell said, "can move the infernal thing in a few moments." He started unbuttoning his greatcoat.

"Murchison and I can do the job," Peter protested. "The log is wet, and you'll dirty your clothes, sir."

"A little honest dirt never hurt anyone," was the calm rejoinder. "Let's see to this. Murchison, take the far end there. You'll act as anchor man, and we'll swing the trunk toward your side of the road. Peter, give me a hand."

In a moment all three were straining as they slowly lifted the tree. As they raised it to their shoulders and started to carry if off the road, a tall, slim figure appeared from behind the screen of brown foliage behind them.

"Don't move, gentlemen," a pleasant baritone voice instructed them. "Remain precisely where you are."

Staring in openmouthed amazement, they saw a heavily armed, elegantly dressed man approaching them. In his right hand he carried a cocked dueling pistol, and two more were jammed into his broad belt. In his left hand was a long sword that shone blue in the wintry sunlight. The stranger wore a jaunty, narrow-brimmed hat which sported a long silver plume, and over his face was a mask made of silver-colored silk. Over his shoulders was flung a white cape, and beneath it, the essence of flamboyance, he was attired in white breeches and jacket of fine white broadcloth, superbly tailored to show off his handsome tall frame. There was a ruffle of white lace at his cuffs, and his spotless stock was of creamy white silk. His boots, a rich brown, lent the sole note of color to his costume.

Only his dark eyes showed through his mask. His hat covered his hair so completely that it was impossible to tell its shade or texture, but his long, slender hands were without callouses, indicating that he was unaccustomed to manual labor. He carried himself with an insolent air as he swaggered toward the trio, who watched him helplessly while they balanced the fallen tree on their shoulders. Peter Staples looked as though he wanted to hurl himself at the interloper, and Murchison's face was a deep reddish purple. Only William Pepperrell was in command of himself, and it was to him that the highwayman addressed himself.

"I've been anticipating this occasion for some time, Master Pepperrell," he said smoothly, tucking his naked blade under his arm and carefully unbuckling the merchant's own sword. "You'll forgive my familiarity, but I leave nothing to chance." He hurled the weapon in the underbrush, then proceeded to remove a pistol and sword from Peter. These he tossed out of harm's way, too, and Murchison's heavy pistol quickly followed. "Ah, that's better. Now all of us can relax, knowing that no one will be hurt." His voice was pitched deliberately low, in the manner of an actor trying to disguise his normal way of speaking.

"Damn you," Peter growled, "you'll hang for this effrontery. You can't attack a man of Colonel Pepperrell's importance with impunity. Every militiaman in Maine, every soldier in Massachusetts Bay will be on your trail."

The Gentleman bowed in mock solemnity. "I shall heed your warning, young sir," he said, "and I assure you that I shall take every precaution to protect my neck, for it is very precious to me." His nimble fingers searched through Peter's clothing, and he removed a gold watch and a fat wallet with casual dexterity.

Pepperrell watched him with an air of seeming benevolence. "There is no need to search me for my valuables," he said mildly. "You'll find the sum of forty pounds in a small moneybag in my upper right hand breast pocket. My watch is in my fob pocket."

"Thank you, Master Pepperrell." The highwayman sounded grateful. "Those who co-operate with me have no cause to regret it." He found the moneybag and juggled it for a moment. "You'll suffer no more than a momentary inconvenience, to be sure. Here, sir, I'm returning five pounds to you. That should be ample to pay for food and lodging on the remainder of your journey. Your agents in Boston will provide you with funds when you arrive there. As for your driver, I shall take nothing from him. I make it my policy never to accept money from those who are poorer than I."

"Your solicitude is very touching, young man. If you are brought before me in my capacity as king's magistrate-in-chief for the Maine District, I shall recommend clemency. I will urge that you be hanged immediately and not be made to suffer the additional penalty of a one-hundred-stroke whipping first."

"I'm glad we understand each other so well, sir." The Gentleman moved off a pace or two and glanced casually in the direction of the carriage. "Now, if you'll forgive me for a moment, gentlemen, I want to pay my respects to the ladies."

Peter Staples dropped his hands from the tree trunk and glared at the man. "If you harm Mistress Pepperrell or her daughter, I'll kill you here and now!" he cried.

The highwayman chuckled appreciatively, but the sword was again in his left hand and the point was poised a scant two inches from Peter's throat. "Place your hands on the sapling," he directed crisply, though an echo of amusement remained in his voice. "That's better. I assure you, my hot gallant, that my last intention in this world is to cause the good ladies any harm, much less to show them any lack of respect. If I were you, however, I would have a care. I assume you value your own skin. You are in grave danger of losing it." He allowed the tip of the sword to touch Peter's Adam's apple lightly, then he moved off down the road, walking backwards.

Watching him, the helpless trio saw that he continued to eye them and that he held the pistol ready for instant use. William Pepperrell smiled, and he spoke as much for the benefit of the robber as for the instruction of his companions when he said, "Take him at his word, it's better to be safe and alive. We'll have our vengeance, though it be not today."

The Gentleman raised his sword in a salute of appreciation, then stood a short distance from the open door of the carriage and called out softly, "Be good enough to come out, ladies, and forgive me if I fail to doff my hat in your presence."

"If you touch Mercy," Peter shouted, "you'll have to kill me first!" Dropping his hands from the sapling, he started down the road.

But the highwayman reacted instantly. His pistol cracked, and the ball tore through the crown of Peter's hat, knocking it to the dirt. In almost the same motion he jammed the weapon into his belt and removed the second pistol, which he cocked expertly with his thumb. Peter, momentarily stunned, stood still.

William Pepperrell was alarmed but did not lose his head. "Peter, come back here," he called sharply. "And don't behave like a damned idiot. He has no intention of harming either of the ladies."

Peter's face was flushed, and he continued to stand his ground stubbornly, glaring at the Gentleman. He opened and closed his fists repeatedly, but the highwayman's fresh pistol held him in check. He was powerless, and at last he had the sense to realize it. "All right," he muttered finally through clenched teeth. "But if he as much as touches Mercy, I'll track him down if it takes the rest of my life."

The Gentleman laughed. "Be good enough to rejoin Master Pepperrell. Your antics amuse me, but I don't have all day to loiter on a public road."

The aide turned, moved back up the road, and took his place along the length of the sapling. Pepperrell, vastly relieved, smiled thinly. "Mary, you may come out now.

You too, Mercy. Do exactly as he instructs you. And Peter, there will be no further need to demonstrate your bravery. I propose that this unpleasant incident be concluded as quickly as possible."

Mary Pepperrell descended without a word, her head high, two bright spots burning in her cheeks. Mercy, to whom the incident was exciting beyond her wildest dreams, jumped lightly to the ground, her eyes shining. The Gentleman studied her for an instant, his dark eyes intent. Then he bowed again to her mother.

"My felicitations, Mistress Pepperrell," he said, and Mercy thought she detected a very faint but distinct trace of a foreign accent. "Your husband's fame and your own reputation for generous hospitality are widespread, but word should be trumpeted from the hilltops that your daughter is the most beautiful girl in all of the New World."

Neither his pistol nor his sword intimidated Mary Pepperrell. "Keep a civil tongue in your head," she snapped. "And you'll oblige me by refraining from ogling Mercy. Of all the brazen——"

"I'm abashed, ma'am," he interrupted, and if he was laughing at her he did not show it, for his tone was truly penitent. "Mistress Mercy, I trust your name fits your character and that you'll prove it by speeding me on my way. Be good enough to open the secret compartment in the floor of the carriage for me, my hands being otherwise occupied, and give me your mother's diamond bauble. She was wearing it when she left Kittery, but as it isn't on her wrist now, that's obviously where she's hidden it."

Mercy gasped, her mother paled, and there was a mutter from the men. The highwayman could not possibly know of the existence of the hollow beneath the floor boards, yet he had spoken with certainty, and either by accident or some weird circumstances he had fathomed the secret. But Mercy was not going to succumb meekly.

"I don't know what you're talking about," she said.

His eyes regarded her unblinkingly through the mask.

"Raise the floor boards," he commanded, and there was a ring of authority in his voice. "I hate to become unpleasant or nasty toward those with whom I—do my business. But when necessity dictates, I never shrink from my duty. Now open the compartment!"

The girl stood firm, breathing hard. Her eyes were defiant, and her lips, compressed into a straight, grim line, looked like her mother's. William Pepperrell broke the deadlock. "Do as he bids you, Mercy," he called. "Never argue with a criminal when he's armed. And you, young man—take the diamonds, but leave me my papers. They're of no value to anyone but me."

Mercy turned her back on the Gentleman, pried loose the floor board, and brought forth the leather bag containing her father's documents and her mother's diamond bracelet. Standing erect again, she whirled and held the pouch at arm's length, as though the highwayman were something unclean.

"Don't bother to sort the contents. I haven't the time!"

"Here," she said. "Take it and be gone." She drew back her arm and threw the pouch at him as hard as she could, but he caught it neatly.

"Contempt makes you even prettier," he declared softly, and again she thought she caught the inflection of a foreign accent. "Two favors before I go."

Holding the leather bag with his sword under his arm, he reached out and caught hold of the thin gold chain of a small, heart-shaped locket that encircled Mercy's neck. He tugged, the chain broke and the locket fell into his hand. "Please," Mercy said, "there's little value in my trinket. You can't get more than a few shillings for it."

"I have no intention of selling it," the Gentleman replied. "I shall keep it as a memento of our first meeting. In return permit me to bestow a small gift on you, Mistress Mercy. This is a little out of my line, but I must demonstrate to your young friend down the road that I take orders from no one."

He stood directly in front of her now, though he kept

the pistol trained on Pepperrell, young Staples, and the coachman. Bending toward the girl, he lifted his mask part way up his face, to a point just above his lips. He kissed her hard, fully on the lips, then leaped away. In a moment he disappeared into the screen of trees. "Thank you," he called happily, "we'll both remember that!"

Later, much later, Mercy remembered that she had kept her eyes open when he had kissed her. And, impossible though it was to recognize a man from just seeing the lower part of his face, she did recall, vaguely, that there was a tiny mole in the cleft of his chin. At this moment, however, she stood very still, her mind whirling, her heart pounding.

By the time the men dropped the tree that had rendered them helpless and pursued the bandit into the woods, the Gentleman was gone. Only after thrashing around in the tangle of dead leaves and branches for at least five minutes did they find a small clearing and realize that he had kept a horse hidden there and had escaped along a narrow path through the forest. A real chase was out of the question: the successful fugitive already had an ample head start.

And so Pepperrell decreed that the journey be resumed. The almost inadvertent loss of his documents pertaining to the defense of the colonies in the event of a new outbreak of war with the French could prove to be serious, but he quickly recovered his urbanity, and a stranger peering in through the carriage window at him would never have realized the gravity of the situation. His wife was plunged in gloom, of course, for her bracelet had been her greatest pride.

But Mercy was not concerned with such matters. She sat as though in a trance, and, as the carriage bumped slowly along the rutted road, she could still see the highwayman's eyes on her, she could still feel the strong yet surprisingly tender touch of his lips against hers. And she wondered if his motive had been to defy Peter and teach him a lesson rather than because he had found her irresistably attractive.

TWO

A COLD east wind swept across the Boston Common, but the bite in the air meant very little to a girl who had grown up in Maine. Besides, this was the heart of the largest and most cosmopolitan city in the English New World, and Mercy Pepperrell was fascinated by the sights and the bustle, all so different from Kittery.

Two red-coated officers of the royal garrison strolled by, each with an exceptionally pretty girl on his arm. And although it was only noon, these gay creatures wore silk dresses and fancy bonnets, and even their cloaks were of satin. Both wore rouge on their lips and cheeks, and a large beauty patch was prominent on the chin of one. Mercy marveled, and stared until Peter Staples, who was walking with her, applied a gentle pressure to her arm and murmured something to her. Only then did she realize that these females were doxies, not ladies, and her own innocence struck her as being so amusing that she laughed aloud. She was pleased that Peter, instead of frowning at her behavior, grinned amiably.

Under a clump of trees to the right a group of four

Algonquian Indians had pitched a crude lean-to shelter of untreated bearskin, and despite the heavy traffic past their temporary resting place they had kindled a fire and were unconcernedly frying fish for their midday dinner. Less than a stone's throw from them, two exceptionally well-dressed gentlemen, one a merchant and the other a ship-owner, judging by their heated conversation, were arguing over the prices of a newly landed shipment of skillets, wool broadcloth, and shoes.

Eight little boys, dressed alike in suits of somber black with stiff, starched white collars, trudged silently in a single row, with a very youthful schoolmaster, armed with a birch switch, bringing up the rear. A farmer stalked past, driving four fat, sleek cows to market, and his shaggy mongrel dog darted back and forth across the Common, wagging its tail and sniffing at housewives, sailors, and shopkeepers. A minister and an elderly lady strolled almost aimlessly as they talked in well-modulated voices, and a fisherman, his arm around the waist of a very pretty, very young country girl, stared in openmouthed wonder at the fine homes that lined three sides of the Common. Some of these handsome brick structures were four stories high, but even they were dwarfed by the magnificence of the new King's Mansion, a huge structure of white stone which served as the combined office and home of William Shirley, Governor General of Massachusetts Bay Colony.

Mercy and Peter were moving in the direction of the Mansion, but the girl was in no hurry, though she had been sent out to buy a length of ribbon that her mother needed to trim a new gown for the official reception to be held that day. And Peter, to whom the sights of Boston Common were neither novel nor especially interesting, was dawdling too, but for reasons of his own.

Stealing a glance at Mercy, he thought that she had never looked so pretty. Her green eyes were sparkling, her lovely red hair was flying free in the wind, and there was a deep flush in her cheeks. He barely managed to control an impulse to take her into his arms, but this was hardly the place for a respectable Maine man to demonstrate his affection. Besides, something was troubling him.

"Do you suppose there's time for us to drop in at a coffee shop for a few minutes, Mercy?" he asked rather tentatively, giving no indication of what he was feeling.

"Oh, do you think we could, Peter? I've never been inside one." The prospect of even so mild an adventure excited her as though he had proposed a midnight rendezvous at a somewhat less than respectable inn.

"You don't suppose your parents would object?"

"If we don't tell them where we've been, they'll have no way of knowing, will they?" She took his hand, then remembered herself and tucked her arm through his in a manner more befitting a young lady of quality.

His conscience and his desire struggled briefly, and, when he stole another glance at the girl, the issue was decided. "There's a new place that's recently been opened on Queen Anne Street," he said, "and I'm told it's quite respectable. We might try it."

They increased their pace and a few minutes later pushed open the door of a one-story establishment that had an air of prosperity. The walls and beams were of solid oak, the floors were of scrubbed white pine and a huge, blazing hearth at the far end of the large room bore the inscription cut in the stone above it, "Ereckted in May, *Anno Domini* 1743, by Hezekiah Horley, Prop."

Most of the twenty tables were occupied, although the hour was still early. This was clearly a place where a man could take a young lady without damage to her reputation. There were several family groups scattered about, and at one table two austere middle-aged ladies were drinking tea from dainty cups and eating thick slabs of rare beef set before them on wooden trenchers.

Mercy and Peter found a table in a distant corner, and she beamed at him as he stood behind her and helped adjust her cape. They ordered coffee and debated the wisdom of whether to eat a bite of food as well. Although both were hungry after their walk, they decided against the idea; Governor Shirley's formal banquet was to take place at three in the afternoon, and both knew from experience that they would be expected to do justice to a repast in which at least a dozen courses would be served.

Their coffee was brought to them in steaming pewter mugs, and Peter looked down at the smoke rising from his brew. Suddenly he took a deep breath. "Mercy," he said abruptly, "I'm worried."

"Oh, I'm so sorry." She looked at him quickly, and her sense of well-being vanished. Peter's face was very grave. "Would you care to tell me about it? What's it about?"

"You." He faced her, and the shadows of the hearth fire flickering across the left side of his face made him appear quite handsome. "Mercy, you've grown up. You're not a little girl any more. You're a woman."

"Why, thank you, Peter." She folded her hands demurely in her lap and concealed a little smile of elation. "That's one of the nicest things you've ever said to me."

"I didn't rightly mean it to be nice." His sense of articulation deserted him, and he groped for the right words. "I used to think that you and I—what I mean is, I took it for granted for a long time that when everything was right, you and I, we'd—well, you know what I mean."

Mercy gave him no help whatsoever. She raised her head, and her eyes, a softer shade of green in the firelight, were innocent and wide. She appeared sympathetic and concerned but acted as though she were totally unable to understand his meaning.

Peter struggled on. "Two days ago, Mercy, when we were on the road, I had a mighty bad shock. I mean, when that damned highwayman held us up. If I ever see him, I'll kill him." His lean jawline tightened, and his right fist clenched.

"If he's caught, Peter, you'll have no chance to touch him. Any judge, any king's magistrate in all New England will sentence him to hang. It was terrible the way he took your money, but others suffered more. Mamma's bracelet can't be replaced, and you know far better than I how valuable Papa's military papers were."

"I didn't mean that. I wasn't thinking about myself or your ma's bauble or your pa's documents." The young militia officer took a deep breath and gripped the edge of the table so hard that his knuckles turned white. "I was thinking about when he kissed you, Mercy." He was too embarrassed to look at her.

"I see."

Something in her voice, a softening made him lift his head sharply. "That's what I've been worrying about. You didn't take on like I thought you would. I know you didn't like him, naturally. But all the same, you didn't hit him and you didn't scream. Later, you didn't even cry."

"I'm surprised at you! Saying something like that!" Mercy was indignant, but her tone lacked conviction.

"If I was to ask for your hand, Mercy, I know what your folks would say. Your ma in particular would tell me you're too young. I was hoping to wait another year, until maybe I'm elected to a junior partnership in the Pepperrell Company on my own merits. That way nobody could say I was after you for your money. But it's not safe to wait, and there's the truth. You're ripe as an apple ready to fall off a tree, and if you're not married soon, you're like to get into mischief for sure!"

His earnestness was touching, as was the obvious depth of his sincerity, and Mercy thought it would be cruel to continue her pretense of bland ignorance. "Is this a proposal, Peter? I've never heard of one like it, if it is."

The warmth of her tone made him forget everything but his love for her. "I don't exactly know," he admitted. "I should talk to your pa before I say anything to you. That's how things are supposed to be done, and he'd be right upset if he knew I was being so open and all, the way I'm speaking to you. But you know how I feel, Mercy—you've known it for a long time. I reckon everybody in Kittery knows it by now. So there's no harm with my coming out in the open. I don't want to lose you, Mercy—and there's the truth. It's better that I speak up too soon than wait too long."

She was genuinely puzzled. "Why should you 'lose' me, Peter? I'm not being coy with you, truly I'm not, but I don't know what it is that you fear. There's no other man who interests me, and you know it."

"Not yet, there's not. But that doesn't mean there won't be. Up Kittery way, folks were accustomed to me paying court to you. There's lots of young bucks who'd come around, but they figure it's no use because I've already got a head start on them. And they know," he added grimly, "that I'd thrash them good and proper if they started nosing around your pa's house. What bothers me is that you're too pretty."

Mercy laughed, although she knew it was wrong when Peter was being so intent, so serious. "That's the strangest compliment I've ever been paid."

"Not so strange as all that. You don't even realize what a stir you cause when you walk down the streets here. Or the attention you're causing in this very place. I don't like it. Look yonder, and you'll see what I mean! You notice how that beau is staring at you? If this wasn't Boston and if it wasn't you that's with me," he declared incongruously, his jealous anger muddling his logic, "I'd punch him in the face for looking at you like he's doing!"

The knowledge that a total stranger found her attractive was intoxicating, even though Mercy knew that her pleasure was wicked. She glanced across the room with feigned casualness, and at a far table she saw a man who was indeed admiring her brazenly. Although he was dressed in a deftly tailored suit of conservative, expensive material, she told herself severely that no real gentleman

would show his interest so openly. Yet she had to concede
to herself that his features bore the stamp of the gentry.
His forehead was high beneath wavy black hair, his dark
eyes were intelligent and clear, his nose was patrician, and
his mouth, though a trifle sensual, was firm. He was no
more than twenty-eight or thirty years of age, and his tall
frame was lean and hard.　　　　　　　　　•

Certainly he did not look like someone who would flirt
with a young lady, particularly when she not only had an
escort but when he himself was not alone. Mercy transferred her gaze to the blonde who sat with the stranger,
and felt a trifle uncomfortable. The woman was a shade
overdressed, and her hair was too pale, too striking, as
though she had rinsed it constantly in apple vinegar and
raw lemon juice. Although Mercy was admittedly no
judge, she decided that this female was probably a trollop,
and she turned back to Peter abruptly.

"If that's all that worries you, please rest easy," she said,
placing her hand on his arm, and secretly wondering
whether she was making the gesture for his sake or to
impress the brash man across the room. "I'm a Pepperrell,
Peter, and I don't take kindly to rudeness. Nor would I
care to associate with anyone who shows such cheap taste
in his womenfolk!"

She would have added more, but a barmaid appeared at
his elbow, carrying a pewter platter on which rested two
enormous buns stuffed with currants and glazed with wild
honey. They had not ordered the confections and were
about to tell her as much when she smiled guilelessly.
"These 'ere," she said, "are wif the com'ents of the gent."

She nodded across the room, and to Mercy's surprise
the rude stranger stood and bowed. Before a startled Peter
could find his voice, Mercy addressed the barmaid. "Be
good enough to return them," she said.

"What'll I tell him, mum?"

"There is no message." Mercy's lips formed in a prim
line.

The incident was closed, and she turned back to Peter, who began to splutter indignantly. She tried to soothe him and at the same time to organize her own thoughts. She was angry and felt somewhat cheapened, yet she was flattered, too. She had never experienced an incident like this, and she would certainly have something to tell Amanda Timkins when she returned home!

Suddenly she felt rather than saw someone standing at the table, and looked up to see the insolent stranger grinning at her cheerfully. "I'm sorry you chose not to accept the buns, ma'am," he said in a deep, cultured voice. "But you'll break bread with me—and sooner than you think."

He was gone before an outraged Peter could jump to his feet. The man's companion was waiting for him at the entrance, and they left the shop quickly, not bothering to glance back.

The principal dining hall of the King's Mansion made up in stateliness what it lacked in opulence, and the personal dignity of William Shirley, Governor General of Massachusetts Bay Colony and chief representative of George II in the New World, communicated itself to everyone present. It did not matter that there were only a few inferior paintings on the whitewashed walls, that the table was of sanded pine rather than polished oak, or that the white cloths covering it were of an inferior grade of coarsely spun linen. The gentlemen who had gathered together under this roof were the most influential and able in the colonies, and their consorts were as charming as any of the great ladies who dined at St. James Palace in London.

The governor, a tall, thickset man wearing a heavily powdered wig, led the procession to the table, with Mistress Pepperrell on his arm. Directly behind him, escorting his lady, came Captain Peter Warren, a spare man of medium height, in the glittering gold and blue uniform of

His Majesty's Navy. Fifty years old and of Irish birth, his background was clouded in carefully contrived mystery. It was rumored that he had made his fortune as a pirate and had turned respectable only when he had won the heart and hand of a great beauty from New York, an heiress in her own right. It was also said that he had bludgeoned his way into his high Navy post. His walk was certainly reminiscent of a quarter-deck swagger, but his face was solemn and immobile, as befitted the occasion. If there was an impudent gleam of humor in his sharp eyes, it was lost on Mistress Shirley.

Third in the line came William Pepperrell, courteous and quietly gallant as always, his head cocked slightly to one side as he engaged in a spirited conversation with Mistress Warren. They were the two wealthiest of His Majesty's American-born subjects, but her gown of ivory satin lacked ostentation as it set off her pale beauty, and his slightly old-fashioned suit of black worsted was as conservative as that of the clergymen who were present.

Behind the three leading couples came an assemblage of more than one hundred persons, including jurists, merchants, shipowners and militia leaders. These gentlemen had been convened from Massachusetts and Maine, New Hampshire and Connecticut, and the lieutenant governors of New York, Pennsylvania, and New Jersey were present as observers of the conference scheduled for later in the day. Every ship from England brought tidings that relations with France were steadily worsening, that the squabbles between the great powers over the rights of succession to the Austrian throne were becoming more acrimonious, and word was expected at any time to the effect that Louis XV had ordered his ministers to declare war; the English Parliament, it was believed, would never be the first to issue such a declaration.

Everyone was too polite to mention the topic in the presence of the ladies; the subject would be thoroughly aired later, after the banquet. Nevertheless the threat of hostilities was in the minds of all, and Governor Shirley's guests were consequently even more quietly sober than the occasion demanded. The only gaiety came from the foot of the long table, where the young people were congregated. There Mercy Pepperrell, vivacious Susan Warren of New York, and the three Shirley girls, each surrounded by young officers and aides-de-camp to distinguished seniors, searched for their right places. There was considerable bright chatter intermingled with bursts of slightly boisterous laughter, but the raised eyebrows and faint frowns of their elders were ignored, and no one objected too strenuously. Such conduct would have been considered in the worst of all possible taste at King George's table, but this was America, and even the most staid of colonial leaders didn't mind a touch of informaltiy from the young.

Peter Staples located Mercy's card, designating her seat, and was elated to discover that he had been placed on her right. Looking at her in her *bouffant*, off-the-shoulder gown of pale green silk, he believed that no other woman present, not even the renowned Mistress Warren, was half as pretty. They stood side by side and picked up small glasses of sack, and Peter felt a thrill of pride as his sleeve touched Mercy's arm. She had as good as accepted him only three hours previously, and he believed that William Pepperrell would approve the match. It was exciting beyond measure to think that in a few months she would be his wife.

"God save the King, and bless him!"

The high voice of Governor Shirley rang out, and the guests raised their glasses, sipped, and continued to stand. Now it was Captain Warren's turn, and he fingered the stem of his glass as he looked up and down the length of the table coolly.

"I propose a toast to the doom of our enemies!" he called in a husky voice. "May they be confounded, and may we be victorious on sea, on the land, and in the sight of the Lord!"

"Amen to that!" William Pepperrell declared, thus making it unnecessary for him to propose a toast of his own.

The ladies and gentlemen sipped again, then took their seats, and a corps of servants, most of them recently arrived immigrants anxious to earn a few extra shillings, began to pass huge tureens of soup. No such dish would have been offered at any similar affair in England or on the European continent, and the great of London, Paris, and Madrid would have considered so hearty an offering inappropriate. Here, however, everyone eagerly awaited his huge wooden bowl, and no dinner of importance would have begun without it.

The base of the soup was beef and venison, and chunks of both meats floated in the rich stew. They had been simmering in enormous cauldrons since the preceding day, and the meat was tender and juicy. In the morning, slices of onion had been added, and a little later chopped turnips, potatoes, and beets had been dumped into the pots. To these had been added wild Indian herbs, cut very fine, and kernels of autumn corn, which had been sliced from the cobs. There were green vegetables, too, including beans, peas and lettuce, and at noon baskets of succulent clams had been added, along with diced squares of bacon.

As a general rule, particularly in polite society, the ladies contented themselves with a single serving, but no gentleman would insult his host by refusing a second helping and possibly a third. At regular intervals along the length of the table were freshly baked loaves of bread, which were passed from one guest to the next, each breaking off as much as he wanted with his fingers. And Governor Shirley, though an Englishman, observed the local custom of giving each male guest a tumbler of rum instead of the wines that were customary abroad. The governor, of course, enjoyed this libation of the West as much as did any of the others. After all, he had already spent the better part of a quarter of a century in Boston.

Mercy, hungry after her long and exciting morning, began to eat her soup as soon as a steaming bowl was placed in front of her, and only when the man on her left addressed her in a resonant baritone voice did she remember her manners; until now she had absently forgotten to see who was beside her there. There was a trace of amusement in his tone, and, she thought, a touch of condescension.

"Do all young ladies from Maine eat this incredible dish with such relish? And if they do, how do they manage to keep such tiny waists?"

A retort was ready on Mercy's lips, but she forgot it as she looked to the left. Sitting next to her was the young man from the coffee house. She experienced a sensation so sharp that it was almost a physical shock, and the intensity of his dark eyes further disconcerted her. Lowering her head in confusion, she could only murmur, "I don't believe we've met, sir."

"We have not," he replied firmly. "Naturally, I know you, as who within hundreds of miles does not? There I have the advantage of you, and that is both the reward and the penalty of beauty. Permit me to introduce myself, so we may balance the scales. I am Jack Duppan, of London and more recently of this city."

Although his interest was flattering, Mercy didn't like his glib, self-assured approach. The men she had known were blunt, plain-spoken, and honest, and Master Duppan's sophistication was as distasteful as it was overwhelming. She would have nodded and turned back to Peter, but something familiar about this intense stranger struck a responsive chord. She realized that she had recognized him because of his rudeness earlier in the day, but her feeling was based on more than that, and she decided to draw him out. "You say you're engaged in commerce in the Massachusetts Bay?"

To her surprise, he laughed heartily. "No, ma'am. I did

not say any such thing. Actually, I'm a man of some leisure at the moment. I'm looking for a good place to invest some funds."

Mercy felt as though she had been doused in the icy waters of the Piscataqua River. So that was Master Duppan's game: he was pretending an interest in her merely to get to her father. There were many men in the colonies who would stop at nothing if they could acquire an opportunity to invest in Pepperrell & Company. She favored the brash intruder with a cold stare and deliberately turned her back to him as she concentrated on her soup. Peter was engaged in a lively debate with a young naval lieutenant, Captain Warren's aide, on the relative merits of land and sea artillery, and she could not break in on him without being obvious. Duppan apparently read her thoughts, however, and spoke softly in her ear.

"Under no circumstances would I attempt to put my money to work in the Pepperrell empire. Had I desired that, I could have arranged it easily enough through Governor Shirley. I'm afraid that your esteemed father's methods, though certain, are a little slow for my taste. I prefer to make a tidy sum quickly."

Fascinated by his candor, Mercy twisted around in her chair and stared at him. "You can also lose quickly, sir."

"Of course I can." He grinned disarmingly, and the girl wondered how many of her sex had told him that he looked uncommonly dashing and handsome when he smiled. "But if I've had a little fun, I don't mind. The game is always worth playing for its own sake."

"Is it, indeed?"

"Of course. Winning or losing is always something of an anticlimax to me." His grin broadened, and Mercy noticed for the first time that there was a long, thin scar along his right temple. Although she knew little about such matters, it looked as though he had acquired it in a duel; on the other hand, if he was the rake he seemed, it was always possible that he had suffered a knife wound at some time. "This is hardly the time to explain my quaint philosophy to you, Mistress Mercy. So I wonder if you'd care to meet me a bit later in the day? I'll not be included in the council of war that the Governor General will call, and we might inspect some of the sights in the new wing of the Mansion together. I hear it has only recently been completed and furnished with goods that were brought from London in the holds of two snows only a fortnight ago. The ships," he added impudently, "undoubtedly flew the Pepperrell ensign."

If only Peter would finish his harangue with the lieutenant! Mercy looked straight ahead, debated what to reply and then spoke primly. "I shall be expected to attend my mother," she said.

"Oh, rubbish." Duppan's ability to puncture a fabrication was disconcerting. "There'll be music of a sort on a fiddle, and a few people will play whist. But your mother will want to hear the latest New York gossip from the lovely Mistress Warren, and if you're there they won't be able to speak freely."

A laugh bubbled up in Mercy before she could stop it. "You may be right, sir. But I shall attend her all the same."

"As you will!" He shrugged and seemed to lose interest in the subject. "However, if you should change your mind, you'll find me in the second-floor library, the private one, at precisely six o'clock."

He turned away from her and devoted himself to the Shirley girl on his other side. And he did not address Mercy again through the rest of the meal, to her relief—and annoyance. It was after five o'clock when the dinner came to an end, and even those most interested in food had no desire to eat again that day. The soup dish had been followed by a course consisting of broiled sea bass and boiled potatoes. Then had come roast venison steak, wrapped around fresh apples, partridge stuffed with parsnips, and a deep-dish cherry pie.

Governor Shirley had a few matters to discuss in private with Master Pepperrell and Captain Warren prior to the meeting of the council, so the remaining gentlemen therefore either moved to the drawing room for port or took a brisk walk in the Common, and the ladies retired to Mistress Shirley's parlor. Conversation was listless, and the young, unmarried women soon became restless. Their evening was just beginning, for the business session to be held later promised to be a long one and the aides and other young men not asked to attend would have several hours to spend as they chose. Peter Staples would have to be there, of course, in his capacity as secretary of the war council, and that would leave Mercy without an escort.

Susan Warren and the eldest of the Shirley girls were whispering in one corner of the room, and Mercy was about to join them when she glanced at a gilded clock on the mantel and saw that it was only fifteen minutes before six o'clock. She told herself fiercely that she had no intention of keeping a rendezvous with Master Duppan in the library, that the very idea was repugnant to her. Nevertheless she decided, perversely, to pay a brief visit to her own chamber in order to comb her hair and dab a little rice powder on her nose.

Saying nothing to anyone, she slipped out into the corridor and made her way to the staircase. As she passed the dining hall she saw her father with the Governor General and Peter Warren, still seated at the long table and deeply engrossed in conversation as they puffed on *segaros* recently arrived with a cargo of molasses from the West Indies. She was glad that they did not see her, and she felt a tingle of guilt as she hurried to the stairs.

Candelabra were nailed to the walls at long intervals, and a few flickering tapers provided the only illumination as she mounted slowly to the fourth floor, where the room assigned to her was located. Her parents had been given a suite elsewhere in the Mansion, and she was glad that she was nowhere near them, though she could not define her reasons.

It was bitterly cold in the corridor and little warmer in her own small room when she opened the door. A small bed of coals glowed in the tiny fireplace and gave off a feeble heat and a faint light, and Mercy decided not to tarry. Taking a straw from a mug on the chest of drawers, she held it in the coals until it flared, then straightened to light the candles that stood on each side of the little mantel. The flames leaped up, and something bright, located between the two tapers, caught her eye. She caught her breath and stood very still, numbed.

Lying on the wood of the mantel was her mother's diamond bracelet.

THREE

"GENTLEMEN," William Pepperrell said, stubbing out the butt of his *segaro* and lighting a fresh one, "we're fooling ourselves if we fail to face facts. I say we tell the council that war is certain. If we mince words, if we try to prepare but pretend on the surface that there's still a chance London and Paris will settle their differences amicably, a great many innocent people are going to die."

Governor Shirley stared out at the window beyond him that looked out onto the Common and absently scribbled on the white tablecoth with the nail of his right index finger. "Every man who'll hear us tonight is a colonial leader," he declared peevishly, "and if we talk about the inevitability of war, the French up in Louisburg and Quebec will have heard our words within a week. They'll step up the pace of their own preparations, and before we know it the fighting will start, even before there's a formal declaration."

"But if we hide our heads in barrels of salt pork, every town, every settlement, every outpost from Maine down to Pennsylvania will be in danger," Pepperrell argued.

"You know the way those damned French fight, Governor. They've doubtless sent agents out to the tribes already, passing out rum and rifles and wampum belts. They'll send every Indian in Canada down to scalp and burn, and some of our own red men won't need much encouragement to war against us."

Captain Warren, who had remained silent for several minutes, nodded in vigorous agreement. "You're right, Will," he said. "Down our way the Seneca and Mohawks will begin their raids as soon as they hear their cousins' war drums."

"The Algonquians are pacified," Shirley said stubbornly. "There'll be no trouble in Massachusetts Bay."

"Then you're fortunate here, Governor, very fortunate." Pepperrell's tone was deceptively mild. "Up my way, we never know what the Penobscot will do. Every time we lick 'em they come back for more. But I can promise you this—Massachusetts Bay won't be spared. Every community, every cabin on the fringe of the wilderness will be in flames if we don't give the council fair warning. These men need time to alert every militia platoon and squadron on the frontier to the danger!"

"And the French are prepared for action the very moment they hear from Paris that war has been declared," Warren added. "You can depend on that! I have positive information that their supplies and ammunition are in order and that they've secretly been getting reinforcements in both men and matériel from France during the past six months and more."

"What's the source of this information of yours?" The Governor General looked skeptical.

"Young Duppan. I don't like the scoundrel, you understand. He's the worst damned landsman I've ever seen. He doesn't know a mains'l from a bowsprit, believe it or not!"

"Who's Duppan?" Shirley was patently unimpressed.

The Irish sailor chuckled. "A guest in your house at this very moment, Governor. You may recall that I asked you to invite him because I've found him useful. He's supplied me with considerable information on the doings of the French."

"Oh yes. The fellow who arrived from London with various letters of introduction to all of us."

"That's the one. I don't care for him at all. Tried to explain a naval engagement to him one day, and I might as well have been talking the language of the North African Berbers." Captain Warren looked disgusted. "But the information he's given me seems to be accurate, so for all our sakes I'm afraid we'll have to be civil to him."

Pepperrell had been following the conversation with mild interest. "What's his motive in giving you this information, Peter—and how did he happen to come by it?"

"Oh, he's spent a considerable time in France. And he hates 'em. I wouldn't say he's a patriot, of course. I've paid him for the data he's given me." There was contempt in Warren's voice. "But if even a little of what he's told me is true, there's not a chance in the world that England and France will be at peace six months from today."

"That's precisely what my own agents in London write to me," Pepperrell agreed.

The governor spread his hands in a gesture of helplessness. "All right, gentlemen, all right," he said wearily, and the other two exchanged covert, satisfied glances. "I've been hoping that war could be avoided, but if it's coming, we'd best be ready for it. We'll tell the council the basic situation. Now then, how much do you suggest that we reveal of our military plans?"

"That depends on what we intend to do. I've never been in favor of a campaign against Quebec, for example," Pepperrell said easily, unbuttoning his waistcoat and making himself more comfortable. "Peter, what do you know of Louisburg?"

"Only that it's impregnable," was the prompt retort.

"You've traveled in that part of the world, of course, and I haven't. So you have the advantage of me," the merchant said calmly. "Have you ever dropped anchor at Louisburg?"

The ranking seaman in the New World snorted derisively. "Drop anchor, you say! Let me teach you a lesson in simple geography, Will. Louisburg is the strongest fortress ever built by man in the New World. In fact, all of Cape Breton Island is a natural fortress, you might say. Here. Let me show you what I mean." He leaned forward, seized several dirty dishes and began to set them up in front of him.

"Here's the island, at the entrance into the Gulf of St. Lawrence. Here, about thirty leagues distant, on the opposite side of the entrance, is Newfoundland. The island is virtually a continuation of Nova Scotia, and is separated from it by the Canso Strait, which is very narrow. And here," he added firmly, "is Louisburg, at the southeastern tip of Cape Breton. It guards the approach to all Canada. If you're thinking of attacking Quebec by sailing an expedition past Louisburg, forget it. Her guns would pound a fleet to bits. I couldn't do it, the Sea Lords themselves couldn't do it."

Pepperrell devoted himself to a close inspection of the lighted end of his *segaro*. "I said nothing about sailing past Louisburg, Peter," he remonstrated mildly. "Those are your words, not mine. I was merely dreaming a bit, I suppose. And it just seemed to me that anything made by man can be destroyed by man, that's all."

Warren loosened his stock and stared openmouthed at the wealthy gentleman from Maine. "Are you suggesting that we attack Louisburg itself, Will? Are you proposing that we destroy the fortress there?"

"Wondering, Peter. Neither suggesting nor proposing, merely wondering."

The former pirate laughed hoarsely. "If we could do it," he said softly, "we'd be the wonder of the world."

"The war would end the moment the French garrison struck its colors," Pepperrell said soberly. "Quebec would capitulate immediately. And King Louis' ministers at the Louvre would sign any peace treaty that London might care to dictate. Thousands of women and children who live near the wilderness would be spared death or captivity. And a war that might pauperize us all would be finished practically as soon as it was begun."

His gentle words inflamed Captain Warren's imagination, and the volatile Irishman jumped to his feet, upsetting his chair. "It would be worth the try!" he cried. "The odds would be incredibly high, almost impossibly high against an expedition. But if it were handled right, there's just a chance it might succeed. The gamble would be worth it! And Will, you're a cunning rascal."

"There *are* one or two things to be said in favor of my dream," Pepperrell admitted. "For one thing, if we kept the whole plan secret, the French could read themselves blind, studying our previous correspondence and preparing the defenses of Quebec. But they would never know we were intending to capture Louisburg until we opened fire on the fortress."

"Both of you," said Governor Shirley in a tight voice, "are mad. As I've sat here listening to you, I've wondered if I were actually in the King's Mansion, listening to the two most influential and respectable of all His Majesty's subjects in America, or whether I had stumbled into a pit where a pair of chained lunatics were babbling. Gentlemen, I beg you to use your intelligence and forget this insanity!"

"We're making no plans, Governor, we're just dreaming a bit." William Pepperrell brushed some pie crumbs from his knee.

"Aye, and a bright, fair dream it is," Warren added, perching jauntily on the edge of the table.

The governor folded his hands over his paunch and sighed. "Permit me to mention a few obstacles," he said patiently. "In the event of war, London will certainly send an officer of the rank of major general to command our army and a senior captain to take charge of our sea forces. Warren, you're a Navy man. And Master Pepperrell, you're the ranking militia colonel. Surely you both realize that no sane commanding officer would give his approval to such a wild venture!"

"In my dream a strange thing happened." William Pepperrell spoke so softly that the others had to strain in order to hear him. "The Governor General has the power in time of war to make whatever military appointments he believes necessary. All that would be required would be a stroke of a pen to make Peter here a temporary commodore. That way he'd outrank any senior captain the Admiralty might send."

The sheer audacity of the suggestion stunned Governor Shirley, and he laughed in spite of himself. "And by another pen stroke I suppose I could promote you to lieutenant general so you'd rank higher than anyone who might be sent over from England."

Pepperrell beamed innocently. "That might be a considerable help, too. But there's no sense in pursuing this line of thought seriously, not at the moment. Before you outline any further objections, let me just tell you flatly that it would be impossible to make an expedition ready until we learned a few facts about Louisburg." He held up his right hand and began to toll off points with his fingers. "We'd need to know the size of the garrison and the number, the caliber, and the location of the fortress' batteries. We'd require information on her food supply and on how long she could withstand a siege. Oh, yes—there'd be a vast amount of data to be acquired before we could consider the project seriously."

"You realize, I trust," Governor Shirley said acidly, "that the French guard Louisburg as carefully as they watch over the person of their king. Have you found any way to glean the information we'd need for such an attack?"

"Not yet, sir, not yet," was the cheerful reply. "However I find myself dreaming with great regularity of late, so it's entirely possible that I may find a solution to the problem before long. Now, as I don't want to hold up our associates too long, may I suggest that we call the council into meeting? And Peter—perhaps you and I can sit down together tomorrow, if you've nothing better to do, and we might amuse ourselves by dreaming aloud to each other. If the governor should eventually see fit to give us joint command of an expedition to reduce Louisburg, we'd be wise to settle as much as we could in advance."

Mercy moved very slowly toward the private library on the second floor of the King's Mansion. She saw that the door was open, but she hesitated for a long moment, again debating the wisdom of what she was doing. Logic insisted that she should go to her father with her suspicions about Jack Duppan, but she would be laughed at if she had no more proof of his guilt than her insistence that she recognized his eyes and his voice. Although her mother's precious bracelet had been placed in her room, that did not necessarily mean Duppan had put it there. And until she had more specific evidence against him, it would be a waste of time to tell anyone what she knew.

If she spoke out prematurely it was even possible that he might have an opportunity to cover his tracks, so the best course of action was to outwit him, perhaps trick him into admitting that he was the highwayman. She knew there was a certain amount of danger in confronting him with what she believed was the truth, and she felt a chill of fear as she stood just past the library door. But she consoled herself with the thought that he had wanted her to know his identity, that he had put the bracelet in her room deliberately, knowing that she would rise to the bait and come here, even though she could never prove conclusively to her parents that it was he who had stolen and then returned the gems.

Nothing could really happen to her in this house, she reminded herself severely. After all, this was the home of the highest official in the colonies, and at this very moment there were magistrates, chiefs of colonial assemblies, and distinguished soldiers gathered together only a few doors distant. If she screamed, they would all come to her assistance. But it should be unnecessary, really, to call for help. She was a Pepperrell, and not even the boldest of criminals would dare to harm her.

Partly comforted, she took a deep breath and walked quickly into the library. Jack Duppan was already there, and stood with his back to the door, his hands clasped behind him as he stared into a blazing fire at the opposite end of the room. The rustle of Mercy's skirts betrayed her presence, and he turned quickly, then smiled when he saw her.

"Ah," he said, "you've come! I was beginning to think you wouldn't be here." He advanced part way across the chamber, and then, sensing her insecurity, stopped on the far side of an oak table on which books and various English journals were piled.

"I feel quite at home in here," Mercy said inanely, and heard her own voice continue to say the last things that were on her mind. "It's so like our library at home."

"I hope to have the opportunity to inspect it at some future time." His smile broadened, and his teeth looked very white in the firelight.

The girl put one hand behind her and grasped the arm of a chair for support. "Was there any special reason you wanted to see me, Master Duppan?" She wished that her voice would stop trembling.

His smile vanished and he regarded her seriously. "You Americans are all so blunt," he said, his tone light despite his sober expression. "You're obviously afraid that I intend to make love to you. That would be presumptuous—and premature. I asked you to meet me because you're a very lovely girl and you appear to be quite intelligent as well. It's a most unusual combination, and I'd like to know you better."

"I would be less than intelligent if I were so gullible as to swallow so blatant an attempt at flattery. As for my appearance, I see myself in the mirror daily, and I am not particularly enthralled with the way I look." Mercy's retort came to her lips, and she discovered that she was enjoying herself. She had almost forgotten that this was the most notorious thief in New England's history, and that she had come here for a specific purpose.

"I'll be pleased to debate the matter with you, ma'am." Duppan bowed and waved toward a divan that stood at right angles to the fire. "Shall we sit down and begin our argument?"

Under normal circumstances Mercy would have refused so bald an invitation. No lady would sit so close to an escort, particularly when unchaperoned. Her parents would certainly disapprove, but she told herself that she was here for the single purpose of unmasking this two-faced charlatan. So she bobbed her head in agreement, not trusting herself to speak, and preceded him to the divan.

He sat down beside her, but she noticed that he took care not to crowd too close to her, and she was grateful for his tact. It was difficult to believe that so charming a gentleman was in actuality a ruthless robber who preyed on innocent people. Unsure what to say, she remained silent, and he, too, said nothing. Glancing at him from beneath her lashes, Mercy saw that he was looking down at her hair.

"When the flames leap high," he murmured, "it has a golden cast. At other times it's a deep red, as bright as the fire itself."

"You sound as though you've never before met a girl whose hair is the color of mine, Master Duppan, and that's something I find hard to believe."

"Looking at you, I'm convinced it's the truth, ma'am."

His eyes were on her, and she thought of the silver mask he had worn when he had appeared out of the forest on the Lynn road. Steadying herself, she returned his gaze unblinkingly. "Thank you for the bracelet," she said faintly. "Mamma will appreciate its return."

Jack Duppan's expression scarcely changed, but even his slight reaction was not what Mercy had expected. A tiny frown appeared on his forehead, and a faint look of bewilderment came into his eyes. "Perhaps I didn't hear you correctly," he murmured. "Or you might be confusing me with someone else."

"The bracelet that was stolen from Mamma on the highway," the girl blurted out. She was rattled and a little angry; he was confusing her, and she didn't enjoy being made to look like a fool, particularly on so important a matter and by so handsome and fascinating a scoundrel.

"I'm really afraid I don't understand you." Duppan leaned forward, seemingly anxious to recapture the mood that he had been building so carefully and that Mercy's digression had momentarily shattered.

But she jumped to her feet and glared at him haughtily. "Are you trying to deny, sir, that you're a highwayman?"

Laughing, he rose, too, and stood close to her, far closer than was customary for normal conversation. "I can neither affirm nor deny anything until I know the nature of the charge you're bringing against me. To what do you refer when you speak of some highwayman? And has anyone ever told you that you look outrageously beautiful when you're upset?"

Mercy could feel the color deepening in her cheeks, and she hated herself for displaying her feelings so blatantly. In a vain attempt to recapture her dignity, she pretended not to have heard his compliment. "Surely the name of the Gentleman is not unknown in the circles in which you travel, Master Duppan. And surely you're not going to plead ignorance of the existence of the most notorious thief who has ever made Massachusetts Bay unsafe for decent, law-abiding folk."

"How curious. How very curious." His tone was a trifle patronizing, but his dark eyes were still tender, as though he treasured her and had never before gazed at so precious a girl. "In some manner beyond my wildest imaginings, you seem to have mistaken me for a very wicked criminal. I don't know whether to be amused or annoyed with you. I'd flattered myself that I'd made a fair impression on you, ma'am. What have I done to deserve your scorn?"

The fleeting thought struck Mercy that if she were truly mistaken, she had already made herself ridiculous, but she dismissed her doubts. Duppan took a step forward and she retreated hastily toward the fire. "Now you mock me, Master Duppan."

"Mock you when I have been hoping to win your favor? Mock you when I preferred your company to that of anyone else at this gathering? Mock you when I am disturbed at an accusation that would hurt me deeply if it were not so absurd? It is you who mock, ma'am, not I."

His ability to twist her words and her thoughts into new shapes made the girl a little giddy. But she was determined to finish what she had begun. "My mother's diamond bracelet, a personal gift from His Majesty, was stolen the day before yesterday by the highwayman who is known as the Gentleman," she declared, speaking slowly, emphatically.

"I mourn with your mother on her loss."

"Not five minutes ago," she continued bravely, "I found that bracelet in my room upstairs."

"I rejoice with your mother on the recovery of her valuable property."

"Really, Master Duppan!" Exasperated, Mercy wanted to strike him across his arrogant face and remove that superior, condescending smile.

"Perhaps," he said, "the bauble was not stolen at all. Perhaps it was merely misplaced and has now been found again."

"I know better than that, and so do you, sir. Why do you deny that it was you who held us up at gun and sword point?"

"I fear you are even younger than I had guessed you to

be. Or else young ladies in the Maine District are more inclined to romantic delusions than I have ever encountered anywhere in my travels. Delusions though they be, you display great charm in expressing them, ma'am. In fact you remind me of an actress of great talents who held audiences at Whitefriars enthralled—"

"I will not be compared to a play actress on the stage!" Mercy was incensed anew; it was common knowledge that women who displayed themselves in the theater were no more than trollops.

"You have more than compared me to a villainous robber, Mistress Mercy, but I've taken no offense." Duppan drawled his words, and the girl thought she caught the same faint foreign accent that she had heard on the road outside Lynn. "You have made a grave accusation against me, one which would rightly send me to the gallows if it were true." He sauntered nearer and gazed for a long moment into the fire. "Your beauty and your youth are your protection against my ire, of course." He turned and bestowed a dazzling yet tender smile on her. "How could I possibly bear malice against anyone who looks as fresh and as appealing as you do?"

There must be some way to break through his barrier of complacent self-assurance, she told herself. It was like a nightmare: she was certain of his guilt, but she could not smash through his bland protective shell. And what infuriated her was that he dared to make love to her besides. Perhaps, she thought, she could use his amorous intentions to good advantage. The idea left her a little breathless, but she decided to try it, to act quickly.

Stepping closer, she lifted her face to his. "Do you deny," she asked softly, "that you kissed me?"

His smile deepened as he looked down into her eyes. "Had I ever kissed you, ma'am, my treatment of you this evening would have been far different. I would have stilled your chatter by kissing you again—many minutes ago!"

"It was you! I'm sure of it!" Mercy reverted to a childish

stubborn insistence, unable to think of any better retort.

The smile faded from Duppan's lips, and a look came into his eyes that made her shiver. "Even a lady can force a gentleman to forget both her station and his own, Mistress Mercy. You give me no choice but to prove to you that your suppositions are false."

His arms moved swiftly around her, but she fought him desperately, beating against his chest with her fists and trying to squirm out of his grasp. His experience in the handling of reluctant women seemed to be vast; certainly it was expert. Before Mercy quite realized what was happening, she found herself powerless. Her arms were pinned at her sides, and she could not escape him.

Duppan kissed her, hard. In spite of the violence of his embrace he was curiously gentle, too, and after a moment Mercy stopped struggling. Without realizing it she was returning his kiss hungrily, and she knew only that he aroused a passion in her that she had never before felt toward anyone.

At last she opened her eyes, and instantly felt a stab of recognition. There, in the cleft of his chin, was the tiny mole she had seen when he had first kissed her on the road. There was no longer any question that he was the highwayman.

Then he smiled at her and kissed her again, and it suddenly didn't matter to her that this man was a desperate criminal. If anything, she thrilled all the more to his embrace because she knew him for what he was.

He released her suddenly, so abruptly that she almost lost her balance. They stood close to each other, and Mercy, unable to avert her gaze, sensed anew the tenderness as well as the bold strength of this man. It was Duppan who broke the spell. He smiled, simply and without a trace of mockery, and backed gracefully across the library. Then he bowed deeply, turned on his heel and walked out of the room.

Mercy continued to stand very still as she listened to his

fading footsteps. She felt that she had cheapened herself and had made a fool of herself in the bargain. Although she was positive now that Jack Duppan was the Gentleman, the knowledge was small consolation. Her heart still pounding, she thought that she had no proof she could present to anyone else—and she had put the highwayman on his guard.

FOUR

THE DAMP cold of the sea penetrated the woods above Kittery, and there was a thin lacquer of ice over the fir trees and pine, cedars, and oak. Ice was crusted over the snow on the ground, too; it hung in glistening drops from the bending, heavily laden bushes and it filled the crevices in mounds of dead underbrush. The forests were silent in winter, too, for the bear and the squirrel hid, the deer walked warily, the raccoon moved about softly and the birds had fled for a time to a more comfortable wilderness. There was no sound but the crackle of a fire in a hollow, but the hissing of the flames was a cheerful noise, and Andy Pepperrell grinned happily as he squatted on his haunches and spread his fingers near the warmth.

Mercy, he conceded to himself grudgingly, was not too inept a companion for a day's outing, even if she was a girl. She had kept pace with him for four hours as he had hunted for rabbit, and he had to admit that it was convenient to have a female along to act as cook. He was hungry, and Mercy did make as tasty a rabbit stew as anyone in the district. She was absorbed in her task, stirring the pot that was held in place over the fire by forked sticks, and Andy thought secretly that she looked far prettier here in the outdoors than she did when she dressed like her mother and the great ladies who visited the Pepperrell mansion. She was dressed in honest buckskins, which she had tanned herself four years ago and which she had almost outgrown. It made Andy a little sad to think that she no longer looked like a young boy in the faded, limp leather; the figure that changed the shape of the buckskins so drastically fore and aft was certainly that of a woman.

But the bright red that the cold brought out in her cheeks was a decided improvement over the rouge pot that she had used in the house ever since her return from Boston, and her head looked cleaner and firmer with her hair hidden under a tight-fitting stocking cap than it did with curls swirling around her shoulders. And the moccasins which had been given her by the Saco Indians last year fitted her feet more snugly than did the ridiculously fragile shoes on which she teetered and minced about whenever anyone came calling.

All in all, she seemed more like her old self, and Andy thought that the moment might be propitious to bring up a subject on which she had told him just enough to whet his curiosity but not enough to satisfy it. "Merce," he said tentatively, taking care to keep his tone casual and not quite looking at her. "When you were in Boston with Mamma and Papa," he began.

"Mmmm?" She took a pinch of marjoram from a little ammunition pouch she used for herbs and added a scoop of snow to it, then tossed the mixture into the pot.

"About that fellow Duppan." He saw Mercy stir, and there was something about the way she twisted her shoulders that he didn't like. "When you told Papa he was the Gentleman, are you sure Papa thought it was as funny as all that?"

"He laughed, Andy." There was that flat, defensive

note in her voice again; she apparently resented any reference to the matter.

"You know how Papa gets. Sometimes he laughs when he doesn't think something is funny at all!"

The girl stirred the stew more vigorously. "Papa laughed. Governor Shirley laughed. And Captain Warren cried, he laughed so hard. They were all positively rude to me."

"If I was a highwayman," Andy answered thoughtfully, "the first thing I'd do would be to wangle an invitation to the governor's. That way everybody would think I was respectable. And I could keep right on robbing, but nobody would ever believe it was me. Did I tell you that Bill Leonard was over from Elliott yesterday, Merce? He says the Gentleman is at it again. Held up a whole convoy two days ago. Took all their money. Papa should have nabbed him right off!"

"I've already told you, Andy." Mercy's voice was even more distant than before and slightly muffled, as though she was suffering from a head cold. "I was so mad at Papa I could have slapped him. He practically patted me on the head and told me to go mind my own business."

"But Peter didn't laugh!" This was the part of the story Andy liked best. Unlike the suitors who had swarmed around his elder sister, Elizabeth, and those who now found excuses to call at the house and pay their respects to Mercy, Peter Staples did not ignore a young boy or consider him fit only for the company of women. Peter had taken Andy on numerous hunting trips, and they had even gone together on a three-day journey up the Piscataqua by canoe last spring when William Pepperrell had sent his aide on a trading mission into Indian country. It had been the only time Andy had ever been permitted to travel without one or both of his parents, and the memory of that expedition was still bright. "Peter took you serious enough, I bet!"

"Yes, Andy. He did. I've told you already that Peter

spent all the next day trying to learn about Master Duppan. He couldn't find out anything about him that
amounted to much, though three different people swore
he hadn't left Boston for a week."

"They could be the Gentleman's helpers. The ones
who get rid of the jewelry and watches and things he
steals." In his growing excitement, he leaned close to the
fire but seemed unaware of its heat.

"That's precisely what I thought. But Peter said there
was no way of telling."

"He thought they were pretty disreputable folks,
though. Especially the woman. Tell me about that part
again, Merce."

"There's nothing to tell." Mercy pursed her lips primly,
and for an instant there was a marked resemblance to her
mother. "Peter merely said she wasn't a lady and that
gentlemen didn't associate with that sort of person."

"Maybe he'll tell me about it the next time we go
upriver together." Andy tried to look important. "There's
some things us men can't talk about plain and open in
front of girls. But," he added generously, "if Peter tells me
anything he hasn't said to you, I'll let you know about it
after. Provided it's fit for your ears, Merce."

Mercy smiled absently. "Thank you, Andy."

There was a silence again, and then the boy sighed. "I
sure wish I'd been there with you when you faced that
Duppan, Merce. I'd have smoked him out proper! I sure
wish I'd been there."

"It's just as well you weren't." She looked away quickly,
and her brother could see only the back of her stocking
cap.

"You never did tell me the last thing he said to you.
Didn't he try to hit you—or shake you—or anything?"

"I've already told you all there is to tell, Andy." Mercy
sounded positively waspish. "And talking about it bores
me. Can't you think of anything else?"

"Sure." His voice grew gentle, as his father's did when

William Pepperrell was engaging in negotiations that required delicacy and finesse. "For instance, you act so mad and you try to keep everything so secret that I get to thinking maybe you're kind of stuck on that Duppan!"

"That's nonsense, and you're a horrid little boy!" She was very angry, but there was a curious softness to her temper.

Andy was disturbed by this seeming contradiction in her mood, but he knew he had struck home, and his voice grew scornful. "I was right! You really are stuck on him."

"If I hear one more word of your stupid rubbish, just one more, I'm going straight home, Andrew Pepperrell. And you can cook this rabbit for yourself."

The boy looked down and aimlessly traced a pattern in the snow with the forefinger of his right hand. He looked so sad, so contrite that Mercy forgave him and smiled at him. "We won't quarrel any more, Andy," she said. "Let's just forget the whole thing."

"I reckon we'll have to forget it," he replied heavily. "I was kind of hoping that we would really fix that Duppan proper, you and I. I figured that between us we could get all the proof that a magistrate would need to hang him. Even enough for Papa, if he should be sitting on the King's Bench. But seeing you're so stuck on the fellow, I'll have to do it alone. I guess that's all there is to it."

It was dusk when brother and sister returned to Kittery, and as they approached the mansion from the inland road to the west, they heard a commotion in the stable behind the main house. Mercy was tired and dirty after the day's outing and would have gone straight to her room to scrub herself with hot water and dress for supper, but Andy, ever curious, insisted that they stop. And without waiting to see if she was joining him, he pushed open the heavy stable door of rough oak. Two of the Pepperrell retainers, a groom and one of the gardeners, were standing, clubs in their hands, shouting at a tall, impassive Indian, a handsome light-skinned warrior, dressed in the conventional buckskins of the settlers.

The man seemed totally unimpressed by the threats of the servants, and stood with his arms folded across his chest, a disdainful half-smile on his lips. Andy prided himself on his ability to distinguish a native's tribe at first glance, but this brave looked like no representative of any nation within one hundred miles of Kittery; he was at least half a head taller than the Penobscot, and far more slender than the big-boned Saco or the Algonquian of Massachusetts Bay.

No one noticed the boy, or was even aware of his companion who, her interest now aroused, hovered behind him in the entrance. Andy felt called upon to assert his dignity as the sole son and heir of the most prominent man in Maine. "What's all this ruckus?" he demanded, trying hard to sound like his father.

The groom and the gardener both turned, and when they saw him they started to speak at the same time. The latter finally prevailed, thanks to a powerful pair of lungs. "Master Andy," he said indignantly. "Look yonder!"

Andy looked toward the rear, and Mercy gasped in admiration. Even in the half-light both could recognize the beauty of one of the most remarkable horses they had ever seen, a coal black stallion with a sleek coat. The animal was tremendous, and stood easily nineteen hands high; at this distance he looked as though he could carry at least three grown men on his straight, broad back simultaneously.

"Master Andy," the gardener said, "this here ignorant natural is insistin' we can't touch that critter. But we can't leave a stallion loose to amble around. We got three mares comin' in from the fields, and this here beast will make a shambles of the barn, that he will. But this natural is so blame stubborn he won't listen to nobody."

The smile was gone from the Indian's lips, but a faint glint of humor remained in his black eyes. "Nobody touches horse of great warrior," he said, and Andy noted that his voice was pitched higher than that of any men of the local tribes. "Only great warrior puts hands on Avenger. If stranger comes near, Avenger will kill."

The boy moved closer to the huge mount and studied him critically. It was certainly possible that the beast was a killer. There was strength in his shoulders and long, slender legs, and his eyes were stormy and wild. "Move your horse into a stall yourself, then," he commanded the Indian.

But the man did not budge. "Great warrior visit white chief," he said. "Warumba stay here."

"You're Warumba. But this horse belongs to someone else—who's up at the house seeing my father?"

The brave contented himself with a nod, then deliberately turned his back. The two servants looked to Andy for guidance, but it was Mercy, silent until now, who settled the issue. "Come along," she said quietly to her brother, "we'll get the heathen warrior to put the animal out of harm's way himself."

They walked to the mansion without speaking, though Andy paused for an instant and sniffed appreciatively at the odors coming from the brick kitchen buildings that were laid out in a triangle behind the main house. It was William Pepperrell's custom to receive visiting native dignitaries in the office he maintained in his home, but no tapers were lit in that little chamber, and Andy led the way to the drawing room, which was blazing with the lights of a score or more candles. This was the most sumptuous and impressive room in the house, and was rich with furniture that had been carried to the New World in the holds of Pepperrell ships. Its polished walnut chairs, upholstered divans and thick silk drapes were unique in the Maine District, and few of the crude settlers' cabins could compare in size with this single chamber.

It was surprising that William Pepperrell should entertain an Indian here, and still more astonishing to hear the tinkle of glasses behind the half-opened doors, for a law which Pepperrell himself had initiated and guided through the Massachusetts Bay legislature strictly prohibited the sale, gift, or service of intoxicants to the natives. This warrior, Andy thought, must be a mighty personage indeed.

As he looked around the edge of the door, he heard Mercy mutter something to herself. Then, without a word of explanation, she fled up the broad, carpeted stairs to her room, her face fiery.

"Andrew!" His father's voice was sharp.

The boy came into the drawing room slowly; there were times, he thought, when Papa had an ability to see through walls. He glanced at the stranger who stood in front of the hearth with a tumbler of snow-chilled rum in his hand, and at first glance the man did look like an Indian. His hair and eyes were dark, and his heavy, fringed buckskin trousers and shirt were typical of a tribal warrior's winter clothing. But this man was certainly white, and his free hand, resting lightly on the bone-handled hilt of a curved knife in his belt, was that of a gentleman unaccustomed to hard physical labor.

"This is my son. Andy, shake hands with Master Jack Duppan."

The realization that he was facing the man who was, in his own mind at least, the most notorious thief in all of North America was almost too much for the youngster, who stood spellbound, gaping rudely. But Duppan, as usual, was equal to the occasion. Setting his glass on a table with a resounding thump, he first held out his hand, and, when the boy ignored it, he tousled Andy's hair. "I've been hearing about you, Andy," he said warmly. "Matter of fact, I brought you a little something." His hand moved so quickly it was almost impossible to follow it, and, before Andy quite knew what had happened, he found himself in possession of the Indian knife.

On close inspection the handle proved to be carved, with little figures of men on the hunt, on the warpath, and tilling the fields arranged in a simple but handsome pattern. And the blade itself was of sturdy English steel, honed to a razor-fine edge. Never had Andy owned so valuable a weapon, and he glanced uncertainly at his father. Only when the elder Pepperrell smilingly nodded his consent did the boy find his voice.

"You sure you don't want to keep it?" he asked, trying to conquer a feeling of gratitude and telling himself it was wrong to be friendly toward a vicious criminal.

"I told you, lad. It's for you. But take good care of it. That knife has kept me alive in the wilderness for months at a time."

"Thanks." Andy fingered the blade, secretly elated that his mother was not present, for she would have insisted that he was too young to keep it. Then a sudden thought struck him, and his pale eyes grew round. "Have you been in the wilderness, Master Duppan? I thought you were new arrived in the colonies."

Guest and host exchanged brief glances. "Where did you get that idea?" Duppan picked up the tumbler, sniffed and sipped appreciatively.

"Oh, Mercy told me." The words were out before he could stop them.

William Pepperrell frowned, but the tall man laughed as though someone had just said something particularly witty. "That's a girl for you!" he said at last, still chuckling. "I swear, I never yet met one who didn't get the simplest things all mixed up."

Andy looked up at him in new admiration. Here was a man who obviously felt as he did, and anyone who had that much good sense wasn't likely to be a highwayman. On the other hand, Mercy *had* said that he was a newcomer to North America, that he had spoken of recent events in London as though he had been there. It was patent that anyone who wore buckskins with such easy

grace, who possessed a native knife that was a real trea-
sure, and who traveled with an Indian companion was no
stranger to the frontier.

"Jack, why don't you send him out to see your horse?
The boy has a way with animals, and though there must
be twenty head in my stables, not one of them can compare with your stallion." It was extraordinary for one as
formal and punctilious as William Pepperrell to address
anyone but his oldest and most intimate associates by their
Christian names.

But his words reminded Andy of his original mission.
"That beast of yours needs to be moved, or the stables will
be torn down. We have some mares out for an airing, and
they'll be back most any time. I told that Indian about it,
but he says nobody except the great warrior can touch the
beast. I s'pose the great warrior is you."

"Like all members of his race, Warumba is inclined
toward occasional exaggeration. Will you pardon me for a
moment, sir?" Duppan's respect for the master of the
house seemed genuine.

"By all means, Jack. And I trust that Mistress Pepperrell
and our daughter will have joined us by the time you
return."

"I'm looking forward to seeing them both and to renew-
ing our acquaintance." A faint curve of one corner of
Duppan's mouth suggested that he was thinking more
than his words had implied. He bowed with the practiced
grace of a courtier, and even though the gesture was
faintly ludicrous coming from one in the crude dress of
the wilderness, he carried it off. Then he turned and
walked silently out into the corridor.

Andy waited until he was sure that Duppan had not
paused to eavesdrop. Then he turned to his father, his
eyes glistening. "Papa," he said, barely able to suppress
his excitement, "that's the Gentleman!"

The elder Pepperrell's thoughts had been far away, and
he raised his head absently. "What's that, boy?"

"He's the Gentleman. The highwayman. Master Duppan——"

"Rubbish! You've been listening to the romantic babblings of your sister!" Papa seemed thoroughly annoyed.

"Peter Staples thinks he is, too—and Peter is no romantic babbler." It took considerable courage to sass the senior officer of the Maine militia, who also happend to be a strict parent.

"Peter," was the slow, considered reply, "is a very competent, very able young man. He is utterly lacking in imagination, at times, and I'm sorry to say that Mercy supplies him on such occasions from her own fertile store. He'd so giddy about her that he'd believe anything she told him." He stared at his son with patient good humor. "Suppose Mercy told you that the way to hunt for bear is to stalk the brutes. Would you believe her?"

"Anybody knows you set bait for bear and let 'em come to you!" Andy was anxious to show off his knowledge, but at the same time he recognized the point that his father was trying to make.

"Very well, then. Let's hear no more about a man who will be a guest in our home for several days."

The boy thought he could lose nothing by making one final try. "S'pose I was to tell you all that Merce and me figured out, Papa. Would you——"

"I'll tell you precisely what I'd do." Pepperrell's voice invariably became cold and uncompromising when he had made up his mind. "I'd cane you, which is something I haven't done for several years. Jack Duppan was a guest of the King's own Governor General in Boston. He's doing a great service for the colonies in the war that's coming with the French. And he's now in Maine on legitimate business. He's my guest. I'll therefore listen to nothing that would dirty his name—any more than I'd tolerate scandalous talk about members of my own family. Understand?"

"Yes, Papa." Andy was almost convinced; he had never

known his father to be wrong in his judgments of men, and besides, Duppan seemed to have sound sense.

"Go clean yourself up for supper, then. And remember, Andy—I vouch for the man." Suddenly the bleak expression was replaced by a quiet smile. "And keep that knife out of sight, boy. It'll be out of the house for good and all if Mamma catches you with it."

Andy grinned, and, after carefully hiding the blade under his shirt, mounted the stairs to his own room. A tub of cold water stood in the corner, but only a small fire of pine wood burned in the hearth, so he decided not to bathe. It would be sufficient if he washed his hands and face; with a guest in the house it was improbable that his mother would realize he had not bathed.

He used the time he had thus gained to test his new knife on several scraps of firewood, and found it extraordinarily sharp. Then his collection of pheasant and grouse eggs caught his eye; one of the stupid immigrant maids had moved them, and he was so annoyed that he spent the next quarter of an hour rearranging them. The sound of a melodious bell awakened him from his reverie, however; this was the warning that supper would be served in another ten minutes, and he threw off his hunting clothes and donned more civilized attire with such feverish haste that he completely forgot to wash.

Then he bolted down the stairs two at a time; if he showed up late at table, he would be subjected to a severe lecture, an experience that was always uncomfortable but that would be especially mortifying in front of Jack Duppan. Thinking about the man, Andy realized that he had completely reversed his opinion. It was now important to him that Duppan think well of him. He glanced into the drawing room, but it was empty. Perhaps he was already late, and he ran down the corridor toward the dining room, hoping against hope that there was still a minute or two to spare. His parents made it their custom to spend a few moments privately in each other's company just prior to meals, and if that was the case then only Mercy, Duppan and whoever else might have been invited to supper would already be seated at the table.

A single candle was burning in a tiny chamber on the near side of the dining room that Mistress Pepperrell used for the sewing and fitting of her clothes and those of her daughters, and Andy slowed his pace as he heard a murmur of voices within. It was unusual for anyone to be in the sewing room at this hour, and he was curious. Then he distinguished Mercy's voice and a deep baritone, and proceeded on tiptoe.

His sister and Jack Duppan were standing together near the window, and they were so close to each other that Andy's old sense of uneasiness returned. It was one thing for his sister Elizabeth to be a married woman; she had always been grown up, as far back as Andy could recall. It was something else for Mercy to behave like the wenches who waited on table at the seafront taverns in town.

And she certainly was acting like a doxy now! Her eyes were big and round, her stance was deliberately provocative, a teasing smile was on her lips and she swayed near to Duppan, then moved away again, almost like a dancer. The man was enjoying himself, too. The expression in his eyes, the grin on his lips were extraordinarily similar to those of the men who flirted with the tavern wenches, and Andy felt a new wave of resentment against this intruder.

It was impossible to hear what the couple inside the sewing chamber were saying to each other, for their voices were pitched very low, and the boy edged closer to the door. Suddenly Duppan laughed, and Mercy's reply floated out into the corridor.

"Now you're laughing at me!"

"Never, ma'am. I swear it." He, too, had raised his voice.

"I'm not a child, and I won't be treated like one." Mercy sounded as though she were angry, but Andy knew that tone of old and realized she was just pretending.

"Indeed you're not a child, ma'am. And I have no intention of treating you like one. Not now or ever."

To Andy's amazement, Duppan took Mercy into his arms and kissed her. And the boy was further astonished by his sister's response. She didn't strike this bold adventurer; she didn't kick him. She didn't even protest. Instead she seemed incapable of resistance. Their bodies pressed tightly together and they kissed each other so long and so hard that Andy wondered how they could possibly breathe.

He had seen enough, and walked on into the dining room, a feeling of bitterness engulfing him. He hated Duppan, and was more sure than ever now that this crafty fellow was the highwayman. Duppan's game was easy to discern, too. He had lulled Andy's suspicions with the gift of a knife, just as he was confusing Mercy now with his kisses. But he wasn't going to get away with it, Andy vowed.

If it was the last thing he ever did, he was going to find proof positive that this clever devil was the Gentleman. It would be pleasant to watch him swing at the end of a stout rope.

FIVE

It was lonely on the cliffs, with the waves below pounding against the rocks and sending up a freezing spray. And although Kittery was only two hours' ride away, the area was as bleak and deserted as though no man had ever before set foot here. Andy Pepperrell shivered, wondered if at any moment he might be murdered, and secretly wished he were safe at home. Last night he had eagerly accepted Jack Duppan's request that he act as a guide for the visitor and lead him to a spot up the coast known as Lobster Cove, a protected inlet where Andy and his friends often swam and fished in the summer.

The opportunity would be perfect, the boy had told himself, to learn something about Duppan's activities. But on sober reflection now he was not so sure. If the fellow had anything to hide, he would hardly ask the son of William Pepperrell to come with him. But, Andy reasoned, if Duppan had any idea that a seemingly innocent youngster suspected him of being the Gentleman, there was no better place or opportunity to get rid of someone who might eventually help send him to the gallows.

The rocks were slippery, the drop from the empty cliffs to the sea was sharp, and the Indian, Warumba, who had accompanied the pair on the trip, was walking only a few paces behind Andy. All the savage needed to do was to sneak closer and shove; if the fall failed to kill Andy, it would certainly stun him, and the sea would do the rest. The boy glanced nervously over his shoulder, and, as usual, Warumba's face was expressionless. But Duppan, bringing up the rear, grinned and waved encouragingly, and Andy conquered an impulse to break and run.

His imagination hadn't begun to bother him until they had left their horses behind at the edge of a small wood, and, as long as he had been on the familiar back of his mare, he hadn't been troubled. But it was different now, and never before had he felt so helpless. Even the knife Duppan had given him the preceding evening and which he wore so proudly in his belt would be of little use if these dangerous characters decided to kill him.

The sight of Lobster Cove directly ahead interrupted his reverie, and a sense of relief stole over him when he saw the placid waters of the snug harbor. Even the towering, jagged rocks of the ninety-foot wide sea entrance to the Cove looked reassuring because he knew them so well. He stopped short, and in a moment the others joined him. "There's Lobster Cove," he said, feeling a trifle foolish over his fears.

"Thank you, lad." Duppan clapped him on the back and grinned. "If you start back for town, you'll be there well before noon, in time for dinner."

"You don't want me to stay and show you the way back?" The boy was deeply disappointed; the Cove was deserted, and there was no sign of life in the woods on the far side. He had hoped to learn something on this little trip, but he was being sent back to Kittery knowing no more than he had when he had climbed out of his bed shortly before dawn.

Duppan's smile deepened. "Warumba and I can find

our way, and we might be out here for some time. You go on back, Andy. And tell your father I'll definitely see him at supper tonight. Be sure you give him my message, or he might wonder what's become of me if I don't return until late."

The boy swallowed his chagrin and nodded. "Yes, sir," he said. "I'll tell him."

Warumba started down the side of the cliff toward the beach of the Cove, and Duppan gave Andy another friendly slap before following. For several minutes the boy stood and stared after them. Once Duppan turned and waved, and Andy returned the salute feebly, then started to retrace his steps along the heights.

It would not be good, he told himself, to stay within sight of the pair for too long. But he walked with dragging feet, his mind racing furiously. Obviously Duppan and his companion had not come to this isolated spot in midwinter merely for the outing. There was some purpose to the visit, and even though it was probably anything but sinister, in that he himself had come with them, he had to learn their reason. How he would accomplish this end was beyond him, however.

In his desperation he suddenly remembered that somewhere on the slope to his right there was a short cut to Lobster Cove. Several of the older boys had once discovered a natural tunnel that ended in a cave which opened onto the far side of the harbor. As he recalled it, the rocks inside the tunnel and cave had been slimy, the interior had been filled with bats' nests, and the roof had been so low that a boy had been obliged to crawl on all fours to avoid bumping his head.

Nevertheless, he began to search diligently for the entrance as he crept down the side of the cliff, bending low. At last he stumbled across the opening, which was not difficult to find once a person knew where to look. Brambles slashed his clothing as he made his way to the entrance, but he ignored the stinging cuts on his face, his legs, and his arms as he dropped to the ground and made his way inside on his hands and knees. The air was fetid, the cold was numbing, and it was so dark that Andy could not see more than a few inches in front of his face.

At this moment he almost turned back, but his memory of Mercy returning Duppan's embrace renewed his courage, and he at last conquered his terror, took a deep breath, and pushed ahead, feeling his way cautiously as he scrambled across the rocks. Twice something feathery brushed across his face and he was on the verge of screaming aloud, but his fear of discovery was greater than his dread of whatever creatures made this underground passage their home, and he was able to stifle his cries.

Only once before had he negotiated the tunnel, and on that occasion he had been accompanied by two other boys; they had shouted encouragement to each other and had joked loudly at their own fears. This time the journey seemed interminably long. But at last a tiny pin point of light showed up ahead, and Andy crawled more rapidly, secretly gloating at his own cleverness and bravery. The light became broader, and the last thirty yards presented no problem whatsoever. The harbor entrance to Lobster Cove was direclty ahead now, and the opening of the cave was a comfortable two and one-half feet high, only partly obscured by a small boulder.

Somewhere in the distance he heard the screech of an owl, and a moment later the sound was repeated from a point not so far away. Andy's heart pumped harder; what he had just heard was the call of the snow owl, a harsh and high-pitched noise that was utterly distinctive. But it was impossible for any snow owls to be in the vicinity. In fact, there were probably none in all of Maine. These unusual white birds flew down from Hudson's Bay one winter in every four, and they had filled the woods around Kittery only last year. Something definitely strange was going on, and he crawled faster than before, discarding discretion for speed.

When the boy reached the entrance he lay on his stomach, panting, but when he saw two savages appear out of the woods on the north side of the beach, he completely forgot himself. In the lead was a heavily painted warrior, and behind him came a figure in a thick feathered cloak who, at this distance, looked like a young boy. Duppan and Warumba made their way down the cliff, and arrived at a spot no more than ten feet from Andy's hiding place. They stood there and began to shout to the approaching pair. The brave called out something unintelligible and waved with his free hand; in the other he carried a heavy sack that aroused Andy's curiosity.

The cloaked figure and Duppan began to run toward each other; a second later they were in each other's arms, only a short distance from the cave and Andy saw to his astonishment that this newcomer was a girl. The feathered cape slid unnoticed to the ground as she returned Duppan's embrace fervently, and Andy had to admit to himself that although she was an Indian, she was just about the most strikingly attractive female he had ever seen. Her single garment of faded buckskins fitted her tightly, revealing a swell of firm breasts, an incredibly tiny waist, and long, slender legs. Her skirt ended just above her knees, giving her the illusion of added height, and Andy thought she was considerably taller than Mercy.

While it was never easy to judge an Indian woman's age, this girl was certainly young; there was a suppleness about her, an elastic grace that no middle-aged squaw could boast. And when she and Duppan broke apart, Andy saw that the wench was truly beautiful—by any standards. Her amber skin was paler than that of most Indians, her lips were full and very red, and her eyes were soft and luminous. Her straight black hair hung down to her shoulders, and in her ears she wore loops of gold which set off her high cheekbones and her short, straight nose to perfection.

In fact, as Andy looked at her he felt vague stirrings that

were far from unpleasant, and for an instant he forgot his self-appointed mission and the fact that Duppan had similarly embraced his sister only a few hours previous. Then the whole party drifted closer to the opening of the cave, and the boy shrank back into the interior. He could not see as easily, but his chances of being discovered were lessened and he could still hear everything that was being said.

"Tani has missed the great warrior." That was the voice of the girl, husky and caressing. "For three moons Tani has awaited the great warrior. When he would not come to her, she has come to him."

"I'd have come to you in another month or two, Tani. You know I've never broken a promise." Duppan's voice was confident, easy.

"Tani will not leave him again." Duppan laughed, but his tone indicated that he would tolerate no opposition. "I'm going back to Kittery tonight."

"No! Tani says no!" Some folks claimed that Indians never displayed their emotions, but this girl was openly agitated.

"And I say yes. We've waited a long time to be together, and we'll have to wait a little longer. There's too much at stake, and we'd be stupid to risk everything we've tried to achieve. Trust me, Tani. I've never let you down, and I won't now."

Andy's heart was pounding so loudly that he could not hear the Indian's reply. There was no doubt left in the boy's mind that Duppan was engaged in some kind of activity outside the law. Although nothing he had said so far necessarily indicated that he was the Gentleman, he was certainly playing a shady game of some sort.

The warrior who had come with the girl was opening the big sack that he carried, and Andy's attention was distracted. To the boy's disgust, the contents were nothing more mysterious than food. The Indian pulled out a large chunk of red meat, several large potatoes, a few onions,

and a big earthenware jug. These he spread out on the
deflated sack, then began to help Warumba collect
driftwood for a fire.

Andy promptly lost interest in these proceedings.
Meantime Duppan and the girl had moved off down the
beach, their arms around each other's waists, and although they were talking earnestly, he could no longer
hear what they were saying. Annoyed, he decided to wait
for the next development. So far he had learned nothing
of value, but something might happen that would be
interesting and important.

All that happened in the next few hours was that
Warumba and the other warrior cooked the food, and the
girl and Duppan then joined them in eating a hearty
meal. The only significance in all this that Andy could
discern was that the girl must be someone of consequence, for under ordinary circumstances no brave would
ever prepare food if a squaw was present to do the work for
him. Otherwise, the boy knew only that he himself was
miserable, that the odors of venison steak and of potatoes
roasted in coals made him even hungrier than he ordinarily would have been, and that the sight of the quartet
consuming their dinner was a torture more exquisite than
any he had ever known.

The damp, fierce cold seemed to penetrate his bones,
and his back and leg muscles ached from the burden put
on them by his cramped position in the cave. Again and
again he was on the verge of abandoning his attempt to spy
on Duppan and to return home. But that would mean
admitting defeat, and worst of all he would look silly in his
own eyes. And so he repeatedly forced himself to stay on a
little longer; occasionally either Duppan or one of the
Indians would glance out toward the entrance to the Cove
and beyond, as though waiting for something, and these
rare gestures encouraged Andy.

Then, after more than three hours, his patience was
rewarded. Warumba jumped to his feet and began to

speak quickly in the strange Indian tongue as he pointed out to sea. The others stood, too, the remains of their meal forgotten. The girl's feather cloak blocked Andy's view for several minutes, but at last she moved slightly and he saw a single-masted fishing sloop with a dirty gray sail anchoring just inside the entrance to the harbor. A tiny gig was lowered from her side, and two men rowed toward the shore. To the boy's amazement they did not beach their little craft, and they seemed to exchange no conversation with Duppan, who had walked down to the shore.

Instead, one reached into the pocket of his rough pea jacket and threw what appeared to be a weighted package wrapped in oil paper. Then the men turned the gig around and headed back to the sloop, which they promptly boarded. Meantime Duppan opened the packet and drew out a single sheet of parchment, which he read briefly, refolded carefully and carried to the fire. Andy could see his face clearly for a few seconds, but his expression was one the boy could not define. His features looked strained, yet in a strange way he looked rather pleased, too.

The Indians asked him no questions, and he apparently told them nothing as he squatted down again before the fire. Then, suddenly, he threw the parchment into the center of the flames and prodded it with a stick until the paper crumbled to ashes. By then the sloop had hoisted her anchor and was sailing out of the harbor mouth, aided by a fresh west wind. Neither Duppan nor the Indians looked at her again, and all four resumed their meal as though nothing had happened.

Andy decided he'd had enough. He could not even pretend to understand what he had just seen, and he was certainly no closer to proving that Duppan was the highwayman. All he had in return for his day's activities was a cold, aching body and an empty belly. What was more, he might meet Duppan and Warumba on the road unless he left soon, and in that event he wouldn't know how to answer their questions as to why he had not returned home hours earlier.

Disgusted with himself, he backed away from the opening, turned around with great difficulty in the cramped cave and started back in the direction from which he had come so long ago. At least he would have the pleasure of taunting his sister, and despite the possibility that he might be heard crawling through the cave, he could scarcely control a laugh that bubbled up in him. He would enjoy seeing the expression that would appear on Mercy's face when he told her of Duppan's duplicity with the Indian girl. Mercy would hate herself for having been so free with her kisses, but she would hate Duppan even worse. The ways of adults were admittedly unpredictable, but Andy knew his sister well enough to be sure she would be raging mad.

William Pepperrell stood with his back to the fire that roared in his study hearth, a tumbler of ice-cooled white rum in his hand, and faced his guest. "It's too bad you couldn't get here yesterday, as we'd planned."

Captain Peter Warren, resplendent in the blue and white and gold uniform of a senior officer in His Majesty's Navy, perched on the edge of a book-littered table, his weather-beaten face a network of deep lines. "I should have sailed in a frigate of my own command," he said heavily. "The damned captain of that damned snow didn't know how to handle his ship in a blow. I hate snows, anyway. A two-masted brig is a clumsy ship. Even so, I'd have arrived here at supper time last night if I'd been on the quarterdeck, I can tell you. But I'd still be floundering around at sea somewhere if I hadn't climbed into my uniform, taken the merchantman's authority away from him and put the damned snow into Kittery harbor myself. That's the trouble with these civilians, Will. One day or another doesn't mean a thing to them. I can tell you that when my commission as commodore of the colonial fleet is authorized, I'm going to be damned chary of the captaincies I'll hand out to the masters of merchantmen. I'd rather put a lieutenant with battle experience in command every time!" He took a gulp of rum, and although the aged liquid was fiery, his face did not change expression; he might have been drinking water for all that he reacted. Suddenly he shrugged and laughed. "However, I shouldn't complain. We have the rest of the week to talk."

"So we do," his host agreed. "But unfortunately Duppan won't be able to remain. He's leaving tonight."

"The devil you say!"

"I'm afraid I do. He returned from a day up the coast only a quarter of an hour before I had word that your brigantine was docking. I tried to explain to him that we both need all the time he can give us, but he insisted he had to leave this very night."

"What's so all-fired important to the young whippersnapper?"

"He didn't say," was Pepperrell's mild rejoinder, "and he's not the sort of man who confides his personal business in anyone. The most I could get out of him was that he'd tell us everything that he could remember about the French and their plans, and he said he was positive this one evening would be enough."

"I suppose it'll have to be," Warren grumbled.

"Under the circumstances I've asked young Staples to join us. As secretary of the council he can take notes on anything that needs to be put on paper. And I've asked him to bring his records with him, in case there's anything we might want to look up."

The naval officer stared at his friend incredulously. "General Pepperrell," he said, "I think you've lost your mind. You're certainly not going to confide our intentions with regard to an attack on Louisburg to Jack Duppan! Hellfire, damnation and brimstone—we hardly know the man! We——"

"Easy, Peter. Easy." Pepperrell sniffed his drink and sipped appreciatively. "You know me well enough to understand that I'm going to confide in no one. You and Governor Shirley and Peter Staples and I are the only men in all the colonies who know that Louisburg will be the object of our attack. Even your ship captains and my regimental commanders will think that we're going to strike Quebec. Until we actually put out to sea and hold a flag-ship conference."

"Then I don't see——"

"I'm never one to waste motions, Peter, as you know. After Duppan leaves us tonight, we'll sift whatever information he's given us, and we'll have Staples right here to refresh us on any data we want checked."

Warren grinned sardonically. "And here I expected to have a long night's rest in one of the noted Pepperrell beds," he declared in mock-tragic tones. "We'll be at it most of the night, Will."

"So I expect," was the calm reply. "I think I've anticipated that, too. I've asked Staples to spend the night."

They drank in silence for a few moments, and there was no sound but the crackling of the burning logs in the fireplace. "We'll need to be damned careful how we question Duppan," Captain Warren said at last, gazing thoughtfully at his tumbler. "Although he's a landsman, he's clever enough to be a first-class sailor, if only he'd put his mind to proper things. And if we start asking him about Louisburg, he's likely to start splicing bits of hemp until he's made a stout rope."

"Have you any reason to doubt his loyalty, Peter?" The question came quietly.

"None. On the other hand, the fewer who know the secret, the better. My last dispatch from London said the French minister went home to take the waters at Aix-les-Bains for the rheumaticks a month ago. The embassy has been left in the charge of that imbecile, de Guiche. And that can only mean that King Louis is planning to declare the war at any moment."

Pepperrell shook his massive head sadly. "Business will suffer badly," he said, then brightened. "However, if you and I can take Louisburg, there'll be an end to the suffering very quickly."

"And if we fail," Warren replied cynically, "you and I won't be on this earth long enough to know the difference. Even if we should survive Louisburg and come slinking home, we'll be thrown into madmen's pits and be stoned to death by every one of the King's subjects from Kittery to Charleston."

Mercy could remember few evenings that had ever dragged so miserably. She had come to her own room immediately after supper, when her father, Captain Warren, Peter and the despicable Jack Duppan had retired to the study. Her mother would have enjoyed hearing her read, but Andy would have been present and she had grown sick of his gloating expression long before supper had been finished. Her humiliation was complete, and she wanted to suffer it alone.

At first, when Andy had told her he had seen Duppan kissing an Indian girl at Lobster Cove, she had flatly refused to believe him, even though she secretly knew that he was telling the truth. But he had been so insistent, so explicit in his descriptions of all that he had seen that she had finally been forced to admit openly that Duppan was a careless deceiver.

She was still unsure of how much Andy knew about her own indiscretion in having allowed the bold visitor to kiss her the preceding evening, and she was pathetically glad that the boy was sufficiently sensitive not to tell her blatantly that he had somehow learned she had made a complete fool of herself. But Andy played a small part in her present thoughts.

She stood inside the partly opened door of her room, listening to the men below as they brought their conference to an end, and she could concentrate on nothing except a picture of Duppan. She had been angry and mortified at supper every time he had smiled at her, every time he had paid her one of the gallant compliments that seemed to come so easily to him. It had been galling to realize that in a matter of a few hours he had exchanged her caresses for those of some uncouth savage female, and it was bitter even now to know that much of her anger was prompted by sheer jealousy.

And she was ashamed of herself for eavesdropping, for having remained fully dressed when she should have gone to bed. But she was determined that no man, particularly an adventurer and criminal, could treat her affections lightly and escape without reproof. When the meeting ended she intended to return downstairs and would pretend she had left something in the conference room.

Then she would find some way to indicate to Duppan that she wanted a word with him alone. She was sure that a man as devilishly clever as he had repeatedly proved himself to be would invent some excuse to pass a few minutes in private with her. She wouldn't need much time with him, just enough to tell him she thought him contemptible.

An owl screeched at the far side of the lawn, then repeated his call. Mercy clenched her hands, remembering what Andy had told her of the signal between Duppan and the Indian girl. The cry she had just heard was definitely that of the snow owl, yet she could scarcely believe Duppan's mistress would come to this house for him. Be that as it may, something very strange was happening.

Not bothering to throw a cloak or even a shawl over her shoulders, she dashed out into the corridor and was past her parents' room and the chamber of Captain Warren to the back stairs. At the foot of those stairs was a covered passage that led to the so-called "guesthouse," the original mansion built by her grandfather, and in it were the servants' quarters and a number of spare rooms which were used to accomodate overflow guests like Peter.

The cold air shocked Mercy and she shivered as she ran along the walk, avoiding patches of ice. A complete plan had formed in her mind. at the top of the guesthouse was an old-fashioned watch tower which Samuel Pepperrell had erected as a lookout for hostile Indians in the days when Kittery had been a wilderness village. When the weather was clear there was an unobstructed view of the surrounding area from the top of the tower, and Mercy felt sure that tonight, with a bright three-quarter moon shining, she would be able to see whoever was signaling to Duppan.

She crept up two flights of stairs, grateful to be indoors again and hoping she would not encounter any of the servants. It would be embarrassing to explain her presence here, and she could think of no excuse that would be satisfactory. So if she should run into someone, even her mother's long-nosed personal maid, she would tell nothing and would let the curious assume what they would. Her own curiosity was the more urgent.

Peter's room was located at the base of the tower stairs, and as Mercy passed his door she was glad he was not there. She dreaded having him, of all people, know what she was doing. It was increasingly likely that she would some day marry Peter, and it would be excruciatingly humiliating if he ever learned that she had stooped to spy on Duppan.

Emerging through a trap door onto the watchtower platform, Mercy almost abandoned her project. The wind was even sharper here, and the rough-hewn, five-foot high pine logs that formed the circular wall of the tower hemmed her in, made her feel cut off from the entire world. She had not been up here since she had played as a child, and she had forgotten how desolate it was. Snow, dry and powdery, was thick underfoot, and her new party slippers were soon soaked. Something swung back and forth slowly before her eyes, and she had to repress a scream, realizing just in time that the object was an old crow's nest which the wind had loosened from the pavilion roof and which was now hanging by a single vine thread.

The venture seemed as futile as it was adolescent, and Mercy began to retrace her steps to the trap door, placing her feet only where she had already left an imprint. She smiled ruefully at her folly; her feet were already wet, and her concern for her shoes was stupid.

Then she heard the owl cry again, and she forgot herself, hurried to the wall, and peered out into the night. About two hundred yards away, near a fringe of trees on the far side of the front lawn, she saw a figure on a horse. It was not possible, at this distance and in the moonlight, to see whether the mounted individual was a man or a woman.

She stared out across the snow, blinking, and even as she began to speculate about the unmoving rider, she heard the front door of the main house open, and the distant rumble of voices floated up to her. The top floor of the new building cut off her view of its entrance, but she guessed that Duppan was leaving, and even as she waited impatiently for whatever was to come next, she was sorry that she had not kept to her original idea and inveigled him into spending a few moments with her. Now she would probably never see him again, and deep regret was mingled with her relief.

It would certainly be better for her peace of mind that she would have no more to do with him, that she would not be in a position to be tempted by him. Her rival, although only a savage, was welcome to him.

Her rival. She smiled thinly at her own absurdity. She had to be honest with herself and admit that it was her own fault that she had allowed Duppan to make love to her. He had not courted her in the accepted manner, nor had he made any commitments, any promises. His bold approach had swept her off her feet, and if she had acted with almost the abandon of a trollop, she had no one but herself to blame. If she had not been a lady, and William Pepperrell's daughter, she might have even allowed Duppan to take her to bed, though she had to admit in all honesty that while the idea of having an affair with him had occurred to her repeatedly, he had never even hinted at a real desire to seduce her.

That made her angry, too, for she was sure he was having a real affair with the Indian girl, and it was insulting that he had not made similar advances to her.

Having reminded herself of the native girl who was undoubtedly Duppan's mistress, Mercy's distress grew more acute. No amount of rationalization could hide the uncomfortable fact that she had cheapened herself, but she tried to argue that her own inexperience had been responsible. Never before had she met such a fascinating man, so complex and unusual a personality. He was sophisticated where the other young men of her acquaintance were gauche, he was in such complete control of himself that he commanded others. It was unique for any man to take her and her attraction to him for granted, even while he flattered her, and she wished that Peter would dominate her more, that he would be a little less the humble supplicant for her favors.

No, that was wrong. Peter was honest and reliable, and his very steadiness and sobriety were a guarantee of marital happiness. What was wrong with her, she wondered, that she shrugged away the qualities in a man that she had been taught by her parents to admire and respect? There was something very much the matter with her, and she would have to draw a tight rein on herself.

She heard the sound of hooves, and a few seconds later Duppan rode into view. He sat his saddle insolently, and his ease was that of a man who had spent years of his life there. Mercy was annoyed to discover that she had difficulty in catching her breath as she watched him move down the path that lay about fifty feet to the north of the guesthouse. She could see his features clearly from here, and she told herself fiercely that anyone so sure of himself was ugly.

Nevertheless she felt the same pull to him that had so long plagued her, and a new sense of panic swept over her. She was again about to abandon her post, but she reminded herself sternly that no Pepperrell ever admitted failure, and she remained behind the log wall, miserable and shivering.

To her amazement, Duppan rode toward the rear of the guesthouse rather than toward the gate, and the figure at the far side of the lawn came toward him rapidly. After a few moments Mercy, watching intently, saw that this other person was a man. He was dressed in buckskins which he wore loosely, in the Indian fashion, and she decided that he was probably Duppan's retainer, Warumba. If she had used her head from the start, she would have realized that he was the logical person to have been waiting for his master.

The pair came together just beyond the original kitchens of the old house, which were now used for the storage of grains and meats, and they halted their mounts, then remained where they were, unmoving. If they said anything to each other, their voices were not audible from the tower. Mercy was bewildered for a few seconds, and then she divined what was afoot.

Duppan, as she had good reason to know, was the Gentleman. And her father was the wealthiest man in all of North America. Even a child could figure out the rest: the highwayman was going to rob this house!

She fled from the tower, forgetting to close the trap door in her haste, and hurried down the stairs. There was a light under Peter's door now; that meant he was in his room, and that help was close at hand. Mercy stopped short and tapped softly but urgently.

"Just a moment!"

She heard a chair scrape, and Peter walked to the door and opened it. To Mercy's relief, he was still fully dressed, and a single glance was enough to indicate that he had been writing in a big book which was opened on a square pine table. In his right hand he still held a quill pen.

"What's the matter, Merce?"

The girl stepped quickly into the room, and spoke softly; there were servants sleeping on this floor, and they would get the wrong impression if they heard her in Peter's chamber. She explained quickly what she had seen, and only when she was halfway through her recital did she realize that Peter would wonder why she had been up in the watchtower in the first place. However he was too polite to ask, and he heard her through without question. In fact his consideration for her was such that he left the door ajar, even though a chilly breeze swept in from the corridor and nullified the heat of the little hearth fire.

When she finished her tale, Peter was silent and stood frowning slightly, tapping the quill thoughtfully on the edge of the table. "I'll grant you that neither of us has ever trusted the man, Merce," he said at last. "But I've got to admit that he was very helpful tonight. He gave us considerable information that will be useful to us when we march against the French. And there's nothing really significant in his having circled back to the house. The obvious explanation is that he forgot something—and simply came back for it."

"If that were the case," she replied heatedly, "why did he come around to the rear of the guesthouse? Why didn't he just ride straight up to the front entrance, as any ordinary person would do?"

A new voice spoke directly behind her. "Because, my dear, I had private business here and didn't want to be interrupted."

Mercy looked around, startled, and saw Jack Duppan standing in the frame, a pair of pistols in his hands. He kicked the door shut with a gentle tap of his booted heel, and leveled one pistol at Peter, the other at the girl.

Peter was the first to recover. "What's the meaning of this, Duppan?" he demanded, and Mercy was pleased at the quiet strength in his voice.

Before the intruder could reply, a dark figure appeared at the window, and an instant later Warumba raised the sash from the outside and leaped into the room. Mercy wanted to scream, but so much happened in the next few seconds that she had no chance. The Indian held a short tomahawk in his right hand, and he sprang at Peter, who had almost no chance to defend himself, and struck the young officer over the back of the head with the flat side of the weapon. In almost the same breath Duppan jammed the pistols into his belt, took firm hold of Mercy and, despite her violent struggles, stuffed a large linen handkerchief into her mouth. The gag was not completely effective, but she could make no more than a faint, muffled sound, insufficiently loud to attract the attention of even the coachman or the gardener who had the adjoining rooms.

Duppan could use both hands to hold Mercy now, and she was powerless in his strong grip. She tried to kick him, but he stood to one side, still pinning her arms to her sides, and he chuckled lightly. Then he took a strip of rawhide from his Indian confederate and quickly bound Mercy's hands behind her back.

The smile faded as he turned to Warumba. "Take Captain Staples at once," he commanded. "Use the stairs. I'll join you in a moment."

For the first time the girl was aware that Peter lay in a crumpled heap on the floor. Warumba picked him up, Duppan opened the door, and the Indian departed silently, carrying his burden. The man who had been a guest in this house less than thirty minutes previously regarded his recent host's daughter quizzically.

"It's unfortunate for you that you chanced to be here when I chose to call," he said. "But you've seen far too much, and from the snatch of conversation I overheard,

you have been observing my movements. You're less
naïve than I'd thought, my dear—or else incredibly innocent. In either event you're too dangerous to leave here, I
regret to say. I'd leave you behind if I could, I swear it.
Much as I enjoy your company." He shook his head
sorrowfully. "Women are a terrible nuisance at times.
And I certainly didn't expect I'd have to deal with you
tonight. Oh, well. A man does what he must."

Although Mercy's hands were tied, she still had the use
of her legs, and she tried to make a quick break for the
door. But Duppan had apparently anticipated such a dash
and stepped in front of her. With seeming effortlessness
he picked her up and slung her over his left shoulder,
holding her behind the knees so she could not kick. "If
you didn't have a gag in your mouth," he whispered, "I'd
be tempted to kiss you again. Please, Mercy—be a sensi-
ble girl and don't make a fuss. I have no wish to hurt you
or mistreat you, but if you don't behave, I'll be forced to
become rough with you. And that's something we'd both
regret."

Glancing around the room he saw the open ledger on
the little table. He stepped over to it, not relaxing his grip
on Mercy, and looked down at the writing, leafing
through a few pages as though to assure himself of the
contents of the volume. Then he whistled softly under his
breath, closed the book with a snap, and placed it carefully under his free arm. He blew out the little lamp on the
table, and, carrying the girl as though she weighed almost
nothing, he stepped cautiously into the corridor.

Mercy knew that unless she attracted help in the next
few minutes it was likely that Duppan would successfully
carry off this outrageous abduction. But the gag remained
firm, she could not free her wrists from the leather thongs
that held them in place behind her back, and she was
utterly powerless in Duppan's grasp. She was badly
frightened, worried about Peter, and bewildered by the
strange turn of events. Duppan was certainly the notori-

ous highwayman who had held up the Pepperrell family on the road. There was no doubt of any kind left in her mind on that score. Yet he had, to the best of her knowledge, taken no money and had seemed intent only on stealing the book in which Peter had been writing.

But she was given no immediate clue as to what was happening. Duppan stole down the back stairs and came out into the open. Warumba was already mounted on the gelding, with the unconscious Peter thrown across the pommel. Duppan, still carrying the girl, mounted his stallion, and the two horses started off rapidly and boldly through the front gate. As they cantered north along the deserted road facing the ocean, the lights in William Pepperrell's study continued to wink brightly and cheerfully.

SIX

DUPPAN and Warumba increased their pace as soon as they were out of sight of the Pepperrell mansion, and they rode hard for more than two hours, in spite of the burden on their mounts. The stallion was in the lead, and Mercy, perched on the saddle in front of Duppan, had to concentrate her full attention on keeping her balance. Although the man kept one arm around her to steady her and to hold her securely, she was in constant danger of falling as the huge beast cantered along the sea road. She could feel the great power of the animal, but knew that Duppan was not giving him his head for fear he would slip on the ice that was crusted underfoot.

Nevertheless their progress was unimpeded, and with each passing minute as Kittery fell farther behind, hopes of immediate rescue became dimmer. The girl could not tell whether Peter had been seriously injured by the tomahawk blow, or even whether he had yet regained consciousness. Warumba's gelding was some yards to the rear, and Mercy was afraid that if she twisted around to look, she might slip and be seriously injured.

The cold was intense, and her silk gown was little

protection against the elements. She shivered repeatedly, and at last Duppan extracted a thick buckskin shirt from a saddlebag and managed to wrap it around her. But even the leather was not enough, and she had to lean against Duppan and take warmth from his body. She told herself repeatedly that she would rather freeze, but her will to live was greater than her pride and she found herself constantly nestling against his chest, much to her annoyance.

She was unable to speak, for the handkerchief was still stuffed in her mouth, and Duppan, devoting his full attention to the perilous job at hand, did not address her. It was hard to think with the wind whistling through her clothes, with the surf crashing against rocks and the hooves of the horses thundering and jarring. There were tears on Mercy's cheeks, whether because of the cold or her plight she did not know, and she could not wipe them away. She hoped they would not freeze on her face and disfigure her; even in her peril she could not forget her appearance.

At last Duppan turned inland and followed a narrow, twisting path through the forest. The horses could only walk here, picking their way daintily, and Mercy discovered that it was somewhat warmer, as the snow that lay heavily on the bare branches of the trees acted as a blanket and cut the full force of the wind. The stallion was breathing easily now, unperturbed by his double burden, and for the better part of an hour he walked sedately, responding instantly as Duppan guided him through the endless maze of oak and cedar and birch and spruce.

It was somewhat easier now for Mercy to organize her thoughts, but she remained utterly bewildered and knew only that the man whose arm encircled her was a criminal of the most dangerous sort. The abduction of Peter Staples had been carefully planned, but she could not imagine the reason; similarly, the ledger that Duppan had stolen from Peter's table surely had little monetary worth. There were priceless paintings, objects of art worth many hundreds of pounds, expensive items of silver and wrought gold in her father's house, and she could not understand why the thief had taken none of them.

The mystery would be clarified eventually, she supposed. Meanwhile she could only commiserate with herself. Her own capture had been accidental rather than intentional, but she could not even guess what was to become of her. She was furiously angry with herself for feeling as she did about this incredible experience: even though she felt a great sense of fear, so intense that it bordered on dread, she was enjoying herself in a perverse way, too. All that really bothered her at the moment was her acute physical discomfort, which had eased somewhat. The very nearness of the rogue in the saddle behind her, the firmness of his arm around her waist and the intimacy of his breath on her cheek disturbed her as no lady should ever be aroused, and although she knew it was wrong, she could not control herself.

She conquered a ridiculous desire to laugh, and a few minutes later began to feel sleepy. She had difficulty in keeping her eyes open, and she thought vaguely that when she returned home no one would ever believe this part of her story. It did not cross her mind that she might not be returning home. After all, she was the daughter of the wealthiest and most powerful man in the colonies, and no one, not even Duppan, would dare to do her real harm. Her innocence was her greatest protection, and she dozed.

When the stallion pulled to a halt Mercy awoke, and had no idea whether she had slept for hours or for only a few minutes. Duppan and Warumba had stopped in a small clearing, and although the moon was waning she could still see clearly. The first thing she noticed was that three new horses were tethered to trees that marked the far limits of the open space. She herself was still in the saddle, but Duppan was standing on the ground, and facing him was a wildly angry Peter, his hands secured behind him.

The girl was so relieved that he was alive and unhurt that it was several seconds before his heated words sank in.

"You'll never get away with this, Duppan!" he was shouting. "Every militiaman in New England will be after you. And you'd better know, we don't treat spies here like they do in Europe. You won't be given the courtesy of a firing squad, or even of a hanging. The boys will tear you apart, Duppan. And King Louis won't be able to help you!"

So that was it; this adventurer was a spy for the French! Mercy was instantly wide-awake, and a score of details, hitherto meaningless, became clear to her. Before she had a chance to digest and analyze the information, however, she became aware of someone regarding her with naked hostility. Blinking slightly in the semi-darkness, she saw two figures on the far side of the clearing. One was a tall Indian brave and the other was an extremely attractive young squaw in a feathered cloak, who stood very still and watched Mercy with blazing eyes.

This was undoubtedly the wench whom Andy had seen with Duppan, and Mercy returned the glare contemptuously. For an instant she thought that the woman would spring at her, but Duppan took immediate command of the situation. He issued a series of angry, guttural orders in a strange Indian tongue. The squaw brought a shorter version of her own cloak out of a saddlebag, handed it to Duppan and then ostentatiously turned her back on him.

Meanwhile Warumba and the strange warrior picked up the protesting Peter and deposited him in the saddle of one of the fresh horses. He tried to call something to Mercy, but one of the braves cuffed him hard across the mouth to silence him. All then mounted, and Duppan took his place behind Mercy on the back of the stallion. He arranged the short cloak around her shoulders, and, even though she resented the gesture, the garment was surprisingly warm. He then removed the gag from her mouth and called out another order. The unfamiliar warrior took the lead, Warumba rode next, holding the reins of Peter's horse, then came the Indian girl, and Duppan brought up the rear.

He addressed Mercy before she had a chance to tell him what she thought of him. "My deepest apologies," he said to her in a soft, caressing tone, speaking close to her ear. "I know you're undergoing great distress, ma'am, but it can't be helped. We'll stop for some food and a proper rest a little later in the day, after we've put a few more miles between us and the good people of Kittery."

"You're detestable." Mercy could think of nothing more devastating at the moment, and if her hands had not been tied she would have turned and slapped his face. As it was, she sat upright, trying not to touch him, and stared straight ahead, not deigning to look back at him.

"I'm in hopes that you'll learn to change your opinion of me." As usual, the scoundrel sounded absolutely sincere. "I hadn't planned to take you with us on this little journey, but your presence in the quarters of the vigorous and handsome Captain Staples gave me no choice. Had I known that a lady of quality was to be with us, I would have made other arrangements. Under the circumstances, you'll be forced to share our crude existence, for which I hope you'll accept my regrets."

He was so audacious that Mercy didn't quite know how to respond. But she made up her mind not to quibble with him; at all costs she would maintain what little of her dignity was left. "No one is more despicable," she said slowly, "than the man who spies for personal gain in times of peace."

"Ah, but we're at war," he answered calmly. "Only yesterday I received word that not quite four weeks ago Louis XV signed the necessary proclamation. The news should arrive in Boston and Kittery any time now."

Shocked, the girl turned part way around in the saddle. "How could you have learned of so important an event before anyone else heard of it?"

Duppan chuckled. "Your energetic little brother of course told you of having guided me to a spot called Lobster Cove yesterday. He may even have witnessed a small vessel putting into the harbor to meet me. That boat met me by prearrangement, to bring me instructions from my superiors. It brought me those instructions—and I'm now carrying them out. It also brought me notification that a state of war exists between our mother countries. If I were to tell you how the details were planned to send the word to me so quickly, you would scarcely believe me. But you must admit that we are clever."

"So clever, Master Duppan," the girl retorted, "that you'll end your days on the gallows."

"Not Duppan, if you please, ma'am," he said imperturbably. "Permit me to introduce myself under my right name. I am Jacques Duphaine, known in some quarters as the Marquis de Grémont. As nobility means so little in this New World, I seldom use my title and am known simply as Monsieur Duphaine. You, of course, may call me whatever you please."

"It will please me most when I have nothing whatsoever to do with you," Mercy said, her composure at last breaking. "When are you going to return me to my home? And when are you going to set Peter free? I demand——"

"I am the last man in this world to refuse the demands of a lovely lady—that is, when I am in a position to comply with them. In this matter, however, I'm afraid my hands are tied as tightly as your own." He smiled slightly at his own joke.

It was plain that he intended to reveal nothing, and Mercy asked no more questions. She told herself that she long ago should have recognized his faint accent as French, just as she should have forced her father to listen to her suspicions about him. Now, thanks to her carelessness—and, she had to admit, her infatuation for him—the English colonies would suffer, her own family would be hurt, and she was in the greatest jeopardy of all.

There was no further attempt at conversation, for Duphaine-Duppan seemed content with silence, and the little party continued to push through the forests. By daybreak the horses were tiring, and Mercy was so exhausted that she would have fallen from the saddle had Duphaine not kept his hold on her. Every muscle in her body ached, she was still chilled and discovered that she was hungry as well. She caught an occasional glimpse of Peter now, and she could tell from the way that he slumped forward on the back of his mount that the strain was telling on him, too.

Even the Indians were dispirited, and only Duphaine's energy seemed boundless. Whenever the others flagged, he called encouragement in a voice that was alive and vital, and it seemed to the dazed Mercy that his strength alone kept the group in motion. It was at least an hour after dawn, perhaps considerably longer, when the horses were halted and the entire party dismounted. Duphaine gallantly lifted Mercy out of the saddle and cut the leather thongs that had held her wrists for so many hours. He seemed to know that she was too listless now to strike him.

When she would have approached Peter, the squaw girl stepped in front of her and brandished a small, double-edged knife. Duphaine immediately came between them and said something to the native girl in her own language; judging by his tone it was scathing, and she winced. She backed away, still holding the knife, still staring at Mercy with smoldering eyes. Watching her in return, Mercy had to concede that she was exceptionally attractive—for a natural.

Looking around, Mercy saw that they were making camp in a natural hollow scooped out of the side of a hill near the summit. The semicircular wall of the depression provided a partial protection from the elements, and the charred remains of a number of campfires indicated that this place had been used as a retreat before.

"I suggest, ma'am," Duphaine said courteously, "that

you take advantage of our stop to rest and sleep. Don't try to escape, if you please, as I've charged Tani with responsibility for you, and she'd like nothing better than to chase you through the snow and trees down yonder and drag you back here by your hair. You might even be hurt a little." He stopped and grinned in the friendliest manner. "For some reason Tani seems to be jealous of you."

Mercy refused to rise to the bait, and stood in ankledeep snow, swaying dizzily. Warumba was building a fire, the other warrior was tying up the horses, and Peter had been dumped unceremoniously on a clear patch of ground some thirty or more feet distant, too far to exchange words of any significance. Duphaine gave the girl a moment to gain her bearings, then took her firmly by the arm and led her to the rock wall of the hollow.

"I can't offer you as comfortable a bed as the renowned feather mattresses of your family's home, but in my humble way I'll try to return the hospitality of your parents to me." Duphaine called out something to Tani, and the Indian girl approached slowly, carrying a blanket, which she thrust at him; then she stalked off, her head high, her long feathered cloak gathered around her.

"Here you are, ma'am." He spread the blanket on the ground, first kicking away a few stones. "Wrap yourself in it, and you'll soon be comfortable. The fire will help, too. And I give you my word as a gentleman," he added hastily, seeing the expression in her eyes, "that no one will molest you."

He stalked away, and Mercy, too tired to argue or disobey, sat down on the ground and pulled the blanket around her. To her relief it was reasonably clean, and she smiled wryly as she thought that even had it been grimy, her silk gown was ruined after the long and arduous night. She stretched out on the ground, and the warmth of the blanket cradled her. The flames of the fire that Warumba had made leaped higher, and their heat dispelled the bitterness of the wintry Maine air. Thoughts crowded through Mercy's head, but they were disconnected, jumbled, and almost before she knew it, she fell into a deep sleep.

Judging by the position of the sun, it was late afternoon when she awoke. The fire was still blazing, and as she sat up she saw that Peter was stretched out on the far side of it under a blanket, wide-awake and watching her. Mercy stood and tried to brush out some of the wrinkles in her gown, Duphaine's buckskin shirt, and the short feather cloak that covered her. She longed for a comb, a mirror and a little privacy, but all were obviously being denied her. Tani appeared at her side and beckoned sharply.

"Come," the Indian girl said, and led Mercy to the woods at the edge of the clearing. While the English girl tried to make herself presentable, Tani watched her stolidly for a time, then turned, cut a long, thin branch from a nearby tree and expertly stripped it of leaves.

A sense of uneasiness stole over Mercy; she could not guess what was in store for her, but the malevolence of the other girl's expression was plain to read. Suddenly Tani reached out, shoved Mercy's shoulder and pointed in the direction of the fire. "You cook!" she commanded.

Mercy was startled, and for an instant she stood still. That moment was all that Tani wanted, and before Mercy quite knew what was happening the Indian girl had slashed her viciously across the ankles with the switch. Mercy danced away in pain and alarm, unconsciously retreating toward the fire. Again the switch lashed out, and in trying to avoid its supple, cruel sting she stumbled and fell to the ground.

Tani, standing above her, struck again, and Mercy felt the blow through her skirt and petticoats. "You cook!" the young squaw again directed.

Warumba and the other warrior, who had been paying no attention to the two women, now stood to watch the fun, laughing loudly. Mercy struggled to her feet, trying to avoid the repeated slashes of the switch; she had been humiliated enough, and only one thought was in her mind. She was going to repay her savage torturer with interest.

Only half-aware of what she was doing in her rage, she reached out, and her left hand caught hold of Tani's long, thick hair. Mercy pulled with all her strength and was rewarded by a howl of pain. Then she caught a glimpse of a flash of steel, and saw that Tani had drawn her little two-edged knife. Warumba was upon them before she could use it, however, and his technique for settling the dispute was as effective as it was crude.

He cuffed Tani across the side of the head and she fell back. In almost the same motion his right hand shot out and he shoved Mercy with such force that she staggered, slipped and sat down, hard, on the ground. She would have risen to her feet and continued the fight, had not Peter called out to her.

"Do what they tell you, Merce. Don't argue with them. Don't dispute them. They have the better of us now, and it does no good to attack naturals when they hold the upper hand."

Mercy's anger cooled, and Warumba nodded in solemn agreement. The bad blood between the women could have resulted in tragedy, and he looked relieved. Mercy stood slowly, brushed snow and mud from her clothes and glared at Tani, who stood a few feet away, watching her stoically. Again it was Peter who broke the deadlock.

"Don't make them angry while Duphaine's away!" he shouted. "Come over here and do as the wench has told you. There's a kettle here—and some food. And I reckon they'll let us talk while you're fixing it—if you seem meek enough."

There were tears in Mercy's eyes as she walked toward the man whom she would have married in Kittery one of these days had not tragedy struck in the form of Jacques

Duphaine. "Are you all right, Peter? That blow on the head last night—"

"Oh, my head is right sore," he replied, attempting to sound cheerful. "But I have a tough scalp. I figure it'll need to be tough," he added in a lowered voice, then spoke again in a louder tone as he directed Mercy to the kettle and the slabs of venison and bear meat piled up beside it.

She began to prepare a stew at once, and Warumba rejoined the other brave nearby. Both warriors sat in watchful, seemingly indolent silence, but neither interfered with the conversation of the two whites. Tani edged closer and remained standing, her eyes never leaving Mercy. Her own temper had dissipated, however, and her knife was no longer in her hand. If Mercy ignored her, the chances of a new flareup were remote.

"I don't think you rightly know the spot we're in," Peter said quietly. "The devil who's captured us is French——"

"He told me," Mercy replied, thinking that never before had she so appreciated Peter's even disposition. "His real name is Jacques Duphaine, and he says we're at war."

"Yes, and I'm a prize of war," her suitor said grimly. "Merce, you have no idea how critical a spot we're in. Duphaine has my council book!" He paused, saw that she failed to grasp the significance of his words, then resumed. "I was working on my notes for the intercolonial war council. And wherever the notes are incomplete, they intend to force me to tell them whatever details are lacking."

Mercy gasped, unable to speak. Like everyone else in Maine and Massachusetts Bay, she had heard countless stories indicating that the French in Canada were devils incarnate, and she had a mental picture of Peter being put to the torture on the rack in some Quebec dungeon. She closed her eyes and shook her head.

"Don't you worry about me," he said soothingly. "I can take care of myself just fine, and any day one man from

Maine can't stand up to a whole regiment of French, you just let me know. It's not me I'm worrying about. It's you. And the whole war plan. Merce, they aren't going to watch you near as close as they're watching me. We're due north of Kittery, and no more than five to ten miles inland, I'd say. Sometime in the next day or so, soon as you get the chance, you slip away. Get down home as fast as you can. And tell your father and Captain Warren that the enemy has taken me."

"I'll try, Peter," Mercy's voice trembled slightly.

"You've got to do more than try! If we don't outsmart Duphaine, we're likely to lose this war!"

SEVEN

THE PALE winter sun had disappeared behind the usual midafternoon clouds when Jacques Duphaine returned to the little camp. The others had finished eating and were, at Warumba's insistence, trying to sleep; the brave had explained to the captives that the journey would be resumed at dusk, and that they would again ride all night, so they rested while they could. Mercy, wrapped in the blanket, could not sleep, however. She felt the ever wary eyes of Tani on her, and she wondered if the creature would try to kill her after she dropped off. It was obvious that the Indian girl considered her a rival for Duphaine's affections, but Mercy considered it beneath her dignity to tell the woman that she was welcome to the scoundrel.

Minutes before Duphaine rode into the compound Warumba and his brother warrior were on their feet, their long rifles ready. They relaxed their vigilance when he moved out of the cover of the trees, and Mercy, who had planned to ignore him when next she saw him, sat upright and stared at him in astonishment.

He was dressed in the white breeches and cape of the

Gentleman, with the silver mask covering his face. He removed the plumed hat that he affected when he wore this costume, and when he jumped to the ground he patted two large saddlebags that drooped at the stallion's sides. Significantly, both were full. After calling greetings to his companions, he removed the bags and walked straight to Mercy. Stopping in front of her, he whipped off his mask, bowed elaborately and thrust the heavy leather pouches toward her.

"You'll be interested in these, ma'am," he said, grinning.

The girl shrank away from the offending bags. "These contain stolen property."

"They're for you, Mercy. Take them."

"I wouldn't dream of it," she replied indignantly. "Do you think for one minute that I'd sink so low——"

"Do as you're told." The smile faded abruptly from Duphaine's lips. "You've caused Avenger and me considerable trouble on your account, and you'll take the gifts I've brought for you!"

He pulled open the pouches and hauled out clothes in profusion. There was a heavy wool skirt with a fur-trimmed jacket to match, a heavy and serviceable cloak lined with beaver, a pair of soft boots made like a man's, and, most surprising of all, three extremely pretty dresses. The highwayman watched Mercy closely as he removed the objects of apparel, and when he had finished he stood above her, frowning.

"You can't travel in the clothes you're wearing now," he said grimly. "It's a wonder you didn't freeze last night, and I'm not going to risk having you fall sick and slowing us down on our journey. The other things are for your use after we arrive at——our destination. If you could see yourself now, you wouldn't be acting so high and mighty. You're supposed to be a lady, but you don't look like one. Your gown is torn and dirty, and neither that old shirt of mine nor Tani's little cloak is particularly suited to your type of beauty." He paused, and the grin reappeared on his face. "You'd thank me nicely if you knew how much trouble you've caused me. There aren't many people riding in and out of—the town that's closest to us, especially at this time of year. And I had to go to a great deal of bother to find someone roughly your size. You should be grateful to me, not angry."

In spite of herself, Mercy began to laugh. Duphaine was being so open, so bland that she felt ridiculous in maintaining her haughty attitude. He would surely hang some day, and then she would have her final satisfaction.

Right now, of course, an immediate problem faced her. She had to either refuse the clothes or accept them. Her conscience warred with her common sense, and her femininity finally tipped the scales. She looked down at what had been a delicate, attractive dress. She glanced at the things Duphaine had brought her, and she could not take her eyes from the beaver-lined cloak. After last night's ride she knew what was in store for her, and she thought longingly of the snug warmth the cloak would provide.

"All right," she said abruptly. "I'll take them."

"Good." Duphaine roared with laughter, but stopped when he saw her expression. "I beg your pardon, ma'am," he added hastily. "The thought just came to me that now you're my partner in crime. You've joined the Gentleman's band!"

The party pressed north again through the second night, and Mercy had a mount of her own now, a spirited little mare that Warumba led out of the woods shortly before sundown. The animal had patently been stolen, but the girl asked no questions and made no complaints. She was relieved at having been released from the embarrassment of spending the long hours in intimate contact with Duphaine, and she found considerable satisfaction in the use of a saddle, which had been taken from Tani and given to her. The Indian wench was forced to ride bareback, and the incident did little to improve the feeling between the two girls.

Peter's words were ever present in Mercy's mind, but

she had no opportunity to escape. Duphaine now assigned the task of keeping watch over her to Warumba,
who kept his gelding only a pace or two behind her mount
all night. The Frenchman devoted his own attention to
Peter, whose hands were again bound when the journey
resumed. Twice when Mercy tried to speak to him on
short stops, both Tani and Warumba approached her
menacingly and cut her off, and it seemed likely that
Duphaine had decided to permit no further conversation
between the captives.

When morning came they stopped to sleep, and this
time they found refuge in a huge, dry cave set high in the
bleak rocks behind a broad expanse of wild beach. It was
obvious that Duphaine and his companions had used this
place before, for they had come to it knowingly, and the
charred remains of what had been a large cooking fire
were scattered just outside the entrance.

Mercy was once more assigned the task of preparing
breakfast, and Peter's bonds were cut so that he could join
the others. To the surprise of everyone but herself, she
cooked a particularly succulent venison stew, a dish she
had watched her parents' servants prepared many times.
Peter complimented her warmly, and the Indians greedily
ate serving after serving.

But Duphaine sat apart, ate alone, and addressed no
one. He had not said more than a dozen words to any of
the group throughout the night, and had not once looked
in Mercy's direction. She had at first thought that he was
annoyed with her, and then realized that he was preoc-
cupied. She hoped that he was worried, that something in
his plans had gone amiss, but there was no way to determine whether or not something unexpected had really
happened.

The one encouraging sign was that Peter had become
aware of the Frenchman's mood, too, and seemed to be
developing some plan of his own. At any rate he smiled
cheerfully at Mercy while they ate, though she knew of

nothing to be happy about, and when they finished and moved into the cave, he winked at her surreptitiously.

The two girls were assigned the innermost portion, and Duphaine placed Peter and himself some twenty feet nearer the entrance, taking the precaution of tying a thong to his prisoner's right wrist and looping the other end over his own. Warumba and the warrior whose name Mercy did not know took up positions just inside the entrance and apparently intended to take turns keeping guard.

Sheer physical exhaustion numbed Mercy, and she fell asleep almost immediately, reasonably sure that Tani would not try to knife her while Duphaine was near. She had seen the Indian girl look at him often, and her expression was always one of fear as well as of love. And that fear would control her and prevent her from giving in to her primitive urge to do away with someone she believed to be a rival. Mercy's last conscious sensation before dropping off was to feel a sense of pique over the way Duphaine had ignored her through the night and at breakfast. Although she wanted nothing to do with him, now or ever, it bothered her that he could be so indifferent to her.

She was awakened by the sound of voices, and she heard Peter and Duphaine talking. Rather than interrupt them by allowing them to know she was awake, she pretended she was still sleeping, for the tenor of the conversation indicated that Peter was putting some carefully devised scheme into operation.

"You admit, then, Duphaine," her father's aide was saying, "that you think of yourself as one of the gentry?"

"I am a gentleman." She sensed a certain stridency beneath his calm tone.

"Then you're willing to abide by the code of gentlemen, I'm sure."

"There are many interpretations of codes, Monsieur le Capitaine Staples. As your country and mine are at war, the ordinary rules do not apply. Were we at peace, you and Mademoiselle Pepperrell would not now be my honored if reluctant guests."

There was a brief silence, and Mercy, opening her eyes slightly, saw that both men were standing. Peter faced his captor, his expression earnest. "A gentleman," he said carefully, "never takes unfair advantage of an opponent. He tries to insure, always, that someone else has a sporting chance."

"We are agreed so far," was Duphaine's cautious reply.

"You gave me no such chance. Your natural yonder knocked me unconscious before I had a chance to defend myself."

"I see. And you would like such a chance now?"

Mercy held her breath and tried to conquer a feeling of panic. She remembered, even if Peter did not, that Duphaine was extraordinarily skilled with a pistol. But she controlled herself with the thought that he planned whatever he had in mind, and he was never one to act rashly or unwisely. "I'm offering to meet you in a fair trial, Duphaine," Peter said. "If I kill you, Mercy will be free to return home. And if——"

"One moment, Monsieur le Capitaine. You speak of fairness. You might kill me, but you know I will not knowingly kill you, for you have a value to my employers. A very great value."

Peter laughed with seeming indifference. "You might as well kill me for all the information that either you or your French generals will get out of me, Duphaine," he said recklessly. "However, if you win, we'll both go along with you peaceably, and will make no attempt to escape. But if I win, the girl is to be set free. What do you say?"

Mercy jumped to her feet and spoke before she could stop herself. "No, Peter!" she called. "Don't do it! He'll cheat you in some way. He'll trick you——"

To her surprise Peter ignored her, waving her away as though she were a child meddling in the affairs of her elders. "Well, Duphaine?" he asked. "Will you fight me, or are you afraid?"

The Frenchman was very much aware of Mercy, and grinned at her amiably before turning back to his adversary. "Monsieur le Capitaine Staples," he said, "I salute your courage though I deplore your wisdom. You have judged me correctly, of course, and know I cannot resist your challenge."

Peter nodded in quiet satisfaction. "Good," he said grimly. "As you're the challenged party, you have the right to name whatever weapons you please."

Duphaine answered at once. "Few men anywhere are my equal with the pistol," he said in a voice that was matter-of-fact, without a trace of the ego that his words implied. "So I might kill you, and you're of value to me only if you're alive. Tumblerough might give both of us much satisfaction, but it is not a fitting medium for a duel between men of blood. That leaves swords as the alternative. You've had experience with them?"

"Enough to run you through."

Mercy knew that Peter had taken daily lessons in the art at a *salle des armes* in London during the eighteen months he had spent abroad, and her sense of depression lifted. Peter had been clever, far more adroit than she had dreamed he could be, and had deliberately maneuvered his opponent into this position. There was truly a chance now that he could win her freedom, but a few lingering doubts remained in her mind. She approached and put her hand on the sleeve of Peter's torn jacket. "Don't trust him," she said loudly. "He'll do anything to keep you with him, Peter. So, please—don't trust him."

"I'm sorry, Merce, but I've got to take the risk. It's the only way out for us. I don't know how else to get you back to Kittery safely. You can take word to your father about——"

She lost patience with the stupidity of males. "He can't afford to let you win," she replied heatedly. "If he can't beat you fairly, he'll find some other way! Don't you understand, Peter?"

"Have you any better suggestions, Merce?"

Duphaine smiled at both of them like an indulgent father. "I give you my oath in the presence of my friends," he said, a trace of amusement in his voice, "that I will duel fairly with the courageous Capitaine Staples." He beckoned to the listening Indians, who moved closer. "The lovely Mademoiselle Pepperrell will act as judge of the sword fight," he said loudly. "If—at any time during the duel—she decides that I am cheating, you are to stop the fight. And the penalty will be my forfeit of the engagement." He turned back to Mercy, and his face was solemn. "I have given my promise, ma'am. If I cheat in any way, and you alone are to decide on my fairness, you will then be free to return unmolested to your home in Kittery."

He bowed, then carefully removed his buckskin overjacket and slowly rolled up the sleeves of his lawn shirt. Meantime Peter, too, removed his jacket, looking pleased at the success of his stratagem. Mercy was far from satisfied, but she could no longer object, for Duphaine seemed to be meeting all of her conditions. But something still did not ring true, and she stood in uneasy silence as the Frenchman uttered a short command and Warumba, a dubious expression on his face, rummaged in a blanket roll and returned with two long swords, double-edged.

Duphaine took them and offered them to Peter, hilts foremost. "These are somewhat less than perfect weapons for duelling, Monsieur le Capitaine Staples, but they are the best I can provide on such short notice and under the circumstances in which we find ourselves."

"I insist you take first choice, Duphaine." Peter disdained to even glance at the swords.

"On the contrary, I am familiar with both, so I shall have somewhat the better of you, no matter which you take."

His argument was reasonable, and Peter examined the blades critically. The one on the left had the more ornamental hilt, but he judged the other to have a better balance. At any rate, it was made of English steel, and he had often used a similar weapon at the *salle*. He took it unhesitatingly, and it felt good in his hand. Without another word he and Duphaine walked side by side into the open.

Mercy hurried back into the inner recesses of the cave for her cloak, and, by the time she emerged into the clearing, she saw that the others were all waiting for her. Peter was cutting through the air with his sword, testing it, but Duphaine stood still, holding his blade as one would a walking stick, with the point digging into the ground. The two braves and Tani were some feet distant, and though the men's faces were wooden, there was a malicious gleam of satisfaction in the wench's eyes that increased Mercy's sense of disturbance.

Before she could probe the feeling, however, Duphaine bowed low to her. "Our judge is ready," he said. "In the absence of seconds, have you any instructions for the principals in this encounter, ma'am?"

She was so bewildered that she didn't know what to say but Peter answered for her. "Let's dispense with the humor, Duphaine," he declared roughly, his voice heavy with anger. "You know the rules as well as I, so I suggest we begin. Merce, move back to the cave entrance, and keep out of the way."

He barely gave her time to comply before lifting his sword in a brief salute to his opponent. Duphaine answered with an extravagant flourish, then leaped forward in an all-out attack. Watching him move with the speed and grace of a wild animal, a hint of a smile at the corners of his mouth, Mercy suddenly realized that he had goaded her deliberately in order to arouse Peter's anger and thus make him more susceptible to defeat at the outset of the duel.

But the year and a half practice in London stood the young man from Kittery in good stead. He held his ground, parried the Frenchman's bold thrust, and himself attacked with an unorthodox upward cut as Duphaine recovered and moved back into position. Both men laughed, to Mercy's astonishment.

"My felicitations, Monsieur le Capitaine," Duphaine said. "You were very quick."

"Just quick enough, Duphaine. On guard!"

They circled each other warily, treading as lightly as they could on the frozen ground. Each had gained a wholesome respect for the abilities of the other in the few seconds they had crossed swords, and neither was taking unnecessary chances; there was too much at stake. It seemed to the fascinated, horrified Mercy, who had never before watched swordplay, that Peter was certainly Duphaine's equal, and she secretly applauded him for his sharp thinking in having precipitated this situation. For the first time she felt there actually was a possibility that within a few minutes she would be free.

Twice Duphaine cut at his opponent, but the blows were apparently not intended seriously, for Peter merely danced out of the path of his enemy's sword, not bothering to protect himself with his own. It was almost as though Duphaine were nervous and lashed out because he was unable to hold his blade still. Then, without warning, Peter took the offensive. He moved in warily and slashed wickedly at the Frenchman's face, then his body, using the sword in the fashion of a cavalry saber.

Now it was Duphaine's turn to show his defensive skill, and he handled himself adroitly, easily, as he beat aside a series of lightning blows, parrying each with calm and precision. Peter lunged, and the Frenchman feinted. Suddenly, unexpectedly, he slipped on a small patch of ice and fell to one knee; he still held his sword in his right hand, but he appeared to be helpless as Peter moved in on him. Mercy closed her eyes for an instant, expecting Peter to run the scoundrel through. To her amazement he stood five feet from the Frenchman and raised his weapon in salute. Even as she admired his gallantry, the girl thought that his gesture could be costly, both to her, personally, and to the English colonies.

Duphaine regained his feet quickly and lifted his own blade. "*Merci*," he said.

Peter nodded and immediately returned to the attack. The rhythm of footwork and bladework had been interrupted, and he wanted to regain the initiative before the other could completely recover. But Duphaine was expecting such a maneuver and was ready for it. He turned aside Peter's thrusts, and each time that he parried he recovered and slashed out brilliantly himself. Gradually, almost imperceptibly, Peter was forced to retreat.

And Mercy, watching, began to realize at last that Duphaine was actually the better swordsman by far. Until now he had been playing with his opponent, testing his strength and his skill. But, having almost lost the encounter and his life when he had slipped, he was obviously determined to take no more chances. He cut, thrust and slashed so repeatedly and with so many variations of each move that the girl could scarcely follow the path of his blade, and she marveled that Peter was able to protect himself as well as he could.

Then Duphaine cried out in triumph. In almost the same instant Peter's sword flew out of his hand, soared high in the air and landed some twenty feet or more away. The Frenchman had accomplished the disarming of his opponent with such consummate skill that he made it look easy.

The two men stood facing each other, and Duphaine continued to hold his sword outthrust. Peter did not move. "It's your privilege under the code to run me through," he said, not flinching. "You've disarmed me fairly, and I'm beaten."

"I do not use my blade against an unarmed man, Monsieur le Capitaine Staples." The highwayman's courtesy seemed to Mercy to be somewhat exaggerated. "And as I have undergone some difficulty in securing your person, I have no intention of killing you."

They bowed to each other, and Warumba hurried to the spot where the sword had fallen and retrieved it. Neither he nor the other brave showed their reactions to the outcome of the duel, but Tani was openly delighted. Her eyes sparkled and she was smiling broadly, but Duphaine was as unaware of her as he was of Mercy.

"I trust it will not be necessary to remind you, Monsieur le Capitaine," he said to his recent adversary, "of the conditions which you yourself named for this exercise. Do I have your pledge that you will make no attempt to escape?"

Peter smiled ruefully. "You have my pledge," he replied. "Of course you understand that as soon as we arrive at our destination, I will consider myself released from my bond."

"Of course," Duphaine said, and there was a faint undercurrent of mockery in his words.

"However, I can speak only for myself. Merce," he said, turning to the girl, "you needn't feel bound by what I've promised. I didn't ask for your agreement to abide by the terms of my duel, and you're under no obligation. If you want to try to escape at any time, your honor isn't involved. However," he added heavily, "I'm afraid there's precious little you can do. That's why I thought of this fight in the first place. It was the only way that I could figure out for you to get free. And now I've failed us both."

Mercy was too miserable to speak and could only incline her head. Peter had been gallant and honorable, but his chivalry had availed him nothing, for Duphaine, when presented with a like opportunity, had not permitted his opponent to rearm. As unscrupulous in a duel as in everything else, he merely paid lip service to the code of gentlemen.

He had still another surprise in store. Sweeping off his hat with a typically flamboyant gesture, he grinned, first at Mercy, then at Peter. "You have failed more than you know, Monseiur le Captaine. It had been my intention to set Mademoiselle Mercy free and to start her safely on her journey home as soon as it was possible for me to do so." There was no judging from his expression whether he was in earnest or was mocking them. "However, as I have won a fair fight by fair means, she will now accompany us on the remainder of our journey."

Peter showed his deep chagrin plainly, and he struggled to find a suitable reply. But Mercy spoke before he had a chance. "You may have been fair," she cried to Duphaine. "But you certainly weren't chivalrous! When you slipped on the ice, Peter gave you another try. But when he lost his sword, the duel was over!"

The Frenchman's lips tightened, but his eyes were still sparkling. "Staples," he said calmly, ignoring the girl, "you have the potential of becoming a master swordsman. Your eye is keener than mine, and all of your instincts are right. But you've had too little practice in actual combat. A man learns best when his life is at stake. That's when his wits sharpen." He turned unexpectedly. "Warumba, give him his blade."

The Indian wanted to object, did not dare, and complied, though reluctantly. Peter seemed quite pleased at being given another chance, but Mercy's apprehension increased, though she could not define her reasons for it.

"Take up your position!" They faced each other, raised their swords and saluted. "Now," Duphaine instructed, "when I maneuver so, and place my tip inside your guard, your natural response is to feint, is it not? You wish to restore the balance."

"Of course." Peter was concentrating completely.

"I must therefore divert your attention. I must create an incident that will cause you to forget. I have the advantage over you. I must distract you from guessing the meaning of my grand counter-feint. What do I do? I use whatever resources are at hand. Here there is ice. Voilà! I slip on the ice!"

He skidded and dropped to one knee, almost precisely

as he had done before. "Then the next time I feint—I do not slip!" Peter burst into laughter, but Mercy could not share the joke. So Duphaine had only pretended to slip! Sick at heart, she realized that Peter's gallantry had been an empty gesture. His wily opponent had tricked him in order to more easily disarm him. There had been no doubt as to the outcome from the very start.

Mercy had heard enough. As Duphaine continued his explanation, steel rang against steel, but she did not listen. Instead she turned and walked into the cave, telling herself fiercely that she would never understand men or their ways. Both victor and vanquished were shouting in pleased excitement, but she knew only that Peter's bright scheme had failed and that her future was as black and hopeless as his own.

EIGHT

BOTH captives were surprised when the journey was not
resumed after sundown, although cooking utensils and
other paraphernalia had been packed. Warumba disappeared shortly after eating a hasty dinner, walking rapidly
north along the beach until he passed from sight where
the land curved sharply in a vast semi-circle into the sea.
Duphaine, Tani, and the remaining warrior all seemed to
be waiting for something as they sat afterwards around the
fire, and occasionally one or another wandered down the
beach and stood for a time peering off into the darkness
before returning, shrugging and lapsing into silence.

There was virtually no conversation as the evening
dragged on. Duphaine seemed tense and nervous and was
lost in his own thoughts, the Indian brave was habitually
quiet and Tani took her mood from the Frenchman. She
said little, but continued to keep a close watch over
Mercy. Peter had no appetite for small talk, and the
exhilaration he felt after his abortive duel gradually gave
way to a sense of depression.

Mercy wanted to comfort him, to put her hand over his

as he sat before the fire, his elbows propped on his knees. But she could not speak freely before Duphaine, whose very presence made her uncomfortable. She knew she should be as pleasant and charming as possible to him, for she was completely at his mercy, but she could not bring herself to dissemble. Sometime soon she would have the chance to tell him in detail of the contempt and loathing she felt for him, but, perversely, she could not and would not express her opinion before others. It would do her no good to give him the tongue-lashing he deserved, but she could think of no other relief for her sense of outrage, and when the propitious moment came, she would tell him precisely what she thought of him. She felt sure that every woman he met flattered him, so it would be satisfying, though futile, to puncture his inflated conceit.

It was at least four or five hours after sundown when a high, shrill birdcall sounded in the distance. Duphaine, Tani, and the warrior were on their feet instantly, and the Frenchman put two fingers to his lips and answered in kind. A few minutes later Warumba reappeared, followed by a burly, heavy-set man wearing clothes that were something of a contradiction, for although the material of his breeches and short overcoat was rough and heavy, they were superbly tailored. The newcomer walked with the rolling gait of a sailor, but when he drew near, Mercy saw that his complexion was very pale, unlike that of virtually all of the seamen who sailed under her father's flag.

The man and Duphaine shouted greetings to each other, embraced, and then, after the fashion of men, began to pound each other on the back. A moment later they were conversing together rapidly in French. The girl understood little of the language, and as both were speaking softly, she could catch no more than an occasional word. The new arrival glanced once or twice at Peter and nodded as though pleased at Duphaine's coup in having captured so prominent an enemy.

Then, she knew, they were discussing her. The newcomer looked at her, and even though the night was too dark to see clearly, her flesh crawled under his glance. Never had any man dared to show his lust so openly, so brutally, and she wanted to shrink into the cave, to remain there until she died. But Duphaine caught the impact of the fellow's look, and his reaction was immediate.

He took hold of the man's coat with one hand, waved an admonishing finger under his victim's nose and addressed a few words to him in a tone that was barely audible. But the intent of his words was clear: Mercy was not to be molested, and anyone who came near her or annoyed her would be responsible to him.

Although the burly man was at least thirty pounds heavier than Duphaine, his respect for the mercurial highwayman was obvious. He stepped back in alarm, began to apologize profusely, and finished a long outburst of oratory by removing his stocking cap and bowing to the girl. She realized suddenly that, although he was steady on his feet, he was drunk. She pretended to be unaware of his very existence, but actaully she was going through a considerable inner turmoil. Against her better judgment, she felt a new surge of warmth for Duphaine. Although he had flirted with her, abducted her, and forced stolen property on her, he was making it clear that he was her protector, that he would permit no one to treat her other than as a lady, and she felt grateful to him.

Fortunately, for her pride's sake, there was no opportunity for her to demonstrate her feelings. The horses were gathered together, and after saddlebags were piled on their backs, they were led off up the beach by the brave and a reluctant Tani, who indicated that she preferred to remain near Duphaine but whose wishes were firmly overruled.

The rest of the party then proceeded on foot, and Peter and Mercy were required to walk in the lead, with the others a few paces behind. This was their first chance to speak privately in many hours, but for several minutes they said nothing as they trudged along the cold, hard sand. At last the girl broke the silence.

"Do you know where they're taking us, Peter?"

"Not for sure, but I reckon it'll be Quebec."

"Surely they aren't going to force us to walk all that distance," she said, alarmed. "We'll never make it all the way up there without the horses, Peter! We'll freeze to death first. We——"

He put a hand on her arm to quiet her. "We aren't going to walk, Merce. There's a ship of some kind waiting for us up yonder, around the bend of the beach. That's why we've been waiting half the night. Duphaine had a previous rendezvous with her, and with that man who met him. He's Duphaine's superior. Didn't you hear them jabbering away at each other?"

"My French isn't good enough for all that."

"It'll soon have to be." Peter laughed without humor. "You might have a long spell in Quebec, Merce. When they hear your father's been made a lieutenant general, they'll keep you as a prize hostage, maybe until the end of the war. But don't you worry," he added hastily, seeing her dismay. "They won't dare harm you. The daughter of General Pepperrell is no ordinary prisoner."

She knew better than to ask the question that forced its way to her lips. "What about you, Peter? Will you be all right, too?"

He shrugged, and she slipped her hand through his arm. The last time they had walked together in this way had been on the Boston Common, and that seemed like something that had happened in a dream. Mercy wanted to cry, but for Peter's sake she could not. The injustice of what was being done to them overwhelmed her, and her sentiment became transformed into fury. She wanted to turn, hurl herself at Duphaine and kill him with her bare hands. Suddenly she began to tremble, and Peter hugged her arm closer.

"Don't worry about me, either," he said, misunderstanding her lack of self-control. "Like I've told you before, I can take care of myself fine." He paused and took a deep breath. "I reckon they'll throw me into a dungeon and try to beat or starve me into telling them what I know. It's what we do to prisoners, too, you know, so you needn't be shocked. But, Merce, there's just one thing. If—when I come out of wherever they're going to hold me, will you—be there for me?"

"Yes, Peter, I will." She barely whispered her commitment.

He wasn't sure he had heard her correctly. "You'll wait for me?"

The power of speech deserted her completely, and she could only nod affirmatively.

Never had a proposal of marriage been made or accepted under such unusual circumstances, but Peter was equal to the occasion. He stopped short, put his arms around Mercy and kissed her soundly. At first she felt cold, almost lifeless. Then all of her frustrations of the past few days came to the surface, and she suddenly found herself returning Peter's embrace fervently. Until this moment he had never aroused her, but the passion that swelled in her now was like a wind so irresistible that she could not keep her balance.

Then a cold, ironic voice broke the spell. "Very charming, my young friends, and very touching," Jacques Duphaine said. "Unfortunately the tides do not wait for romance, so I fear we can pause no longer."

The snow *Dauphine* was as snug a two-masted merchant vessel as any ship ever made in French yards, but her passenger accommodations were somewhat less than luxurious, and the captain was more interested in his cargo than in the comfort of his guests. The horses were herded onto the aft deck, Peter was hustled below, and Mercy, to her horror, found herself sharing a tiny, cramped cabin with Tani. There was just enough room

for two bunks, one above the other, and if both stood at
the same time there was scarcely enough space to crowd
past each other. When Mercy arrived, led by the captain's
steward, Tani was already ensconced in the lower bed,
and she made it instantly plain that she considered the
arrangement eminently unsatisfactory, too. She sat up,
glared and looked as though she were about to spit on the
deck.

Mercy wanted to back out, to take herself anywhere but
here; however the steward had already gone, closing the
door behind him. There was no choice but to see the
experience through, in spite of Tani's evident aim of
making it as unpleasant and uncomfortable as possible.

"Great warrior has ordered that Tani must share in this
room."

"No one told me about it. I understood that I was to
have a cabin to myself." Mercy debated with herself the
wisdom of undressing and decided to remain fully clothed
for the night.

"Tani does not wish this. But Commandant
Tediere—he who met the great warrior on the beach—
has filled his belly with brandy. And the great warrior has
ruled in secret that Tani is to sleep here."

"There's nothing can be done about it, then?" Mercy
was increasingly indignant at the effrontry of this savage,
but realized it would be hopeless to prolong the argument.
She sighed and shrugged. "Neither this voyage nor the
choice of a cabin mate was of my making, but I assure you
that if you don't make yourself obnoxious we'll get along
fairly reasonably."

Trying to maintain her dignity, she climbed into the
upper bunk. Tani made a grunting noise that could have
been a sign of either agreement or contempt and blew out
the single candle before Mercy had settled in her bed. The
gesture was a deliberate one, and in trying to arrange the
beaver-lined cloak over herself, Mercy bumped her head
on the low, curving bulkhead; if she were a man, she
thought, she would curse violently.

The *Dauphine* weighed anchor on the midnight tide, and the creaking of lines and tackle, the unaccustomed motion and the shouts of men on the deck, kept Mercy awake. She could not have slept under any circumstances, she told herself as she huddled beneath a single blanket and the beaver cloak, shivering. She was entering a new phase of her life, but all she knew was that she was probably being taken to New France. Never had she faced such dark uncertainties, and she dreaded tomorrow.

She tossed restlessly in her swaying bunk and reflected bitterly on the part that chance had played in her life. Had she not decided at the last minute to go with her parents on their pre-Christmas trip to Boston, she never would have encountered Jacques Duphaine on the highway. And in that case she would at this moment be safe in her own bed in Kittery instead of being launched on a dangerous and unwanted adventure.

All the terrible things that were happening to her were the direct fault of Jacques, and she hated him with an intensity she had never felt toward anyone. Although she was forced to admit to herself that he continued to fascinate her, that he excited her as some people were aroused by strong drink, she could not envision any permanent relationship with him. But there was little chance of that; he was not, she told herself bitterly, the marrying kind. And even if he were, he would be a most unsuitable and unsatisfactory husband. She forced herself to stop that sort of thinking, and she reminded herself sternly that there was no profit in it, that Jacques could mean only trouble and heartache for her.

It was far wiser to occupy her mind with mental pictures of Peter, and for some minutes she allowed herself to dwell on the various things that might happen to him. His future was far more precarious than her own, and she realized that she would never cease worrying about him until both of them were returned home in a prisoner exchange.

She had gained a new appreciation of Peter on this harrowing journey, and she thought she understood him now, for the first time. She would not again take him for granted; she had learned the quality of his character, the depth of his courage, the intensity of his quiet strength. If he failed to arouse her as Jacques did, that could only be a sign of her own immaturity and was no reflection on Peter.

As a child, Mercy had loved sailing in one of her father's brigs to Boston or New York, and the steady motion of the *Dauphine*, the rise and fall of the ship, the rhythmic creaking of timbers, lulled her, and she became drowsy at last. She felt the same sense of snug security she had known as a little girl, and although she knew the notion was ridiculous she enjoyed it, and at last she slept.

A series of harsh, jarring noises awakened her, and for a moment she thought she had been having a nightmare. But the sounds, soft but persistent, continued, and a chill of fear swept over her. It was very dark, and she knew it was still night but had no idea of how long she had slept. As her eyes became accustomed to the gloom she realized that there was an alien presence in the little cabin, and that the noises below were the sounds of a violent fight.

Peering hesitantly over the edge of the bunk, she saw Tani, clad only in the thin undergarment that she customarily wore beneath her buckskin dress, fighting a savage but losing battle against a man. The intruder was powerful, broad-shouldered, and he was silently, insistently forcing the Indian girl onto her bunk. She clawed at his face, kicked at him wildly, but to no avail. His superior strength was too much for her, and it would be only a matter of time before she would of necessity succumb to him.

Strangely, Tani made no outcry as she fought. Perhaps she was conserving her strength, perhaps she was a victim of her own femininity and was trying to avoid embarrassment, to beat off her attacker without awakening the rest of the ship's company. Whatever her motives, Mercy could not remain neutral, a mere bystander.

Almost without thinking she hurled herself off the edge of the bunk and fell with full force onto the man's neck and shoulders. Surprised at this unexpected onslaught, he twisted his head around, cursing volubly in French. Mercy caught the strong odor of brandy on his breath, and in almost the same instant she recognized the man as Commandant Tédière.

The ship sank into a trough, then heaved convulsively as she rose on the sea's swell, and the man lost his balance and tumbled into the lower bunk, both girls falling with him. He began to lash out with his fists now, his lusts forgotten in his new rage at having been interrupted. His frustration gave him added strength, and he was more than a match for his two slender opponents. But Tani, elated at the help she had received, fought him with renewed vigor, and her nails raked his face, his throat, his neck.

He needed both his hands to fend her off, and rolled over onto one side, pinning Mercy beneath him. For a moment she was too stunned to move, to think or to react. She felt as if the breath were being slowly squeezed out of her lungs, and the faint rays of night light that filtered in through the glass of the small porthole began to shimmer before her dazed eyes.

She tried to push Tédière away, but his weight, combined with that of the frantic, struggling Tani, was too great to be budged. Mercy thought her left arm was crushed and that her side was being ripped open. The figures above her continued to pummel each other, and finally she realized that something hard and unyielding was pressing into her ribs. At last it dawned on her that Commandant Tédière was wearing a pistol in his belt, and for the first time she felt a faint glimmer of hope.

Slowly, painfully she freed her hand, which was pinned at her side, and after several agonizing moments

she was able to take hold of the butt of the weapon.
Tédière realized vaguely what she was doing but could not
release his hold on Tani. Mercy drew the pistol slowly
from his belt, then wanted to scream at the top of her
lungs when it slipped from her grasp and clattered to the
deck.

She could not reach it, and her last chance seemed to
have vanished. Yet she knew instinctively that her only
hope of survival lay in retrieving the weapon, and she
reached down, groping. Tédière was fully aware of her
intent now and tried to kick the pistol to the other side of
the cabin. As he lurched, Mercy found her opportunity,
and she inched her right shoulder from beneath him, and
her fingers closed around the barrel of the gun.

She gripped it hard, raised it, and unhesitatingly
brought the butt down with all of the force she could
command. There was a sickening thud as the metal struck
the back of Tédière's head. The man went limp, crumpled, and slid to the deck.

Tani was on her feet at once, kicking viciously at his
inert body. Mercy thought she had killed him, but he
groaned, and she placed a restraining hand on the Indian
girl's arm, and Tani became calmer, desisting at last.
They stood together, panting, supporting each other as
they stood close together and stared down at the man they
had vanquished. Mercy was never able to remember how
long they remained there, but she recalled that she continued to hold the pistol and that Tédière lay very still.

When he finally moved, both girls were startled, and
Mercy took a tighter grip on the gun. Tani tensed, too,
and held her short knife, which she had recovered from
somewhere, but neither weapon was needed. The man sat
up slowly, blood oozing from a dozen deep scratches on
his face. The fight was gone out of him, and he pulled
himself painfully to his feet, then lurched to the door,
opened it, and disappeared down the deck without utter-
ing a sound. He was certainly sobered; whether he was
penitent or deeply resentful it was too dark to tell.

Mercy stepped forward and slid a latch into place; she had not noticed it previously, and the knowledge that the commandant would need to batter down the door before he could re-enter gave her a partial sense of security. Tani moved to the single, narrow chest of drawers the cabin afforded, removed a tinder box, and lighted the taper set in a wrought iron holder on the top.

The flame leaped up and the two girls looked at each other. Both were bruised, the hair of both was in wild disarray and their clothes were ripped. Suddenly Mercy began to laugh helplessly, and in a moment Tani joined her. Unable to control themselves, they sat on the edge of the lower bunk and rocked back and forth until tears came to their eyes. The Indian girl was the first to regain her control.

"Wild pig think Tani you," she said.

"You saved me, Tani. Thank you." At the thought of the gross seaman Mercy shuddered as though some unclean thing had crawled across her.

"Great warrior take care of pig. Great warrior carve out his heart with long knife." Tani spoke calmly now, as though the death of Commandant Tédière were an unimportant but accomplished fact.

"No, Tani! If we say nothing, I think he'll be inclined to forget this whole incident. The men would laugh at him, and he wouldn't want to appear foolish to them, I'm sure. But if we challenge him, there'll be more trouble."

Tani considered the matter in silence for a moment. "Yes," she said at length. "You right." She smiled, although her lower lip was out. "Pig will do no more. If he try, Tani and sister-of-red-hair will beat him again."

The tensions of past days were gone, and Mercy smiled too. "I don't think we'll forget this night."

"Tani will not forget." The Indian girl stood, and, although she was exhausted, she held herself erect. "Tani had done good for sister-of-red-hair. And sister has saved life of Tani. Tani will repay debt, in time to come."

Peter

BOOK TWO

NINE

THE SNOW plowed majestically through calm seas, heading north, and Peter was certain now that her destination was New France. He stood at the rail of the aft deck, staring down at the gray-green water as he told himself for the hundredth time that neither persuasion nor force would cause him to reveal the plans of General Pepperrell and Commodore Warren to the enemy. Like every other New Englander he had heard stories about the tongue-loosening equipment lodged in the cellars of the notorious prison at Quebec, but he promised himself that even under extreme torture he would say nothing about the coming campaign against Louisburg. The success of the enterprise would depend on the maintenance of absolute secrecy. If the French should learn of what was coming, they would have ample time to prepare their defenses accordingly, and the inevitable result would be a catastrophic defeat for the English colonists.

The future of all North America, as Peter saw it, depended on his ability to keep his mouth shut under duress.

The notes in his journal as war council secretary, the record book which Duphaine had so calmly stolen, were cryptic, and, although the French would certainly glean that an expedition would be sent against them and might even piece together enough data to guess at the size of the force, there was no word that even hinted at the joint military-naval destination.

It was just barely possible that Mercy might know something of her father's plans, and that was his major concern. She could have overheard his private conversations, or he might have relaxed and allowed an unguarded word to slip out in the privacy of his family circle. And if she did know anything, the French would never rest until they had extracted every last crumb of information from her. She would never willingly reveal any plans to them, of that much he was sure, but her ignorance of military matters was such that she might say too much without realizing what she was doing. Yet his own dilemma was sharp: even if he had an opportunity to question her privately, he could not alert her to the danger without telling her the secret on which the entire future of the English colonies depended. He had pondered the problem from the time they had first been kidnapped, and as yet had found no satisfactory solution; there was no choice, apparently, but to continue to hope that General Pepperrell had been his usual discreet self in her presence.

Mercy could take care of herself, and Peter comforted himself with the thought. Granted that he had long been in love with her, his admiration for her had only grown during these last trying days. Her coolness and her courage were an inheritance from her father, but her strength was her own; she had matured in this short span of time, and Peter realized that if he survived the period to come, she would be the best of all possible wives.

What was to be done with her when they landed at Quebec was a worry to him, too, although he had been careful not to voice it aloud to her. Under the normal rules of warfare, both of them would be honorably treated. However, he had no illusions as to what was in store for him, and he could only hope that Mercy would be accorded the dignified treatment that a lady of rank and stature deserved. But it was possible that she might be in for a rough time, and he seethed in impotent rage when he thought how powerless he was to help her or protect her.

The knowledge that her abduction had been unplanned and unwanted did little to soothe him, though he could not blame Duphaine for bringing her along. In like circumstances, he had to admit, he might have deemed it wise to take the same precautionary measure. Peter's sense of frustration grew, now that Duphaine had intruded on his thoughts. The real cause of his unhappiness over Mercy was caused, he knew, by her open interest in the bold French adventurer. Were she anyone but Mercy Pepperrell, he would swear that she was infatuated with the wretch. But it was impossible that she, of all girls, would really develop romantic inclinations toward a tawdry highwayman, spy, and opportunist.

Of course he could not blame Duphaine for sparking to Mercy as he did. Any man in his right senses would be attracted to her, and Peter had spent two years patiently eliminating every eligible bachelor in the Maine District from the competition for her hand. But Duphaine was different, and the very qualities that made him unique increased the dangers of Mercy's vulnerability to him. When she looked at him a sparkle came into her eyes and her cheeks grew flushed; she had never in her life reacted like that to any other man, not even her future husband. Peter had to concede, grudgingly, that he was jealous of the wily Frenchman, and it was no help to know that after they debarked at Quebec and were separated, Duphaine would be free to see her, to woo her, to make love to her whenever he pleased.

Mercy would never consent to marry him, Peter was

convinced. But she was inexperienced in the ways of
sophisticates, and it was agonizing to think that her
naïveté, which had always been one of her greatest
charms, might cause her to blunder into Duphaine's
bed. If that should happen, Peter told himself fiercely, he
would kill the man.

He stood now with his fists clenched, looking at the
water with unseeing eyes, and he did not hear someone
approach behind him on the deck. The voice of Jacques
Duphaine startled him.

"It is too far to swim to Kittery, my friend. Be grateful
that you have been permitted a little time to breathe fresh
air, thanks to my intervention. If Commandant Tédière
had been given his way, you would be locked in the hold,
a very unpleasant place."

Shocked by the sudden appearance of the man who had
been so much on his mind, Peter stared at the Gentleman, who lounged against the rail, smiling companion-
ably. Duphaine's clothes were more suitable for a levee at
Versailles than for life aboard a cramped brig, but he wore
his lace-cuffed shirt, his embroidered jacket and
breeches, his white silk stockings and gold-buckled shoes
with such an air that he appeared neither ludicrous nor
foppish. Apparently he had slept well, for the marks of
fatigue were erased from his face, and he was as buoyant,
as full of energy, as he had been on the day of Governor
Shirley's dinner in Boston.

Peter could not share his good humor. "Duphaine,"
he demanded bluntly, "what's to become of Mistress
Pepperrell and what's in store for me? I have a right to
know."

The Frenchman adjusted the ruffle of his stock.
"You're in no position to speak of your rights," he de-
clared mildly; "but I'll not dispute the point with you.
Your own fate I leave to your imagination, my friend.
You'll find that French generals are fair and liberal men.
But they have a great thirst for knowledge, and when it is

withheld from them they are inclined to show the stern side of their natures. I know, I know," he added hastily when he saw the expression on Peter's face, "you are a man of principles. You must remember that if you truly believe in a cause, you must be willing to suffer for that cause. I think it only fair to warn you."

"And you, Duphaine—in what do you believe?"

"The cause of Jacques Duphaine," was the quick retort. "I would never do what you have evidently made up your mind to do. No nation is worth personal unpleasantness or injury."

Peter was gaining a new view of his captor. "I reckon you don't love your country, then," he said slowly. "But if that's true, why have you risked your neck for her?"

The highwayman laughed, genuinely amused. "My country? I risk my neck for the things that matter, my friend—for gold and for women. Nothing else is of importance."

"Only one woman means anything to me." Peter's jaw tightened. "And you haven't yet told me what's going to happen to her."

The grin faded from Duphaine's lips. "I give you my solemn promise as a gentleman," he said, emphasizing each word as though taking an oath, "that no harm will befall her. She is under my personal protection, and I will take every step necessary to insure that she is respected."

Peter examined him carefully. Duphaine seemed completely sincere. But now was the time to speak of the things that weighed so heavily on his mind. "If she should be abused or mistreated or—or insulted," he said, "I'll kill the man who has hurt her. I'll kill him with my bare hands."

"That will not be necessary, for I shall dispose of him first. I appreciate your anxiety, but I assure you that my concern equals your own."

There was no opportunity to probe his meaning, for he held out his hand, and Peter took it. Both gripped hard,

and the New Englander suddenly thought that he liked
Duphaine. The man was a scoundrel and a thief, but it
was impossible not to respond favorably to the impact of
his personality and his charm. "I take you at your word,"
Peter said.

"Ah, but you understand that I exclude myself." The
broad, confident smile reappeared. "Never have I known
a more fascinating creature than Mercy, and it would
be impossible to restrain myself from paying court to her."

"You're damned frank, I must say." Peter was so jarred
that he didn't quite know how to react.

"To you I am frank. Remember I was no more than a
yard or two behind you when you kissed her on the beach.
I envied you. I live for the day that you will envy me, my
friend. But if you are sure of her love, you need have
nothing to fear. I will never take unfair advantage of her,
and if Mercy ever comes to me, it will be only because she
herself wills it."

Peter's relief was boundless. "Then I'm not afraid,
Duphaine."

They took each other's measure, almost as they had
done when armed with swords, and suddenly both
laughed. "When the war ends and the capital of New
France has been moved to Boston," the highwayman
said, "you and I will hunt together for wild game. It will be
great sport."

"It will," Peter agreed heartily. "We'll make it a definite
engagement on the very day that the banner of St. George
is planted on the heights of Quebec and we annex the
colony in the name of His Britannic Majesty."

Duphaine broke the impasse gracefully by taking a
slender gold watch, probably a stolen piece of jewelry,
from his fob pocket. "You and I have a more pressing
meeting to attend first," he murmured. "Commandant
Tedière has ordered that I bring you to him, allowing him
time to make himself presentable. By now the pig should
be as presentable as one so gross can ever be. Come
along."

They strolled down the deck together, looking all the world like two friends. Peter glanced at his companion, ready to ask a question, then thought better of it and reframed the words. "Do I gather that my personal inquisition is about to begin?"

The reply was prompt—and unexpected. "Paul Etienne Tédière is an ass. He is also ambitious, a dangerous combination. For years he has wanted to be head of the secret police in Paris, a position as far beyond his capabilities as it is close to his dreams. This war offers him his last real chance, and I have stolen his glory. The capture of you and of your fine military journal is my achievement, not his, and although he is nominally my superior, I report only to the highest authority. And so I have refused to give you or your journal into his custody. However, we French are the most polite people on earth, so there are amenities to be observed. Paul thinks he can bully you into revealing vast quantities of military information before we land, and that he can share in the credit for my achievement."

"If that's what he's counting on," Peter replied grimly, "he's wasting his time."

"My thanks for protecting my interests." The left corner of Duphaine's mouth twisted down, as it always did when he became wry. "But do not forget what I have told you about him. Despise him, as I do. But remember, as I also do, that he is as treacherous as he is stupid."

They arrived at the door of a cabin second only in size to that of the *Dauphine's* captain, and Duphaine knocked perfunctorily, then raised the latch and entered, with Peter directly behind him. The first thing that struck both was the stale odor of the compartment, for Commandant Tédière was keeping his square window tightly closed, although the morning weather was unexpectedly mild. Clothes were strewn on the bed, on the floor, and across two chairs on the far side of the cabin, and Tédière, dressed in a food-spotted dressing gown, sat at a small table with his back to the door as he finished a breakfast of boiled mutton and ale.

"What do you want?" he muttered in a voice made hoarse by his overindulgence of the preceding night.

"That's no way to speak to guests, Paul." Duphaine's manner was a subtle blend of respect and derision. "Captain Staples and I are here at your request."

Tédière continued to chew on a chunk of mutton. "You'll not be needed, Jacques, so leave us. Staples, come here."

Duphaine put a restraining hand on Peter's arm. "Surely you won't deprive me of the pleasure of your company, Paul," he said, his tone bantering but his meaning very clear. "And it occurs to me that you gentlemen haven't yet had the pleasure of a formal introduction. Commandant Tédière, I present Captain Staples." He emphasized Peter's military rank, pausing for an instant after speaking the word.

The burly man shoved his chair away from the table, stood, and turned, annoyed that he had been shamed into behaving civilly. His face was a network of deep scratches from his encounter with Mercy and Tani, his left eye was discolored, and a heavy bruise showed on his forehead. And the realization that his visitors were gaping at him did nothing to improve his disposition. "You know I achieve my best results when I work alone, Jacques," he rasped.

"I also know you and your results." Duphaine leaned against the door, balancing himself as the ship rose and fell gently on the calm sea. "If I am to protect myself, I must protect the person of Captain Staples." His eyes became hard, and when he spoke again, his voice was flinty. "He's my prisoner, you know."

"He is the prisoner of France, and I am the representative of His Christian Majesty."

"There are those who might wish to quarrel with your representation, but I'm in too friendly a mood." Duphaine's hand rested lightly on the hilt of his sword.

"Nevertheless, at the risk of quibbling with someone whom I admire, let me remind you, Paul, that he is not yet the prisoner of France. He is in the possession of Jacques Duphaine, Marquis de Gremont. And he will remain in my keeping until such time as I am suitably rewarded by those who have a better claim than you to being the official representatives of our beloved Louis. If you've forgotten my circumstances, Paul, allow me to refresh your memory. Unlike you, I receive no retainer from our generous king, who sees fit to reward me only after each of my exploits."

Tediere did not choose to reply, but turned instead to the New Englander, who had been following the conversation avidly. "Take off your hat in the presence of your betters, Staples," The command was harsh and abrupt.

But Peter did not budge. "Looks like I've got to do a mite of reminding myself," he drawled, his voice softening deceptively as it always did in a moment of crisis. "I'm an officer in the Maine militia, operating under a patent of His Majesty of England to the Massachusetts Bay Colony. I'll be pleased to salute an officer of an enemy nation, just as your Duc de Villars saluted our Marlborough a few years back. But I'll take off my hat to no man except my king and the minister of my church."

The atmosphere became explosive as Peter and the commandant glared at each other. Tediere, his authority flouted, grew very red in the face and had difficulty in controlling his breathing. "You damned peasant," he said at last, "I'll——"

"Easy Paul." Duphaine, who had been enjoying the spectacle, decided that the moment had come to intervene. "Captain Staples is right, you know. He's entitled to full honors. The Prince d'Anjou has been very strict about the observance of formalities ever since he became First Marshal of France. And now that his son has married that farm girl—what was her name?—His Highness has been very sensitive to the word 'peasant.'"

"All colonials are peasants. As for you, Duphaine, I've had my doubts about you for some time. If you're the Marquis de Grémont, what are you doing in New France, tell me that? Why aren't you at Versailles, enjoying life? One of my first tasks when I return to Paris and take up my new position there will be to examine your official dossier carefully." He puffed out his chest and pursed his thick lips in an attempt to regain his dignity. "And Staples, take heed of what I tell you. I'm the man to be placated, not this gaudy peacock."

"I don't rightly reckon I'm the sort who does much placating to speak of," Peter said mildly. "If you knew folks down in Maine, you'd know we all suffer from a peculiar affliction. No amount of medicine cures it, and no doctor has ever been able to find a way to fix it up proper. We've got us a stiffness in the joints that's just fierce. Stops us from bending our knees to anybody there is."

For an instant the commandant looked as though he would hurl himself at the prisoner. "I know that swine from Maine need taming," he said curtly. "I'll bring you to your knees fast enough, and that damned wench, too."

Peter and Duphaine exchanged a startled glance: the marks on Tédière face began to have a new significance. There was a long, pregnant silence, and Peter drew a deep breath. "What do you know of Mistress Pepperrell?" he asked, his voice barely raised above a whisper.

"Enough." Tédière smirked, but instantly regretted it, as there was a cut from one of the girls' fingernails across his lower lip.

Peter took a single step forward, and Duphaine tried to stop him but could not. Raising his right hand, he smashed his fist into the commandant's fleshy face. Tédière tried to protect himself, but Peter's left caught him in the ribs, and another hard blow that raked him across the temple ended the brief encounter. He reeled back against the bulkhead, lost his balance, and slid to the deck, groaning.

"You're a madman," he muttered, wiping a trickle of blood from his face, "so you shall have to be treated like a madman. I'll make you sorry for this as long as you live." Lurching to his feet he ran to the door and out onto the deck beyond, shouting for the captain.

Peter would have followed, but Duphaine took hold of his arm and held him firmly, shaking his head in exasperation tinged with cold amusement. "You are a fool," he said. "I applaud what you have done, and I salute your bravery, but you are a fool. Now you will be sent to the hold in chains, and I will spend many tedious hours persuading the captain to release you on the grounds that you are my prisoner. Mercy needed no help, you know. The scars of battle on Tédière's face are a sign that she was well able to look after herself."

"I'll teach that filthy—"

"You've done sufficient teaching for one day, my friend. Your excursion into the realm of education has made it certain that your lot will be a hard one. And you have complicated beyond measure my task of protecting Mercy from harm."

TEN

JACQUES DUPHAINE was as good as his word; Peter had to
concede him that much. And he had certainly gone to
considerable trouble on his prisoner's account. After
twenty-four hours in the ship's brig, Peter had finally been
set free, thanks to the highwayman's eloquence in persuading the captain that the captive was his, not Tédière's,
and that the attack had been provoked. Peter was grateful,
for the cell had been uncomfortable, dark, and rat-
infested, the chains that had been clamped on him had
been painful and cumbersome, and the slops he had been
fed had been inedible. It was good to be comparatively
free again, but he knew he would strike the commandant
again if the opportunity should present itself. The mere
thought of Tédière continued to anger him, and, come to
think of it, there was little at the moment that wasn't
annoying.

It was irritating, for example, to have exchanged no
more than a few perfunctory words with Mercy. Now, as
Peter emerged from the tiny cabin he shared with
Duphaine, he looked eagerly up and down the length of
the deck, hoping to catch at least a glimpse of her. But she

was nowhere in sight, and the deck was deserted except for two sailors who were scrubbing the pine boards with holystones. Disappointed anew, Peter moved to the rail; the day was gloomy and contributed to his depressed mood. The skies were leaden and overcast, and the sea, churned into a gray froth by fresh winds, reflected the darkness overhead. There was a strong hint of snow in the air, and the *Dauphine*, her twin sails filled, plunged from trough to crest and down again in an unending series of swells.

Although it was agony to be so close to Mercy yet not speak to her, Peter thought that Duphaine had probably been right when he had suggested that they avoid each other's company. There were many on board who would report every move and every gesture of the enemy pair immediately on landing, and it seemed reasonable that Mercy would have a far easier time if the authorities were ignorant of her close relationship to an officer who was privy to all of his high command's secrets. On the other hand, Peter could not help but wonder if Duphaine had not merely invented a seemingly logical excuse for reasons of his own, personal or mercenary, to keep him apart from Mercy. While it was difficult not to like the highwayman, it was impossible to trust him.

And it was confusing as well as unsettling to observe that Mercy and the Indian girl, Tani, were always together, whether on deck or in their cabin, and that they seemed on the best of terms. They had apparently made their peace, and there was an understanding of some sort between them. Peter was anxious to learn the details, but, the few times he had seen Mercy, Tani had been with her and it had been impossible to ask.

Peter began to pace the deck restlessly, and tried in vain to confine his thoughts to the immediate present. He was determined to achieve his escape as soon as possible after landing and to make his way south again. The forests of French Canada held no terrors for him, and he was confident that once he broke free he would be as good as at home again. The big problem would be to get out of the prison in Quebec, but he was sure that others had done it before him, and nothing would stand in his way. If possible, he would take Mercy with him, though progress through the wilderness would be slow with a girl as a companion, even one as adept at forest living as a native of Kittery who was raised on the frontier. If he could not work out an escape for both of them, it might be necessary to leave her behind, and that made sense, too. Duphaine had told him repeatedly that she would be treated with honors befitting the daughter of New England's most prominent man, and there was no good cause to think otherwise. But—and he grinned wryly at the realization—all of his thinking was premature. It was impossible to plot an escape from a jail he had not yet seen.

The lookout in the crow's-nest sighted land, and his shout brought the snow to life. The crew poured out of the fo'c'sle, and men scurried up the lines. The *Dauphine's* captain, hastily buttoning his jacket, relieved the officer of the watch on the quarter-deck, and the helmsman, a lean-faced Breton, took over the wheel from his assistant. In a few moments Duphaine emerged into the open, wearing the gaudy white costume he affected as the Gentleman, and he sauntered over to Peter, pulling on his gauntlet gloves as he strolled. Warumba and the other brave, who had been nowhere in sight since the time of embarkation, a considerable feat on so small a vessel as a merchant brig, appeared suddenly through an open hatch.

A short time later Mercy came onto the deck, attired in one of the gowns Duphaine had stolen, a peach-colored dress of thin wool with a slender skirt in the vogue started by the Princess of Wales. The beaver-lined cloak was thrown over her shoulders, and althought the garment was heavy and cumbersome, she looked exceptionally graceful in it and carried it with an air all her own. Tani, in buckskins, was close on her heels, and both girls moved at once to the rail. Only Commandant Tedìère remained out of sight.

Peter was confused by all the authority, which seemed to indicate that a landing was imminent. Quebec was at least thirty-six hours distant, up the St. Lawrence River, and a ship would sail past innumerable visible islands en route to the capital of New France. Yet the *Dauphine* was still ploughing through open seas, and Peter turned to his captor, a question forming on his lips.

But Duphaine anticipated him. "You will soon see the glory of all North America," he murmured. "Visibility is poor today, so we are closer to our destination than you might think. Look there!"

He pointed ahead and slightly to the right, and the elements joined him in making the moment a dramatic one, for the sun appeared briefly through the heavy clouds, and the haze lifted. Less than a mile distant a number of buildings and church spires indicated the presence of a town, unidentifiable at this distance. Before Peter could ask the name of the place, however, he caught a glimpse of a mammoth, multi-sided wall of gray stone located some distance to the left of the community, and he caught his breath. The pile of masonry seemed to reach toward the sky, and even at this distance it was possible to make out the gaping holes that could only be gun apertures. Three sturdy towers rose from somewhere behind a bulwark of the wall, and from the tallest of these the banner of France, lilies of gold on a field of white, whipped in the stiff breeze.

Peter's eyes met Duphaine's, and the Frenchman grinned and nodded. "Yes," he said, "that is it. We have already penetrated deep into Gabarus Bay."

Neither the sight of the imposing man-made structure nor Duphaine's words made any impression on Mercy, who was curious and puzzled, and Peter turned to her soberly. "Merce," he said, his voice tight, "that's the strongest fortress on earth. Nobody has ever conquered it, nobody has ever escaped from it, nobody has ever set foot inside it except those that the folks who run it want to let in. They're taking us—to Louisburg."

The brig's unexpected destination was only the first of a series of surprises. The vessel docked at a long wharf located at the eastern end of the town, and Commandant Tedìere, appearing at the last possible moment in official uniform, made it clear that he intended to take charge of the valuable prisoner. But Duphaine, who had apparently bribed the bosun, was the first person ashore, and no sooner had he set foot on the dock than a series of mishaps involving lines and tackle held up the rest of the passengers for the better part of a quarter of an hour.

The highwayman was thus enabled to hold a long and earnest private conversation with a tiny, unprepossessing gentleman of middle years who had stood apart from the crowd that had gathered. This frail, ascetic-looking personage, it developed, was none other than Governor Duchambon, deputy of King Louis on Cape Breton Island and the second-highest ranking offical in all of New France. Men in Maine and Massachusetts Bay who had met him in Quebec invariably scoffed at his flowery manners, his exaggerated sense of gallantry and tendency to treat inferiors as though they were nobles of consequence in attendance on the royal family at Versailles. But Peter was secretly elated that Henri Duchambon had risen from nowhere and was determined to behave toward others with a consideration that had been denied him, personally, until he reached his present eminence.

When the passengers finally disembarked, the governor kissed Mercy's hand, bade her welcome to his island fortress domain, and loudly proclaimed for the benefit of all that she would be his personal guest until suitable living accommodations were found for her. He was equally courtly and sympathetic toward Peter, whom he treated like an honored visitor rather than a war prisoner. Commandant Tédière was virtually ignored by Louisburg's first citizen, who provided a carriage for Mercy and invited Duphaine and Peter to accompany him on spirited mounts which members of his entourage immediately brought forward.

The three Indians who had played so important a part in the lives of Peter and Mercy disappeared from sight immediately after the landing, and when Mercy expressed her disappointment at not bidding farewell to Tani, both Governor Duchambon and Jacques Duphaine shrugged; Tani and the two braves were all members of a tribe that lived in villages across the straits in Acadia, and their comings and goings were, by French standards, erratic, unpredictable, and illogical. Duphaine commented lightly that Tani would some day reappear in Louisburg as suddenly as she had vanished, and with that Mercy had to be content.

The road from the town to the fortress was paved with neat cobbles made of square, wooden blocks, and as Peter rode behind Mercy's carriage, flanked by the governor and Duphaine, he saw that the bay was large and sheltered, and, judging by the boats of all sizes anchored along the shore line, sufficiently deep almost everywhere to give an invader his choice of a landing place. Inlets dotting the coast were protected by artillery batteries set inside circular stone walls that afforded protection from land attacks as well as from sea marauders, and the entire area was patrolled by soldiers.

Of the greatest significance was that these troops were men of New France; they carried the long rifles that were familiar to Maine settlers, and they were tough frontiersmen, as tough as their neighbors to the south. The invasion, if ever it materialized, would be more difficult than either Pepperrell or Warren had imagined.

Duphaine obviously realized the depth of Peter's interest, and reaching out, slapped the New Englander on the back. "If you could tell them in Boston what you're seeing, fat old Shirley could be persuaded to make out a new commission for you as a colonel, eh, Peter?"

Governor Duchambon, riding on the prisoner's right, chuckled appreciatively. "That is Jacques' way of telling me he demands a colonelcy from me for bringing you to me, Monsieur Staples. As you have doubtless learned, our Jacques is infinitely resourceful." His attitude toward the highwayman was one of admiration and affection, but completely lacking in respect.

A sound of derision came from the left. "Our revered governor is resourceful, too. But—as usual—he credits me with too little intelligence. He hopes to dangle the prize of a high commission before my eyes, and would brevet me with a gold epaulet this very day—"

"Indeed I would." The governor looked past Peter at Duphaine, his clear hazel eyes sparkling, his waxed mustaches almost bristling.

It was Duphaine's turn to laugh, and he did, derisively. "You hear him, Peter? He thinks me a fool. He knows I am eager to win a commission as a colonel, and he counts on my desire clouding my judgment." For the first time he addressed the governor directly. "Your Excellency forgets that I know full well Paris would never confirm my appointment in such a high rank. I must perform a whole series of singular deeds of valor on the battlefield before my enemies will relent and permit my advocates to plead my cause at court."

"Listen to him, just listen to him!" Duchambon was enjoying himself immensely. "If you heed the rogue, he actually has a standing in the eyes of His Majesty. His pretentions are like—like a soufflé without filling!"

To Peter's amazement, Duphaine was completely disconcerted. His dark eyes gleamed with cold anger, and the healthy ruddiness of his face faded and for a moment became a waxen pallor. His right hand closed over the pommel of his saddle as though he intended to tear it off, and after glancing slowly, murderously past Peter at the governor, he lapsed into a moody silence, which neither Duchambon nor the prisoner broke.

At last he spoke, and there was an ugly rasp in his voice. "I'll thank Your Excellency to reward me in gold—louis d'or—at double our usual rate of payment, as is fitting and proper in time of war."

Peter eyed him obliquely and thought that never had he encountered so strange a person. Duphaine gambled wildly with his life, yet he took his risks in spying for the French out of no motive of patriotism and apparently held no official position in the government of New France. He acted as an espionage agent for his country for the identical reason he had robbed unwary travelers near Boston: in brief, he was working for money. But there was more to this man than was yet clear; an ordinary rogue and highwayman would not become so disturbed at a sly allusion to his lack of standing at a royal court. So it seemed likely that there was something complex in his background.

It was more than intriguing to speculate on Duphaine, Peter reasoned. Escape from Louisburg would be far more difficult to achieve than from Quebec, as he would need a boat to take him from the island to Acadia, the peninsula which the English called Nova Scotia, and the savages there were reputedly fiercely hostile to all whites except the French, who had long pursued a careful policy of cultivating their friendship and encouraging their enmity toward the settlers who swore fealty to King George. The odds against a successful escape were therefore very high, and Peter told himself that if he could acquire the key to Duphaine's character, it might be possible to win his help. Paradoxically, the very man who had made him captive might assist him to freedom.

If it were only money that Duphaine wanted, he would be susceptible to a bribe, and Peter was prepared to offer him a handsome sum from the treasury of Governor

General Shirley and from the personal coffers of William Pepperrell. Both strongboxes, he felt positive, would be opened for such a purpose. Yet, if only the desire to accumulate wealth motivated Duphaine, he could be a rich man by now, for he could have collected considerable sums from the English colonists by giving them the data they wanted so badly. Instead, Peter knew, he had received only a pittance from Commodore Warren in return for bits and pieces of information. There was something he wanted other than money, and if the New Englander could only learn what it was, he might be enabled to return to General Pepperrell with data that would be priceless in the coming campaign.

In any event, Peter vowed, nothing would persuade him to reveal the plans of his superiors to the enemy. Louisburg was going to be the toughest nut that any invading force had ever tried to crack, and, if the French should discover the Pepperrell-Warren intent, thousands of men from Massachusetts Bay and Maine, New Hampshire, Connecticut, and New York would lose their lives. The palisades loomed directly ahead now, and, looking up at the forbidding walls, Peter quietly marveled that men could have overcome the obstacles of the wilderness and of isolation to build such a fortress.

The entire enclosed area was greater than that of a dozen town squares in New York or Philadelphia. The walls were more than one hundred feet high and were made of huge slabs of stone easily four feet thick. The trio of watchtowers commanded the approaches from both sea and land and afforded a view of Acadia across the Canso Strait. A surprise attack against such a place would be almost impossible to achieve, and the defenses were so stout that a comparatively small number of men could defend the citadel successfully. The size of the fortress' armaments shocked Peter, too. He could see the muzzles of a score of cannon poking through apertures, and the biggest of these were eighteen-pounders. On the near side

alone, Peter estimated at a quick count, there were at least
six of these monsters, and his heart sank. In all of New
England there was not one gun of such a caliber.

A troop of cavalry rode through the heavy, metal-
reinforced gates, and these men were not local settlers but
the famed *ami* of the regular French Army, tough veterans who had signed for ten years' service in the colonies
and who were reputedly the best-disciplined and most
rigorously trained fighting men in all of the New World.
They trotted rapidly in a long column four abreast, and
each man carried a naked saber, holding it vertically
before his face at precisely the same angle that his
brothers-in-arms were saluting with their weapons. Their
helmets were silvered, their tunics were a bright green,
and their breeches were white; the officers wore plumes
and cockades in their headgear and multicolored sashes
across their chests.

The sight was awesome to people from Kittery who had
seen no more than a handful of red-coated English regulars in Boston, and, even as Peter blinked and sucked in
his breath, Mercy forgot her training as a lady and leaned
out of the window for a better view. Then, in a sudden
gesture of impudent defiance, she twisted around, looked
back at Peter and shouted over the clatter of hooves on the
cobbles.

"Aren't they the little dandies?" she called.

Although it was unwise to provoke their hosts, Peter
could not refrain from answering in kind. "One squad of
your Pa's own regiment could take care of them fine,
Merce."

Duphaine, ever fond of bravado, laughed appreciatively, and the governor allowed himself a watery smile.
But a moment later Duchambon was all business; the
leader of the troop, a tall major who would have been
handsome had he not been handicapped by a badly reced-
ing chin, rode up to him, wheeled, and fell in beside him.
They conversed in low tones, and, although Peter

strained hard, he was unable to catch the drift of their talk. The troop caught up with the party, split into columns of twos and executed a brilliant about-face as they formed an escort on either side of the road. A moment later the entire party swept through the gates and into the citadel.

Peter was never sure how he was maneuvered out of his position between Duphaine and the governor, but before he quite realized what had happened, both men were continuing behind the carriage but he himself was hemmed in by six husky cavalrymen. They forced his horse to a halt, and an elderly lieutenant, a man who reminded Peter of a schoolmaster who had taught him as a child in Kittery, dismounted and walked slowly toward him. In spite of the fact that Peter was not in uniform, the officer saluted him respectfully.

"If you please, mon capitaine," the lieutenant said in heavily accented English, "be good to join me. On foot."

"But Mistress Pepperrell has gone on—with the others!" Peter was so taken by surprise at the sudden turn of events that he could only speak the first thought that came to his mind.

"That is not your concern, nor mine." The man actually sounded like a schoolmaster reprimanding a mischievous boy. "If you please, mon capitaine."

There was no choice but to leap to the ground and to walk beside the officer, and Peter was so angry that he paid no attention to his surroundings. He could think only that he had been forcibly separated from Mercy, that he had not even been given a chance to say good-by to her. There was no telling when, if ever, he would see her again, and he was furious at the trickery of the French in depriving him of a last moment with her. As a gentleman and a militia officer he deserved that privilege, and he cursed Governor Duchambon, who had undoubtedly given the necessary instructions to the troop commander when they had ridden together outside the walls.

The lieutenant led the way into a large building, and

not until they had been climbing a steep flight of stone stairs for several minutes did Peter's rage subside sufficiently for him to take note of his immediate situation. Only then did he realize that two soldiers armed with cavalrymen's short muskets were directly behind him. Thin slits in the masonry were placed at ten foot intervals and admitted just enough daylight so climbers could distinguish the steps, but there was no other illumination. The lieutenant was wheezing, and Peter felt his own heart pounding; such a long flight of stairs, he knew, could lead only to the top of one of the towers, where a prison of some sort surely awaited him. Although he had known form the time of his capture that hail was the fate that awaited him, its imminence caused a wild sense of rebellion to surge through him, and for a moment his habitual common sense deserted him.

A single leap would bring him up to the elderly lieutenant, who was no match for him physically. And it would be an easy matter to grapple with him, overpower him and use him as a shield. The two soldiers would not fire for fear of hitting their own officer, and there was at least a chance that Peter could take the lieutenant with him as a hostage and could descend the stairs again and break loose. He did not stop to consider that he would still be in Louisburg and that freedom would still be far distant. His emotion was stronger than his reason, and he could not think of anything except hurling himself at the elderly officer, who at this instant represented the enemy incarnate.

Something in Peter's manner, some gesture betrayed him as he was about to spring, and he felt the hard, flaring muzzle of a musket jab into the small of his back. One of the troopers was only three steps away, his eyes cold in the half-light. "*Non, monsieur,*" the man said, prodding Peter again.

There was nothing to do but submit meekly, numbly, and the remainder of the climb was accomplished without incident. When the quartet reached the top, the lieutenant lifted a heavy metal bolt from a door that faced the landing, and Peter followed him into a high-ceilinged anteroom, bare of furniture and almost completely airless. Here, as on the staircase, small slits provided the only light. Three doors faced onto this curious little chamber, and the officer nodded toward one of them, took a key from his pocket, and tossed it to one of his men. The soldier promptly thrust it into an opening that was seemingly well-oiled, for the thick iron key turned easily and noiselessly. A thick door of oak swung open, and the lieutenant indicated with a gesture that Peter was to enter.

"Your new home, mon capitaine," he said, his tone devoid of sarcasm. "It is the wish of His Excellency, Governor Duchambon, and of Major General le Clerc, chief of the garrison, that you should be comfortable here. *Entrez*, if you please. If your meals should fail to satisfy you, tell me your complaints and I shall insure that the chef rectifies his errors at one."

Peter tried to comply with the order, but his feet would not obey his mind, and he remained where he was until one of the soldiers started to move toward him. Then at last he walked, his head high, through the door, which closed silently behind him, and he was alone.

He had expected to find himself in a cell of some sort, but to his astonishment he stood in the center of what seemed to be the living room of a sumptuous little apartment. A thick, patterned carpet in gray and yellow was spread on the floor, and over an enormous window silk drapes of yellow and gray hung in graceful folds. A divan piled high with plump cushions stood against the wall on the left, and over it was a huge, rich tapestry depicting a pastoral scene. Three or four large chairs with carved arms, legs and backs were scattered about the chamber, and on the far side, near an inner door, was a highly polished oak table with a design in mother-of-pearl worked around its edge.

The inner room, though smaller still, was equally luxurious. Dominating it was a large four-poster bed with coverlets of ivory silk, and opposite it stood a large and cheery hearth, which was provided with a generous supply of firewood, a flint, and a tinderbox. There was a large window in here also, stretching almost to the ceiling and facing in the same direction as that in the living room. Still unable to believe that this was to be his jail, Peter walked to the window and looked out.

He was indeed in one of the towers, though he could not tell from here which it might be. Directly ahead and below stretched the foaming waters of Gabarus Bay, and from this height the fishing craft anchored there looked like toy boats. As he watched, a large vessel worked her way up through the choppy seas toward a berth, and when she drew closer he saw that she was either a ship of the line or a large frigate of the French navy. As of less than a month previously there had been no major enemy naval units in American waters, hence this fighting ship must have sailed from her home of Brest or Le Havre to lend the power of her great guns to the war effort. What Commodore Warren would give to know of her presence here!

Peter smiled ruefully and began to count the ship's guns when she sailed closer still. She tacked to starboard obligingly, and he thought that he could make out twenty-four gun ports. If that figure was accurate, she must be a forty-eight-cannon ship of the line, and he whistled in dismay under his breath. Warren's largest was a thirty-gun frigate, and the Admiralty in London, occupied with the major war effort in Europe, was unlikely to send a warship across the Atlantic large enough to challenge the authority of this giant. The future seemed to hold as much threat of trouble to the commodore as it did to General Pepperrell, and Peter made a small wager with himself that at least two or three fast and strong French frigates would cast anchor here in the next few days, too. No admiral could allow a great vessel like this one to sail the seas alone, and her mere presence in these waters indicated that the Grand Admiral in Paris had daringly weakened the home fleet and sent at least a full squadron of warships to stations off the coast of New France.

Realizing anew the helplessness of his position, Peter tore his gaze from the ship of the line and looked out toward the right, where a mass of evergreens stretched toward the horizon. The combination of sea and trees reminded him forcibly of Maine, of Kittery, of his long-nourished hopes and his love for Mercy, and he turned abruptly and strode up and down the entire length of his comfortable prison. Mercy was somewhere below in this great citadel, and he wondered if she missed him even a fraction as much as he ached for her. Throwing himself into the nearest chair, he looked up at the high, domed ceiling with unseeing eyes.

Let the French threaten him or beat him all they pleased. Some day, somehow, he would lead Mercy back to safety and would take his rightful place in the ranks of his regiment. He repeated the promise to himself aloud, and, although the words echoed back to him across empty space, they did not sound hollow to him.

ELEVEN

For two and a half days Peter saw no one except the taciturn soldier who brought him his meals and who was obviously under instructions not to speak to the prisoner. The dull routine was finally broken on the third morning when the living room door was unlocked and Jacques Duphaine, elegant in a buff-colored suit and carrying an ivory-and-gold-topped walking stick, strolled in. "Peter, my good friend!" he said, behaving as though he were a young gallant calling on another in a Paris apartment. "I've missed you these past days!"

"That's a situation that could be easily rectified." Peter, who had been staring down at the sunlit waters of Gabarus Bay, turned and extended his hand. "You might use your influence and have me given freedom of the fort, at the very least, Jacques." He used the highwayman's Christian name easily, genuinely glad to see the rogue and glad of any company after his enforced idleness.

"I fear my word doesn't carry quite that much weight." They exchanged dry smiles. "However, I'm glad they've given you this suite. It's my favorite, you know."

"No, I didn't." Peter sank into a chair and watched his guest, who was wandering around the room, examining furnishings with a critical eye.

"Ah, yes." Jacques' face was sober, but there was an undercurrent of mirth in his tone. "I've twice been given this very apartment as a temporary dwelling. His Christian Majesty took excellent care of me here, excellent." He wandered to the table, on which the remains of Peter's breakfast still rested. "They're taking good care of you, I see," he added, sniffing appreciatively at the dishes. "Oysters stewed in sauterne and served with garlic sauce. Delicious for breakfast. And this looks like kidney-and-mushroom pie. Was it tender?"

"I don't rightly know." Peter had never paid much attention to food and usually ate whatever was placed in front of him. Eating was a matter of satisfying his hunger, no more.

"No, of course not," the Gentleman was sympathetic and understanding. "I remember all too well how my own appetite suffered when I was a visitor here. It's never a pleasure to eat alone. And I see they've provided you with no reading matter. I must send a few books up to you."

"I'd appreciate that." Peter was genuinely grateful, for the time had passed slowly.

"Ever since Tédière has been in charge of the arrangements for the Crown's guests here, there hasn't been a single book in the suite. Tédière is illiterate, I'm sure, so he'd never think of entertainment in any terms except a wench or a brandy jar. But let's pass on to more pleasant topics. One of the purposes of my visit is to reassure you regarding Mistress Mercy's welfare."

"She is all right, then? You wouldn't fool me or lie to me, Jacques?"

"A gentleman does not stoop to lies on the subject of a lady. She is in excellent health. And temper." He smiled wickedly as he sat on the divan. "Some of our more narrow-minded officials who have traveled but little like to believe that you Anglo-Saxons are a cold-blooded people. Mistress Mercy has taught them otherwise. In brief, friend Peter, this fortress was built to withstand any siege, but it trembled under Mercy's wrath when she discovered that you had disappeared by the time she left her carriage and that she wasn't going to be allowed to see you again. I actually felt sorry for poor little Duchambon, I can tell you. For a few minutes he thought—and so did I—that she was going to tear him to bits with her hands." He laughed aloud at the memory.

Peter was elated over Mercy's loyalty and was relieved beyond measure that she was well and safe. But he had not yet learned any details of her situation. "The governor hasn't made her pay for her assault on his dignity?"

"Oh, no." Jacques leaned back against the cushions and made himself more comfortable. "You see, friend Peter, His Excellency may lack a sense of humor, but Madame Duchambon does not, and she witnessed the scene in which your Maine wildcat showed her claws and teeth. A little man always lives in fear that he will be made to look ridiculous, and Duchambon values the regard of his wife. So he has been very careful to adopt an air of kindness and generosity to Mercy. She has been a guest in the apartment of Their Excellencies until this very morning, and they have both treated her as though she were a sister—no, better than that—a mistress of Louis himself!"

The witticism was wasted, and Peter, forcing himself to remain calm, peered across the room. "What happened to her this morning?" he demanded.

Jacques studied his fingernails for a moment, then plucked a thread from his breeches. "Living quarters inside the citadel are rather cramped," he said, almost too casually, "and the Duchambons must hold what little space they have for visiting dignitaries from Paris, even from Quebec, as you can well understand."

"Yes, yes—but what's happened to Mercy?" Peter persisted.

"First you must realize that there are few houses in Louisburg suitable for a lady of quality. Almost the only people who live here, aside from the military, are fishermen and fur traders. And so the problem was not an easy one to solve. And so, though I question His Excellency's decision, I am not sure I could have done otherwise had I been in his position."

Peter's patience was growing thin. "Come to the point!" he snapped.

"Your stay in the Tour du Nord does not improve your disposition, friend Peter. Where was I? Ah, yes. Several miles from the citadel, at the far side of the town, where a handful of gentry have built small mansions for themselves, there resides a young widow, Jeanne le Sueur, who was of course greatly pleased to offer Mercy a haven."

The care with which the highwayman chose his words increased Peter's sense of nervousness and irritation. "Get on with it, Jacques," he growled. "Mercy has gone to the house of this Madame le Sueur, who for unknown reasons is happy to have her there."

"She will indeed be a guest there, but Jeanne's motives are not unknown, my friend. Just the opposite. I have been—shall we say, acquainted with the beauteous Jeanne for a considerable time, and can always see through her with the ease that I look through this sheet of glass, which was brought to New France from Lyons at a staggering expense. Jeanne holds an endless fascination for the officers of the garrison, who are starved for the companionship of well-bred ladies. And as she leads a rather lonely life, she is glad to bring under her roof someone as lovely as herself, though in a different way. Our petite Jeanne understands little in the world except men, but them she knows, and she realizes that her charming guest will create a new flurry of interest among the unmarried gentlemen of the corps. Interest in her salon has flagged of late, but now her drawing room will be crowded again."

Peter's agitation increased, and he arose. "I'm damned if one word you tell me makes me feel good. I'm engaged to be married to Mercy, and here I am, helpless, while she'll be spending her days entertaining young bucks who'll try to make love to her. Damnation, Jacques, I know soldiers, and—"

"But you do not know the incomparable Jeanne le Sueur! She will use Mercy as the magnet to draw the eager to her home, it is true. But once they set foot under her roof, it is she herself who will become the center of attention, and if any man should allow his ardor for Mercy to become too great, Jeanne will cut out his heart and place it on the front stoop as a warning to the foolish. On that you may depend. And you may take my word that Mercy is as safe as if she had been sent to a convent in Quebec."

In spite of his explanation, Peter was not satisfied. "You just finished saying that you weren't sure you trusted the governor's judgment. Why do you question it, if Merce is so all-fired safe?"

"Because, friend Peter, Jeanne is in the employ of that miserable toad, Tedière. She holds her salons in order to report to him all that the officers think and say. Save for Duchambon himself, I alone in Louisburg know this secret, and it was told to me by none other than the bewitching Jeanne herself. Naturally, I would prefer that Mercy be farther removed from the influence of such vermin as Tedière. And that brings me to a more pressing matter."

Peter wanted to continue to speak about Mercy, but Duphaine sat up suddenly on the divan, and his manner was so grim that the New Englander was forcibly reminded of his own difficulties. "If Tedière sent you to me, Jacques," he said between clenched teeth, "you can tell him from me to go to hell."

The highwayman waved a hand expressively, as if to indicate that this was not the occasion for posturing heroics. "I was granted permission to visit you by none other than little Duchambon himself, who hopes I will persuade you to be reasonable. He will come to you in person later today, and will request that you reveal to him the war plans of his enemies."

"I reckon he has better things to do than waste his time climbing up all those steps."

"If you refuse, he will give his reluctant permission to Tédière, who will find other means of persuading you to loosen your tongue."

"I'm prepared for whatever risks are needful."

Jacques ran his fingers through his carefully combed hair. "Life in Maine must be very hard," he said. "Everyone I have ever known who comes from that outlandish place resembles the rocks that fill your countryside."

Peter smiled in quiet pride, and his reply was soft but succinct. "Ever try to break a Maine rock, Jacques? It's been tried by lots of folks, but they're not easy to crack."

"There is no need to suffer when you can spend the entire period of the war living the life of a gentleman."

"I don't rightly care enough for oysters with garlic sauce to be a traitor."

Exasperated, Jacques jumped to his feet and stood close to the New Englander. They were roughly the same height, though Peter, broader-shouldered and heavier, seemed the taller. They glared at each other, and at last the highwayman spoke, using a tone one would employ with a child. "Have I suggested that you reveal the real secrets of your general? I have not. Have I recommended to you that you tell the actual war plans of Shirley and Pepperrel and Warren? I have not."

He would have continued, but Peter held up a hand. "Hold on, Jacques. You're French. You took me prisoner and brought me here. But now you're implying that maybe I ought to make up a pack of lies to tell the governor about my war council's intentions. Even if I could get away with some false stories—and I'm not clever like you are, so I couldn't—I still don't see why you give me that kind of advice. It doesn't fit."

"The breeches I wear always fit perfectly, and so do my jackets," was the smooth response. "You are so naïve, friend Peter. I have already been paid for your capture. A report outlining what I have done has been written and will be sent to France on the next packet ship, and when it arrives in Paris it will doubtless be treated as the communiqués on my other exploits have been treated." A shadow crossed his face, but he quickly recovered his poise. "You see, I hope, that I have nothing to gain from you any longer. I will not be one louis d'or richer if you tell the truth, nor one louis d'or poorer if you lie."

"But——"

"You assume, perhaps, that I am a man without a conscience or a sense of compassion. I am endowed with an abundant supply of both qualities. And it would grieve me if you should be made to pay a penalty for stubborn silence. Particularly when a few graceful evasions and inspired inventions would serve to protect your skin from unsightly bruises."

"I can't do it, Jacques. They'd catch me up in no time. Besides, I swore an oath when I took the King's commission that I'd never——"

"You must do as you think best. I can only warn you. I bid you au revoir, friend Peter. And I only hope that this is not adieu."

Henri Duchambon prided himself on his humanity, but his sense of duty was ever present in his consciousness, and his ambition was great. Some day, if he could prevent jealous subordinates from sullying his name overmuch in their private reports to Paris, he would be promoted to the exalted position of the King's Grand Deputy for New France. In that event he would almost certainly be elevated to the nobility and would be created a marquis, at the very least. Then Louise would surely stop complaining about the dullness of life in this raw wilderness world, for almost all of America would, in a sense, belong to her. She would be the first lady of all that now comprised New France, and he would take her on a triumphal tour of the about-to-be-conquered English provinces.

Louise would like that. And for a time, perhaps, she would stop ridiculing him in public, flirting with his colonels, and snubbing the wives of underlings who were important to him. She would never be truly satisfied, of course, until they returned home and she took her place with the great ladies of the court at Versailles, and she never tired of telling him that this was her ultimate goal, just as she rarely stopped berating him for his failure, so far, in achieving her ambition for her. There were times when he thought that, much as he loved Louise, she complicated his life.

This was one of those times, he told himself as he sat in the little drawing room of the prison suite in the Tour du Nord and gazed with sad eyes at the giant from Maine who was being so recalcitrant. The young man's face was red, but his eyes were steady, and, as he sat with his arms folded across his chest, it seemed unlikely that he would change his mind and tell what he knew of his superiors' plans. Like all who were born on this savage continent, French and English alike, he was as stubborn as he was uncouth, and Henri Duchambon felt a slight twinge of distaste for him.

On the other hand, not even a governor enjoyed making someone who had done him no personal harm suffer unnecessarily. If only he would co-operate, how beneficial and pleasant it would be for everyone. Duchambon could send a detailed report of the enemy's intentions to Quebec, and at the same time dispatch a flood of copies to Paris so that no one else could claim the proper credit for his achievement. The promotion and title would be that much closer, and Louise would love him, or at least pretend to love him for a little while. And this hulking English colonial would spend the duration of the war living in quarters unlike any he had ever before known, eating dishes unlike any he had ever tasted. He would have his choice of all the women Louisburg offered, and even the Pepperrell girl, whom he obviously loved, would be permitted to visit him here from time to time. The governor had explained all this in great detail, but the young oaf seemed incapable of understanding. There seemed to be nothing to do but try once more.

"I appeal to your logic, Capitaine Staples." Logic, indeed. This New England bear didn't know the meaning of the word.

Although they had been going over the same ground for more than an hour, Peter remained courteous. "I'm sorry, Your Excellency," he said politely, "but I can tell you nothing, just as your lips would be sealed if our positions were reversed."

"I can imagine no such circumstance!" Duchambon's patience was wearing thin. "I offer you friendship, young man. Although our countries are at war, I offer you my personal friendship. Henri Duchambon does not offer his hand to everyone. Do you strike it away? Do you dare to reject as your patron the second subject of Louis of France in all America?"

Peter wanted to smile, but felt too tired. "I'd like Your Excellency's friendship," he said evenly, "but if I've got to betray my country, the price is too high."

The governor sighed. Patently he was getting nowhere, and it was high time he returned to his own apartment. Louise was entertaining that newly arrived artillery specialist at tea this afternoon, a handsome devil with a roving eye and a fear of no man's rank or position. He had left them alone far too long already. "That is your last word, capitaine?"

"I'm afraid it is, sir."

"And you will not reconsider?"

"I can't reconsider."

Duchambon stood, and beckoned for his cloak and gloves to one of his three orderlies, who stood wooden-faced and immobile behind him. Then he signaled to his adjutant, a dolt whose single commendable quality was his loyalty. "Ferdinand," he said, speaking slowly as he always did to the man, in order to give him time to absorb even the simpliest of instructions, "issue an order which I will sign. The prisoner, Peter Staples, is no longer to be considered an honorable officer of the enemy's forces. His military rank is therefore nonexistent, as of this date. You will say in this order that he was captured while actively engaging in espionage work against France, and he will henceforth be accorded the treatment we give to spies. Make seven copies, Ferdinand. Be sure to put one in safekeeping in my personal files. The usual distribution for the rest, and the one that goes to Paris to be marked for the personal attention of His Grace."

Sighing again, he adjusted the long cloak, which gave him the illusion of greater height, and walked slowly out of the chamber. The members of his entourage followed, and Peter watched them in silence. He wanted to protest over the change in his status, which was as vicious as it was unfair, but he knew there was nothing he might say that would be heeded. He had been given his chance to play the traitor, had refused, and now he would be called upon to face the consequences.

His time of tribulation came even faster than he had imagined it would. Four burly soldiers filed into the living room as soon as the last of the governor's orderlies had departed, and behind them came Commandant Tédière, a smirk creasing his full face. Obviously he had been awaiting word from Duchambon in one of the tower's other apartments, and it was equally plain that he had been anticipating this moment ever since Peter had struck him. He advanced part way into the chamber, but was careful to keep his men between himself and the prisoner.

"Well, my bully boy," he said jovially, "we haven't seen each other in some days. How have you fared? Have you been enjoying yourself? Have you been content with your lot?"

Peter did not reply, but watched warily as the soldiers fanned out and edged closer to him. He guessed that they were planning to pounce on him, and he decided to make any action they took as expensive as possible for them. Forcing a laugh, he wished he could appear as casual as he was sure Jacques Duphaine would be under like circumstances. His right hand closed over the carved top of a high-backed oak chair, and he stood tensely, waiting.

"You don't talk as much as you did the last time we met," Tedière said, savoring every word. "You were verbose enough then. And busy with your fists, too, as I have good cause to remember. Oh, well, enjoy your little silence while you may. You'll talk before I'm through with you, bully boy. You'll babble by the hour until my ears grow tired."

Although the quartet of troopers wore pistols in their belts, none of them carried weapons in their hands, Peter noticed, and that was all to the good. The odds were against him, but with the exception of a black-hearted corporal, none of the soldiers looked particularly formidable. Patently Tedière was planning to maul him; well, he'd make the man pay for the privilege first.

"I grow tired now, as it happens," the commandant declared, and his voice grew ugly. "The time for jesting has come to an end. Come here!" His face darkened when Peter did not move. "Your first lesson is to obey—instantly—when I give you a command, pig. I said—come here."

"Come and get me!" Peter tensed, ready to spring.

"Take him!" the burly man ordered, and the soldiers closed in.

But Peter was ready, and, lifting the chair with his left hand, he swung it around over his head like a club. The troopers had not expected such a violent reaction, and three of them fell back a pace or two, while the remaining man hesitated. But the New Englander was already in motion, and, advancing on Tedìere, he smashed his right fist into the leering face. The commandant howled in pain and retreated, cursing violently.

The soldiers had recovered from their momentary surprise, and they surrounded Peter, trying to get near him. To their surprise, he laughed as though he were having a good time, and to their further amazement he addressed them in passable French. "Surely you don't object, not if you are loyal soldiers of France," he said, holding the chair in front of him like a shield. "That swine who wears an epaulet commanded me to come to him. And I did."

One of the men tittered nervously, and the sound enraged Tedìere all the more. "Take him at once!" he shrieked. "Show him no mercy!" The men shuffled cautiously closer to the prisoner, taking good care to remain out of reach of the chair legs, however, and the commandant danced up and down in wild, impotent anger. "Damn your stupid little souls," he howled, "do as I tell you and be quick about it or I'll have you flogged, all of you. Any man who fails in his duty will get fifty lashes!"

The soldiers were more afraid of the threatened whip than they were of the reckless young man who faced them so defiantly, and although they were secretly pleased that he had punched Tedìere, they knew that the commandant would keep to his word if they failed to obey him now. They had seen him in this mood before. And so, reluctantly but resolutely, they made a dash toward Peter. He brought up the chair again and aimed it at the largest of the troopers. The heavy edge of the seat caught the luckless soldier across the side of the head, and he dropped to the floor, writhing in pain.

But the others were upon Peter now, and two of them caught hold of his arms while the third dived for his legs. They crashed to the floor and rolled over and over, pounding him unmercifully and being pummeled in return. He had been helpless for so long that this moment offered him the opportunity to get rid of his pent-up rage, and he used every trick he knew as he fought with the savage abandon of one who had wrestled Indian fashion since early childhood, who had grown up in a ship-building town where a boy was respected first because of his prowess with his fists.

He pumped his knees unceasingly, which made it next to impossible for the soldiers to hold him, and he struck repeatedly with his hard fists at the faces that loomed over him, at the bodies that tried to crush the breath out of him. For a time he gave as good as he received and more, and was only dimly conscious of the sharp jabs in the ribs that made him gasp for breath and the slashing blows that cut open his lips and made his face swell. At no time was he conscious of the almost hysterical Tédière, who stood out of harm's way at the far side of the room, alternately screaming encouragement to his men or cursing at them, depending on the progress of the fight.

But his assailants were too many, and, although no single one of them could catch him, their combined strength was too great for him. Finally the room began to grow hazy, objects of furniture blurred before his eyes, and even the afternoon light streaming in through the high window grew dim. He became aware at last of the cutting pain in his body, of the throbbing of his head, and his blows grew weaker, less incisive. When he gave up the struggle altogether he did not know it, and had no idea that he was sprawled on the thick carpet, battered and bloody.

From a great distance he heard the triumphant voice of Commandant Tédière. "Enough! I do not want him to fall asleep quite yet."

Peter opened his eyes with a great effort and saw the heavy-set Frenchman standing over him. "Where are your brave speeches now, bully boy? Show me more of your heroics! Show me how a pig from Maine can fight?"

A booted toe crashed into Peter's ribs, and he groaned

involuntarily. The pain was so sharp that the world went black for an instant; then Tédière kicked him once more, and he thought dimly that he was going to die. Again and again the heavily shod foot smashed into him, but Peter was not aware of it now. He never knew that Tédière continued to kick him long after he lost consciousness.

TWELVE

"Your Excellency," Jacques said, "if you make the right moves, you'll soon be the King's viceroy for all of North America. Think of it. You'll be ruler of a continent. Enough to make a man giddy, eh?"

Henri Duchambon bent his head over a pile of papers on his desk so Duphaine would not see his face. The fellow had an uncanny knack of reading others' secret thoughts and then twisting what he had gleaned to his own advantage. "Permit me to be the custodian of my own career," he replied.

"If I do, you'll go home to Paris in disgrace." Jacques' cheerful candor matched his lack of respect." And so far I fail to see any signs of wisdom on your part. Here you have an opportunity given to few men in your position, and what do you do? You bungle your chance!"

"Duphaine, you'll keep a civil tongue in your head, or——"

"I'm interested in results, not civility!" Jacques jumped to his feet, and, as he moved to the window to stand and stare out at the ships in the bay, the governor was reminded anew of his similarity to some wild animal. There was the same boundless energy and intensity, the same sharp sense of cunning. "I brought you a prisoner who can tell you where the enemy will attack. He probably knows the actual dates of the operation, too. But you put him in the hands of Tédière. Tédière, mind you! And what have you learned? Nothing, absolutely nothing!"

"Be patient, Duphaine. Paul will achieve these results over which you become so dramatic. He's very adept at persuading people to talk."

The Gentleman looked at Duchambon contemptuously. "Peter Staples will not respond to force. You're a patriot yourself, Your Excellency, so you ought to understand the frame of mind of a man who knows that his country and his people will suffer if he fails them."

The governor understood all too well that he was being subtly flattered by the comparison, and he braced himself for a request of some sort. He had seen Duphaine's tactics of mixing vinegar and honey before, and to protect himself he pretended that he was bored. Leaning back in his chair, he yawned and closed his eyes, and hence was totally unprepared for his visitor's unorthodox reaction.

Jacques crossed to the desk in three strides and pounded the polished oak with his fist. "While you sit here daydreaming about the suite you'll be given at Versailles, the important men who'll bow to you in the drawing rooms, and the ladies who'll entice you into palace boudoirs, the one person who can help you to achieve this exalted state of happiness is being put to death. And once the life is crushed out of him, I assure you that he'll be useless to you, Your Excellency."

Duchambon looked up, startled, and wished that the soundrel would not perch so familiarly on the edge of his desk. He wanted to say as much, but the lean, scowling face was only a few inches from his nose and he did not quite dare. "You exaggerate!" he declared peevishly.

"Do I, indeed?" Jacques ran his fingers through his

crisp hair in exasperation. "Tedière has submitted him to the torture every morning for the past ten days. Do you know what that means? Have you ever seen one of those charming little seminars that Tedière conducts?"

"Good heavens, no!" The governor shuddered slightly at the mere thought.

"In another day or two, Staples will be dead. I don't ask you to take my word for it. But when he's gone, you'll have only yourself to blame. I do ask you to remember that I warned you. I risked my life to capture him. I succeeded in bringing off the most brilliant coup in the history of New France. And what have I to show for my pains? A few tawdry louis d'or."

"You took them fast enough." Duchambon hoped his fright didn't show. If what the rogue said was true, his chance to make a brilliant showing was indubitably vanishing.

"I have a few dreams of my own that go beyond money." Jacques' dark eyes blazed, but his voice was cold. "And I tell you plainly, when Tedière fails I shall find some excuse to call him out. Then I'll run him through like the swine he is. That will be small satisfaction, but at least it will be something."

"What would you have me do, Duphaine?" The governor lifted his hands over his head in a gesture of despair. This small sample of the fellow's fury was enough to send chills running up and down the sedate gubernatorial spine: if Staples died before telling his secrets, it was safe to predict that Duphaine would feel so cheated that he would run amok. And then no one would be safe, least of all the second most prominent citizen of New France, who would be given no chance to hide behind the dignity of his office. Duchambon remembered all too well how this devil had caught the Maréchal de Flambiène cheating at cards some months past, had provoked a quarrel with him, and had neatly shattered the reputation of a famous soldier in the ensuing duel. Duphaine had sliced the marshal's clothing so expertly that he Flambiène had finally stood in his underwear before a circle of onlookers, disarmed and humiliated. He had consequently been so ridiculed when he had returned to France that he had put a bullet through his head.

Jacques stood again at the window, staring moodily out past the parade ground through the open gate to the sea, and he seemed not to have heard the question. "What would you have me do?" the governor repeated.

Turning slowly, Jacques showed no elation, and when he replied his voice was quiet and gentle, almost anti-climactically flat. "Let me handle this," he said. "Let me handle it—in my own way."

Metal ground against metal, wood creaked, and ropes moaned as they stretched tighter. Peter knew the sounds so well by now, and, as he kept his teeth clamped together to keep from shouting, from screaming, from babbling like a child, he told himself that the pain was of secondary importance. Had anyone told him that he could think more clearly, more logically while under torture he would have laughed, but it was true. And the realization that he could even contemplate laughter struck him as funny: a gleam of humor came into his eyes.

"Hold!" commanded the rasping voice of Tedière above him, and the bloated face of the commandant bent closer. "I had thought he was again losing consciousness, but he is still with us. Staples, where will the New Englanders attack? Will it be Quebec or Montreal?"

Peter wondered idly how many times he had been asked those identical questions. There had been a day—he could no longer remember whether it had been yesterday or farther back in the dim past—when he had kept his sanity by counting Tedière's almost endless, repetitious demands. It was too bad, he thought, that he had forgotten the total number by now, and it was a pity that he hadn't decided to play the same game today. But it was too

late now: he had been strapped into the ingenious device
hours ago.

"Quebec or Montreal? Which is it, Staples?"

It was sometimes almost impossible to distinguish the
commandant's actual voice from its own echoes which
sounded with such hollow solemnity against the stone
walls of the high-ceilinged chamber. It was this inability
to differentiate that had caused him to abandon the game
in the first place, Peter suddenly recalled. The effort had
been too great and the pleasures too small.

"Turn the wheel!"

There was a moment's pause, then the familiar noises
of metal, ropes and wood. Peter strained against the
boards and thick leather bands that held him, and although he had been consoling himself with the notion
that he was numb, impervious to all feeling, he knew
better now.

"Quebec or Montreal? Tell me, Staples. Just the one
word—that's all I want. Quebec? Montreal? Which is it?"

The routine was suddenly interrupted by a new voice,
lazy and contemptuous, somehow challenging—and
vaguely familiar. "Tedìere, you are a butcher." Peter
wondered if he himself was speaking, then realized that
the remark had been made in a French more perfect than
he himself commanded.

"Get out! I permit no one admission here! Do you
understand? No one!"

Tedìere's rage seemed genuine enough, and Peter
came to the conclusion that he was not the victim of his
own imagination. Reassured, he concentrated all the
harder, trying to place that new voice. It did not occur to
him to look, for he had closed his eyes sometime in the
past few minutes and could not bother to open them.

"Careful, Tedìere! It would give me such joy to skewer
you that I'm not sure I can control my impulses." It was
remarkable, Peter thought, how a man's hearing improved under torture. He was positive the sound that

struck his ears was that of a sword being whipped from a soft leather sheath.

Tédìere became almost inarticulate in his frenzy. "I'll have you on that same table before the day is out! I'll——"

"You'll oblige me by addressing me with the respect due a gentleman. Here is an order signed by Governor Duchambon. You may read it yourself, if you wish. It removes the prisoner from your custody and places him under my authority." There was the rattle of thick parchment and the noise of Tédìere's labored breathing, then the new voice sounded again, and there was a clear note of authority in it now. "So you will be the one who goes! Now, Tédìere—at once! What? You hesitate? Do not tempt me. My blade itches to spank you!"

There was a welter of confusing footsteps, and a door clanged shut. The newcomer spoke again, more urgently. "Release your wheel!" he ordered. "And do it quickly, or I'll cut your damned ropes!"

At last Peter identified that voice: it belonged to Jacques. Contented, he drifted into oblivion.

Mercy tried not to move her hands. A real lady, her mother had always said, allowed them to remain placidly in her lap. And even more important, if she plucked at the lace handkerchief she held, she would certainly betray her nervousness to Jacques, who was sitting back in his corner of the carriage, eyeing her with that casual unconcern that she had come to identify as a sign of alert watchfulness.

"You've tricked me again," she said, trying unsuccessfully to keep from sounding either hurt or reproachful. "You told me you were going to take me for a drive into the countryside, and this carriage is heading straight for the citadel. Yes, and even the carriage itself isn't what you told me it was!" she added, completely forgetting her resolve to match his calm. "You claimed it belonged to you—but there's the governor's official shield, carved into the woodwork. And——"

"I've rarely known a woman so eager to cavil and quarrel over irrelevant details." Something struck Jacques as amusing, but he apparently had no intention of explaining—until he saw the indignation on Mercy's face. "Most beautiful girls," he elaborated, "are content to let a man admire their beauty. But you're unique, and no one can deny it. You combine the appearance of a king's favorite with the occasional disposition of a washerwoman shrew!"

Mercy was unsure whether he intended the remark as a compliment or an insult, but she let it pass. There were more important things to discuss. "Why are we driving to the citadel?" she demanded, maintaining a semblance of dignity despite the incessant bumping and jolting of the carriage.

"One thing at a time, if you please." Jacques patted her hand, then withdrew it before she could accuse him of familiarity. "Did it occur to you that the house of Jeanne le Sueur might be staffed with agents in the employ of Paul Tédière? No? Well, let me assure you that he pays each one of them a wage every month. So I merely said the first thing that came into my mind, just to confuse them. And him. Friend Tédière bears me no love these days." He grinned and managed to look like a small, naughty boy.

Mercy thought of her brother, felt homesick, and had difficulty in composing her features. "I see," she said shortly. "Now will you be good enough to explain——"

"You share one trait in common with every woman I've ever known. Curiosity. I——"

"Be good enough to stop comparing me with your wenches," Mercy said crossly.

"That's my last intention, I give you my word. You are unlike any girl I've ever known or have ever hoped to meet."

His voice was grave, and his eyes were so intense that Mercy averted her gaze. She wanted to shiver and felt flustered, and she was both glad and sorry when the carriage swept inside the west gate of the citadel and pulled to a halt. At least there was no need for a reply, and for that much she felt grateful. Jacques opened the door, jumped to the flagstones and helped her to the ground, then offered her his arm.

Mercy took it and with her free hand tugged Jeanne le Sueur's thick silk cape more tightly around her. The atmosphere of the fortress was so grim, so desolate that she always felt depressed when she came here. And it was no different in this section, which she had never before visited, than it was anywhere else. Uniformed sentries paced up and down cobbled walks, their muskets on their shoulders, their tread measured, their necks stiff. As a rule Mercy enjoyed seeing them eye her, even turn and look after her in defiance of their military orders, but today was different. She still didn't know why Jacques had brought her here, and his evasion of the subject irritated her to the point where she forgot the sentries and her feminine ego.

Before she could again press her question, Jacques led her to a heavy iron door set into the very wall of the citadel itself. There seemed to be some sort of blockhouse here, and as they entered it three soldiers jumped to attention and saluted. This was surprising in itself, for Jacques had no military status. There was no time to ponder the matter, for directly ahead now was a stone staircase that dropped sharply into the underregions of the citadel.

Mercy caught Jacques looking at her, and she saw an expression on his face that startled her. He composed his features quickly, and his eyes became hard, almost indifferent. But a feeling of dread stole over her as she continued to picture the strange mixture of pity and calculating elation with which he had been regarding her.

His side had stopped aching, and he no longer felt the excruciating pains in his legs, the agony in his arms, but Peter didn't care if he lived or died. Today was one with yesterday and tomorrow didn't matter: the days had merged into the gray haze that surrounded him. His world was the tiny cell in the dungeons beneath the citadel, and he was too weak, too tired to allow his thoughts to wander beyond the damp stone walls that hemmed him in. A vermin-infested straw pallet and a slop jar were his only "furniture," the dim light that illuminated the little room came from a slit in the thick metal door and the iron chain on his right ankle bit into his flesh; all reminded him constantly how low he had fallen.

Once each day a guard thrust food into the cell, and for a time he had tried to husband his strength by eating the dry bread, the watery cabbage soup, the occasional thin stew that was his fare. But in recent days he had become as indifferent to food as he was to life itself, and he no longer bothered to haul himself from the pallet. Standing was such an effort that he trembled for hours after each attempt, and it was easier to remain where he was, suspended in lethargy. He invariably became dizzy when he sat up, too, so it was far more satisfactory to remain horizontal.

Only one real pleasure remained in life: the contemplation of his glorious victory. In spite of all to which he had been subjected, he had revealed no military information of consequence to his captors. He vaguely remembered the last time he had been in the torture chamber, when Jacques Duphaine had superseded Tedière, and Jacques, he knew, was more humane. Jacques would not subject him to those terrible indignities of flesh and spirit but would leave him here to die in peace. And it would be peaceful, for the enemy had not forced him to break his silence, and he knew he had triumphed under conditions so appalling that they would have been beyond the scope of his imagination only a few weeks previously.

Fortunately, his physical condition served to insulate him now from the worries that had almost driven him out of his mind during the early days of his imprisonment. He could think of Kittery, of his former position with the Pepperrell enterprises, and remain completely detached, for he believed that he was no longer the Peter Staples who had cared about such matters. And through bitter experience he had disciplined his mind not to linger on Mercy any more, for on this one subject alone he still maintained some measure of feeling. When he thought of her he invariably wept, which was not only weak and childish but left him shaken for the rest of the day. And so it was better to dismiss her from his mind, just as he hoped that she would soon forget him. His life was finished, but Mercy had many years to live.

He heard the key grate in the lock of his door, but he did not turn. He would not bother with cabbage soup today; in fact, the mere idea of eating the stuff made him ill. The door opened, and light filtered into the cell, and when someone spoke from the doorway he was certain beyond all last doubt that he was at last truly out of his mind. He could swear that the voice was Mercy's.

Then the door closed again, and somewhat to his surprise he discovered that he was weeping. Sternly, repeatedly, he told himself that his imagination was running wild. Yesterday it had been Jacques, today it was Mercy. The end was obviously near, and he was glad. It was best this way.

THIRTEEN

MOST of what happened immediately after Mercy was shown a glimpse of Peter in his cell remained blurred and hazy in her memory afterwards, and it was at least a quarter of an hour, perhaps much longer, before she could think clearly again. Scattered incidents, a few details, did impress themselves on her mind, however. She later remembered that Jacques had pocketed the key to Peter's cell after closing the door, and she recalled that the highwayman had been anxiously solicitous as he had stood with her in the bright sunlight of the world of reason. He had said little but had watched her closely for signs of hysteria or fainting, and had kept a firm but gentle hold on her arm until he saw the normal color return to her cheeks.

Then he led her along a stone walk to a severe, two-story building in the center of the citadel's compound. This seemed to be barracks of some sort, and, like all structures inside the fortress, its exterior was made exclusively of stone. They moved through the corridors in silence and at last came to a room not much larger than

Peter's cell. A small cot was ranged along one wall and a plain chest of drawers stood opposite it near the small, high window: the sole concession to luxury was a woven Indian rug on the floor. The walls were bare of ornamentation, but Jacques' swords, pistols and a collection of knives and tomahawks were suspended from pegs on the inside of the door.

The Gentleman bowed Mercy to a seat at the foot of the bed, his manner as ostentatious as though this were a ballroom at his king's palace at Versailles. "Welcome," he said, "to the Maison Duphaine. This is my home, my office, my world."

On the top of the high chest lay a locket that looked suspiciously like the one Jacques had taken from Mercy by force on the road near Lynn so long ago, and beside it stood a miniature of a woman who, at a glance, seemed to be Jeanne le Sueur. Before Mercy could identify either the jewelry or the portrait, however, Jacques whisked both objects into a drawer, then faced her with a smile so pleasant that this might have been a social engagement.

"I trust you're comfortable, Mercy."

She worded her reply slowly, carefully. "France deserves to be wiped from the face of the earth. I never knew that such horrible things could be done—to any human being." She could not bring herself to mention Peter's name.

"France is not to blame," Jacques replied with quiet conviction. "There are men like Paul Tédière in every land. I know." He paused and seemed lost in his own thoughts for a moment or two before continuing. "But Peter is no longer in Tédière's charge. He has just been given over into my care, and I give you my word that——"

"Never mind. He won't live long." Tears would have been inadequate, and Mercy was dry-eyed.

"With care, he can live." Jacques was very emphatic, very sure.

"Why did you take me to his cell? Why did you show him to me?" The questions were out before she could stop them, and she no longer cared whether her voice trembled.

He rested an elbow on the top of the chest of drawers, and, although his pose was one of elegant repose, his eyes were serious. "I don't suppose that you know anything about your father's military plans, do you?" he countered.

"I am William Pepperrell's daughter, not his confidante," Mercy replied scornfully, wondering why he had chosen to ask such a strange question.

"But Peter was his aide-de-camp. A secretary of the colonial English war council. Peter knows which of our fine cities you father intends to attack—and when."

Mercy understood now, and she was filled with contempt—and pride. "You may kill him, but he'll tell you nothing."

"So Tedìere has learned. Myself, I have never stooped to murder. It does not become a gentleman." Jacques touched his stock, then lightly adjusted his cuff. "I prefer other methods. Peter loves you, and if you were to persuade him——"

"You can't mean that!" Mercy stared at him, then began to laugh. "How abysmally ignorant you really are, in spite of all your pretentions! If you think for one moment that a Maine man would compromise his honor——"

"If it were not for me, Peter Staples would now be dead," Jacques interrupted savagely. "I was able to persuade the governor to give him over into my custody on the grounds that I could persuade him to reveal what no one else has forced him to tell."

"And what made you think that you could——"

"Think? I merely hoped. There are few men anywhere half so shrewd as I am. I have taken a gamble. If I succeed, the results are worth it to me. It should be obvious to you that I have much to gain."

It was indeed clear to Mercy that Jacques thought of himself first and that all other considerations were minor. A wild idea occurred to her and began to grow in her mind, and, although her heart pounded violently, she kept her features composed. "What will happen," she asked, "when Governor Duchambon discovers that your efforts have produced no more results than Tédìere's?"

Jacques shrugged and chuckled faintly. "Duphaine will be called a braggart, but that will not be anything new, I can assure you, Mercy. My enemies have compounded some epithets for me that are worse than——"

"I'm not interested in you!" she said peevishly, regretting the words almost before they were out of her mouth. She had to tread lightly, she reminded herself, and started anew, her tone calm and sweet. "I meant to say—what will happen to Peter then?"

"If he's lucky he'll be allowed to starve to death in the dungeons. If he's less fortunate, friend Tédìere will finish him off far more quickly."

Mercy decided to go ahead with her idea; if she wavered or reconsidered now, she would never do it, and she stopped listening to that part of her which protested so vehemently. Standing, she took a deep breath. "Then Peter will be truly safe only if he escapes from Louisburg."

"Impossible." Jacques saw the gleam in her eyes, the flush on her cheeks, and eyed her curiously. "He's unable to stand on his own feet, much less escape."

"I'm only supposing now. If he were somehow restored to health——"

"In a dungeon cell?" Jacques was incredulous.

"No. But somewhere. The details don't matter for the moment. Suppose he regained his strength. Could he escape then?"

"Not one prisoner has ever escaped from Louisburg in the history of the fortress." Jacques seemed to be humoring her.

"Not one prisoner," she responded, "ever had the right help, then."

Unable to believe Mercy quite knew what she was implying, he stared at her long and hard before he spoke again. "Why would I give him such help?" he demanded bluntly.

"Because you put Jacques Duphaine above honor, country, any of the things that other men hold dear."

"That has been my necessary lot." There was no self-justification in his tone. He made the statement simply, factually, then hooked his thumbs into his belt. "What have I to gain by somehow seeing to it that Peter becomes strong and healthy again, and then—in some extraordinary way—spirit him out of the fortress?"

"If any man can do it, you can."

"My thanks for your compliment, Mercy. But why would I take such a risk? I can see what's to be won if I can find out the military information Peter knows. But this——"

The moment to reveal what she had in mind had come, and Mercy put out a hand to steady herself against the wall. "I am an heiress in my own right," she said, unaware that her voice had risen slightly. "And some day I will inherit a rather large fortune from my father—"

"The wealth of few nobles in either France or England can match that of William Pepperrell," Jacques murmured, his eyes hard and alert. "Go on."

"You've hinted from time to time—no, you've more than hinted that you don't find me unattractive." This was the most difficult part, and Mercy could not control her breathing.

"You're the loveliest creature I've ever seen, and I've told you as much countless times."

"Then—I'll marry you—after you've helped Peter to escape." There, it was said.

Jacques reacted at once. Stepping forward, he took Mercy into his arms, kissed her gently, and then moved away. Turning, he reached into the top drawer of the chest, took out a quill pen, ink, and a sheet of parchment. He wrote a few words, and the room was very quiet save for the scratching of the pen. "Here," he said, offering the sheet to Mercy, "this is a simple confirmation of our agreement."

She studied it for a moment, then looked up, her brow puckered, her eyes guarded. At this moment she was very much William Pepperrell's daughter. "This seems in order. You'll sign a like statment for me?"

"There's little chance that I'll try to back out, is there?" he countered, laughing. "But I'm hardly likely to give you power to have me hung."

"Hung?" Mercy was all innocence.

"Precisely. If I sign such a statement, I'm proved traitor any time you care to take the document to little Duchambon. This will be the only written record, if you please. And I insist on it merely because I am all too familiar with the ability of a woman to change her mind." Jacques dipped the quill into the ink jar and held it out to her.

Mercy signed her name, and as there was no sand available she waved the parchment back and forth to dry it. She was scarcely able to think about the bargain she had just made: the self-recriminations, the doubts and worries, the bitterness and regret would all come later. Now all she knew was that something would soon be done for Peter, that there was at least a chance he would be alive and free in the not too distant future.

Jacques took the paper from her, examined it carefully and held it up to the light when he looked critically at her signature. Watching him, Mercy was secretly glad that her father had insisted that she learn to write: Jacques had taken her prowess for granted, and it pleased her vanity that she had shown herself capable of compliance with her demand. Now, if he kept to his part of the agreement, she would become his wife. She lowered her eyes as he folded the parchment and placed it in an inner pocket of his tunic.

"My dear," the highwayman said, "we are now officially—though secretly—betrothed."

Tedière definitely was useful, even valuable, but there were times when he went too far. This had been a trying day, and Governor Duchambon tried to curb his growing irritation as he gazed across his desk at the bloated face of the commandant. "I do not wage war on young ladies!" he said sharply.

"Your Excellency does not understand." Tedière's voice was unctuous, his manner ingratiating.

"I understand all too well that my career would be at an end if I permitted Madamoiselle Pepperrell to be imprisoned and turned her over to you for torture! France would never stop talking about such a scandal. And His Majesty would never forgive such a *faux pas!*"

"But——"

"This girl isn't a mere nobody, Tedière! Her father is wealthier than the Duc d'Orléans! And he commands the enemy army! Do you realize what he would do in return? Why, if my Louise were ever captured, I——" He stopped short and shuddered.

"Your Excellency," Tedière said, his voice soothing, "it has never crossed my mind to subject the wench——"

"*Mademoiselle* Pepperell!"

"—Mademoiselle Pepperrell to the treatment which we reserve for criminals. Permit me to explain more clearly. Staples told nothing, even under the greatest pressure I could apply. Such a man will never be broken by that braggart and liar, Duphaine, no matter what tricks Duphaine tries. And if Your Excellency will forgive my temerity, I feel very deeply that you made a grave error in turning over so important a prisoner to that—that poseur."

The governor held his temper in check only because he suspected that Tedière knew that he had kept more than his share of last year's fur revenues. "Staples was almost in his grave by the time you finished with him. If Duphaine can learn the information we seek, I stand to gain a great deal. If not, I lose nothing. But what has this to do with your revolting notion of imprisoning Mademoiselle——"

"Staples loves her, Your Excellency. Whenever my— ah—treatment drove him out of his mind, he talked about her constantly. While we would actually put her in no danger, Staples might be far more willing to reveal the secrets he holds if he *thought* she was in danger." Tédière paused delicately and licked his puffy lips. "The girl is young, and I presume she is robust. So a few weeks, even a few months in a cell would do her no real harm."

Duchambon was silent for several minutes as he weighed the matter carefully. The idea, he had to admit, was as clever as it was unscrupulous. And it might possibly work; as with so many of the commandant's schemes, the potential results were worth the adverse comment that would be caused by the brutality of their achievement. "You are resourceful, Tédière, very resourceful," he said cautiously.

The heavy-set man beamed at the compliment. "I thought Your Excellency might begin to see the possibilities of my little plan. And there need be no unpleasant repercussions, either."

"No?"

"The Pepperrell girl need never be told the reason for her imprisonment. After a time, Staples will either speak up or he will not. In either eventuality, we then do away with him." He snapped his broad fingers and grinned unpleasantly. "He will have been the one person in possession of the truth, and his lips will be closed, permanently."

"But," Duchambon persisted, "what of Mademoiselle Pepperrell herself? She will know she has been confined in a cell and that her existence has been at best rather hard—"

"At the proper time Your Excellency will set her free, personally. You will go to her cell and unlock the door with your own hand. You will apologize profusely. You will claim that until that very day you knew nothing of what happened. And you will prove your good intentions by having the stupid wretch responsible for the mistake beaten and thrown into the same cell she has occupied. She will be a witness to the whole incident."

"One moment, Tedière." The governor was slightly confused. "Who will play the part of the author of this terrible error?"

The commandant shrugged and a far-away look came into his eyes. "It will not be a part, Your Excellency, and there will be no need for play acting, I promise you. My lists are always crowded. I never lack candidates for the dungeons."

The fastidious Duchambon had heard enough for one morning and rose suddenly to his feet, terminating the interview. "Your suggestion has merit," he said abruptly, "and I shall give it my consideration. Naturally, I shall discuss all this with Jacques Duphaine, as I don't know how Mademoiselle Pepperrell may fit into whatever he has concocted to entice information from Staples."

Tedière wanted to protest, but the expression on his superior's face indicated that the governor was fond of Duphaine, so he said nothing. He had already accomplished more than he had dared hope, and he was content to wait. Meantime, he thought as he bowed his way out, he would be wise to take his usual precautions.

Later that day a sentry who was in his employ and whom he had stationed outside the governor's office reported that Duphaine had been summoned to the governor's office and that a violent argument had ensued. The guard had heard little of the conversation, but was able to pass along sufficient information to indicate that Duphaine had been opposed to the arrest of the Pepperrell girl, and had so antagonized the governor by the vehemence of his dissent that Governor Duchambon's attitude had hardened.

Eminently pleased, Tedière at first felt sure he was right to bide his time. But in the ensuing days two things happened that distrubed him somewhat. Most important, his agents told him that Duphaine had disappeared from Louisburg for more than seventy-two hours; it had been impossible to follow him, for he was as clever as an Indian at covering his trail in the Acadian forests. He had returned as unexpectedly as he had vanished, had gone straight to Jeanne le Sueur, and had been closeted alone with her for an hour or more.

At least, Tedière reasoned, there was little cause for concern in this last development. It was considerably less than unusal for Madame le Sueur to entertain some man.

Jacques

BOOK THREE

FOURTEEN

"Love's but a frailty of the mind," an English poet
     scribbled:
Oh foolish scrivener who at the sweets of Paradise has
     but nibbled,
In cold disdain you judgment pass from the lofty seat of
     the mighty
And blindly close your eyes to the gentle, loving glory of
     Aphrodite.
The cold, the damp, the gloom of London rotting in your
     bones,
The busy, busy buzzing of your merchant English
     drones
Have robbed you of the wonder bursting, dazzling in the
     night,
That tender, yielding passion that is every woman's
     right.
The warm, sweet scent of wooded hills, the quiet of the
     dawn
When lovers lie, enraptured, their cares and troubles
     gone,
This ecstasy, this blissful wedded state of heart and
     mind,

This fragile, elfin, glowing flame that flickers in the
wind:
This is love! this is love! We know it as we dance
The dance of life in this heaven, our own beloved
France. *

JEANNE LE SUEUR'S knowing, mocking voice filled the
drawing room as she accompanied herself daintily if not
expertly on the harp, and her audience, composed almost
exclusively of regimental officers from the Louisburg garrison gave her their rapt attention. Some looked at her in
open adoration, others were frankly lascivious, and a few
of the younger men seemed dazzled, overwhelmed. Only
Jacques Duphaine was indifferent, and he seemed preoc-
cupied with thoughts of his own as he lounged in an
overstuffed chair, an expression of faint cynicism on his
face. Watching him, then glancing at the others, Mercy
felt sure he had once been Jeanne le Sueur's lover.

The song finished, there was a burst of applause and
Jeanne began another. Mercy was piqued at the concentrated devotion of the audience; as the only other woman
in a gathering of twenty men she felt that she deserved
some acknowledgement of her presence, and she felt dull
and inadequate. The sensation was new to her and it
annoyed her, but she could not feel any real jealousy. If
she were a man, she knew, she would be fascinated by
Madame le Sueur, too. In any land her long, wavy blonde
hair, her enormous violet eyes, and her lush, ripe figure
would proclaim her a beauty, and in any land she would
be a favorite of men, for she had a knack, a positive
instinct for saying and doing what was pleasing to the
opposite sex.

* Translated by the author from Augustine Mirlieu's satiric, free sonnet,
To an English Poet, On Love. Intended as a light literary thrust at
Congreve, it became a patriotic anthem in France during the War of the
Austrian Succession (King George's War, in the colonies.) Written in
1719, it was put to music more than twenty years later by an unknown
composer.

Only Jacques treated her with an easy familiarity, an amused disrespect that bordered on contempt, but that was his way with all women, and perhaps signified nothing. Certainly Jeanne was different with him than with any of the other men who had filled the house in the time that Mercy had been here, however. She often lost her temper with the Gentleman, though with others, even those who sometimes forgot both themselves and the fact that she was a lady, she was tolerant and gentle. She played the gracious, untiring hostess even to immature ensigns ten years her junior, but she never offered Jacques as much as a cup of wine from her plentiful cellars nor a bite of food from her bountifully provisioned larders. Yet he came to the house often, made himself at home and helped himself freely to whatever refreshments he wanted.

Someone was trying to attract Mercy's attention and she glanced up to see Jacques eyeing her. He indicated by a tiny nod that he wanted to speak to her, and with a flick of his fingers he motioned toward the adjacent room, the dining chamber. Jeanne was still singing and Mercy arose carefully from her chair, holding the taffeta skirts of the rose-silk gown that her hostess had loaned her so the petticoats would not rustle. A few of the officers looked her up and down speculatively as she passed them, but she pretended to be unaware of their smiles of invitation as she made her way to the dining room.

Jacques was already waiting for her. "The sun and wind of Cape Breton are kind to you, Mercy," he said, his voice pitched low in order not to disturb the singer or her audience.

"I prefer the climate of Maine," she retorted softly.

"I haven't called you out here to exchange quips with you." Jacques regarded her soberly, his eyes humorless. "I must leave Louisburg again, this time for ten days, and I wanted to say good-by to you."

Illogically, Mercy felt a stab of disappointment and forgot her resolve to behave impersonally. But she said nothing and continued to regard him steadily. He would tell her whatever he chose, no more and no less; he would always be like this, she knew, and she had a foretaste of what was in store for her if he kept to his bargain to free Peter and she married him.

"Governor Duchambon is going to Quebec," he said, turning his face away from the door so those in the drawing room could not read his lips. "He's not particularly fond of me at the moment, so I'm going with him in the hopes of improving my position with him. I tell you all this candidly so you won't think I've forgotten you. Or our agreement. Or Peter."

"Has his—condition improved, Jacques?"

"Turn this way so they can't see your face out there!" he commanded, and when she was slow to obey he took hold of her arm impatiently and pulled her around so that she was looking toward a bay-shaped window seat. "That's better. No, he's still in the same cell. I've been unable to do much for him as yet. To be frank with you, I've been distracted by a more urgent matter, but I hope to be in a position to help him more substantially when I return."

Jacques smiled, and Mercy grew indignant. Peter was desperately in need of attention, and the highwayman's attitude seemed to be unnecessarily callous. "It strikes me," she said, "that nothing is more urgent——"

"I'll handle this in my own way," he interrupted firmly. "I intend to make you my wife, and I know the conditions that must be fulfilled first."

Neither of them realized that the music had stopped and that they were not alone in the dining room until the husky voice of Jeanne le Sueur sounded very near. "What an intimate little fete-à-fete," she said.

Jacques bowed, seemingly unperturbed at the interruption. "Jeanne, my angel," he murmured, "you have excelled yourself today. I can only recall one occasion when I've heard you in better voice."

The widow's violet eyes grew angry at the hidden meaning of his words, which she obviously understood. "Join us in the drawing room, then, and you'll hear some amusing additions to my repertoire."

"Your repertoire is endless, my sweet Jeanne, but I'm afraid I must deny myself the joy of worshipping at your throne today." He peered out the window at the faint mid-March sun. "Governor Duchambon waits for no man when he sails to see the King's deputy in Quebec."

Jeanne laughed, and her eyes were veiled. "I wish you Godspeed," she said. "I hope you have the success that marks all of your enterprises. You go in the knowledge that your interests in Louisburg will be well protected."

To Mercy's astonishment Jacques took hold of the widow's wrist, a white line forming around his mouth. "If they are not," he responded, his voice icy, "I shall know where to place the blame and how to compensate for failure."

He dropped Jeanne's arm, and there were red blotches where his strong fingers had gripped the smooth, white skin. Turning his back to her in a gesture that could be nothing but deliberate rudeness, he lifted Mercy's hand and kissed it first on the back, then on the palm. "Until we meet again," he said.

Before Mercy could reply, he grinned, saluted her in an offhand fashion and was gone. Jeanne watched him as he threaded his way through the throng in the drawing room, her eyes narrowed. With her left hand she gingerly massaged her bruised wrist. "The Marquis de Grémont," she said, and her voice was bitter.

Mercy looked at her quizzically. "You've known each other for a long time."

"Too long."

"I see." Mercy felt uncomfortable.

"No, you don't. And it's just as well. I advise you to forget him, and I only wish that I could." Jeanne turned and faced the younger woman. Although it was rumored that she was in her late twenties, perhaps even thirty, she did not look it. Her skin was clear and fresh, and she carried no excess weight on her small-boned frame. "Jacques' departure comes at just the right time," she said carelessly. "He has a penchant for being nettlesome, you know. He takes a positive delight in it. That gown," she added suddenly, "is all wrong."

Mercy took a single step backward. She had secretly thought the bodice too tight, the neckline too revealing, and although she knew that her mother would never approve of such a dress, she had told herself that the standards of the French were different from those of a New England matron. So it was doubly disconcerting to hear Jeanne le Sueur confirm her fears. She mumbled something in her dismay, but the widow did not hear her.

"I believe I know what will be suitable for this evening. I have a creation that was made to my measurements in Paris last year, in contrasting black and white silk. You're bigger than I am, so it will be rather a snug fit, but that should make it all the more piquant." Jeanne pursed her sensuous lips and looked at Mercy from beneath lowered lids. "There's red beading on the hemline and along the darts, but I don't think it will clash with your hair. We shall see. As soon as we rid ourselves of those buffoons and stumbling gallants in there." She lifted a shapely, delicately painted eyebrow in the direction of the drawing room.

"There's no need to bother on my account."

Jeanne did not hear the remark. "Of course black and white may be too severe for you. I'm not sure that you're old enough to get away with such a gown, but he always likes a sophisticated touch, so it's sure to be becoming—for the occasion."

"He?"

"Oh, didn't I tell you? You have an admirer who will call on you at supper tonight." Jeanne's eyes widened innocently. "I have an invitation to dine with the lieutenant colonel of the Chartres battalion at his officers' ward, a great honor, so you'll have to play hostess here in my stead."

"Who is this—admirer?" Mercey tried to keep her voice steady.

"I thought you knew." Jeanne reached out and patted her arm soothingly. "You've made an enormous impression on one of the most powerful men in New France, someone who can do you a great deal of good. One word from him, and you'll be permitted to write that letter to your parents that you've been begging permission to send."

"Who is he?" Mercy persisted, fearful that she knew the answer even before she heard it.

"Why, Paul Etienne Tédière, of course. Between us, he's positively enamored of you." Jeanne's tone and manner were disarming, but neither she nor Mercy was fooled.

There was a long moment of silence. "I'm afraid," Mercy said with dignity, "that I shall be indisposed this evening. As Commandant Tédière seems to have made his arrangements through you, I would appreciate it if you'll notify him that I can't possibly see him."

The change in Jeanne was startling. She stepped forward quickly, her eyes hard, and she thrust her face close to Mercy's. "You idiot," she said fiercely, "you insane little idiot! Don't you realize what his favor could mean?"

Mercy tried hard to remember that she was a Pepperrell, with a tradition behind her of stature and honor. She would terminate this distasteful discussion with dignity as well as finality. "What is it you would have me do? If it's what you imply, I utterly refuse——"

"I made no demands on you, idiot. I am not a man!" Jeanne paused as a captain in the drawing room shouted something to her, and she turned for an instant and favored him with a brilliant smile. "Be patient, my pets. We'll rejoin you in a moment!" she called, then the smile faded as she again faced Mercy. "All men are alike, all of them have the same desires. But the power belongs to you, if you have the sense to use it. You're a woman, and you have a woman's weapons! Use them! Look at me, child, and see where I've come with no influence, no weight to tip the scales except my natural charms and my natural wit. You're endowed with far more than I was at your age. What does it matter if you let Paul make himself ridiculous over you? If it isn't Paul, it will be someone else!

"You can improve the lot of your lover—or whatever the prisoner may be to you," she added hastily as she saw Mercy stiffen, "and you can win so much for yourself, too. Don't throw away your chances. Force the men to throw themselves away for you instead!"

Without waiting for a reply, Jeanne scooped up her trailing skirt with one hand and walked slowly into the drawing room, her hips undulating slightly, just enough to be provocative, not so much as to be vulgar. She had worked long and arduously to perfect her stroll, which was justly famous through New France.

Mercy could not face the officers waiting in the other room, and a surge of masculine voices at Jeanne's approach created a sudden sense of panic in her. Almost without knowing what she was doing and certainly without conscious thought she slipped into the corridor, hurried up the stairs to her bedchamber and from a satinwood cupboard took the beaver-lined cloak that Jacques had stolen for her. This perfumed house with its overly feminine, frivolous trimmings suffocated her, and she needed to think. A New Englander, even one who had been raised in a wealthy home, could not set her mind in order in this atmosphere. Mercy fled down the stairs and into the open; the air was sharp and cold, almost like the good, bracing air of Maine.

She walked briskly, not bothering to look where she was going but drawn instinctively toward the sea, and after some minutes she found herself at the edge of a bluff overlooking the eastern end of the bay. She was out of breath, and it occurred to her fleetingly that she had been walking rapidly, perhaps even running. There were times, she thought, when a girl had a right to feel sorry for herself, and she sat on a long, flat rock overlooking the water and stared blindly at the hazy line of the horizon.

With Jacques not here to protect her or advise her, she was at a complete loss. There was no way to avoid Tédière and his advances without incurring his further enmity, and she was convinced that her previous treatment of him was at least partly responsible for the suffering he had inflicted on Peter. The question was whether the commandant was more dangerous as a foe or a friend, and the thought kept occurring to her that he was at the very least an official representative of established authority. And this was important to a Pepperrell, accustomed to a world of order and reason.

Perhaps she should have placated him. It was possible that she had blundered, that she had sacrificed her whole future when she had made her bargain with Jacques. At best he was an opportunist, at worst an outright criminal. In any event he held no position with the government of New France, and lived by his daring and ingenuity. She might have been wiser, in her anxiety to help Peter, to turn to Tédière for assistance. And the mere hint to herself that if Jacques had held Tédière's job she would have gone to him unhesitatingly was as painful as it was disturbing. If she honestly had so little respect for the Gentleman, why had she been so quick to offer herself to him in return for Peter's freedom? Did she really *want* to become his wife?

A cold wind from the west swept across the island, but in her distress Mercy did not notice it any more than she was aware of the passage of time. In her anguish she knew only that she was alone, forsaken, and at last she wept. Day turned into night and still she sat, frightened and lonely and miserable. She did not hear soft footsteps behind her, and she raised her head only when someone touched her shoulder. Gasping, she looked up into the strong, lovely face of Tani.

"Great warrior send Tani," the Indian girl said, dispensing with formal greetings. "Great warrior say Tani's sister need help. Tani here, Tani help. You come."

She held out her hand to Mercy, who stood meekly, unresisting. Together they walked slowly into the dusk.

FIFTEEN

A COMPANY of Connecticut militia drilled in a vacant lot on Queen Caroline Street, three more small frigates had dropped anchor during the morning in Boston Harbor, and word had just been received from Rhode Island that the colonial leaders there had voted funds to convert five speedy merchantmen into men-o'-war. The Common had been converted into a huge armed camp, and each day saw the arrival of battalions, companies, and even straggling platoons from all of New England, New York, and New Jersey. Tents had been erected for the officers, the men had thrown up crude lean-to shelters for themselves, and scores of fires burned every day.

These fires and the accompanying odors of cooking food had come to dominate Boston life, and some matrons in the Back Bay complained of the smell of frying onions and ham, of boiling oatmeal and roasting beef, but no one paid them any heed, least of all their busy husbands who were provisioning the army. The Americans, as the soldiers were beginning to call themselves, were at war with New France, and everything was being subordinated to the supreme effort of making final preparations to crush the enemy.

The troops cheerfully suffered the privations of serving without pay while the royal governors and colonial legislatures wrangled over funds, and they good-naturedly accepted the crude conditions of their day-to-day living without complaint. Their unflagging buoyancy was a never failing tonic to Lieutenant General William Pepperrell, who had aged considerably since the mysterious disappearance of his daughter and his trusted aide. He sat now in the parlor of the house he had rented for his wife and himself facing the Common, and, as he watched the men from Connecticut marching toward their bivouac in the cold, driving rain, he marveled that they were singing lustily. These were his men: he was responsible for their safety and welfare, and the very least he owed them was his full concentration. He was learning, through great effort, to keep his personal sorrow locked away in the inner recesses of his mind.

Tugging at his scarlet uniform tunic, he smiled apologetically at Peter Warren, restless as usual, who paced up and down before the fire in the parlor grating. "I'm sorry, Peter. I missed your last point. My mind was wandering, I'm afraid."

The commodore continued to walk as briskly as if he were on the quarter-deck of his flagship. "They caught another damned French spy hanging about the docks last night," he repeated with what for him was considerable patience. "Woke me up to tell me about it, and I received the bastard in my nightshirt. Five minutes was enough, more than enough for me. I had the execution orders drawn at once, and he was hanged from the *Invincible's* yardarm at dawn."

Pepperrell leaned forward slightly in his chair. "Did you learn anything?"

"No, Will. It was the usual. Those blundering dunderheads up north bungled it again. Sent down a poor devil who barely spoke English and who could be spotted by a child as an enemy agent. He was doing it for the money, of course, and as always the great minds in Quebec hadn't given him a ha'penny. They were waiting for him to bring in results. They don't know the meaning of patriotism up there."

"Sit down, Peter. You set my disposition on edge when you never hold still. This is the fifth spy we've taken in the past two weeks. It strikes me that the Royal War Committee of New France is becoming desperate."

Warren laughed sharply and paced more rapidly than before. "Wouldn't you be desperate if you were in their boots? Thanks to your foresight the three wilderness raids they've attempted have been repulsed. They lack our man power, so they can't launch a real invasion against us. But enough of their spies sneak back to them with word that you're assembling an army of four or five thousand men and that I have almost one hundred ships in my fleet already! I'd be scared, too, if the only place my strength was superior was in sea power." He paused and frowned, then struck the open palm of his left hand with his right fist. "If London doesn't send me those ships of the line and the new frigates by the end of the month, we aren't going to get them, Will. And that means I'll have to make do with the damndest collection of scraps, odds, and ends that have ever put to sea."

"My own correspondence with Lord Percy leads me to believe you won't get them, Peter. They're too concerned with their own war in Europe."

"Shortsighted baboons!" The commodore's lean face became puffy with anger. "I'll lend 'em my captain's glass so they can see across the ocean. Unless I get reinforcements I can't risk a major battle between here and Louisburg. If Admiral Delaire finds me, those huge tubs of his will blow my decrepit little fishing boats right out of the water and straight to hell!"

"All the more reason, then, why we must keep our target a complete secret. Only you and I and Governor Shirley know it."

"And Peter Staples." Warren regretted his words before they were out of his mouth, for Pepperrell turned pale and sank back into his chair.

"Yes. And Peter Staples," he said, then smiled with a visible effort. "I've sent an open request to regimental commanders asking them to give me their views on the best route to Quebec. And I've invited their opinions regarding a diversionary attack on Montreal. That should keep the enemies' spies busy for a time."

Again Warren laughed, a trifle more warmly. "I've sent out word to my captains, too. Their chart makers are to submit all known data to me on the seas between here and Quebec. I'm to have this infomation without fail when I return here next month. Will, you and I are either the cleverest men in Christendom or the worst damned fools who ever drew breath."

An uproar over Mercy's disappearance greeted the governor of Louisburg on his return from Quebec, but Henri Duchambon was in no mood for uproars. He had just been through a trying experience, one that had nettled him as well as shaken him, and his mind was occupied. The King's ministers in Paris had seen fit to send a committee of five blue-blooded incompetents to Quebec to take charge of the war effort in the New World, and the governor still marveled at their pomposity, at how little they knew but how rigidly they clung to their opinions.

Had it not been for Jacques Duphaine, the garrison at Louisburg would have been denuded of its regular troops, for the nervous commissioners had been adamant in demanding protection for their persons, and for this purpose they naturally wanted the renowned regiments stationed on Cape Breton Island. Duchambon, seeing his influence and importance badly impaired by such a transfer, had despaired. But luck—and Duphaine—had intervened.

Admiral Delaire, commander of the Western Fleet, second ranking officer of the entire navy and first cousin of Madame de Brissac, the King's current mistress, had amazed the governor by greeting Duphaine as an old and dear friend. It did not matter that both had maintained a curious, tight-lipped silence on the place and circumstances of their previous acquaintance: what counted was that Duphaine whispered a few well-chosen words into the Admiral's ear. And the old sea dog had obliged by roaring and ranting so effectively that the commissioners had decided to look elsewhere than Louisburg for their escort. Colonial levies, it was hastily decided, would serve the ministers' appointees rather than the regiments from Louisburg.

So it transpired that Duchambon, deeply grateful to Jacques, was not of a mind to hear calumnies heaped on him. Commandant Tediere tried to insist that Jeanne le Sueur had played a role in Mercy's disappearance. But the governor quickly learned that a score of officers had been Jeanne's guests on the very day of the unfortunate incident, and that she had never been out of their sight until long after dusk, though Mercy had vanished in midafternoon. As for Jacques, he had been a member of the governor's own party for almost two weeks, and no further proof of his innocence was required.

It was he who suggested that Mercy had probably decided to try to make her way back to New England, and all Louisburg, the governor included, agreed. No one had come to know her well in the short time she had been on the island, and the officers of the garrison, after saluting her courage and deploring her lack of common sense, promptly forgot her. As Duphaine intimated here and there, any woman who tried to make her way alone all the way to Maine could not possibly survive the hazards of the journey.

The male prisoner was far more important than the girl, Jacques told the governor, who agreed heartily. After all, it was Peter who held the key to the future of New France.

The room was vaguely familiar and the four-poster bed, soft and comfortable, convinced Peter that he was dreaming. The deep mattress, the clean linen sheets and the blankets of light wool were too good to be true; he was no longer in his right mind, but if this was delirium, he wanted to stay this way, always. Most of the time he slept, but whenever he awoke the woman was there, feeding him hot, nourishing broths, smoothing his pillows, tending to his every need with infinite, gentle patience. Whenever he opened his eyes she was there, her long, blond hair gleaming in the sunlight, her full, red lips smiling at him, her violet eyes watching him with tender concern.

By the second week of this inexplicable new status he had come to take the presence of the woman for granted; at one time or another he had thought first that she was his mother, then Mercy, then an aunt who had looked after him when his parents had been carried away by the plague. Now he knew she was none of them, but it seemed as though she had been close to him all of his life. He watched her as she knelt at the hearth, her simple wool gown of pale gray swirling gracefully about her as she stirred a little kettle of soup, and he thought that never had he known anyone so sweet, so tireless, so lovingly compassionate and generous.

Then he glanced out the window, and with a sudden sense of shock realized that this was the apartment in the Tour du Nord which he had occupied in the first days of his imprisonment, before he had been handed over to Paul Tedière for questioning and torture. The window was open and the crisp yet soft air of early spring mingled with the delicious odors of chicken broth. Peter knew that he was hungry, that he was alive, and that he wanted to live. Bewildered, he caught sight of his left hand; it was pale and emaciated, the hand of a stranger. And more peculiar still, he was wearing a long-sleeved nightshirt of rich silk, a garment more expensive than any he had ever owned.

The woman rose and tiptoed toward him. She saw that he was awake, looked into his eyes and her face was suffused with relief and happiness. "The Lord is good," she said in a husky voice, her English marked by a charming French accent that was anything but Parisian. "You are your own self again, monsieur."

Peter tried to prop himself up on one elbow, but the effort was too much for him, and the woman was instantly at his side, tucking the blankets more snugly around him. Countless questions raced through his mind, but he asked the most immediate of them. "Who are you?" His voice sounded like a dismal croak in his own ears. "You seem to know me, but I don't think I've had the honor of being presented to you."

She leaned close to him and he caught the elusive fragrance of a scent that was more delicate than any he had ever known. "Hush," she said. "You've been very ill. Twice I've thought you were gone. You've been spared, but you must not tax yourself."

"Why am I in the North Tower? Hasn't Tédière had enough of me? Isn't he through with me yet? Does he think——"

"Ssshh." The woman sat on the edge of the bed, and Peter, looking at her squarely and consciously for the first time, realized that she was years younger than he had thought. She seemed roughly his own age, and she was breathtakingly beautiful. "We French are not all ogres, you know. You have experienced much, but you will not be made to suffer again. Your trials are behind you." She stroked his forearm soothingly, and he thought that never had he felt so light a touch, never had he seen a skin so creamy and white. "Sleep now, you need sleep." She cradled a pillow beneath his head, and he closed his eyes. For the first time in many weeks he smiled.

In the mornings Jeanne usually read aloud, either in English from the works of Dean Swift, with which Peter was familiar, or in French from the *Maxims* of the Duc de la Rochefoucauld, which were new to him. The choice of material was hers, and her favorite was La Rochefoucauld, of whose cynical wit she never tired. Occasionally she would pause after reading an epigram which scalded men for their sordid motives and hypocritical self interest and murmured, "How true, how true," before resuming.

Peter usually napped at midday before eating his dinner, which Jeanne came to share with him as his health improved. And in the afternoons they chatted about anything and everything except the war, which they avoided by unspoken consent. As the New Englander began to grow stronger he was permitted by his nurse to leave his bed for longer and longer periods, and he began to exercise by walking up and down the length of an outdoor parapet on the far side of the tower. When these strolls first began, Jeanne held his arm through necessity, and she continued the practice even after Peter began to feel like himself again; both of them enjoyed the habit, and there seemed to be no real reason to break it.

Jeanne had taken up residence in another and smaller suite in the tower, and the doors between the apartments remained open at all times. In fact Peter was almost inclined to forget that he was still a prisoner until the day he wandered down the stairs and came upon a pair of armed sentries stationed at a small landing platform. Both had promptly presented arms and one had said, "*Non, monsieur,*" in a friendly but firm voice as he motioned Peter back to the tower above. When Jeanne had learned of the incident, she scolded him; all would be well, she had said, if he remained here in her charge. Should he attempt to escape, Governor Duchambon would lose all patience with him and would stand him before a firing squad.

As the inevitable intimacy grew, brought about by constant daily association, Jeanne become increasingly frank about herself. She told Peter that she was the widow of the fur trader, Pierre le Sueur, who had left her ample funds and a large home. She often entertained officers of the garrison, and had become intrigued by their frequent references to the fortitude of the prisoner from Maine. When she had learned that he was to be released from his cell and if possible restored to health, she had applied for the position of looking after him, for there were few women in Louisburg capable of performing the task, and fewer still who were sufficiently free of responsibilities. Only when Peter pressed her for information on the indentity of his benefactor did she become somewhat less than open. She hinted repeatedly that the governor himself had seen fit to grant a partial parole to a brave enemy, but she never said as much in so many words, and at last Peter asked no more.

She freely told him that Mercy, who, she said, had been a guest in her own home, had suddenly and inexplicably disappeared one afternoon. It was commonly believed that she tried to make her way home to Kittery, and Jeanne was blunt in expressing her opinion that Mercy had died en route. Peter was sorrowfully forced to agree with her estimate. It had still been winter when Mercy had gone, and it was inconceivable that a lone girl who knew only a little about the wilderness could make her way through deep forests, through the domains of a score of hostile Indian tribes and arrive safely at a destination hundreds of miles distant in enemy territory.

For several days Peter grieved, but gradually his sense of depression lifted. All that had happened to him since the night he had been knocked unconscious and carried away from William Pepperrell's house seemed so unreal that it was as though these strange things had been happening to someone other than himself, and he felt like a play actor on the stage of London's Drury Lane. The Peter Staples who had been a prospective son-in-law of Pepperrell and a future shareholder in the Pepperrell enterprises was certainly not the man who had been at death's door in the dungeons of Louisburg and was now being nursed back to health by one of the loveliest, most captivating women who walked the face of the earth.

By the time he was able to run up and down the one-hundred-and-fifty-foot length of the parapet without losing his breath, he had come to the conclusion that he desired Jeanne more than anything else in the world. He could never love her as he had loved Mercy, as he would always love Mercy, whether she were alive or dead. But he came to understand that there were different kinds of love, that a man's feelings were never the same toward any two women. Jeanne was warm and wise, intelligent yet always feminine, mature but still young enough to be gay and sparkling and vivacious. She was certainly a lady, though her every look, every gesture, every movement was provocative. And she was here, and he wanted her.

He forced himself to conceal his feelings, however. It would be so easy to take her by sheer force, now that he was again strong. But that would be poor repayment for her kindness to him, he told himself again and again, and if he hurt her he would never be able to forgive himself. Jeanne's life had been a difficult one, according to what she had told him, and only a scoundrel would take advantage of her now. She had been born in Marseille, had grown up in genteel poverty, and had improved her position through her own efforts. She had hinted that she had been intimate with several men and she had often openly declared her contempt for the male, whom she believed interested only in the satisfaction of his physical wants.

When Peter had begun to improve he had read the expectation in her eyes that he would soon try to make love to her. When he had not she had been surprised, then slightly hurt, and, finally, deeply though silently grateful. In the past few days there had been a subtle but very definite change in her, however. She had been reluctant to meet Peter's gaze, had flushed when she had felt his eyes on her and had gone to rather obvious lengths to keep a distance between them. Now, on a balmy, sunny morning in late spring as they sat before the open window in the drawing room of Peter's tower suite, she seemed to have difficulty in controlling her voice as she read from the *Maxims* of her favorite author.

"'Our virtues are most frequently but vices disguised.'" Instead of laughing at this epigram, as she usually did, Jeanne's face showed distaste, and she flipped a few pages. "Here's one I've always liked," she said, her husky voice soft: "'There are few people who would not be ashamed of being loved when they love no longer.' I don't think that's particularly amusing today, do you, Peter?"

He took the book from her and studied it for a moment. "Here's one," he said. "Number 471. 'In their first passion women love their lovers, in all the others they love love.'"

To his amazement, Jeanne jumped to her feet and ran to the window, where she stood with the wind rippling through her light orange gown of chiffon silk. Peter tossed the volume on a table and followed her; only when he reached her side did he realize that she was crying. He was perplexed, but all of his resolves melted away, and instinctively reached for her and took her into his arms.

Even as he bent to kiss her, Jeanne lifted her face to his. Their lips met and the desire that flowed between them was so powerful, so urgent that it was overwhelming. Then, suddenly, the heels of Jeanne's hands were pressed against Peter's chest and she shoved him away. "No," she whispered, "no."

Without another word she turned, ran to the door of the drawing room and opened it, then fled into the corridor and down the stairs of the tower.

SIXTEEN

PETER stood on the parapet walk and looked down at the great fortress of Louisburg, marveling, as he always did, that man could have built so impregnable a structure. From this vantage point he could see the whole of the great citadel: only the sea wall, facing Gabarus Bay, was hidden from his view, and he assumed that its armaments were at least as formidable as those studding the other sides. No wonder the French here were so complacent. They would never dream that this place might be attacked: and even if they knew, they could afford to smile. Idly, just to give himself something to do until Jeanne returned, Peter began to count the guns in the north wall.

She had been gone for at least an hour, and he became increasingly uneasy. She had been very much disturbed when she had raced away from him, and he was sure she had been crying. It was bitter to think that he himself was responsible, that he had allowed himself to become emotionally involved with her and by that same token had permitted her to complicate her own existence. It was poor thanks for the care she had lavished on him, and he felt ashamed. Jeanne deserved far better, and he intended to tell her as much. Now that he was recovered she might find it easier to return to her own house in town.

But, being truthful with himself, he had to admit that he did not want her to go. If it was true that Mercy had died while trying to return to Kittery, and if he himself survived the war, he might even ask Jeanne to marry him. When she came back to the tower he would say something to her that would at least be a hint of his intentions. Her shield of cynicism was proof that she had been hurt in the past, and he felt an overwhelming compunction to show her that he, at least, was honorable. Of course, Jeanne might laugh at him; she undoubtedly knew many men who were wealthier, more prominent, more important than he. But that was the chance he had to take.

He continued doggedly counting cannon, and then suddenly stopped short and stared down at the walls, thinking he had gone mad. A feeling of intense excitement stole over him, and he glanced around surreptitiously, guiltily, until he realized that even if some guard saw him, no one could read his thoughts. Slowly and with infinite care he tuned back to the walls and minutely inspected the northeast corner of the citadel. Jeanne was forgotten now as Peter became the trained military observer who had, miraculously, discovered a chink in the armor of the fortress.

Only from this height and from the inside of the citadel was it possible to note what Peter was seeing, and he studied the masonry until his eyes ached and watered. Louisburg, he knew now, was vulnerable; having been made by man, it was less than perfect!

The generals who had planned the fort and the architects who had built it had not expected a land attack from the northeast, that was certain! Elsewhere the walls were thick and strong, capable of withstanding artillery bombardment and stout enough to turn aside even the most powerful of battering rams. But the citadel's builders had been careless when they had reached the northeast corner, and in addition they had sacrificed caution for speed. It was quite plain here that they had run short of the thick stones they had used everywhere else, and instead of waiting for a new shipment from their quarries across the Canso Strait they had been content to chop the remaining boulders into thinner slices, and the jagged edges of those chunks still showed clearly.

From the tower the wall at the critical corner looked paper-thin, and Peter, squinting hard as he peered down, estimated that the stones were no more than two inches thick. Accurate artillery fire would crumble the entire section, which extended for a distance of about thirty feet along the east wall and perhaps twenty feet on the north wall. A determined assault by a battalion of foot soldiers at that precise spot could, if it followed immediately on the heels of the artillery barrage, bring about the fall of the entire fortress!

Peter's elation was greater than any he had ever known, and he felt proud of the ability and training that had enabled him to discover Louisburg's Achilles' heel. Then, as he remembered his own situation, his joy evaporated and was replaced by a fierce, hopeless sense of depression. He was in possession of information so valuable that General Pepperrell could take the fortress—if he achieved a successful, surprise landing and if he knew what Peter now knew.

But the general was in New England. And Peter was here, locked inside a tower from which there was no escape. Jeanne could come and go at will, but he was a prisoner, not only of the French, but of his own thoughts, which was worse.

> *We're fed weevils in our biscuits, foul water in our*
> *rum,*
> *We breed rats galore aboard us, we get justice 'fore*
> *the drum.* *
> *We sail to far-off places, then back to Hull we come*
> *And find our wives have left us whilst we've been away*
> *from home.*

A score of sailors chanted the old refrain as they spliced lines, mended sails, polished the *Invincible's* cannon and applied fresh paint to her hull as she rode at anchor off Governor's Island, her prow pointed toward the Battery. The crew was in high spirits, and with considerable reason. No other ship of the regular service had been sent from England to join the commodore's command, and that meant that the men of the *Invincible* held undisputed rank in the fleet. Even the lowest apprentice seaman believed himself a cut above the commissioned officers of the merchantmen who were joining the naval militia, and they knew that they would be given credit in the all-important Book of Naval Records that was maintained at the Admiralty in London. Thus they would take the lion's share of any prize ships captured by the whole fleet, and they would be considered responsible for any victories won by any segment of the command, which would entitle them to individual promotions far faster than their luckless brothers who were battling in the North Sea, in the Mediterranean, and off the coast of France.

Although the *Invincible's* men were English-born and had signed on for nine years of service, most of them had been in colonial waters sufficiently long to consider New York their home port. And so they had wenches waiting for them ashore whenever they were off duty, homes of their own to which they could retire, all the comforts which usually came to seamen only after they had served

---

* Justice was traditionally dispensed in the English Navy by officers who stood behind the bosun's four-foot-high drum when pronouncing a court-martial sentence. The drum was otherwise used to sound a battle alert.

thirty years or more before the mast. And here they were, with the war already two months old, and they had yet to hear one of their guns fire more than a practice salvo. Most of these past eight weeks had been spent in port, as a matter of fact, and they had been to sea only twice, when the commodore had sailed up to Boston to confer with the colonial general who was in command of the land forces.

And so the sailors sung happily, enjoying the bright early spring sunshine of New York, congratulating themselves on having achieved the near-impossible, that unattainable of all who wore the King's colors, a perfect assignment. Then, suddenly, they heard the bosun's shrill pipes and, looking over the side, they saw the commodore's gig approaching from the direction of the Battery, and they knew from the silence of the eight oarsmen who manned the gig that something was very much amiss. The bosun's mate and two of his helpers hurriedly lowered "the captain's chair" over the side, the officer of the watch shouted through his speaking tube and brought the first lieutenant hurrying from the wardroom where he had been napping.

By the time that Commodore Warren was only one third of the distance up to the deck, the singing had died away completely, for the men had seen his face, and they knew what would happen to anyone who made a noise that the commander in chief of the fleet thought unseemly. His cheeks looked sunken, there were dark circles beneath his eyes, and the lines in his forehead and at the corners of his eyes were so deep they appeared to be carved in stone.

The officer of the watch stood at salute and the bosun's pipes twittered shrilly as the commodore hoisted himself out of the chair onto the deck and looked around, glowering. Saluting the quarterdeck absently, he caught sight of the luckless midshipman who was assistant officer of the deck. "Mr. Hale," he said, biting off the words, "be good enough to quiet those infernal pipes. They make my head ring." Then he turned to the watch officer, who stood respectfully at attention. "Mr. Johnson, I shall be in my stateroom. I shall receive no one, and I am not to be called under any circumstances."

"Aye, aye, sir." The lieutenant was afraid, judging by the commodore's expression, that something more was coming.

He was right. "The *Invincible,* Mr. Johnson, is not a Portuguese fishing schooner, she is an English man-o'-war. Have those shirts and underpants drying on the rigging removed at once. Holystones," he added, pointing with a white-gloved finger, "are intended for the purpose of polishing sanded decks. They are not receptacles for food. It has also come to my attention that several trollops have been entertained these past nights in the fo'c'sle. That practice is to be stopped at once. If there is any further breach of discipline, all shore leaves will be canceled, and I will resume my old practice of applying the cat personally to any offenders who forget they serve in His Majesty's Navy. And that reminds me. Be good enough to ask the first lieutenant to bring a new cat-o'-nine-tails to my stateroom at six bells. You may also inform him from me that he will incur my severe displeasure if he persists in whistling that prayer-meeting hymn as he goes about his duties. I do not object to whistling, and I am very partial to prayer meetings. But I detest being forced to listen to someone who is consistently out of key."

"Aye, aye, sir." The lieutenant felt like a youthful midshipman again and had to control an impulse to bolt and run.

"Well, Mr. Johnson? Do you fail to understand me? Must I repeat everything I've said? You may carry on, Mr. Johnson!"

The commodore turned and stamped down the deck to his stateroom; the only sound to be heard was the thumping of his boots on sanded pine. When he reached the sanctuary of the cabin he threw his three-cornered hat onto a table, unbuttoned his tunic, and threw himself on his bed. He was growing old, he decided. There had been a time when he could remain awake all night and not feel a thing the next day. But that day was gone, apparently. Yet he had drunk very little at last night's reception for the new commander of Fort Albany.

No, he told himself, it wasn't drink that made him so tired, it was the damnable argument he'd had with Susan after they had come home, a fight that had ended only when he had walked out of his home, slamming the door behind him, and had fled to his own world, a man's world, the *Invincible*. It was not his fault that women found him attractive, and he had not encouraged the wench in the red gown—damn! He couldn't even remember her name. There had been no call for Susan to make such a scene, especially before their own daughters. Granted that he had given her enough provocation in the past. But Susan ought to know that he did not fritter away his thoughts or his energies on flirtations during wartime. He had more than enough to occupy his time without complicating his existence.

He closed his eyes, and the gentle rocking of the ship lulled him. It would be good to remove his boots, but his orderly, who had not expected him today, was ashore. Oh, well. He would remove the damned things himself. Just as he started to sit up, he was outraged by a timid tapping at the door. "Damn you!" he shouted, "what do you want?"

The door opened, and the officer of the watch, miserable and badly frightened, stood trembling, looking as though he wanted to lean against the bulkhead for support.

"You confirm my suspicions, Mr. Johnson," the commodore said, knowing himself to be more than a little unfair for taking out his annoyance at Susan on Johnson, who was a loyal if none too quick-witted officer. "I have long believed you incapable of comprehending a simple order given to you in basic English. I distinctly told you I did not want to be disturbed."

"Yes, sir. I know what you told me, sir." The lieutenant gulped and started over again. "Sir, it is my duty as officer of the watch to report to you in person a contravention of your own regulations. A civilian gentleman has arrived by gig, and he came on board even though I told him that the ship is forbidden to anyone except authorized naval or military officers."

"What do you mean, 'he came on board,' Mr. Johnson? Throw the bastard in irons! I assume that with the assistance of one hundred or so members of the crew you could accomplish the feat, Mr. Johnson!" Forgetting all about his boots, he stretched out full length on the bed.

The lieutenant coughed apologetically behind his hand, but before he could reply, a new voice spoke up directly behind him. "This is sure a cozy boat, if I do say so."

Incensed anew, the Commodore sat up, ready to bellow. None but the most ignorant land lover ever referred to a warship as a "boat." Then he saw his mild-mannered visitor, a portly man with a fat face, dressed in dark gray worsted. He stood in the frame, looking like a modestly successful peddler of pots and pans and he smiled cheerfully, seemingly unaware that Lieutenant Johnson was about to lay violent hands on him. Commodore Warren was on his feet instantly, however.

"Well, come in, sir. Come in!" he said pleasantly, then turned and scowled at the luckless young officer. "Must you stand there all day, Mr. Johnson? And must you gape? Be good enough to leave me alone with my guest."

The door closed hastily, and the lieutenant escaped. Peter Warren grinned and held out his hand. "Colonel Sparhawk, how are you?"

William Pepperrell's son-in-law ambled across the cabin. "Tol'ble well, Commodore." He saw a bowl of fruit on a bulkhead shelf and immediately transferred his attention to it. "It beats all," he said, taking an orange and peeling it with his thumb, "how you folks down here in New York get food we never see up North."

Warren told himself to be patient: Elizabeth Pepperrell's husband was not a man to be hurried. "Help yourself," he said unnecessarily, then added casually, "I'm surprised to see you in those clothes. What's happened to that handsome green uniform I saw your good lady sewing for you?"

"Liz is right handy with a needle, I got to admit," Sparhawk said, chuckling. "But Pa Pepperrell now, he gets ideas, and he's right stubborn about 'em. He didn't want me to go calling attention to myself coming down here from Boston, so he said I was to wear this old suit. I guess I put on weight since I got in the army." He lowered himself into a chair and carefully unbuttoned his waistcoat. "When the war's over, Liz will have to let out blame near everything I own."

"General Pepperrell sent you to me with a confidential message, I gather." The commodore barely controlled a desire to shake his guest until the fat man's teeth rattled.

"He wouldn't trust this one to anybody except family." Colonel Sparhawk reached into an inner pocket and began to fumble with a pile of letters, some of them old and battered. "These are mostly poultry orders," he said shyly. "I made 'em up before I left Boston. That way nobody would think I was on a military mission, as you might say, if I got held up. Here we are." He held out a creased and dirty sheet of folded parchment.

Commodore Warren snatched the document from him, broke open the seal and read avidly. His eyes began to sparkle, the marks of exhaustion disappeared from his face, and he chuckled softly. "Colonel," he said, "I believe I can oblige you with a cabin for your trip back to Boston."

"Say, now—that's right nice—"

"Enjoy your quarters, Colonel. They'll be more spa-

cious than the ones assigned to you on your troopship."
Warren exhaled sharply and grinned as he rocked back
and forth on his heels. "We'll sail tonight, Colonel Sparhawk. I've been urging Will to speed up the schedule, and
he's at last agreed. We'll be in action—before the week's
end." Not bothering to note his visitor's reaction, he
stepped out onto the deck and began to shout commands.
The *Invincible* was at last going to war.

Jeanne knew that she looked ravishing, but the realization did little to allay her nervousness. The color in her
cheeks was too high, her eyes were unnaturally bright,
and Jacques was expert at discerning little things and
drawing right conclusions. So she declined his offer of his
chamber's only seat, the edge of his bed, and with haughty
deliberation moved to his window and stood with her back
to it. The spring sunshine streaming into his eyes might
make observation a trifle more difficult for him. And as
she knew of old that it was best never to be on the defensive
with him, she launched into an immediate attack.

"You needn't play the gallant with me, you know. As
we're quite alone, I suggest that you be yourself."

Jacques regarded her with indolent tolerance. "That's a
very becoming gown. I seem to recall an orange dress in
the wardrobe of the Marquise d'Mailloupy when she and
her lamented husband visited Quebec last year. I gather
that you stole it from her."

Jeanne knew his shock tactics so well; her eyes were
hard to a degree that Peter had never seen. "This is not the
same gown, Jacques. And I did not steal it."

He raised his eyebrows but didn't press the point. "You
look well. Your confinement in the tower hasn't been
injurious to you."

"It has not." Jeanne seemed at ease, but was betrayed by
the nervous tapping of a slippered foot.

"I've been anticipating a visit from you almost daily. It
hasn't been easy for me, you know, countering Tedière's

constant complaint that we've failed, as well as placating the governor and the like. Little Duchambon is losing patience with us, my pet. And Tedière misses that steady stream of gossip that used to find its way to him from your salon. But I assure everyone that if anyone can pry information from Staples, it is you." Jacques' voice, which had been soft, almost caressing, became cold. "You have news for me, I trust."

"No. I have not." Jeanne gazed down at her hands, then looked up defiantly. "I suggest you get someone else to do the job. Peter's little sweetheart from Maine, for example—who disappeared at a very strange time. I followed some peculiar instructions you gave me—and the next thing I knew, she was gone."

Jacques could feel the parchment of Mercy's secret letter of agreement in his inside pocket, and he grinned briefly. "All I know is that she's gone—and that our chances for advancing ourselves in this world aren't going to wait forever. Forget all your sly little suspicions and concentrate on your work or the men down in Boston will be on the march before you've persuaded Peter to tell you anything."

For the first time his tone took on a smooth, persuasive quality that Jeanne knew all too well. He was less sure of himself now, and she pushed her advantage. "Isn't the job dignified enough for your precious little Mercy? Is she too much of a lady to——"

"She'd hardly betray her own father, even if she were here. Which she isn't."

"I know you, Jacques. You're never content to play only one game at a time. You aren't satisfied to sit back and rely on my efforts alone. What other little schemes have you hatched to——"

Jeanne broke off sharply as the highwayman took hold of her wrist and gripped it tightly. "I'm depending on you to get the information I seek, Jeanne."

She wrenched free and glared at him, afraid but determined. "I wish to be relieved of my assignment."

Jacques seemed unable to believe what he heard for a moment, then he began to laugh. "You're in love with him!" he said with finality. "You're in love with Staples!"

"Love?" Jeanne looked as though she would claw at the face that loomed above her, but recovered. "I wish," she said slowly, "that I had met Peter nine years ago. My life would have been very different."

"So would his." Jacques continued to chuckle, then stopped and took hold of the woman's rounded arms, his fingers digging into the flesh. "I've been very tolerant, dearest Jeanne, but there's too much at stake to allow you to indulge yourself in girlish dreams. Either you'll return to the Tour du Nord and devote your person and your charms to the task I've given you—or you'll be sent back to France with the *fleur de lys* brand of a thief marring this lovely shoulder. Which shall it be, eh? Which shall it be?"

SEVENTEEN

MERCY looked down at herself in the water of the little lake and curbed a desire to laugh bitterly. No one in Kittery would recognize her as she was now, and a great many Maine settlers, who certainly wouldn't see in her an heiress of the District's first citizen, would be more inclined to shoot at her with their long rifles. Her fair skin was stained a deep brown with a mixture of herbs, roots, and nut juices, and her hair was dyed a deep, dead black and was held in place with a thin leather band on which had been burned the crisscross design that marked the wearer as an unmarried woman of the Lukai tribe. Her feet, legs and arms were bare, except for a beaten copper bracelet on her left wrist, and in her ears she wore large hoops of beaten cooper which had been given to her by Tani, and she took care to wear them at all times. Indians, she had discovered, were extraordinarily sensitive people, and the slightest gesture, the least indication of forgetfulness or indifference created hurt feelings and further complicated an already uphappy existence.

Her body was covered by a single garment of soft doeskin, a high-necked dress that extended to a point just above the knees. It was the simplest yet most ingeniously devised costume she had ever worn: she wrapped it twice around her slender figure, then fastened it at the right side with thongs which were concealed by thick fringe. And though every line was revealed, there was a modesty about the dress that even her mother would have approved. In brief, Mercy thought as she studied herself, she looked the part of a Lukai squaw maiden. Only the natural waviness of her hair, which had been cut to shoulder length, and the green of her eyes gave her away as a member of another race.

She had lost weight in the weeks she had lived with the savages, and it was no wonder, for although she ate heartily, she had never worked so hard. Nor had she ever been so miserable, so uncomfortable, so lonely. Her mornings were spent in the fields, and she felt that she already knew as much about planting and sowing, weeding and cultivating as her father's gardeners in Kittery. She arose at dawn, and, after helping to prepare a communal breakfast of ground corn and fish, accompanied the other women to the several hundred acre tract where the tribe grew its vegetables. At first the work had been almost too much, but Mercy's youth and energy had stood her in good stead, and she could bend now over long rows of potato plants and clear weeds from the path of cucumber vines for hours on end without noticing the strain. The women sang as they worked, and Mercy knew the chants now and joined in with the others: even though the meaning of some of the words eluded her, singing helped to pass the time and made her feel less like an alien among these barbaric people.

At noon she hurried back to the village, where she and the other maidens were expected to prepare the day's biggest meal for the entire community. The Lukai ate a remarkable variety of foods, including venison and bear, grouse and partridge and wild turkey, cod and tuna and lobster, and a girl who ruined a dish, who scorched a stew or burned a roast, first received a tongue-lashing from the elder women and then was made to run the gantlet of her sisters, who armed themselves with heavy spoons and other cooking utensils of wood. On only one occasion, when Mercy had allowed a cauldron of squash to boil down to a meaningless mush, had she been forced to brave the gantlet, and she had carried bruises from the experience for a week and more. Since that time she had always devoted her full attention to the project of the noon dinner, which was the object of the elders who had conceived the system.

The afternoons were the worst, and she considered the weaving and pottery making as unrelieved drudgery. No conversation was permitted and one of the older squaws, armed with a birch whip, was in constant attendance to insure that each of the maidens performed her quota of work for the day. The standards of craftsmanship were high, punishment was immediate for those who were sloppy or careless, and in spite of the fact that Mercy was totally unfamiliar with the making of either jars or baskets, she was not spared. Obviously the Lukai believed that the birch stick was the best teacher, and it was true that her efforts improved rapidly. As she learned a little of the language of the savages, she discovered that the others hated the afternoons, too, and that many of the maidens were longing for marriage merely to escape this unrewarding, dull labor.

Shortly before dusk there was a break in the day's routine, and this was the time that Mercy disliked the least, when her feeling of depression and dread lifted slightly. The unmarried squaws were free to bathe in the lake, or, if they preferred, to walk three miles to the sea and swim. Their duties for the day were over, and they were required to prepare food for no one but themselves in the evenings. Most of them, thoroughly sick of the cooking fires, were satisfied with a chunk of cold meat and a handful of roasted corn kernels as they sat cross-legged in front of their long lodge and gossiped. And Mercy was surprised that their talk, as much of it as she could grasp, was similar to that of the girls with whom she had grown up in Kittery. The principal topic was the young men of the tribe, and lesser subjects were clothes, jewelry, and their parents. The maidens of the Lukai did not live in the thick mud huts of their mothers and fathers, but they remained under strict parental supervision, which they resented as deeply as did the young ladies of Kittery, whose modern ideas were frowned upon by their elders.

It was a relief to Mercy that the tribe's moral code was severe, for she had remembered all too well the way that Warumba and the other brave who had guarded her on the journey north from Kittery had eyed her, and she had feared endless complications. It was a strict rule of the Lukai, however, that all contact between the braves and the squaw maidens was fobidden, and transgressors were harshly punished: the man was mutilated and whipped, and the girl suffered a far worse fate. She was flogged, her head was shaved and she was cast, naked, out of the tribe. Subsequently, if she was fortunate, she died of exposure in the wilderness; the alternatives were enslavement if she was captured by other Indians or enforced prostitution if the French caught her. And the penalties were applied so rigorously that only one unfortunate couple had been caught in the past two years.

Civilization as Mercy knew it seemed far away, for though the village was located only forty miles from Louisburg on the Acadian peninsula and was the closest of the Lukai towns to the white man, the tribe's relations with the French were at best coldly formal. Less warlike nations had made their peace with the invader, mixed freely with him, accepted his whiskey and guns and powder and diseases in return for pelts. However, the treaty which Ajinga, greatest of the Lukai kings, had negotiated in Quebec gave the tribe the right to expel any who invaded its territories, and in return none but a handful of the ruling hierarchy ever visited either Louisburg or Quebec. The Lukai insisted on the right to live their own lives in their own world, and as a rule trouble arose only when some eager settler cleared land for his cabin and farm in Lukai hunting preserves.

The elders knew of the war between the English and French, and it was their firm intention to remain neutral in the struggle, according to what Tani indicated to Mercy. There was little hope that the village leaders would return the white girl to her own people, for the old warriors wanted no traffic with the despoilers of their forests. They felt they had done Mercy an honor by taking her into the tribe; as a woman it was her place to accept her lot and be satisfied.

The prospect of spending her whole life here was deeply disturbing, yet for the present at least she had no choice but to remain. She had tried, on one occasion, to return to Louisburg, had been caught and severely whipped; it would be senseless to make the attempt again. And she could not possibly risk the long journey down to Maine alone, either by horse or on foot; she knew far too much of forest dangers to risk anything so foolhardy. She was lucky, she supposed, that she had actually been taken into the Lukai as a member of the tribe. When Tani had first brought her here she had supposed that she would be at best a guest and at worst a prisoner, but she quickly learned that neither status was acceptable to these proud people. They had made a place for her in their own ranks, and she had to accept it. Whenever she asked Tani about the possibilities of returning to Maine, her friend merely shrugged.

No attempt was made now to keep her within the bounds of the village's borders, and she was free to wander beyond the hidden posts of the lookouts who were posted to keep the French and the warriors of other tribes at a distance. Her one attempt to escape—and her subsequent punishment—had come early in her stay, before she had actually been taken into the tribe. Today she was a full-fledged squaw maiden, and if she ran away the offense would be considered unpardonable.

She knew what would happen to her if she failed to return some night from a stroll or if she did not show up to perform her duties in preparing the morning's fish. All of this had been made clear to her in the week-long ceremony of initiation which she had been forced to undergo, and the mere memory of those rites still made her shudder. As long as she lived, she knew, she would never be able to forget the feats of endurance, the trials by pain, and the strange rituals in which she had been forced to participate. Even now she became faint when she recalled the torture she had endured when pine needles had been thrust under her nails, the disgust she had felt when she had been forced to drink the blood of a freshly-slaughtered animal.

For the present, Mercy had to concede to herself, she could not complain too bitterly about her day-to-day existence, in spite of her misery and lonely discomfort. She was safe, she was protected, she had plenty to eat, and, although she was determined to return home at the first opportunity, the time was not yet ripe. Meanwhile she needed to be patient, and she tried to become as resignedly philosophical as her hosts were in all things. It was not easy, for thoughts of Peter constantly intruded, and to her annoyance her mind often lingered on Jacques, too.

She was still haunted by her mental picture of Peter as she had last seen him, wasted and unconscious in his cell, and she could only hope that he was still alive, that his living conditions had been bettered, and that he more closely resembled the man she had once promised to marry. She tried to be practical, and that meant she pinned her faith on her agreement with Jacques, whose ambition might keep Peter alive, whose greed might win Peter his freedom.

As for Jacques himself, he was obviously responsible for

her presence in the village of the Lukai, and she had often pondered on his motives in having sent her here. She sometimes wondered whether the threat from Commandant Tediere had been real or whether Jacques had merely devised its shadow in order to make her more willing to leave Louisburg for a life with savages. And though it was plain that he had not wanted her anywhere near the fortress, she could not quite imagine that he knew the Lukai had gone so far as to adopt her into their tribe. Although his tie of kinship with these Indians was a close one, they were their own masters, and while they might listen to him they would not be ruled by him.

Whatever his reasons had been, she was patently being held in as remote and secure a hiding place as he could want during this time when he was working out the details of his bargain and preparing for Peter's escape. Were it not for her deal with him, she would have run away from the village long before now and trusted to luck to help her find her way down to Kittery. But such a rash step, she knew, would more than seal Peter in Louisburg for the duration of the war: it would be the equivalent of signing his death warrant. It was irritating to realize that Jacques was aware of all this and was counting on her remaining because of her concern for Peter.

Now and again she found herself imagining the little details of daily living in a lifelong marriage to Jacques, and she was as frightened as she was excited. Jacques was too strong, too clever for her to change his habits: instead he would probably drag her down to his own level of precarious existence. It would be a sorry end for a Pepperrell, a life far more degrading than the one she currently knew: at least among the Lukai she broke the laws of neither God nor man, as she had been taught and understood those laws. Yet even as she dreaded the time that Jacques would come to her with proof that Peter was free and would demand her hand in return, she looked forward to that day and her self-disgust did nothing to mitigate her eagerness.

And Jacques was insuring that his interests were being protected, of that she was sure. Warumba, whom Mercy occasionally glimpsed in the village, sent her small gifts from time to time through his own squaw. With each packet of smoked dog or elk, each cluster of grapes came the message that these presents were sent in the name of the great warrior, which, as Mercy had good cause to remember, was what the brave always called Jacques.

That was Tani's name for him, too, but the Indian girl never mentioned him, and on several occasions when Mercy had tried to talk about him, her friend had deliberately changed the subject. On any other topic Tani expressed herself volubly, and continued to declare herself grateful for Mercy's timely help in beating off the advances of Commandant Tedière, hence her silence on Jacques was doubly perplexing, for she had certainly made no effort to hide her feelings for him on the long trip to Louisburg from Kittery.

Most of the time she was friendly and pleasant to Mercy, whom she continued to address as her sister. On one or two days of each week she would disappear on errands which she never explained, and her mere absence from the community life and its routines set her apart from the other squaw maidens, most of whom seemed a little in awe of her, a little afraid of her. When she returned from her trips Mercy always felt a trifle uneasy, too, for on these occasions Tani would sit by the hour watching the white girl speculatively, silently, with an expression that at times seemed as hostile as it was penetrating.

Then, by the following morning Tani was invariably smiling and affable again, the cause of her disturbance apparently forgotten. And as the weeks stretched out without incident, Mercy came to believe that her friend was simply moody; it was easier to cling to such a view than to give in to morbid, unprovable imaginings involving Tani and, of course, Jacques.

And so days became weeks. Mercy desperately missed the many comforts and conveniences she had known all her life, but she had to admit to herself that it was easy to get along without them. In place of her many hair brushes, her creams and cosmetics, her colognes and perfumes, she owned a single bone comb. The numerous gowns that had once comprised her wardrobe had been replaced by the one garment which she wore daily, and when the time came to replace it, she would be required to treat the doeskin and sew the dress for herself. There were no books to read, and entertainment was unknown except for the weekly meetings in the council lodge, which began with a harangue from an elder and ended with long hours of chanting and singing, yet she was not bored.

The greatest nuisance she knew was to make and apply a fresh coating of stain to her face and body each week, to carefully grind and use the faintly medicinal herbs which turned her hair black. She would have given up such practices had Tani not insisted that it was necessary to look as much like others in the village as was possible. There were many in the tribe who hated whites and who might do her harm if reminded daily and insistently that she came from the race of those who would destroy the forests and cheat the Indian of what was his. And after a time she came to accept even this.

Mercy was only moderately depressed as she sat one evening before the lodge of the squaw maidens, trying diligently and with fair success to follow the instructions of two of the other girls, who were trying to teach her to cut, sew and decorate a pair of moccasins. Language was still something of a barrier, as Mercy could understand only a part of what was said to her, and all three laughed repeatedly as they tried to make out each other's words. Suddenly they became aware of someone standing above them and both of the native girls tensed slightly for a party of braves had arrived that day from the main Lukai town, one hundred and ten miles to the south, and they were afraid they would be called to the huts of their parents to take part in interminable ceremonies of welcome to distant relatives. Both relaxed immediately when they saw that the new arrival was only Tani, but Mercy realized at once that something was amiss. She knew her friend and benefactress well enough by now to see beneath the surface calm.

"What's wrong?" she asked, slipping without thinking into English and forgetting the chore of moccasin making.

Tani answered gravely in the tongue of her own people. "The elders have ordered Tani to bring to the council lodge the maiden who is known as Rina-hai-kodo." This was the name the Lukai had given to Mercy, and meant "she-of-the-green-eyes."

Alarmed, Mercy jumped to her feet, and the other girls looked at her sympathetically. "Have I done something wrong again, Tani? Am I to be punished for——"

"It is not the wish of the elders to punish their new daughter." Tani spoke emphatically. "But you must be made to look presentable."

Her words seemed to have special significance to the other girls, and all three led Mercy into their lodge, where they carefully combed her hair and secured it with a fresh band, smoothed her short gown and, after much debate, decided to allow her to wear her own earrings and bracelet rather than accept the loan of some of their jewelry. A discussion also began over whether Mercy should don a pair of moccasins for the occasion, but Tani cut it short.

"The hunter waits for the deer," she said cryptically, "the deer does not wait for the hunter."

She took Mercy's arm and guided her out into the night. A bright half-moon guided them as they made their way past the cheerful supper fires that blazed in front of virtually every mud hut. Now that the weather was warm few families kindled their fires inside their homes, and whole families were gathered for the evening meal in the open. The braves ate contentedly, their squaws and children patiently waiting until their menfolk were finished so they could have their turn. Small, naked boys ran shouting through the maze of ceremonial poles in the center of the village that were used for the preliminary torture of captives, but no matter how loud their laughter, the little girls of the community sat in stolid, cross-legged silence near their mothers, observing and thinking but displaying no emotion.

A group of young braves throwing tomahawks at the charred trunk of a dead tree and betting wildly against each other stopped their game to watch Tani and Rina-hai-kodo walk past. Neither girl paid them the slightest heed, although one of the men muttered something under his breath that caused his companions to whoop delightedly. And the game was not resumed until the maidens had passed from view; there was no rule against ogling.

Tani's silence was disconcerting, and, despite the fact that it was bad manners to ask questions, Mercy could stand the supense no longer. "Why have the elders summoned me, Tani?"

"Men do not need to explain their reasons for what they do. The men command, the women obey. It has always been thus."

"But——"

"Tani will be at the side of her sister to explain all that may be required. The elders have so ordered."

Mercy had to be content. At least it was good to know that she would not be alone in whatever ordeal she was going to be called upon to face. She consoled herself with the thought as they arrived at the big lodge, and following Tani's example she folded her arms across her breasts, lowered her head and entered with a show of humility. This was a custom she hated, but it was expected of every squaw, young or old, married or single, and any deviation

from the practice would bring an immediate rebuke—and
a dose of the birch switch. Mercy had learned how to
swallow her pride.

In the center of the lodge a fire was burning brightly,
and a plume of smoke rose lazily toward the hole cut in
the skins of the roof. As usual, most of the fumes remained inside the musty structure, and Mercy had to
control an urge to cough. Never, she thought, would she
become acclimated to the incredibly poor ventilation of
Lukai buildings. The three elderly men who comprised
the village council sat in a semicircle on the far side of the
fire, and Mercy saw that they wore their best feathered
capes over their breechcloths and shirts and that their
faces were daubed with circles of green paint, which
signified that they were entertaining guests of honor and
rank. Apparently the visitors to the village were braves of
some distinction.

The two girls approached, sank to their knees in the
approved manner, and bowed their heads. They were
given permission to rise by someone at the far side of the
lodge, whom Mercy had not noticed before, and as she
stood she saw a huge figure emerge from the shadows.
Never had she seen a man quite so tall or so menacing;
had she encountered him in the forests near Kittery, she
would have fled for her life. But here, in the council lodge
of the Lukai, she waited with seeming quiet, her features
impassive as she had been taught to compose them.

The warrior was half a head taller than either Peter or
Jacques, both of them big men, and the heavy-muscled
legs that protruded from beneath his breechcloth looked
like the trunks of trees. His shoulders were broad, his arms
powerful, his hands huge, and the smears of white paint
on his bare chest and his face made him seem even larger
than he was. His scalp lock, stiff with fresh tar, ran straight
down the center of his head to the nape of his neck, and he
had very recently shaved off all other hair from his head.
His eyes looked black and hot in the light of the fire,

which accented a large nose and thin, determined lips. On one side of his belt he wore a small knife, and a tomahawk slapped against the other leg as he walked.

To Mercy's horror he marched straight to her, grasped her hair with one hand and unceremoniously dragged her closer to the fire. She stood trembling, her heart beating wildly as he circled her slowly, looking her up and down. He was about half-finished with his close inspection when something happened inside her and she felt a surge of anger. No one could treat her like this, and she had every intention of telling the brute as much in the most forcible words she could muster, but a warning cough from Tani, an imploring look in Tani's eyes stopped her. Apparently it would be dangerous to object in any way to his humiliating examination.

Suddenly the warrior stepped forward, swiftly felt Mercy's arms, bent down and pinched the calves of her legs, then straightened again, reached out his hands, pried her jaw open and peered into her mouth. Then, grunting sharply, he took a step backward and addressed a remark to the elders. Although he spoke the language of the Lukai, his accent was different from that of the local village, and Mercy could not understand what he had said. The men were looking at her now, and apparently she was expected to make some reply, but she could not and looked at Tani. One of the elders nodded, and the Indian girl spoke.

"The mighty Moha," she said in a matter-of-fact voice, "has agreed to take Rina-hai-kodo as his squaw."

For a few incredible seconds the words made no sense to Mercy. She heard herself gasp, but the sound seemed to come from afar. The walls of skin and mud danced crazily, then righted themselves. She wanted to speak but could not; it was as though the hands of the giant had closed around her throat.

But Tani knew what she felt, and spoke again quickly, this time in English. "Moha is grandson of mighty Ajinga. Moha is mighty warrior too. Father of Moha is king of all Lukai. Insult to Moha mean death."

Before Mercy could reply, the warrior gripped her shoulder and said something to her in a booming voice. Then, turning away from her abruptly, he spat into the fire. Apparently the interview was over, for Tani sank to her knees and bowed, and Mercy did likewise, her legs shaking. When they came into the open, Tani's wooden composure broke and she smiled broadly, but only a quiet gleam of triumph in her eyes indicated that she might have had a hand in the arrangements.

"You have been greatly honored," she said. "The mighty Moha was pleased with Rina-hai-kodo, and well may the maidens of the Lukai envy her. Moha has expressed his will. You will become his squaw before the leaves fall from the trees."

EIGHTEEN

BOSTON, like any enlightened city, did not believe in omens. But it was unfortunate that Governor Shirley had slipped and broken his leg while walking across the Common for a final review of the troops that were to take part in the campaign against New France. It was too bad that seamen on board several of the ships at anchor in the harbor saw a school of silver sharks not two hundred yards distant, for sailors of all nationalities considered these sea scavengers to be sure harbingers of bad luck. Perhaps it didn't matter that the weather had been unseasonably cold and gloomy for the better part of a week or that a fire destroyed the better part of the new Adams printing shop just as a pamphlet of encouragement for the troops was being set up in type. There was little significance, possibly, in the fact that the Reverend Herkimer Locksley lost his voice in the middle of his sermon in which he had been predicting victory over the foe. And of course only the ignorant and superstitious would find any meaning in the presence of a black pig in the midst of a herd being driven onto a supply ship: there was no difference between black pigs and white, as any farmer knew.

But, admittedly superstitious or not, the residents of Boston were openly nervous, and their faith in the joint enterprise of General Pepperrell and Commodore Warren was shaken. Any intelligent man would of course ignore one or two signs of impending trouble, but only a fool could close his eyes to more omens of disaster than anyone could remember showing themselves in a single day, and that day the official beginning of a campaign! Efforts were made to persuade the military and naval men to postpone their expedition for a week or two, but the leaders of the army and navy continued with their last-minute preparations as though nothing were amiss.

Even the most pessimistic were forced to admit that never had they witnessed such efficiency. The man in charge of this business knew precisely what they were doing, and never had the presence of so large a force disrupted the normal routine of the town so little. Now that the men were leaving, it was difficult to believe that more than four thousand soldiers and almost two thousand sailors, all of them militiamen with a traditional hatred for discipline, had been the well-behaved—as well as profitable—guests of Boston for many weeks. The visitors had been plentifully supplied with cash, which they spent so liberally on food and drink and clothing and useless trinkets that the merchants who had profited the most were among the first to discern omens favoring a delay in sailing. But no one in a position of authority bothered to listen.

And all was at last in readiness for the departure of the expedition. One hundred and seventeen ships, most of them converted merchantmen and large fishing craft, were anchored in the harbor in the positions they would occupy in the convoy, and the water was filled with small craft ferrying troops to their transports. The men from Rhode Island, New Hampshire, Connecticut, and the Maine District were already on board their vessels, and the regiments of Massachusetts Bay were lined up in long rows on the docks. It was their turn now, and the men, tired after a long day of waiting, sat on their blanket rolls in morose silence. Earlier in the day they had spent their time singing lustily, and the Boston volunteers who had been accompanied to the wharves by their wives and sweethearts had postured and swaggered bravely, had boasted in loud voices that they would capture Quebec and return home in a month.

But the families were gone now, and the sergeants at arms wearily toured the embarkation area and chased away the few remaining trollops in search of a last-minute liaison with men whose pockets were bulging with an unexpected payment of their wages. It was rumored that General Pepperrell had provided the money himself, in return for notes from Governor General Shirley and the representatives of the various colonial legislatures. The sergeants at arms knew nothing about such matters; their sole concern was to send away all but fighting men, and to prevent straggling. And they did their job thoroughly though dispiritedly; they, too, had found the day long and trying.

The captains of the ships grumbled as they made personal inspections of their holds and painstakingly checked barrels of powder and casks of lead against long lists. The commodore of the fleet, it seemed, was a stickler for details and had threatened to demote any master whose supply list did not tally with the matériel piled up beneath the decks of his vessel. Many of the younger and more belligerent captains were secretly outraged at the concern of their commander with bags of ground corn and sacks of salt pork at a time when, they thought, he and they should be devoting themselves exclusively to the setting of gun watches. But they carefully kept their reflections to themselves; Commodore Warren would not only demote but would publicly humiliate any officer who dared to express disagreement with his least order.

If the naval contingent knew it was headed by a martinet, the military hierarchy was well aware that it enjoyed better luck. Most of the colonels had been acquainted with General Pepperrell for years, and the majority of them had done business with him at one time or another, just as they had traded with each other. Now, Major General Wolcott of Connecticut, second in command of the expedition, was closeted with the head of the expedition on board the flagship, where both had been given cabins, and the atmosphere on a closely guarded wharf, where the regimental colonels, the commanders of independent battalions and of supporting artillery units, had been gathered for last-minute instructions, was highly congenial. It was significant that the man in the center of the group was Brigadier General Samuel Waldo of York, Maine, Pepperrell's close, lifelong friend. It was equally significant that he handed out long, black *segaros* before he started speaking.

No one had ever looked less like a soldier than General Waldo, who weighed almost two hundred pounds and stood only five feet, five inches high in this thick-soled boots. He gave the appearance of being a successful warehouse owner, which he was, and his mild blue eyes, his fat cheeks, gave no hint that he was also a distinguished veteran of eighteen Indian campaigns. Rolling an unlighted *segaro* in his mouth, he stood quietly and waited for the buzz of conversation to subside. "You, Cap'n Davey Wooster of Connecticut," he said. "You made double good and sure there's nobody here who oughtn't to be here?"

"Yes, General."

"Good enough, then. Dr. Thornton, if any of these gentlemen get the ague or suchlike from the tobacco I've fed 'em, you fix 'em up quick. They got more work comin' than they ever had in all their lives. They got to be fit, good and fit." He looked around the circle of faces, still smiling. "Any of you get to feeling rheumy, I say you swim over to Doc Thornton's ship. He's goin' to be aboard the *Glorious*, which is that dilapidated old hulk of a barge sittin' yonder." He pointed to a small frigate with his *segaro* as he waited for the laughter to subside, then reached into a cowhide pouch slung over his left shoulder and pulled out a stack of sealed parchment documents.

"You know what I was doin' last night?" he asked plaintively. "You know what I was doin' while you were drinkin' too much rum and forgettin' you're all married and respectable-like? Me and General Wolcott, we were gettin' cramps in our hands, writin' and writin' these here papers." General Waldo waved the folded sheets of parchment over his head but continued to clutch them tightly. "Old Will Pepperrell, now, he's the most cantankerous, suspicious old buzzard in New England. I've known him for fifty years and I say it right out. He has aides who can copy papers. But not these papers. You know what I got here? This will tell you exactly where we're goin' and what your order o' battle will be when we get there."

There was a sudden tension among the officers, and young Captain Wolcott, the junior of the group, kept drawing his sword part way from its scabbard, then letting it fall again. General Waldo paused, allowing his news to sink in, before continuing. "These papers are to be opened only after we've weighed anchor and sailed," he said, his smile as broad as before. "Any officer who opens his orders prematurely or any officer who loses his copy will be shot by firing squad the day we strike land. That's General Pepperrell's word, gentlemen, and he means it."

Waldo began to hand out copies of the orders, and there was no sound now except the lapping of water against the wharf, the measured tread of the marine sentries who stood guard over the gathering. Colonel Richard Gridley, the artillery commander, cleared his throat. "Sam," he demanded, puffing hard on his *segaro*, "suppose we have some questions about these orders? Suppose

there are things we don't understand? Are we supposed to
swim across open sea to the *Invincible* to find out what
Will has in his mind?"

"It so happends that your orders are more complete
than most, Dick. Artillery's goin' to be mighty important
to us, and you'll discover that your letter comes from Will
himself."

Colonel Gridley was less than satisfied; his mathemati-
cal mind insisted on neatness and precision. "Let's say
that I have no question myself, then. But what of some of
the others? Suppose that Pitman or Willard here aren't too
sure of what they read. Suppose Colonel Hale or Major
Titcomb are confused? What do they do? And why all this
secrecy in the first place?"

General Waldo seemed to be having the time of his life
as he chuckled, then looked around the circle, beaming.
"The reason there's so much secrecy will be plain as the
ears that waggle on the sides of your heads. Soon as you've
read your orders, that is. And I'd be right grateful if you
lads don't ask me any more. You see, right this minute—
and for the next hour, maybe—I know somethin' you
don't. So that leaves me sittin' right on top of the biggest
keg of powder there ever was. We don't know who might
be listenin' to us. But I do know that Will isn't foolin'
when he says anybody who talks out of turn will be shot.
And confidentially, gentlemen—I don't want to be shot."

Still affable, he walked to the end of the wharf and
signaled to a gig which was waiting for him, and which
approached at once. The others, holding tight to their
orders, quietly dispersed and made their way to the small
boats that were to take them to their ships. The meeting,
such as it had been, was over.

Meantime, on the *Invincible*, General Pepperrell stood
on the starboard main deck, ignoring the bustle of officers
and seamen, unaware of the flurries of signals between the
flagship and the rest of the fleet, unmindful of the members of his own staff who stood only a few feet away and

conferred in low tones as they watched the progress of the embarkation. His head was raised, and he seemed to be watching the dark clouds that raced across the sky, pushed out to sea by a stiff breeze. There were problems and questions that required his attention, but his aides and adjutants knew him, and they sensed that he did not want to be disturbed.

He stood very still, his hands gripping the rail, and only his lips moved. "Lord God," he said softly, "watch over us and bless us in our enterprise. We want peace, not war, and we seek only to do thy will. Help us to overcome our foes so that this senseless struggle may be ended quickly, before innocent women and helpless children on both sides are needlessly slaughtered. Guide us, that we may do the right."

The general paused, and when he spoke again, it was from memory. *"He that dwelleth in the secret place of the most High shall abide under the shadow of the Almighty. I will say of the Lord, He is my refuge and my fortress: my God; in Him will I trust. Surely He shall deliver thee from the snare of the fowler, and from the noisome pestilence. He shall cover thee with His feathers, and under His wings shalt thou trust: His truth shall be thy shield and buckler. Thou shalt not be afraid for the terror by night; nor for the arrow that flieth by day; Nor for the pestilence that walketh in darkness; nor for the destruction that wasteth at noonday. A thousand shall fall at thy side, and ten thousand at thy right hand; but it shall not come nigh thee. . . . Because thou hast made the Lord, which is my refuge, even the most High, they habitation: There shall be no evil befall thee, neither shall any plague come nigh thy dwelling. For he shall give His angels charge over thee, to keep thee in all thy ways."*

Peter tossed restlessly in his bed, unable to sleep. His discovery of the citadel's weakness had recalled him to a sense of duty, to a realization that he was not as far removed from the war as he had allowed himself to suppose. He could drift no longer, but he was at a loss to work out some method whereby he could pass along what he learned about the fortress' northeast corner to his own people. He was still under heavy guard and knew that any attempt to bluster or fight his way out of the tower would end in certain failure. He needed to think about the problem, to work out some careful mode of action that would enable him to help his country and his friends.

But it was almost impossible for him to concentrate. For the first time in his life, personal considerations intruded and clouded his vision. In brief, Jeanne had not returned to the Tour du Nord during the long hours of the afternoon and evening, and there had as yet been no opportunity to sit down with her and talk about her strange and explosive flight. He had heard her entering her own suite sometime after midnight and had been tempted to go to her, but had refrained. The mere fact that she had remained away so long was an indication that she did not wish to see him or speak to him tonight, and the least he could do was to respect her desires.

Nevertheless he held countless imaginary conversations with her, and in almost all of them the scenes ended on the same note: he would take Jeanne into his arms. He knew now that he had long wanted to make love to her, and was disturbed because he had realized the intensity of his feelings only at virtually the same moment it had dawned on him that he could make a valuable contribution to the New England war cause. He tried to analyze his emotional state, but could not decide whether he was still clinging to the remote hope that Mercy might be alive and that they would sometime, somehow come together again or whether he was afraid of the depth of his reactions to Jeanne.

Staring out of the open window, Peter saw the sky growing lighter and abruptly decided he could tolerate bed no longer. Rising, he hurriedly dressed, but only when he walked to the window and looked out moodily did he realize that he had been deceived by the false dawn of early morning. He grinned ruefully at his own stupidity, then the smile froze on his lips. Below him, in the deceptive light that filtered across the bay, he saw a sight too good to be true, yet so real it had to be believed.

Sailing toward the harbor of the town of Louisburg was a large fleet of ill-assorted vessels. And hovering in the distance, her sails trimmed for instant action, was a frigate that provided cover for the smaller and more vulnerable ships. Peter had seen her many times and recognized her silhouette at once. She could be only the *Invincible*.

The invasion of Cape Breton Island had begun.

Darkness descended with startling rapidity as the false dawn faded, and Peter could no longer see Commodore Warren's fleet. The silence was more intense than before, and for an agonizing moment he wondered if he had merely imagined the scene that had been so dramatically etched before him. He had seen just such a sight so often in his dreams that he could scarcely credit the evidence that had loomed before his eyes.

Then he heard a small cannon bark, and from the flash saw that it was one of the guns of the French battery located near the town on the east side of Gabarus Bay. The smile reappeared on Peter's face; Pepperrell and Warren had really come at last. The time of waiting was over, and he himself had been faithful to his trust.

There was no reply to the French from the fleet, and Peter nodded, muttering to himself. Warren's tactics were eminently sound: it would be some minutes before the defenders could be thoroughly aroused, and in the meantime it was wiser to take advantage of the cover of darkness to maneuver the ships toward land. And, he thought, the troops would come ashore at the town, which was far more vulnerable than the fortress. He bobbed his head approvingly again.

The alert battery commander who had discovered the presence of the invaders in Gabarus Bay fired the second of his cannon, then the third, and by that time Louisburg began to come to life. Peter could hear shouts and pounding footsteps echoing from below and knew that in a few minutes the huge guns of the citadel would reply to the challenge of the English colonials. He tried without success to see through the murky gloom, and his tension was almost unbearable. The next quarter of an hour might determine whether the invasion would be successfully launched or whether it would end before Pepperrell's army could be landed.

Slowly, almost imperceptibly, the sky grew lighter, and Peter sucked in his breath. The real dawn was breaking and daylight, at this ticklish juncture, would work to the advantage of the French. Muskets and rifles sounded in several spots at once, then a deafening, earth-shaking roar indicated that the mighty artillery of the citadel had entered the lists.

There was so much to see now that Peter scarcely knew where to look first. The invasion was obviously much farther advanced than he had gathered in the quick glimpse he had been previously afforded. A score of vessels, most of them double-masted snows and single-masted brigantines, already rode at anchor at the wharves of Louisburg town. There was scattered firing in the town itself, but resistance there was a mere gesture, for the troops, French regulars and provincials alike, were quartered in the fortress, not in the civilian community. The road leading from the town to the citadel was already filled with people fleeing to the hulking stone walls for protection. These refugees were unmolested, and Peter was at first struck by General Pepperrell's humanity, then realized that his was a military move, not a compassionate gesture. The citadel would be placed under siege if the landing came off successfully, and the more residents of Louisburg who crowded into the fortress, the more mouths Governor Duchambon would be called upon to feed, the more difficult would become his task.

Searching for the bulk of the invasion fleet, Peter suddenly gasped. The majority of the ships were clustered near the rocky beaches to the west of the citadel, at the farthest point on the bay from the town. The water was filled with boats, and troops were scrambling ashore, setting up a defense perimeter and establishing a foot-hold—out of range of the fortress' great cannon. As he grapsed the daring maneuver, Peter was filled with admi-ration for the ingenuity of Pepperrell and Warren. Only men who could have conceived of an attack on this impregnable spot would have dreamed of taking Louis-burg itself with a comparatively few men, a regiment at the most, and husbanding their strength for a major blow from the unoccupied wastelands on the other side of the citadel!

At least two full regiments were already landed, Peter estimated, and men were making the earth fly as they dug a trench and built up a solid earthwork of Cape Breton rocks and soil before it. More small boats were heading toward the beach, and at the present rate the entire army would be landed in another hour or two.

The *Invincible* and three smaller frigates, patently the most powerful vessels in Commodore Warren's com-mand, rode just out of reach of the citadel's guns, protect-ing the operation. But even as Peter became aware of the tactics of the flagship and her sisters, he saw with dismay that Warren was not going to turn Gabarus Bay into a private preserve without being forced to fight for the right. A monster of the sea, an eight-gun ship of the line was sailing majestically in from the ocean, her gun ports bristling, her decks stripped for action. From a chance remark that Jeanne had made some days previous, Peter reasoned that this must be the *Vigilante*, one of the largest and newest men-o'-war in the French Navy, and his heart sank as he saw her plow through the seas, heading straight for the frigates. The *Vigilante* had probably been stationed in the Atlantic to guard the entrance to Gabarus Bay, but had grown indolent through long days and nights of boring inactivity; Peter could imagine the rage and chagrin of her captain, whose carelessness had permitted the entire enemy fleet to slip past him. He plainly intended to make up for his failure.

Signals flew between the frigates, and the three smaller ships raised their sails and fled, skirting the western shore of the bay as they headed back around to the harbor entrance. And, to Peter's amazement, the *Invincible* inched closer, then closer still to the citadel. She was within range of the fortress' cannon now, and the artillerymen were losing no time in training their weapons on her. The big guns fired at her repeatedly, but they were wide of the mark; her very audacity in edging so close to the huge guns that could blow her out of the water seemed to give her a charmed life, for the moment at least.

The *Vigilante* was close enough to break the *Invincible* into kindling now, but her own guns remained still. All at once Peter understood what Commodore Warren was doing: in a display of incredible cunning and daring, he had deliberately risked his flagship by moving her into the citadel's shadow. She was so close that the *Vigilante* could not fire at her without danger of hitting the fortress!

And the cannon of the citadel also fell silent, one by one, for it dawned on the battery commanders that they might strike the *Vigilante* if they overshot their mark. Meantime the three small frigates, all of them Maine-built and manned by New England volunteers, as Peter realized with pride, had tacked suddenly and had swooped down on the *Vigilante* from the rear, cutting off her escape to the open sea. They were forcing her to stand and fight, but they swooped down on her so quickly that before her gunners could get their range they had moved in to a point where the *Vigilante's* great cannon, which had never been built for anything but a long-range duel, were ineffective.

They began to pepper her at will with their six- and eight-pounders; meanwhile the commodore on the *In-*

vincible had ample opportunity to bring his own twelve-pounders into play. His guns fired at the towering *Vigilante* methodically, in succession, and in less than five minutes his men were scoring hits. Iron balls crashed through the hull of the proud French ship of the line, churned her decks into splinters and knocked her own muzzled cannon out of action. The lesser frigates were showing success, too, though it was more difficult for Peter to see the damage they were wreaking.

The *Vigilante*'s captain tried valiantly to hurl his great man-o'-war out of the reach of these terriers of the sea, but as he sailed fitfully around the bay they clung to him, maneuvering more rapidly, more gracefully than he, remaining ever near to him so he could not bring his ponderous guns into action against them.

After what seemed like a few minutes but was in actuality the better part of three quarters of an hour, the *Vigilante* had enough and struck her colors. The *Invincible* and one of her little sisters closed in immediately, and men stood on the decks of Warren's ships with grappling hooks, ready to board the defeated giant. The commodore had added a badly needed eighty-gun ship to his flotilla without the loss of a single man or a scratch on the hull of a single ship.

But the army, Peter saw, was less fortunate. Although the French had been caught flat-footed, they were rallying and were forcing General Pepperrell to pay dearly for his landing. Cavalrymen, armed with muskets and sabers, poured out of the west gate of the citadel and rode at a gallop toward the beach where the perimeter had been established. Peter counted seven full squadrons of horsemen, and he clenched his fists as he saw the superbly trained Frenchmen fire at the enemy as they rode, then reload and fire again.

The earthworks which the New Englanders had thrown up so hastily offered but scant protection from the onslaught of the cavalry veterans, and Peter could not help but admire the tactics and training of the units that manged to maintain their formations, that swerved away from Pepperrell's lines at the last moment, then charged again. This was the grimmest and bloodiest of close-range fighting, completely unorthodox, utterly merciless. Neither side asked quarter, neither gave quarter, and the casualties were many.

Meanwhile the French were moving horse-drawn artillery out of the fortress, and within a short time six-pound guns were hammering the men from Massachusetts and Maine, New Hampshire and Connecticut. Commodore Warren tried to maneuver some of his ships closer to shore in order to cover General Pepperrell's troops with a curtain of artillery from his ship-borne batteries, but the French gunners proved the accuracy of their aim by smashing two ketches which mounted three-pounders, and the other vessels were forced to withdraw.

But the militiamen continued to move ashore: for every landing boat that was hit by a French ball, five others managed to land their precious cargo of fighting men; for every soldier who was felled by a cavalryman's bullet, another stepped up to the earthworks to take his place and two more toiled doggedly with spades to strengthen the protective mound of dirt and stones that formed the only barrier between them and the horsemen. And, although death struck repeatedly and indiscriminately at both sides, the perimeter was at last secure and the French, unable to eject the enemy and unwilling to sustain further, useless casualities, withdrew.

The cannon were carefully returned to the citadel, and the cavalry formed anew in a solid phalanx to prevent the capture of the guns. But Pepperrell was not going to be tempted into making a rash counterattack. Instead, he continued to send troops ashore, to strengthen his perimeter, to land mortars and set them in place at intervals along his line.

And so, after a single morning of battle, Warren controlled the sea approaches to the great fortress and Pepper-rell had acquired a firm foothold on French soil. Duchambon, taken by surprise, was forced onto the defensive, and demonstrated that he knew it by sending out two companies of infantry under a white flag of truce to collect his dead and wounded. The guns on both sides ceased firing and the French returned slowly to the shelter of the thick stone walls of their proud, powerful citadel. The siege had begun.

Peter continued to watch, transfixed, until someone touched his arm and he looked down to see Jeanne standing beside him at the open window. He had no way of knowing how long she had been there, how much she had seen. "I'll let you in on a little secret," he said, his voice shaking with fierce elation. "It's something I've kept to myself long enough, and it's time I share it with all of my fine hosts. They've been pestering me for a right lot of weeks now, and I reckon the day has come for me to be generous.

"The object of our attack—is Louisburg."

For a long moment Jeanne said nothing but continued to stare out at the littered field of battle, at the growing perimeter of the English colonials, and at the ships so busily setting up their blockade of the citadel in Gabarus Bay. Finally she turned to Peter, and to his amazement she began to laugh. The sound seemed to be compounded of equal parts of genuine amusement and sheer relief.

NINETEEN

AT THE insistence of William Pepperrell's aides, the general's tent was set up in the most protected portion of the perimeter, easily accessible to the beach in the event that the French counterattacked in sufficient strength to force the invaders back onto their ships. Pepperrell hated preferential treatment and explained to his juniors that he had no intention of giving the enemy enough respite to develop an offensive. And when he declared that his own safety was no more significant than that of any of his troops, the aides listened, saluted respectfully, and pretended to agree. Then, when he went off with General Wolcott to arrange for a series of night raids on the French artillery positions located outside the citadel, the officers of his staff quietly erected his tent in the spot they had first chosen for it.

He was so tired by the time he returned an hour after sundown that he seemingly failed to notice its location, and entered without a protest. All was quiet inside for a short time; then the general's personal orderly, Hankorn, who had been his valet in private life, brought him a bowl of thick, steaming soup, a concoction of corn, barley, dried beef strips, and flaked salted cod which was also being served to the troops. Within a quarter of an hour a refreshed commander in chief appeared at the flap and requested the presence of Generals Wolcott and Waldo, and from the spryness of his step and the expression of lively determination in his eyes, the aides knew that their first night on enemy soil would be a busy one. The two deputies hurriedly joined their superior, and the aides settled down to wait.

General Pepperrell made himself comfortable on the cot, General Wolcott occupied the tent's only chair, and little General Waldo perched on the edge of an upended, empty crate that served as a desk. For a few moments no one said anything, and the trio listened in silence to the rattle of muskets, the more pentrating sound of long rifles and the high whine of mortars. Each seemed busy with his own thoughts, and Waldo, who had brought a bowl of food with him, continued to eat placidly with a wooden spoon.

"This soup is awful," he said, carefully scraping the edge of his bowl. "And it's my own fault for forgetting to include salt in the provisions that were sent ashore today. We'll have none until tomorrow, or sugar either. And that means I'll have to drink my breakfast tea plain. If there's anything I loathe and detest, it's tea without sugar."

"I sent two of my Connecticut companies and one of the independent New Hampshire battalions to harass those artillery positions," General Wolcott declared to no one in particular. "It seemed like an excellent idea to keep the enemy awake all night, but it didn't occur to me until now that I'll get very little sleep myself. I'm very sensitive to noises at night."

Pepperrell allowed himself a thin smile. "The army is sitting out there wondering what we're talking about in here, gentlemen. It would never cross their minds that we're doing the precise same thing that they're doing—complaining about living conditions. It's miraculous the way man adjusts to his surroundings and begins to think of his personal comfort as soon as he's out of immediate physical danger. And that reminds me. My lads deliberately disobeyed me and put this tent up practically at the water's edge. They'll move it to the center of the compound at daybreak tomorrow."

His deputies' faces showed thorough disapproval of the idea, but both were too wise to express their opinions aloud; if they agitated the noted Pepperrell stubborn streak, he would move his headquarters to the location closest to the enemy position that he could achieve. General Waldo finished his soup and drew a crumpled sheet of paper from his pocket. "I have Doc Thornton's latest report on casualties," he said, and all pretense of calm and boredom vanished from the tent. "Accordin' to his last count, we've lost sixty-eight dead and two hundred and thirteen wounded, more than half of them seriously."

His superiors were silent and thoughtful, and at last Wolcott nodded. "There's this consolation, Sam, we've lost fewer than we estimated beforehand. But landings don't come cheap. And neither do night operations. The surgeons will be busy before daybreak."

"I'm afraid you're right," Waldo agreed gloomily. "Who ever heard of night tactics?"

"The Iroquois nations from whom I borrowed them." There were no signs of fatigue on Pepperrell's face, and he spoke emphatically. "I realize that neither of you gentlemen quite agree with what I'm doing at the moment. I ask you only to remember that our landing was successful only because we achieved an element of complete surprise. We've partly destroyed Duchambon's feeling that he's sitting in the safest place on this side of the Atlantic. He's off balance, and I intend to keep him off balance. He and his generals have been trained to warfare that stops at dusk and begins again at sunrise. If I keep them stirred all night, every night, they'll never know what to expect."

"Oh, yes they will." Wolcott, the oldest of the officers,

was the most conservative. "There's only one way to take that big pile of stone, and that's to starve out its garrison. And meantime we'll lose valuable man power in night raids and harassing operations. Just between the three of us, I'm afraid that——"

He paused at the noise of the commotion outside, and when it increased in volume, Waldo, who was nearest the entrance, pushed his face through the flap. A grimy young ensign in the blue tunic of Connecticut infantry immediately approached, pushing his way through a knot of annoyed aides. "Sir," the young man shouted angrily, "I don't know what in hell to do with my prisoners and I can't get any help from these——"

"Prisoners?" Waldo blinked, trying to accustom his eyes to the darkness, and finally made out a large group of gesticulating men milling about in the open space that separated the commanding general's tent from that of his lesser officer. "You'd best come inside, son."

The presence of the three senior officers of the army under the canvas roof did not awe the ensign, who barely remembered his military manners and raised his right hand in a vague approximation of a salute. "Nobody in this army wants my prisoners," he said bitterly, "and I don't mind telling you that Sergeant Abe Hubbel and I are getting mighty tired of wandering all over this camp with them. Who discovered these wine casks? I did! And they'll all be gone before I can get back."

General Wolcott was about to reprimand the youth for his informality, but General Pepperrell spoke quickly, before his second-in-comand could utter a word. "First off, lad," he said, his voice and manner serene, "suppose you tell us who you are?"

"Ensign Robin Lawrence, sir. Colonel Richmond's Bristol regiment, Captain Ebenezer Eastman's company. You see, General—we took the battery, and——"

"You *took* it?" Under the circumstances, Pepperrell's calm was monumental.

"Yes, sir." Ensign Lawrence was impatient. "The three

guns that were the first to open up on us this morning. The battery that's located about halfway between the town and the fortress. Captain Eastman, he decided to sneak up on 'em, so's to give 'em a good surprise. We found 'em eating their supper, and we surprised 'em for sure, sir. The company's finishing off the Frenchmen's supper. And their wine. But there won't be anything left for me unless I——"

"Turn your prisoners over to the provost guard, and rejoin your command." General Pepperrell's attitude became suddenly crisp. "My compliments to your Captain Eastman, and tell him we'll dispatch reinforcements to his position immediately." He had to call out his last words, for the ensign was already disappearing through the flap.

The generals were all on their feet now, smiling, and Wolcott's grin was the broadest, for the honor of capturing the artillery position belonged exclusively to his own men from Connecticut. "Duchambon isn't going to like this one bit's worth," he said.

"I won't blame him for that," Pepperrell responded. "General Waldo, I wish you'd be good enough to find accommodations for our unexpected guests until morning. Meantime send off a message to Commodore Warren and ask him to make a snug ship available to take prisoners."

"That's a right good idea, Will." In his own way, Waldo was as informal as the young ensign had been. "We're just borrowin' trouble if we try to set up a prisoner compound on land."

Pepperrell nodded, then turned to his first deputy. "General Wolcott, be kind enough to dispatch another company to the site of the captured battery. The enemy may try to retake it. Oh, and you'd better send Colonel Gridley to inspect the guns. He won't mind missing his evening's chess game when he learns he has a few real cannon."

Waldo and Wolcott reached for their hard-brimmed

hats, but stopped when Pepperrell chuckled. They looked at him inquiringly, and he smiled again. "It seems to me, gentlemen," he said softly, "that our policy of pressing the fight both night and day is already paying dividends."

Peter and Jeanne were still together at the window of the drawing room in the Tour du Nord suite, peering blindly through the night as they tried to puzzle out the meaning of the sporadic rifle fire that broke out first to the east of the citadel, then to the west. Occasionally Peter hopefully explained the possible military significance of the unusual activity, but there was no other conversation between them. Their shoulders touched now and again as they looked down, and whenever this happened they self-consciously pulled apart. A phase of their relationship was drawing to a close, and although neither would admit it, both were aware of it.

Soon, when the initial shock of the unexpected invasion subsided, someone in a position of authority would remember the prisoner in the tower and would quickly conclude that there was no longer any need to give him preferential treatment. When that time came, Peter expected that he would be returned to the dungeons. That would spell disaster for him, but he didn't know how to avoid it. Through the long and exciting hours of the day he had thought of a score of escape plans, then rejected them, one by one. Now that General Pepperrell and the army were actually outside the gates of the citadel, his knowledge of the vulnerability of the northeast corner of the fortress was more vital than ever, but he had yet to evolve a scheme that would give him even a remote chance of reaching the lines of his compatriots.

Jeanne's presence here was partly responsible, of course, for she distracted him. The crowded events of the day had made it impossible for him to tell her how he felt about her, and a reluctance to bring up so delicate a subject at this particular time restrained him still. He knew she must be worrying about the fate of her home and her valuable possessions in the town. Her house was occupied and her material security was threatened by New Englanders, and Peter told himself that even if she had never before thought of him as a personal enemy, she must so regard him now. Nevertheless he could not delay beyond this evening in telling her what was on his mind. Looking down at her shining blond head he realized that nothing he ever said or did would compensate her for the tenderness and devotion she had lavished on him.

It was impossible to make sense out of the rifle fire, and Peter moved away from the window and decided to summon his courage; he would speak up to Jeanne right now. Then he heard a single pair of rapidly approaching footsteps through the open door of the suite, and was faintly relieved. This was probably a guard, bringing his supper and Jeanne's, and he told himself that words would come to him more easily during a meal.

A moment later Jacques Duphaine walked into the chamber. He was wearing the white costume he used in his role of the highwayman, and there were several smears of dirt on his long cape. His sword hung at his side, two duelling pistols were jammed into his belt, and the glitter in his eyes was as sharp as the odor of gunpowder that clung to him. He surveyed the couple before him and spoke abruptly.

"Jeanne," he said. "I want you to go at once to Governor Duchambon. It will hours before he can see you, but I want you to make yourself noticed in his anterooms. When you're finally admitted, tell him you're ill because the enemy has taken your charming little house. Tell him you wish to resign your position as the guardian angel of Peter here, and beg him for a pass through the gates so you can see for yourself whether your house has been damaged. He'll refuse your request, but that's irrelevant. The important thing is that your time will be accounted for, and you won't be implicated here. Well, woman? Why do you stand there? Do as I tell you!"

Jeanne was startled and looked at Peter for advice, but

Jacques crossed the room, took hold of her shoulders and shook her. "There's no time to waste!" he said. "Do you want Paul Tediere to regain custody of him? With the town occupied and the citadel under attack, every officer in the garrison will insist on the removal of an important prisoner from the tower!"

He tried to propel her toward the door, but Jeanne resisted and finally broke free of his grasp. She looked again at Peter, who smiled unhappily. "It would appear as though we've got to trust him, Jeanne. There doesn't seem to be any choice. I don't rightly understand the reasons for all he wants you to do but I'm not as quick as he is."

Jacques found the New Englander's bluntness so refreshing that he laughed aloud. "I am always heartened by the confidence of my good friends. Please hurry, Jeanne—or I shall not be responsible for the consequences."

Ignoring his presence, Peter stepped forward, took Jeanne into his arms and kissed her full on the mouth. When he released her they both became aware of Jacques watching them, his eyes sardonic. Jeanne opened her mouth to speak, but could not, and turning slowly, she walked with dignity to the door. Jacques followed her and closed it behind her, then extended his hand.

"We've not met in some time, Peter, but I've kept myself informed on your progress. Well, first, my congratulations. Your Maine regiments know how to fight."

Peter took his hand, thinking anew that it was almost impossible to hate the scoundrel, yet wondering what new trick Jacques was trying to perpetrate. "Were the Maine boys in today's battle?"

"I rode close enough to them to cut their whiskers with my blade. But there'll be time enough to discuss our exploits when we're old. If we grow old. We'll both be cut off in our early prime unless we move at once. Peter, within the hour you will be either a free man—or a dead one."

His heart pounding, Peter could only stare. Jacques seemed to be in earnest, but this sudden development was incomprehensible. "You're going to help me escape?"

"I am. Now."

"Why?"

"Would you prefer a return to the dungeons? Tédière has little imagination, you surely realize. He'll undoubtedly give you the same cell you occupied before, and I dare say you have no fond memories for the place."

"Just a minute, Jacques." Peter drew in his breath and tried to think clearly. "You very well know where I want to be. But in offering me your help, you're deliberately making a traitor of yourself. I want to know why."

Jacques looked at the agitated prisoner and smiled. "Let us say that I have reasons of my own, private reasons that make the effort and the risk worth my while."

Peter's sense of uneasiness increased. Perhaps some trap had been prepared for him, and he was being urged to destroy himself. The French certainly didn't want him to be alive at the end of the campaign to report to his own people how he had been tortured and abused. It would be far more convenient if he were killed while trying to escape: witnesses to the incident could verify the details later, and the entire French high command of Louisburg would be absolved of any blame.

On the other hand there was always the possibility that Jacques meant what he said, even though he chose to cloud his motives in secrecy. If the offer was genuine, of course, here was the opportunity to report the citadel's weakness to General Pepperrell. Peter decided to take the gamble."

"What do you want me to do?"

Jacques tugged his stolen watch from his fob pocket and glanced at it. "In just five minutes' time, a reconnaissance party of volunteers will ride out of the east gate, which will be opened to them for the purpose. There's been some sort of trouble at the Royal battery—the gunsite located about a mile and a half from here on the road to the town. They haven't answered the last two flare signals sent to them, and we suspect that the enemy has captured the battery."

Peter felt elated, but controlled himself. "Go on," he said.

"Naturally I have volunteered to be one of the four who will ride to the site. As no one would mourn my loss, my generous offer was accepted. My horse awaits me at the gate." He threw his cloak onto a chair and began to unbutton his tunic. "Here. And give me your clothes."

Jacques reached out and ripped the fabric of the fine suit of civilian clothes which Peter had been given. Startled, Peter could only blink at the highwayman. "What—"

"Take off your coat and throw it on the floor. We'll talk as we change. There's precious little time." Jacques handed over his white, tunic, then unbuckled his sword and looked at it wistfully for a moment. "Take this. And my pistols. Can you ride in those shoes?"

"I can ride barefooted, if need be." Still uncomprehending, Peter nevertheless hastened to follow instructions. If there was a trap, it was too late now to back out."

"All right. Now listen carefully. When you reach the foot of the stairs, turn right until you come to a stone wall. Turn right again, and go straight to the end. My horse and saddle are white. You'll recognize them at once. Oh, yes—my hat."

He removed it, set it on Peter's head, then pulled down the brim. "Keep your head low, and there's a chance you'll get away."

He smiled, but Peter's expression was grim. "They'll hang you for this."

"Indeed they will not, for I shall have proof that I defended myself valiantly." Jacques picked up a small arm chair and hurled it with such force against the adjoining bedroom wall that the back cracked and one of the legs broke off. He then deliberately overturned a table and kicked at a rug. "Hit me now, if you will, please," he said briskly, still grinning. "In the face only, of course—where it will show."

Peter hesitated for an instant, and Jacques' expression indicated that if he didn't act at once, all was lost. He drew back his right fist and smashed it into the highwayman's face. A thin trickle of blood dripped down Jacques' chin from his lower lip.

"Again, if you please. And with a little more force this time. If you spare me now, little Duchambon's hangman will not."

Taking a deep breath, Peter drove his left into Jacques' cheekbone, then followed it with a crushing right that caught the Gentleman on the eye. Jacques staggered backward, then slowly crumpled to the floor. "Excellent, excellent," he murmured, his speech thick because of the swelling that was already puffing his lips. "Good luck, friend Peter. My future rides with you."

Peter adjusted the white cape around his shoulders, tugged on the gauntlet gloves, and stepped out into the corridor, closing the door carefully behind him. His flight to freedom had begun.

TWENTY

PETER heard his own footsteps echoing through the vaulted stone corridor and realized he was walking too fast. He would only attract attention to himself, he thought, and slowed his pace accordingly. At the head of the stairs stood two bored guards, one on either side, close enough to touch. Surely they would recognize the prisoner who had been held inside the tower suite for so many weeks, and he did not dare look at them. As he brushed past them they saluted, and he returned the salutation unthinkingly: not until his fingers touched the brim of Jacques' hat at a forty-five degree angle did it occur to him that he had given them what had come to be known as the American salute, a distinctive gesture which invariably annoyed officers of the regular army sent out from England, and which the militia deliberately retained to show its independence of the mother country's traditions.

Fortunately the French soldiers were indifferent and failed to notice, and Peter started down the steps, his heart pounding. He wanted to suck huge quantities of air into his lungs, but refrained; the sound would undoubtedly attract the attention of the guards. He knew he had been lucky, and he had learned a valuable lesson: he would need to be careful of every move, every gesture, or he would betray himself. Jacques had given him the tools of escape, but he had to use them himself. A feeling of panic came over him as he found himself unable to remember the French salute; although he had seen it often, his mind refused to function.

And every second brought him closer to the guards stationed at the next landing. Forcing himself to be calm, he tried to apply reason to the dilemma. Jacques, he thought, was not a member of the French army but a civilian. It was therefore possible that no more than a vague wave, if anything, was expected of him. There was no alternative but to try, and Peter gripped the butt of a pistol with his left hand as he neared the landing. The guards, who had apparently been resting, quickly jumped to their feet and held their muskets in the prescribed vertical position. Peter raised his right hand casually and neither paused nor looked back as he continued to descend the winding staircase. There were no repercussions, and he relaxed slightly; by the time he approached the last landing he was in command of himself, but when he reached the ground and turned right, per Jacques' instructions, tension gripped him anew.

At the end of a short corridor was a door, and as he approached it a soldier on the far side pulled it open and thrust a torch in his direction. It would be foolhardly now to conceal his face, he knew, and he looked at the sentry boldly, hoping for the best. The man seemed satisfied; at least he made no objection as Peter stepped out into the night. This was the first time, he thought, that he had been anywhere but above the ground or beneath it since the day he had first arrived in Louisburg.

Again he turned right and started rapidly down the path, his outward appearance confident and jaunty. He heard the beat of marching feet and peering ahead saw a platoon of infantry approaching, a sergeant at the head of the column. Apparently these were troops returning from sentry duty on the citadel wall, for they were loudly complaining that they were hungry and were expressing the conviction that the rest of their company had already consumed everything edible and had left them only slops.

They were walking two abreast, and there was no room for Peter to squeeze past them on the path. For an instant his mind again refused to function as he wondered whether to step into the dirt at the side of the stone walk or to force them to give way to him. Then he conjured up a mental picture of Jacques, and knew that the highwayman would never voluntarily give precedence to anyone. Increasing his pace and swaggering, he held to the center of the path. The soldiers uncomplainingly swerved and tramped through the dirt, most of them paid no attention to him, and he responded to the glances of the others with what he hoped was a semblance of a carefree grin. So far so good.

The dark shadow of the fortress wall loomed directly ahead now, and slightly to the left Peter could make out the huge gate. Several men were clustered in front of it, and grooms were holding four horses. Two riders were already in the saddle, and the tension of the entire group was evident, even at a distance.

The men turned at the sound of his footsteps, and someone called, "Duphaine! Is that you?"

"Yes," Peter knew there was no similarity between his voice and Jacques', but he had to reply. Silence would have been suspicious when he had been asked a direct question.

"Be on time after this when you take an assignment! Do you expect us to delay the whole war just for you?"

That was a voice Peter would know anywhere: the speaker was Commandant Paul Tédière, who stood no more than a yard to the left of Jacques' white horse, and Peter had to summon all of his will power to keep himself from leaping at the man. But he knew that if he did the victory would be Tedière's, and he controlled his fury as he vaulted into the saddle and pulled the plumed hat lower over his forehead.

The fourth member of the reconnaissance party mounted too, and Peter was in a fever of impatience to start. He could feel Tedière looking up at him; Jacques would certainly answer an open taunt, and this silence was so unlike him that Tedière's interest was aroused. This was the critical moment, and Peter loosened his cloak, then took hold of his sword beneath its folds. Tedière was signing his own death warrant, too, if he recognized Peter now.

So far the night had been mercifully dark, but the moon, which had just risen, began to appear through a haze of clouds, and in a few more seconds concealment would be impossible. One of the horses neighed, and Peter found himself counting the number of soldiers standing at the gate, ready to raise the bar. There were eleven; the knowledge was of no significance, but looking at them helped to keep him from dwelling on his own immediate danger from Tedière.

"Let's go!" one of the others called, and Peter, glancing at him obliquely, saw that this, too, was a commandant. He felt inordinately grateful to the officer.

"One moment, Ballou." Tedière cleared his throat importantly. "Let me remind you that this mission——"

The officer whom he had called Ballou spurred forward. "Open the gate!" he directed. "This is no time for you and your speeches, Tedière!"

"I shall find it necessary to report your attitude to Governor Duch——"

"Report and be damned to you! Open the gate!"

The soldiers strained as they lifted the heavy metal bolt, and three others ran forward to swing the studded oak door wide enough for the riders to get out. Peter maneuvered his horse to the far side of the group, away from Tedière, and he was on the leader's heels as Commandant Ballou moved into the open countryside. The gate creaked closed again, and Peter felt a stream of perspiration trickle down his face and into the collar of his tunic.

Ballou motioned to the others to come close, but Peter stayed as far distant as he dared. At any moment now one of these officers was sure to see that he was not Jacques, and then trouble would begin. In any event, the odds had now been reduced to only three against his one, and that was something for which to be grateful.

"We'll stay together for the first mile," Ballou said, "and we'll separate only when we come to the twisted oak, the scene of last summer's little indiscretion."

The French, Peter thought, were incredible. Here were four men embarking on a mission as hazardous as any group could be called upon to execute in a war, yet the commander of the little expedition spoke in a tone as frivolous and light as he might employ at a fashionable party in an aristocratic salon.

"When we arrive at the oak, we'll separate, fan out and ride as close to the battery as we can penetrate. If it's still in our hands, the first to arrive will instruct the commander there to light a small cannister of gunpowder as a flare signal that all is well. If the position is in enemy hands, we will return to the citadel separately. Those of us who survive. Understood?"

The others nodded, Peter with them. He found it difficult to concentrate on what Commandant Ballou was saying, but this was no time to allow his attention to wander. Failure to grasp the smallest detail could lead to discovery and death.

"Use this gate and no other on your return. And call out the password to the chief sentry officer when you are one hundred feet from the wall. Colonel de Marini is justifiably nervous, and his men will shoot to kill if you're tardy in your response. You all know tonight's password, I trust?" He paused and glanced at Peter with the traditional distrust of the military man for the civilian. "You, Duphaine?"

"Naturally." Peter forced himself to respond quickly, to inject enough venomous scorn into his voice to conceal his accent.

"We ride, then, single file. Luck be with you, my children. I invite you to share a drink with me later tonight, either in my quarters or in hell." Ballou started off down the road.

The others fell in behind him, and Peter, who had hoped to be last, saw that a young cavalryman was reserving that honor for himself. There was no disputing the point, though it would have been convenient, to say the least, if he could have brought up the rear and slipped away unobtrusively in the night. Now he would have to wait.

These Frenchmen knew their business, and there was no talking as they pressed their horses forward at a canter. Their experience had taught them that voices carry in the night, and they were well aware that the clatter of their mounts' hooves on the dry, hard-packed dirt of the road was a sufficient warning to the enemy, if indeed the foe was ahead, that they were coming.

Peter, bending low in the saddle, suddenly realized that the night had grown very quiet. Somewhere in the far distance there was an occasional musket shot, but the nose came from the far side of the citadel, and the immediate area was silent. Several possible courses of action were open to him now, and he debated them as he rode. The first and most obvious was to make an immediate break, hope that his companions were poor shots and that he could shake free of them. Then he would try to make a wide detour around the citadel and attempt to reach General Pepperell's main camp. The idea was tempting but very risky. The French officers were better horsemen than he, and it was very possible that they would catch him, or at the least come close enough to him to put a bullet through him. In addition, he knew, it was unwise to wander alone through unfamiliar countryside at night, when he was likely to encounter patrols of either side who would shoot first and investigate his identity afterwards.

His impulse, of course, was to achieve freedom at the first possible instant, but he reasoned that it would be wiser to wait until he and the three Frenchmen arrived at the place of separation. Then, if he slipped away, there was far less chance that his defection would be noticed. That, he thought as Commandant Ballou slowed his horse to a walk, was what he would do.

The moon had risen a trifle higher now, and Peter saw the silhouette of a gnarled tree some distance down the road. Ballou urged his horse into an open field to the left, and the officer directly ahead of Peter followed. When Jacques' mount would have done likewise, the man turned in his saddle and gestured fiercely in the opposite direction. Peter happily and obediently turned the beast to the right, noting as he did that the cavalryman who had brought up the rear was fanning out even farther to the right.

It was difficult, almost impossible for Peter to realize that at last he was alone, that technically, at least, he was succeeding. The momentum of his horse carried him forward one hundred feet or more, and when he saw a tangled patch of scrub pine, birch and thick weeds ahead and a little to his right, he pushed into it, then halted the horse. The obvious line of action came to him suddenly, and he realized that his mind had been muddled or he would have known long before now that he should wait here for a time: if a flare showed at the battery, he would then beat a hasty retreat, but if the English colonials had indeed taken the site, he would ride forward and join them.

Suddenly a flurry of rifle fire broke the stillness on his left. It was quiet for a few seconds, then the guns sounded again. Peter could see nothing through the trees, and decided to push forward into the open. When he reached clear ground again, he might be able to make out the location of the battery, even though the moon was once more hidden and the night was again very dark.

He came out of the clump of woods at a walk and stood in the saddle in an attempt to see more clearly. A voice called out, unexpectedly close. "There he is! It's another o' them bastards!"

There was a flash, followed by the retort of a long rifle, and a ball tore through the fabric of Peter's cape. The horse reared, almost throwing him, and in the sudden danger of the moment it did not cross his mind that the man who had called out had shouted in English.

"You there!" This was a second voice, and Peter, quieting his mount, saw three, no—four riflemen arise from the long grass, their weapons pointed at him. "Throw down your pistols! Get off that horse and come to us with your hands high. All the way up."

"You damned idiots!" Peter found his voice at last, but did not know he was roaring at the top of his lungs. He had recognized a strong Connecticut twang, and relief was mingled with his wild anger. "Since when do you start shooting before you identify your target? What kind of militiamen do you call yourselves?"

"He speaks pretty good English, Jeb." There was wonder in the tone.

"Yep, he does. For a Frenchie."

"Frenchie be damned!" This was more than Peter could bear, and his rage took possession of him.

"Who be ye, then?"

"Captain Peter Staples of General Pepperrell's staff. Take me to——"

"Hold on, mister. Not so fast, by your leave. What's tonight's password?"

"Password?" Under the circumstances the request seemed outrageously unreasonable to Peter, and although he was not a profane man he cursed intensely, expertly and at length.

"That there was pretty good cussin'," one of the

militiamen admitted, "but it don't solve anythin'. Now them others that was sneakin' up on us was Frenchies, so who's t' say you ain't? Mister, you get down from that there critter quick, and you do just like we tell you or we'll show you some o' the neatest shootin' there ever was. And gettin' hit with a rifle ball close on ain't very comft'ble, I don't mind tellin' ye."

The muzzles of the four long frontier weapons cooled Peter's temper. He was where he had so long wanted to be, where he needed to be, with his own army again. And he told himself repeatedly that unless he behaved rashly now, he was indeed safe at last. He dismounted slowly and lifted his hands above his head.

They disarmed him quickly, treating him more roughly than was necessary, and again Peter had to curb his anger. The men glanced at each other, not sure what to do next, and Peter spoke up at once. "I reckon you'd better take me to your commanding officer."

The notion seemed to make sense, and they shoved him through the high grass toward the artillery position, prodding him occasionally with their rifles. One of them led the horse, who followed quietly, and at last they came to the battery, which, from the outside, seemed to be a duplicate of the citadel in miniature. As the little cavalcade moved inside, a number of men who were lounging about, their arms close at hand, muttered threats in Peter's direction, but he kept quiet and no incident developed. The methods of the men from Connecticut, he told himself, were crude but effective.

After a short walk on a stone path he was pushed into a blockhouse that stood between two large cannon, and inside he saw an officer, a captain, sitting and reading an official document by the light of two candle stubs stuck onto the window ledge. The man was short, unshaved and wore spectacles: Peter guessed that he was a small merchant in civilian life. "Well, boys, you got one!" His Connecticut accent was as unmistakable as the hostility in his eyes as he glanced at Peter.

"I'm Captain Staples of General Pepp——"

"Shut up!" The captain was matter-of-fact. "Tell me about it, boys. You, Hiram, you talk first."

The militiamen explained the circumstances of Peter's capture carefully, and only when they had finished did the officer permit his prisoner to say a few words. As Peter tried to launch into the story of how he happened to be in Louisburg, the captain held up his hand.

"That's enough, mister. Maybe you're what you say you are, maybe not. That's up to headquarters to decide. Take him there, boys. Go the long way. And no risks. At the first sign of a trick, kill him!"

He turned back to the paper he was reading, and the troopers led Peter back into the night, out of the battery compound and into the open countryside. Woodsmen all, they made their way across comparatively strange terrain with remarkable ease, and although Peter was even less familiar than they were with the region, he kept his sense of direction and realized they were truly taking a roundabout route to the perimeter where the bulk of the army was encamped. The walk took an hour and a half and seemed even longer, for every minute was nerve shattering. Peter knew he was safe enough unless the party encountered a French patrol, in which event the men from Connecticut would shoot him instantly. In similar circumstances he would accord identical treatment to a prisoner, of course, but the knowledge held little solace for him.

At length they arrived at the perimeter and made their way through a maze of tents and past long rows of men sleeping in the open. Here at last was real safety, but Peter was too numb now to enjoy the moment. He had looked forward to this time for so long that he felt nothing but weariness, and as he plodded behind one of the Connecticut militiamen he yawned repeatedly.

Here and there men were awake and chatting quietly, and as Peter's guards made their way toward the shoreline, where the high command was quartered, they passed the bivouac area of one of the Maine companies, that of Captain Ami Cutter. Two sentiries recognized Peter and ran to him, shouting wildly. Soon others joined in, and his back was slapped, his hand pumped repeatedly. The men from Connecticut were somewhat taken aback but were determined to follow their orders to the letter, and although the march became something of a triumphal procession, they neither lessened their watchfulness nor relinquished their charge until ordered to do so by Major Christopher Ellis of Kittery, who first stood wide-eyed in the entrance of his tent after being awakened by the commotion, then threw his arms around the old friend whom he had believed to be dead.

Ellis took complete charge of the situation and led Peter at once to the private tent of the sleeping General Pepperrell. At least a score of men followed and stood about outside; among them were the Connecticut infantry troopers, who grinned sheepishly when they discovered that they were being regarded as heroes for bringing Maine's long-missing officer safely to camp.

Peter walked into the dark tent, and Ellis lit a candle with a tinderbox, then moved back to the flap. The general was not a heavy sleeper, and in a few moments he stirred, then opened his eyes and sat up abruptly.

Peter saluted smartly. "Captain Staples standing at report, sir," he said. "Sorry I'm a mite tardy, General."

William Pepperrell blinked and rubbed his eyes. "Bless my soul!" was the most he could muster.

TWENTY-ONE

AN ALL-DAY staff conference was held immediately after Peter's return, followed by a council of war in the evening. Regimental commanders attended, as did the principal officers of the independent units, and, when General Pepperrell asked for a vote, it was unanimously agreed that the attack should be concentrated on the northeast corner of the citadel, in accord with the information that Peter had brought to the army. It would first be necessary to surround the fortress, however, and this was a move that would have been undertaken in any case. Thanks to the range and power of the citadel's great cannon the encirclement was inevitably going to be costly, but the invaders knew they had to pay the price, and unit after unit moved out into the open fields, then literally dug in for their lives as the great guns opened fire on them.

Each day for a week the siege lines inched closer and closer to the walls, and at last the time came when Colonel Gridley decided that the cannon which had been captured in the French battery outside the fortress could be put to use. The walls of the mightiest structure in the

New World were at last within his range. A bombardment was opened and the French replied so furiously that the earth trembled and foraging parties sent out by General Wolcott to hunt fresh meat reported that there was no wild life in the immediate vicinity, deer and bear having retreated to the far reaches of the island.

Peter reserved for General Pepperrell's ears alone the full story of what had happened to Mercy, and the commander vowed that when he brought Louisburg to its knees he would hang Jacques Duphaine. In vain Peter tried to explain that Jacques had done all in his power to help and protect Mercy, and that he himself would have been dead long ago had it not been for the intervention of the highwayman. In fact, he argued that if the citadel should be taken because of his discovery that the walls were weak where he had noted them, at least part of the credit should belong to Jacques for having helped him escape. But the general, grieving anew for his daughter, quietly swore vengeance and refused to heed Peter's pleas.

But the fall of the fortress seemed far distant; the fight continued day after day, and the French gave more than they received. General Wolcott's infantry and General Waldo's sappers were successful in throwing a cordon around the entire citadel, but the defenders were plentifully supplied with ammunition, and whenever an attack was attempted it was repulsed by a withering fire that resulted in heavy casualties for the English colonials.

And Colonel Gridley was plagued by troubles. One of his captured guns was smashed by a heavy ball from an eighteen-pounder, which landed on the barrel of the cannon: as luck would have it, fire started and the gun's nearby powder cache exploded, killing nine of Gridley's best artillery experts. The remaining two cannon, which had been dragged into new positions a quarter of a mile from the northeast corner, subsequently were forced to suspend their fire for forty-eight hours when they ran out of ammunition. None of the naval flotilla's shot fitted the

weapons, and operations came to a virtual standstill while
Colonel Gridley hastily built the equivalent of a crude
foundry and recast his iron in the larger mold.

There was always the danger that heavy reinforcements
would be sent to Louisburg from Quebec or from France
itself, and despite Commodore Warren's fortuitous capture of the man-o'-war, his forces would be no match for a
major fleet. If he should be attacked, the most he could
hope to do would be to remain in Gabarus Bay, where the
maneuverability of large ships was limited, and where,
though he might be bottled up himself, he might
nevertheless continue to stand between the fortress and
whatever relief might be sent to her. But as the days
dragged on and no French fleet made an appearance, the
commodore concluded that either Quebec had not yet
heard of Louisburg's plight, which was unlikely, or that
Admiral Delaire had too weak a force to risk a showdown,
which was more probable.

Several gaping holes finally appeared in the masonry of
the citadel's northeast corner after Colonel Gridley resumed his barrage, but the French continued to inflict
such fearful punishment on any attackers who dared to
approach that General Pepperrell refused to see his men
slaughtered and directed that the all-out assault would
have to wait. Tempers became frayed, bitter quarrels
sprung up between individuals and even units, and one
night it was necessary to put in a hurried call to the fleet to
send several hundred "pacifiers" ashore when a riot broke
out between a Massachusetts Bay battalion and two companies of New Hampshiremen.

And through it all Peter discovered that he had little or
nothing to do other than keep a record of the steady stream
of messages that passed between General Pepperrell and
Commodore Warren, who remained on the water, having transferred his flag to the captured ship of the line.
The work was dull, and it seemed absurd that he, who
knew more about Louisburg than any other man in the

army and who had greater personal cause to hope for her reduction, should be forced to sit and play an inactive role in the siege. General Pepperrell had told him repeatedly that no commands were open, and he had to content himself with the job of a glorified file clerk.

At least he was in a position to know everything that was happening, and, as he sat in front of the tent he now shared with two other staff officers and made notes in a large book spread out on a rough-hewn table, he listened to the familiar thunder of the citadel's guns and watched the leaves of a nearby elm quiver in the afternoon sunlight. Had anyone told him six months ago that war could be so boring, he would have laughed. But it was no laughing matter now to be idle when he wanted revenge on those who had treated him so cruelly. He pushed up the sleeves of his shirt, wiped his forehead, and then raised his head as he saw someone approach.

He started to smile when he saw Matthew Thornton, chief surgeon of the expedition, but the medical man's prematurely lined face was grave and Peter instantly sobered. Dr. Thornton strolled over to him and threw a long sheet of paper on the desk. "Here are today's casualties, Peter," he said without preamble. "You'd best show the list to the general in chief when he returns from his inspection."

Peter looked down, saw that the parchment was filled with name after name and whistled softly. "I didn't know there was a major engagement today."

Thornton shook his head and ran his fingers through his gray-streaked hair. "We're now fighting a worse enemy than the French. These men are dysentery victims."

"All of them today?" Peter was incredulous.

"They've all fallen victim today."

"Then—if we don't do something soon—we'll have no army capable of mounting an attack?"

"So I told General Pepperrell this noon. Peter, if you see Sam Waldo, ask him to loan me two or three more regimental surgeons, will you? I told them we needed twice the number of doctors on this expedition, but nobody listened to me," he added without bitterness as he started to wander away. "I've never yet seen an army with enough medical men."

When he was gone, Peter picked up the list and studied it for names he knew. Suddenly a strange light came into his eyes, and his mouth set in a grim line. He arose abruptly, folded the list carefully and carried it in his hand as he walked the thirty feet to General Pepperrell's tent. He was there twenty minutes later when the army chief returned. Several officers were with him, but it was obvious that Peter wanted to speak to him in private and he dismissed the others after giving them brief instructions regarding the movement of three regiments.

He glanced quickly at the list, then looked up. "I know," he said. "I've been hearing about nothing but illness for the past three hours. Ordinarily I'd have waited a few weeks longer and tried to starve the French out of their garrison. But I can't. We're going to attack at dawn tomorrow, Peter. There's no choice, and I've asked Colonel Gridley to open that gap in your wall as wide as he can." Something in his aide's attitude caught his attention. "There was something else you wanted to see me about?"

"Sir," Peter said carefully, "if you'll take another look at the sick list, you'll see that Captain Ephraim Baker is among the sick. Fourth company, York regiment. His first lieutenant is Bray Dearing. Now, Bray's a good officer but he's too young and too inexperienced for a command. That company is mostly from around Kittery, sir. I know them and they know me. So I thought——"

Pepperrell put a hand on his shoulder, silencing him. "I know what you've thought. Peter, you'd have been my son-in-law if Mercy——" He broke off sharply. "Anyway, that's what Mistress Pepperrell and I always hoped." He looked away for a moment and his fingers tightened. "All

right, lad. Draw up the orders yourself and report to
Colonel Bradstreet. You realize that as that's my personal
regiment, it will lead the attack?"

Peter grinned broadly, though his eyes remained serious. "That's what I hoped, General."

Colonel Gridley made no attempt to conceal the intentions of his commander, and, indeed, he could not hide
them. His two big cannon maintained an incessant barrage throughout the night, and he used his ammunition
recklessly, prodigally. A half-battalion was assigned to the
special task of carrying water to him, and whenever his
cannon became too hot he doused the barrels, then resumed his operation. Under cover of darkness he moved
his mortars to within three hundred yards of the citadel,
and they, too, maintained a steady fire. However, no
single mortar was allowed to remain in the same place for
more than a quarter of an hour at a time, for fear its firing
flashes would pinpoint its position to the enemy and make
it an easy target.

The French replied steadily, methodically, with their
guns, but few of the defenders dared approach the break in
the citadel wall, for Colonel Gridley had directed that ten
of the mortars be loaded with "grape" or scrap metal to
prevent repair squads from sealing up the ever widening
hole in the masonry.

No one on either side was sleeping, no one could sleep
in this prelude to battle. William Pepperrell and his lesser
generals stood on a slight knoll behind Gridley's guns, and
even Commodore Warren had come ashore and joined
them. Several of his ships, he told them, had taken
advantage of the night to sail close to the citadel's sea wall
and to hurl their iron at her. Granted that their efforts
were puny and ineffectual, but they created something of
a diversion, kept the French guessing, and added to the
uproar.

Nearly fifteen hundred militiamen, comprising approximately half of Pepperrell's task force, awaited the coming of dawn when they would storm the fortress, and of these the happiest was Peter. He sprawled on the grass, his company on either side of him and behind him, and watched the display of deadly fireworks from a vantage point less than a quarter of a mile from Colonel Gridley's cannon. He had smeared his face and hands with dirt, Indian style, to make himself less visible, and beside him were a Penobscot tomahawk, which he would hang from his neck by a thong, a long rifle, and a sword. The blade was the one Jacques had given him and which had been returned to him some days previous by an apologetic Captain Eastman of Connecticut, and, as he touched its hilt, Peter grinned quietly. The thought of such a time as this had sustained him through long hours of torture in the citadel's dungeons.

Glancing up at the sky, he estimated the time until dawn, then raised himself on one elbow, "Sergeant O'Connell!" he called sharply, raising his voice so he would be heard over the din of the artillery.

Someone touched his arm and he saw the grime-streaked face of the Fourth Company's sergeant major. "Right here, sir."

"Sergeant, pass the word along. No man is to eat any biscuits or drink any water until after the attack. Tell them they'll get sick if they do."

"Yes, sir." The sergeant, a foreman in the Pepperrell shipyards at Kittery in peacetime, sounded calm and confident.

"We'll soon be home again, Tim." Peter felt a fierce surge of kinship with O'Connell, with every man in the company.

"That we will, Peter, that we will." The sergeant chuckled, punched him affectionately on the upper arm, and crawled off into the darkness.

A light drizzle began to fall, and Peter frowned. "Mr. Dearing!" he shouted to his first lieutenant, who was lying a scant four feet distant. "Tour the company area. Make sure every man's powder horn is dry!"

The lieutenant said something unintelligible and started off. It was unlikely, Peter thought, that Maine men who lived close to the wilderness would be foolish enough to allow their powder to become damp, but in the tension of this hour someone might become forgetful. It was better to be careful and save lives.

Again he squinted up at the sky, but the rain clouds made it even more difficult than before to gauge the approaching dawn. There was another interminable wait; the artillery of both sides continued to drum methodically, and Peter felt inexplicably sleepy. Then he heard and subsequently saw a young ensign running across the field, and he was instantly alert.

The youth, no more than sixteen years of age, was calling at the top of his voice as he sprinted past the lines of resting men. "York regiment! Convene at your assembly point!"

The time of waiting was over.

Peter stood, hung the tomahawk around his neck, buckled on the sword, and picked up his rifle. Men on all sides of him were doing the same, and he began to walk forward to the prearranged position from which the attack would begin. He needed to give no order; the company followed him to a man, Lieutenant Dearing dropping back and taking his proper place at the rear. It was unnecessary to tell these veterans who had often skirmished with naturals in the forests to spread out: they instinctively moved apart and crouched low as they first walked, then trotted forward.

Two men squatted in the scorched grass directly ahead now, and as Peter drew nearer he made out a pair of silver epaulets in the gloom. This was Colonel Bradstreet; they had come far enough. He stoppped, and so did his men. French cannon balls were falling here and there in the area, and the militiamen hugged the ground, shielding their faces whenever a heated chunk of iron crashed into the earth.

The sky began to brighten, almost imperceptibly at first, but Peter was no longer aware of time. He saw Colonel Bradstreet jump to his feet, and at the same instant the soldier with him blew a long, piercing blast on his trumpet. Peter started to run straight toward the gap in the citadel wall, and his last calm, conscious thought was of Mercy: every enemy he killed would be for her.

It seemed as though the bulk of the French garrison was massed to meet the infantry attack. Of necessity Colonel Gridley's guns had fallen silent now, though the citadel's cannon kept up their fire and drowned the sounds of rifles and muskets. Regular French troops and provincials alike were stationed on three levels of the high walls, and still others waited behind the rubble of the dark, yawning hole at the corner.

Pepperrell's troops did not return the fire of their foes, however. The New England militiamen were under instructions to make every shot count, and they were not wasting ammunition and powder on stone. They swept onward, and when a man dropped another took his place. Nothing could halt the momentum of the first wave, not even the cauldrons of boiling oil which the French on the parapet hurled down.

Peter, carried forward by his own impetus and that of the few who were ahead of him, realized dimly that the artillery had done its job thoroughly, that the breach in the wall was now wide enough for a full company at a time to climb across the debris into the fortress. He did not know that he was shouting, that he brandished his long rifle as he ran. Nor was he aware of the heavy fire the French were pouring down on him and his comrades. A man to his left dropped with a bullet through the throat and one to his right screamed and fell when struck in the groin, but his own wild surge carried him across a mass of broken stones and splintered timbers into the citadel.

The enemy was ahead of him now as well as on the remaining parapet on both sides, so he crouched quickly behind a boulder that had once been a portion of the wall's base and peered around it cautiously. The muzzle of a musket appeared around the corner of a partly demolished building some thirty feet away, then he saw the gold visor of a French infantryman. Peter drew in his breath, took a bead on the soldier and fired. A grim smile cracked his face as the figure crumpled, and his tension vanished. Calmly now he primed his rifle.

New Englanders by the score were hurtling across the rubble, pausing, firing and moving forward again. Peter looked around, saw a number of familiar faces, and realized that his own company was one of the first to break into the fortress. It was impossible to give instructions in this uproar, but the men, experienced frontier fighters, needed none. All they knew was that the advance was continuing: each was eminently qualified to look after himself. Sergeant O'Connell, for one, was kneeling behind a fallen oak beam, laughing maniacally as he shook a charge of powder from his horn into his rifle.

The situation was changing so rapidly that Peter was unsure, for the moment, what to do next. At least two full battalions of New England infantry were doggedly climbing the inner steps of the parapet, and, judging by the casualties they were inflicting on the foe above them, they were doing as well as the high command had hoped they would. Other companies were pushing deeper into the fortress which until now had been considered impregnable. Suddenly Peter saw Colonel Bradstreet, standing alone and urging his men forward. If any man was the hero of the attack, it was he, for in spite of his advanced age, in spite of the epaulets on his shoulders that made him a natural target, he stood in a completely exposed position, coolly directing the advance of his units.

Peter hesitated no longer. Brandishing his rifle, he raced toward the colonel, his men following. Bradstreet waved him on, shouting something Peter couldn't hear above the din. Ahead now was a network of buildings, some of them four stories high, all made of heavy stone, and through an arched passageway Peter saw a parade ground beyond, apparently set inside a quadrangle of sorts. It was amazing how little he knew of the geography of the citadel, despite all the time he had spent here. But that was unimportant now: what did matter was that he saw a large-scale fight in progress inside the quadrangle, and he ran through the passage, firing his rifle at the nearest French target.

Several hundred men were milling around on the field, and what had been an organized battle was rapidly degenerating into a series of vicious hand-to-hand encounters. Peter and his company were swept into the struggle as soon as they appeared, and every man needed all of his strength, his skill, and his wits to stay alive. There was no time now to reload a rifle, and Peter cast the weapon aside. His sword would be more valuable, he thought, and drew it just in time to parry the thrust of a saber stroke from a very young, very fierce dismounted French cavalryman.

The next few minutes were extremely confusing: again and again Peter found himself in the center of a melee, then discovered that he was alone as the tide of the battle swept elsewhere. The noise of rifle, musket, and pistol fire was deafening, but it did not occur to him that a bullet might strike him down at any moment; he was too deeply engrossed in slashing away at every French uniform he saw to think of himself.

Suddenly a familiar face loomed in front of him, and Peter stopped short. His sword was already poised, but he could not bring himself to strike at Jacques Duphaine. The very weapon he held was Jacques', and he had the highwayman to thank for his freedom, for his life itself. Jacques, a long blade in his right hand, an iron-hilted poniard in his left, was obviously enjoying himself. There was a cold gleam in his eyes, a broad smile on his lips as he took on first one New England officer then another, almost simultaneously. Neither was a match for him, and he easily wounded one, then disarmed the other.

He became aware of the presence of someone else, whirled and saw Peter. His reaction was immediate and instinctive. Without a pause he lifted his blade high in a flourishing salute, and Peter raised his own weapon in a like gesture. There had been a time when, more than all else in the world, he had wanted the opportunity to fight a duel with Jacques. He had his chance now, but could not take it, just as Jacques would not cross swords with him.

But there was not time to stand and contemplate what had passed and what might have been. A French infantryman swung the butt of his musket at Peter's head, then dashed forward, intending to grapple with his foe. Peter jabbed hard with his sword, and the soldier fell back, bleeding profusely. Dimly Peter realized that his hat was gone now, that if the man's aim had been a half inch more accurate he would have been knocked senseless.

The fight had moved down the parade ground again, and Peter started toward the area where the desperate men of both sides were locked in combat. He moved closer to the walls of the building on his right, figuring that he would be less conspicuous there, less likely to be made the target for a stray French marksman's bullet. Then, suddenly, he realized that the enemy had ceased fire and was fleeing from the field. The break came so unexpectedly that Peter stopped short, and even as he watched, a sense of panic spread rapidly among the French forces. Individuals threw down their weapons and surrendered, and a few moments later a whole company of infantry that had been deployed in an areaway between two buildings raised a white flag and marched abjectly onto the parade ground.

This was no moment for elation, however. Peter realized that Jeanne le Sueur was very much on his mind, that he was deeply concerned over her safety. It was possible that she was still quartered in the suite she had occupied in the North Tower, and so, after quickly orienting himself, he ran in the general direction of the tower entrance. He had to make his way through a series of connecting passages, and twice lost his way but doggedly kept going. Here and there he heard bursts of rifle and musket fire as General Pepperrell's victorious forces cleaned up isolated pockets of resistance, but he was only dimly aware of this final stage of the fight.

At last he found the familiar entrance to the tower, and, his sword in his hand, he mounted the deserted stairs two at a time. When he reached the top he paused for a moment to catch his breath and to look around. The door leading to Jeanne's rooms was shut, but the entrance to the quarters in which he himself had been held prisoner was open, and he heard a noise inside. Advancing cautiously, he peered into the living room.

Flames were blazing high in the fireplace, and Peter saw that someone was burning papers. A man, muffled by a long cloak, was hastily shoving handfuls of documents into the hearth. The figure was one he would know anywhere, and Peter's heart pounded hard against his ribs.

"Good morning, Tédière," he said, and was surprised at the hoarseness of his own voice.

The commandant jumped to his feet and as he turned he reached for his sword. He could not draw it speedily, however, for his movements were hampered by the long cape of black wool that he wore over his uniform. It was obvious that he had donned the garment as a disguise; it was the type of cloak common among moderately successful merchants, and Tédière had plainly hoped to be mistaken for one of the numerous civilians who had taken refuge in the citadel during the siege. Peter smiled at him comtemptuously.

"There's nowhere you can run. I've caught you." He flexed his wrist and the sword responded; it felt like part of his arm. "I don't rightly reckon that we'll bother with any of the usual preliminaries. Let's begin."

For a moment Tédière did not move. His sword pointed toward the floor and he stared with expressionless, unblinking eyes at Peter. Then his left hand moved inside the cape.

The New Englander saw the gesture and laughed. "You want to get rid of your cloak, do you? That's all right with me. I don't want it said that I took unfair advantage, not even of you."

A malicious glint appeared in the commandant's eyes as his left hand moved again and appeared in the open. In it he held a long, slim pistol, cocked. "You don't think I'd play at swords, do you, Staples? Not when I can rid myself and the world of you this way. It's something I should have done long ago."

Death was in the muzzle of the pistol, but Peter leaped forward regardless, slashing at Tédière with his blade. Two pistols fired, almost simultaneously, but it was a second or two before Peter quite realized that a weapon other than the commandant's had been discharged. The duelling pistol's ball whistled harmlessly over his head, and in the same instant Tédière crumpled and fell in a disordered heap at his feet.

Peter could only gape: he had not touched the man with his sword, yet Tédière was dead. Then he heard a faint sound behind him, turned and saw Jeanne. She was holding a pistol, which she flung to the floor, and before Peter could quite recover his wits, she fled.

He heard her retreating footsteps, and suddenly he pulled himself together and followed. He shouted, but she did not answer, and although he raced down the stairs she managed somehow to remain ahead of him. By the time he emerged from the tower into the open, Jeanne had disappeared.

He began to search for her, and hurried down the walk for a distance of perhaps fifty feet. He saw no sign of her, and as he began to retrace his steps he became aware of the insistent blare of a trumpet, playing the rallying call of the English army. And so, reluctantly, and for the moment only, he abandoned his hunt for the woman who had saved his life by killing Tédière.

When Peter arrived back at the parade gound, still clutching his sword in his hand, he saw several white flags fluttering from bayonets affixed to rifles. And to his right the militiamen of New England were forming in orderly rows and marching off. A moment or two passed before it was borne in on his consciousness that a truce of some sort had been struck.

TWENTY-TWO

"WE'VE beat 'em fair and we've beat 'em proper," General Waldo said emphatically, "but they'll try t' diddle us out o' victory by makin' conditions and more conditions t' peace terms. That's why Will Pepperrell wants me t' ride into the citadel and have a little talk with that governor that's sittin' in there, try' t' pretend he ain't lost Louisburg. Will says there's nobody ever cheated out o' a ha'penny yet on a barrel o' salt cod or a keg o' molasses, so I'm the one who's been given the job o' goin' in and makin' this Frenchie realize he's been beat. And seein' you had a mighty big hand in all that's happened, we kind o' agreed you'd be the best aide-de-camp there is in the army t' go with me. What do you say, Peter?"

"There's nothing I'd like better, sir." Peter was still stunned by all that had happened earlier in the day, and he could not quite realize that it was only early afternoon. He took another bite of jerked beef and nodded his head. "I'd appreciate going with you, General."

Sam Waldo grinned broadly as he scooped up a hand-ful of ground corn. "That's sort o' what we figured. Seein' that you wasn't exactly treated like an honored guest while you were in the citadel, Will and old Wolcott and me, we thought it'd be poetic justice, so t' speak, t' have you come along when I tell 'em their fortress is the property o' George II now. Soon as I finish eatin', I'll be ready t' go."

"All right, sir." Peter stood hastily and made the rounds of the cook fires that were blazing in the fields behind the citadel. His tunic was torn, his hat and sash were missing, and his boots were badly scuffed. As a member of the offical delegation he would need to look presentable, and would borrow necessary items from brother officers.

Thirty minutes later the army was lined up in a long, double row facing the citadel and Peter, more splendidly attired than ever before in his life, joined General Waldo, mounted a horse that had been specially groomed for the occasion and started off toward the fortress. A strange silence had settled down over Cape Breton Island as the little procession, headed by a sergeant on foot, carrying a white flag, neared the scarred walls of the fortress. Waldo, seemingly unconcerned and unimpressed, hummed a tune off key under his breath, and Peter had to suppress a grin. The general was one of the best educated and most widely traveled men in all of New England; he had found it convenient to pose as a simple rustic for so long that the rule had become part of him. Governor Duchambon was going to have his hands full.

French troops stood at rigid attention along the remaining portions of the north and east walls, and, as the horses picked their way across rubble, Peter saw that other companies were drawn up inside. A French colonel, mounted, waited for Pepperrell's representatives near the rock where Peter had paused in his headlong dash earlier in the day. Salutes were exchanged, the sergeant from Massachusetts Bay lowered his white flag and sat down to rest, and the colonel silently led the guests through a maze of streets inside the citadel. Soldiers stood at attention along the route, which was lined with numerous civilians, among them many women, and Peter searched the crowd eagerly for Jeanne, though ostensibly looking neither right nor left. But he saw no sign of her, and at last the colonel halted before an imposing house that seemed to be set into the fortress' sea wall.

He dismounted, still not having spoken a word, Waldo and Peter did the same, and the door of the house opened. On the threshold stood Henri Duchambon, wearing the dress uniform of his high office. The general saluted him perfunctorily. "Waldo o' New Hampshire, representin' General Pepperrell and Commodore Warren. And this here lad with me, I got an idea you already know him"

"Welcome, gentlemen." Even in defeat Henri Duchambon was gracious and self-controlled. "Captain Staples, it is a pleasure to see you once again. Come in, won't you?"

He led the way into a drawing room, General Waldo followed and Peter brought up the rear, carefully permitting the dour French colonel, who outranked him, to precede him. A buffet and a wine punch were set out on a gleaming oak table, and the display was impressive. The punch bowl was of heavy silver, as was the service, and two long, embroidered runners were of the finest linen. And the delicacies that were being offered were fit for the table of a king. There was a loaf of *pâté* filled with truffles, smoked oysters, Polish ham cut razor-thin, cold breast of partridge in claret jelly, and hot slices of beef filet simmering in chafing dishes with mushrooms and Burgundy. The food shortage caused by the siege had apparently not been felt in the governor's household.

Duchambon insisted on serving his guests personally, then took General Waldo off to an inner chamber for private conversation. The colonel, bitter in defeat, walked to the far side of the room and ostentatiously studied a painting on the wall. Peter stood with a cup of wine in his hand, faintly bewildered by the incongruity of the situation. Only a few hours previous, death had been everywhere in the citadel; now the war seemed very far away. In fact, once the terms of surrender were arranged, it was likely that the entire fight in the New World would be at an end. Pepperrell and Warren had accomplished the impossible.

Some kind of an altercation was taking place just outside the front door of the house, and the voice of a sentry was raised in protest. Before the silent colonel could investigate, however, all became quiet again, and a moment later Jacques Duphaine strolled into the drawing room. There were no signs of fatigue on his face, and it would have been difficult to guess from the spring in his walk that he had spent the better part of the day in mortal combat. He was freshly bathed and shaved, and he wore a splendid suit of oyster-gray satin nonchalantly. He crossed the room quickly to Peter, and they shook hands like two old friends. The colonel, after a perfunctory glance at the newcomer, resumed his examination of Governor Duchambon's works of art.

"My luck still rides high!" Jacques said enthusiastically. "I knew it the moment I saw you riding toward us with that potbellied little general. Peter, it's good to see you. You look fit."

"So do you." Peter wasted no time on formalities. "How is Jeanne? She saved my life this morn——"

"I know. She did you and the rest of the world a service when she rid it of Tédière. But don't flatter yourself, my friend." There was a twinkle in the highwayman's dark eyes. "Jeanne wasn't being a heroine for your sake. She had a score of her own to settle." He wandered over to the table and began to sample first the ham, then the partridge, eating with his fingers. "My congratulations to Will Pepperrell," he said casually. "This victory will make him famous throughout the world. I'm very happy to be associated with him."

Peter laughed in spite of himself, then sobered. "Jacques," he said earnestly, "you've done me more than one favor, and the least I can do is return the compliment. General Pepperrell intends to hang you within thirty minutes of the moment that he takes possession of the citadel."

"I imagined he'd feel that way, but he'll change his mind fast enough when he learns that Mercy is alive. And safe. She is, Peter. I wouldn't try to fool you on anything so important."

A long minute passed before Peter could speak. Mercy was alive! His thoughts, his plans, his hopes were dramatically revised. There was only one girl whom he truly loved or ever could love: Mercy. His feeling for Jeanne was deep and warm, but it was not all-consuming, as was his love for Mercy. He would be grateful to Jeanne always for nursing him back to health and for saving his life. But he could never marry her now that he knew Mercy was alive; the shadow of the one real love of his life would inevitably darken and eventually spoil any other marriage, even to someone as compassionate and sweet as Jeanne. He knew now that he was one of those men who was capable of loving only one woman, ever.

"You hope to trade your life for Mercy's." He could barely whisper the words.

"I wouldn't put it that way." Jacques' seeming indifference was maddening. "Let me just say that not even as patriotic and loyal a man as Pepperrell would want to execute a member of his own family." Jacques reached into an inner pocket and pulled out the creased agreement which Mercy had signed.

Peter studied it in silence as the room whirled. The signature was undoubtedly genuine and his elation at discovering that Mercy was indeed alive gave way to black despair. He understood now why Jacques had helped him to escape; he knew, too, that Mercy had sacrificed herself and her happiness for his sake. But there was nothing he could do for her in return. He wanted to smash his fist into the highwayman's complacent face, to destroy that self-satisfied smile of triumph. But a brawl would serve no useful purpose. He needed to think, to devise some way to outwit this fiendishly clever rogue, but even as he searched his mind for some way out, he knew he was beaten. Louisburg had fallen to Pepperrell and Warren, but Jacques had won the most precious prize of all.

"You can't do it," Peter said gruffly. "Even if the general should agree to pardon you, which I very much doubt, there are a dozen officers after your scalp. They know you for a spy, and they'd shoot you on sight. And they'd be hailed as heroes in Massachusetts Bay, where a reward has been posted for the man who was holding up travelers near Lynn."

Jacques seemed totally unconcerned. "I've already guessed as much and more," he declared lightly. "And so I propose that as a protection to Mercy, a special clause should be included in the terms of capitulation giving me the right to leave the citadel masked. Then I can go to Mercy and bring her back to her father unharmed."

"After you've first held her to her bargain and married her, of course!" Peter's voice was thick with helpless rage.

"Of course. I have myself to protect, too. I suggest you take up the matter with my father-in-law-to-be as soon as General Waldo has finished discussing the peace terms with him. You'll find him very willing to go along with my plan."

"Hold on a minute. Do I gather that Mercy is somewhere outside Louisburg?"

"That's right."

"Then I'm coming with you to fetch her, Jacques. For all I know you're just making up a story to save your own hide. I'll go with you to wherever Mercy is, and I'll stay with you until she's reunited with General Pepperrell. And I warn you, if you try any tricks, I'll——"

Jacques laughed happily. "We've made a bargain. Though I'd think you'd be the last, the very last who'd want to come with me when I claim my bride."

At sunrise the following morning the French regiments marched out of the citadel in full-dress uniform to the accompaniment of their garrison band. Arms were stacked, officers offered their swords to the victors and were then permitted to keep them by a gracious William Pepperrell. Governor Duchambon delivered the keys of the fortress to his conquerors, then the gentlemen of both sides retired to the great hall of the citadel for a banquet. The civilians returned to their homes in the town of Louisburg, and the New England militiamen promptly sought the acquaintance of the island's daughters.

The defeated regiments were not unhappy, for the regulars were being sent home to France under the terms which Governor Duchambon had accepted, and the provincials, almost all of them conscripts, were being released and would soon rejoin their families in Quebec and Montreal. The only people who truly seemed to mind the fall of Louisburg were the permanent residents of Cape Breton Island, who watched with long faces as the fleur-de-lis was hauled down and the banner of St. George took its place.

After a campaign marked with so much hostility on both sides it was surprising how little animosity was shown during the ceremonies that marked the shift of power from the French to the colonial English. Only one brief incident marred the early morning occasion, but tempers subsided after a brief flurry of excitement. The tension first rose when a strange, lone figure emerged from the citadel on horseback, a man who neither marched with the army nor walked with the noncombatants. He was dressed in simple, faded buckskins, but on his face he wore a silver mask that was familiar to a score of New Englanders as the identifying insignia of the highwayman known as the Gentleman. General Pepperrell had feared just such an insolent gesture on Jacques' part, and, thanks to a series of elaborate precautions, the men who would have broken the truce and fired at the scoundrel were forcibly restrained.

By prearrangement Jacques rode straight for the western end of the formation of New England troops, where Peter awaited him. But, with attention no longer diverted to the highwayman, something happened that upset Jacques' neat calculations. Eight horsemen, all of them officers of the general-in-chief's provost guard, sat their mounts directly behind Peter. And as Jacques approached they quietly surrounded him, overwhelmed him and took his weapons from him. He had the good sense not to struggle, and the feat was accomplished so smoothly that not more than a score of people on the field realized what was taking place. For the majority, the drama of French capitulation was all-absorbing.

Peter approached the cordon surrounding the prisoner and saw that Jacques was smiling insolently, seemingly undisturbed by the turn of events. "I warned you," the New Englander declared solemnly. "You underestimated him just as I thought. He agreed to let you come out of the citadel masked because he was afraid you might otherwise have sneaked away before the surrender terms became final. And he doesn't believe he's behaving dishonorably by seizing you, not after all the tricks you've pulled. The general is an outraged father before he's a gentleman, you know." He paused to let his words sink in. "If you know what's good for you, Jacques, you'll tell him everything you can about Mercy, and quickly."

The Gentleman shrugged eloquently but said nothing as he was led away. The last Peter saw of him he was laughing as though highly amused by some private joke.

The ceremonies of surrender continued, and thereafter Peter was busy supervising the embarkation of a full regiment of French troops who were to sail on the afternoon tide for Le Havre. It was late when he finished, and dusk was falling when he finally made his way to General Pepperrell's tent; in a typical gesture of courtesy the commander was not moving into more elegant quarters in the citadel itself until Governor Duchambon departed for home.

The general was dressing for the victory banquet that was to begin within an hour, but he looked up quickly when he saw his visitor. "I've already had words with him," he said, anticipating Peter's question, "but he wouldn't tell me anything. I tried for an hour, but he wouldn't respond to threats any more than he would to promises of leniency if Mercy was returned at once. So I'm following the only course left open to me, Peter. I don't believe in violence, but I've prescribed a touch of corporal punishment for Master Duphaine in the hopes it will loosen his tongue. And tomorrow morning you and I will interrogate him together. He'll talk before I'm through with him"

Peter wanted to say that he knew from personal experience that force alone could not compel a man to reveal information he was determined to keep hidden, but he did not trust himself to speak, so merely nodded and withdrew. He could think only of Mercy, and the banquet, which he otherwise would have enjoyed, proved to be so dull that he left early and returned to his own quarters. As a company commander he had a tent to himself, and he was grateful for the privacy; so much depended on the coming morning's examination of the prisoner that he could not have tolerated any more gaiety tonight from wine and victory flushed brother officers.

It was a long time before he fell asleep, and it seemed as though he had just dropped off when he felt someone standing over him, shaking him. He muttered something under his breath and would have turned over, but a familiar voice awakened him immediately. "I don't have all night, friend Peter," Jacques said.

Sitting up on his cot, Peter blinked, then stared incredulously as he saw the highwayman, cocked pistol in hand, not three feet distant. Jacques was dressed in the uniform of a first lieutenant of Maine militia, and aside from an angry red welt across his face he looked as carefree as ever. Someone else was present too, and, straining to see in the dark, Peter made out the figure of the long-departed Indian retainer, Warumba. The brave was dressed in buckskins, but on his head he wore a distinctive low-crowned, soft-brimmed hat of the kind habitually used by Maine natives hired as scouts by militia regiments.

"Get dressed," Jacques commanded in a low voice. "I'm going for Mercy, and I thought you'd like to come along."

The situation was so bewildering that Peter couldn't grasp it all at once. "How did you know where to find me?" he demanded.

"I asked a sentry, naturally. One of the few who is sober tonight."

"And how did you escape? Where did you get those clothes, and how did Warumba there——"

"You inquire too deeply into my trade secrets, friend Peter." Jacques grinned pleasantly, then poked his pistol at the sitting figure. "Are you coming or aren't you? If not, we'll be on our way. And I warn you, if you try to give an alarm, I shall be forced to kill you. I wouldn't like to take your life, but when my own is in the balance, I wouldn't have too much choice."

Peter debated swifly with himself. Unarmed, he could not cope alone with both Jacques and Warumba, and he was certain that the highwayman meant every word about protecting himself. There was no way of guessing why he had decided to take Peter with him, and this was not the time to probe. Any risk was worth seeing Mercy again, to be in a position where he might be able to help her. Peter reached silently for his shirt and breeches.

Three saddled horses were waiting outside, and the trio mounted at once and moved off; Warumba took the lead and the others rode side by side, Jacques with his pistol laid with seeming carelessness across the pommel so that it pointed directly at Peter. The sounds of singing could be heard in the distance, and there was a faraway babble of

shouts and raucous laughter. The few men who had
returned to camp were sleeping soundly, and, when the
little party reached the limits of the perimeter, no sentry
appeared to challenge them. As always, Jacques seemed
to know precisely what he was doing; certainly he could
not have chosen a more opportune moment for his escape.

Once they reached open countryside they spurred their
horses to a canter, and after a short ride they reached the
Canso Strait, where they searched the shoreline for a few
moments, then found what they were seeking, an un-
gainly but sturdy barge which Warumba guided expertly
to the Acadian side. Here the raft was hidden in a mass
of high weeds, and Jacques addressed Peter for the first
time.

"You'll feel better carrying these," he said, handing the
New Englander his sword, long rifle, and knife, which he
removed from a bulky boot-roll. "You could shoot both of
us, of course, but you won't. If you did, you'd never see
Mercy again."

Peter accepted the weapons, marveling anew at
Jacques' incredible sleight of hand. He had not even seen
the highwayman take them from his tent. There were
innumerable questions that weighed on his mind, but
Jacques and Warumba gave him no chance to ask them as
they pushed rapidly along a well-defined trail through the
forests, stopping only to rest their horses occasionally. At
these times Peter tried hard to find out where he was being
taken, but silence met all of his attempts at conversation,
and he finally gave up the effort.

Jacques gave no indication of where they were going
until early afternoon, when a tall, light-skinned Indian
suddenly materialized out of the forest and stood on the
trail awaiting them. He and Jacques exchanged a few
words, then the natural disappeared silently through the
trees. And Jacques turned at last with an explanation.

"We are," he said, "in the land of the Lukai."

Twenty minutes later they arrived at the tribe's village,

and here Jacques was greeted joyously and affectionately by dozens of natives. Peter, searching the crowds for Mercy, realized that only men were present; no squaws were in sight and, strangely, no children. The New Englander was himself the object of considerable curiosity, which he endured impatiently. Perhaps, he thought, Jacques intended to trick him after all: there was nothing to prevent these savages from doing away with him; Jacques would not then be called upon to produce Mercy alive and well and could disappear into the wilderness where not even the long arm of William Pepperrell could reach him.

But such a development was unlikely, Peter conceded to himself as he dismounted and allowed a middle-aged brave to lead his mount away. Mercy's signature on the agreement had been legitimate enough, and Jacques would not have gone to such lengths to invent this particular ruse for the purpose of saving his own neck. There certainly seemed to be no immediate danger: a serious talk of some sort was taking place between Jacques and several braves.

Apparently a feast was in preparation, for two oxen and four or five deer, all strung on poles over individual fires, were being roasted, and from several huge kettles came a faintly sweet odor that Peter recognized at once as that of an Indian favorite, dog meat. At last the tribesmen stopped speaking to Jacques, who turned to Peter with a grave, thoughtful expression on his face.

"Your siege made it impossible for me to visit this place in recent weeks, and I'd say we've arrived just in time. Moha came here only yesterday, and his wedding to Rina-hai-kodo is set for the rise of the full moon, in four days from now. That, friend Peter, is Moha." He pointed to a giant warrior, naked except for a loin cloth and smeared with paint.

Mystified and more on his guard than ever, Peter merely nodded and waited for a further explanation. It was not long in coming.

"Rina-hai-kodo is known in the world in which she was raised as Mistress Margery Mercy Pepperrell."

"This is carrying a joke too far." Peter reached for the long rifle slung over his shoulders, but Jacques' hands restrained him.

"They'll tear you to pieces if you as much as point a weapon at him!" His voice was low but urgent. "That's not the way to handle this. Moha is the son of a great chief, and he chose Mercy himself as his squaw. This situation requires a certain delicacy—"

"Delicacy be damned!" Peter could tolerate no more.

"We'll both be killed if you don't control yourself. And keep your voice down! They don't understand English, except for Warumba, who'll do as I tell him. Peter, there's only one way to prevent Mercy from marrying Moha. He's my blood brother, you understand, but I agree with you that it would be a trifle too much for the loveliest girl—and wealthiest heiress in all of the New World to become his wife. Moha must be challenged to a trial by individual combat."

"But this is the most——"

"Mercy is now a full member of the Lukai. If we don't do this their way, we'll be put to death."

"All right." Peter's eyes became hard. "I challenge him. Tell him that."

Jacques smiled lazily. "I'm sorry, but I've already reserved that right for myself." When Peter tried to protest, his voice grew a shade louder. "She is going to be my wife. It's a man's right to fight for what is his."

There was nothing left for Peter to say, and he stood in impotent silence as Jacques addressed the braves in their own tongue. His tone was strident, his manner haughty, and his words had an immediate effect on his audience. Moha approached him, and they stood only a few inches apart, staring at each other. Then, abruptly, the brave turned on his heel and stalked away.

Inside of a few minutes the village became active.

Squaws and children began to appear now, and several elders marked out a rectangular line in the open space not far from the ceremonial stakes. They defined an area approximately eight feet long and six feet wide, and several of the younger men dug a ditch, narrow but deep, to mark the boundaries. Jacques and Peter were left alone, and the highwayman removed his tunic and boots as he stood in his breeches. The soft June breeze played across his bare chest, and he grinned as though anticipating a pleasurable experience.

"If anything should happen to me," he said quietly, "I wouldn't advise you to try single-handed to rescue Mercy. I'd go back to General Pepperrell and ask him to send a full brigade of troops against the Lukai. They might kill Mercy, but that's the chance you'd have to take." Before Peter could reply he reached out, plucked the New Englander's short knife from the sheath at his belt and tested the weapons's weight and balance in the palm of his hand. "This is a better blade than mine," he said. "May I borrow it?"

At that moment Peter saw Mercy approaching, and he knew her only because she cried out an involuntary greeting. She was with a large group of Lukai maidens who were being shepherded into place on the far side of the rectangle by several older squaws armed with birch switches, and when she tried to step forward two of the women promptly lashed at her legs and forced her back.

Peter would have gone to her at once, but Jacques took hold of his arm and held him firmly. "No! Strangers are not permitted to talk to Lukai women. And there's nothing this crowd would like better than to see you neatly burned to death as a preliminary to my fight. They're in a real holiday mood."

A deep-seated sense of recklessness swept over Peter. Mercy was here, almost close enough to touch, yet he was not being permitted to go near her, and the situation was so absurd that he felt tempted to do something rash.

However, he knew that if Jacques did not survive the fight with the Lukai warrior, Mercy's future would depend upon his own ability to return to General Pepperrell with word of her plight. And it began to look as though even then he might have a difficult time extricating himself from the village; the braves, who were beginning to gather, were regarding him with open hostility and several of the younger men deliberately jostled him as they strolled past him, obviously seeking some excuse to make him a participant rather than a mere onlooker.

So Peter had to content himself with looking at Mercy. Although she certainly didn't look like herself with her hair blackened and her skin darkened, she was still the loveliest girl he had ever seen. Her eyes, warm and alive and luminous, were unlike those of any other woman, and though she was thinner, her Indian dress revealed that she had lost none of her supple and strong yet completely feminine grace.

The entire population seemed to have assembled now, and when Moha appeared the men raised their right arms as a sign of encouragement and the women shrieked their approval. Peter watched Mercy looking at the warrior, who had smeared a thick coat of grease over his body, and he saw that fear and disgust were in her eyes. In his right hand Moha carried a curved, bone-handled knife that was at least three inches longer than Jacques' blade, but the highwayman didn't seem to mind. He walked quickly to the edge of the ditch, lifted his dagger as though it were a sword in a salute to Mercy, then stepped inside the quadrangle.

Moha moved with powerful dignity into the little arena, then he and Jacques stood at opposite sides, staring at each other. No signal of any kind was given, but the Indian suddenly leaped forward, the knife in his right hand lifted high. Jacques side-stepped neatly, and Peter noticed that he held his dagger now in his left hand. Again Moha advanced, and this time the highwayman was ready for him. Meeting the savage's rush head on, Jacques coolly lashed out with his right fist, striking before Moha could slash at him with the knife. From the sound of the impact, the warrior's nose was broken. He dropped to the ground as though he had been hit by a bullet, and in almost the same instant Jacques was on top of him. Again his right fist crashed into the brave's face; then he held his short knife poised over Moha's throat.

The crowd was very still, and Jacques called out something to them in their own tongue as he jumped to his feet and stepped over the ditch. The Indians were murmuring to each other now, smiling and nodding, and Peter saw that Mercy, who had understood what Jacques had said, looked relieved. Moha continued to lie on the ground for several seconds, and his tribesmen ignored him as he arose and walked away; he turned his bleeding face from them, his shoulders sagged, and it was plain that he had lost face in the tribe, that he would need to perform some feat of particular valor at some future time to redeem himself.

Jacques handed the dagger to Peter. "Thanks for lending this to me," he said, hastily putting on his tunic. "You'll see that I didn't soil it."

"What was it you said to these people?" Peter demanded.

"Oh, I simply told them that I won't take the life of a blood brother. Naturals are simple, as you know, and something dramatic always appeals to them." Jacques caught the eye of Warumba, who hurried to him. After a brief exchange of words the Indian dashed off, and Jacques turned back to Peter. "We'll leave at once," he said crisply, "before they have a chance to change their minds and become ugly."

The old squaws no longer maintained their watch over Mercy, and she walked slowly toward the two men, who meant so much in her life. Peter wanted to take her in his arms, but he saw Jacques smiling at her, and he merely stood, trembling. She would soon be the Frenchman's wife, and it would be pointless and improper to shout his love for her. She and Jacques said something to each other in a low undertone, then she turned to Peter, and for a moment he was speechless. With a great effort he managed to become coherent.

"Thank you for what you've done for me, Mercy."

She tried to reply, but could not, and her eyes filled with tears. Peter would have reached for her, but Jacques stepped between them, smiling cynically. "Our horses are waiting," he said lightly, "and Warumba has a mare for Mercy. I suggest we leave immediately."

They mounted and set off at once, with Jacques in the lead, Mercy behind him and Peter bringing up the rear. As they neared the fringe of trees that marked the edge of the village clearing, the girl twisted around in her low Indian saddle and took a last look at the place that had been her home for so many weeks. But she avoided Peter's eyes, and when she again pressed forward her back and neck were rigid, unyielding. Peter guessed that it was a struggle for her to keep the bargain she had made with Jacques, but he knew he would be tormented for the rest of his life wondering whether she had really preferred the highwayman all along.

They rode without pause for several hours, and only when it began to grow dark did Jacques draw to a halt at the top of a small hill. They seemed to be near the coast, for the soil underfoot was sandy and almost bare of vegetation; they had emerged from the forest, and there were no trees within one hundred and fifty yards on any side. Jacques dismounted, helped Mercy to the ground and continued to hold her hand. Peter, who had been about to join them, hesitated and stood uncertainly some feet away.

Mercy tossed her head in a reminiscent gesture that made Peter's heart ache, and faced Jacques defiantly. "Why did you come for me?" she asked. "And if you think by securing some sort of temporary release for Peter from the citadel you've lived up to our bargain, I———"

Jacques laughed and there was a wistful quality in the sound. "Your father rules Louisburg now. But I helped Peter to escape some time ago, as he will testify."

She turned, bewildered and seeking corroboration, and Peter realized that she knew nothing of the tumultuous events of recent weeks. Jacques tightened his hold on her and spoke again in a strained voice. "He is far freer at this moment than am I!" Leaning toward Mercy, he cupped her chin in his hand. "I have kept my word and could demand that you marry me. But I will not. You are beautiful, lovely and sweet beyond compare, wealthy and established in this world's highest places. I am only Jacques Duphaine. The Marquis de Grémont." He spoke the words as though they were a curse, and pain, sharp and deep, was mirrored in his eyes.

He took a step forward, kissed Mercy savagely, then released her suddenly and walked to his horse. Mounting, he rode a few paces, halted and cupped his hands together. The cry of the snow owl echoed across the desolate wilderness of Acadia. Then he sat very still, as if waiting for someone or something.

Peter and Mercy watched him until it suddenly dawned on them at the same moment that they were free of all commitments, free to do and live as they pleased, free to be together. Their arms encircled each other and they kissed hungrily. At last they were at peace.

When the moved apart they saw that someone had joined Jacques. They gaped when they recognized Jeanne le Sueur, dressed in drab buckskins in place of her usual finery. The French couple turned and waved, and in the gathering twilight Peter and Mercy could barely make out the expressions on their faces. As usual Jacques was smiling mockingly, but on Jeanne's face was a haunting look, sad but courageous.

In the distant underbrush there was the distinct sound

of approaching horses' hooves, and Peter reached for his rifle, then relaxed when a single figure emerged into the open. It was Tani, astride an Indian pony. She rode straight to Jacques, and they spoke intensely for a few moments: they were too far away for the startled New Englanders to hear what was being said. Then, suddenly, Tani swung her pony into line behind Jeanne, Jacques spurred his horse, and all three disappeared into the forest without a single backward glance.

Mercy felt a surge of exhilaration at being alone with Peter. This, she knew beyond all doubt and for all time, was her man. Their marriage would be as secure and as solid as the Maine rocks on which they would build their home. Their sufferings had given them an understanding of each other that would insure the permanence of their regard and affection for each other. She would be Peter's wife as long as she lived, and that was right.

Yet, as she watched Jacques ride out of her life, a momentary sense of emptiness stole over her, and in that instant she knew that it would return fleetingly from time to time, even after she became a mother and a grandmother. No man could have been more wrong for her than Jacques, and it would have been impossible to achieve a successful marriage to him. Yet she felt a lingering regret for what had not been, for what would not and could not be. She had tasted insolence and bravado, wild courage and unmatched cunning. She had known a man who had lived by no code other than one of his own making, and she knew that in years to come she would live more joyously and would savor each experience more intensely than if the highwayman had never ridden across her path.

A cool breeze had sprung up, and Peter put his arm around her shoulders. "Your pa has been waiting for a long time, Merce," he said. "Let's go home."

POST SCRIPT

Few men ever achieved world renown more suddenly than did Lieutenant General Sir William Pepperrell and Rear Admiral Sir Peter Warren, the first conquerors of Louisburg, and few giants have subsequently been forgotten so soon. Their audacious capture of the great island fortress in 1745 won them honors almost without end: both were made baronets, both achieved high permanent military rank, both were regarded as heroes in America and in England so long as they lived, and for a quarter of a century their joint reputation was unique throughout Europe.

Their brilliant achievement was snatched from them and Louisburg was returned to France in the peace treaty which ended King George's War, and it remained for Lord Jeffrey Amherst to take the great fortress again in the final French and Indian War. He, rather than Pepperrell and Warren, is today remembered as its conqueror. In their own time, however, they became awesome figures. Sir William, the first native-born New Englander ever to be created a baronet, was the single most powerful man in the English colonies, and his happy, full life was marred only by the premature death of his son, Andrew.

Warren, who spent most of his life in London after the fall of Louisburg, was one of the most colorful persons ever to set foot on New World soil. A one-time Irish buccaneer who became "respectable," he cemented his ties with America by his marriage to Susan, daughter of the prominent James Delancy of New York. And his influence on the growing country was even greater than he himself knew it would be when, in 1734, he brought his nephew, William Johnson, over from New England to manage his estates in the Mohawk Valley.

The Pepperrell-Warren campaign was important beyond its own day, for Louisburg was a proving ground for men who achieved greater prominence during the American Revolution and in the period just preceding it. Major General Wolcott of Connecticut became governor of that colony, and his son was a signer of the Declaration of Independence, as was Dr. Matthew Thornton, Pepperrell's surgeon. Colonel John Bradstreet, later a major general, was a hero of the French and Indian War; so was Pepperrell's close friend, Samuel Waldo. David Wooster was the first major general of Connecticut troops in the Revolution, and was killed in action near Norwalk. And Colonel Richard Gridley traced and superintended the battery thrown up on Bunker Hill the night preceding one of America's most memorable engagements.

With the exception of these and other obviously real persons, such as Governors Shirley of Massachusetts Bay and Duchambon of Louisburg, all characters in this novel are the product of the author's imagination, and any similarity between them and any real people, living or dead, is purely coincidental.

I am deeply grateful for much of my source material to Usher Parsons, sole biographer of New England's only baronet, who wrote his *Life of Sir William Pepperrell* just one hundred years ago.

The reader will, I believe, be interested in the terms of capitulation demanded by Pepperrell and Warren in their joint letter to Governor Duchambon. Attention is particularly invited to provision 6.

We have before us yours of this date, together with the several articles of capitulation on which you have proposed to surrender the Citadel and other fortifications of Louisburg, with the territories adjacent under your government, to his Britannic Majesty's obedience, to be delivered up to his said Majesty's forces now besieging said place under our command: which articles we can by no means concede to. But as we are desirous to treat you in a generous manner, we do consent to allow and promise you the following articles, namely:—

1st. That if your own vessels shall be found insufficient for the transportation of your persons and proposed effects to France, we will supply such a number of other vessels as may be sufficient for that purpose, also any provisions necessary for the voyage which you cannot furnish yourselves with.

2d. That all commissioned officers belonging to the garrison, and the inhabitants of the town, may remain in their houses with their families, and enjoy the free exercise of their religion, and no person shall be suffered to misuse or molest any of them till such time as they can conveniently be transported to France.

3d. That the non-commissioned officers and soldiers shall immediately upon the surrender of the town and fortress, be put on board his Britannic Majesty's ships, till they all be transported to France.

4th. That all your sick and wounded shall be taken tender care of in the same manner as our own.

5th. That the commander-in-chief, now in garrison, shall have liberty to send off covered wagons, to be inspected only by one officer of ours, that no warlike stores may be contained therein.

6th. That if there be any persons in the Citadel garrison

which may desire shall not be seen by us, they shall be permitted to go off masked.

7th. The above we do consent to, and promise upon compliance by you with the following conditions:—

[1] That the said surrender and due performance of every part of the aforesaid premises be made and completed as soon as possible.

[2] That as security for the punctual performance of the same, one of the batteries of the Citadel, shall be delivered, together with the warlike stores thereunto belonging, into the possession of his Britannic Majesty's troops before six o'clock this evening.

[3] That his said Britannic Majesty's ships of war, now lying in the port of Louisburg, shall be permitted to enter the Citadel's harbor without any molestation, as soon after six of the clock this afternoon as the commander-in-chief of said ships shall think fit.

[4] That none of the officers, soldiers nor inhabitants in Louisburg, who are subjects of the French King, shall take up arms against his Britannic Majesty, nor any of his allies, until after the expiration of the full term of twelve months from this time.

[5] That all subjects of his Britannic Majesty, who are now prisoners with you shall be immediately delivered up to us.

In case of your non-compliance with these conditions, we decline any further treaty with you on the affair, and shall decide the matter by our arms, and are, etc.,

Your humble servants,
P. Warren,
W. Pepperrell

Don't Miss these Ace Romance Bestsellers!

_____#75157 **SAVAGE SURRENDER** $1.95
The million-copy bestseller by Natasha Peters,
author of Dangerous Obsession.

_____#29802 **GOLD MOUNTAIN** $1.95

_____#88965 **WILD VALLEY** $1.95
Two vivid and exciting novels by
Phoenix Island author, Charlotte Paul.

_____#80040 **TENDER TORMENT** $1.95
A sweeping romantic saga in the
Dangerous Obsession tradition.

Available wherever paperbacks are sold or use this coupon.

ace books,
Book Mailing Service, P.O. Box 690, Rockville Centre, N.Y. 11570

Please send me titles checked above.

I enclose $. . . . . **Add 50¢ handling fee per copy.**

Name . . . .

Address . . . .

City. . . . . State. . . . . Zip. . . . .

74a

D.E. STEVENSON
ROMANCES

"Finding a re-issued novel by D. E. Stevenson is like coming upon a Tiffany lamp in Woolworth's. It is not 'nostalgia'; it is the real thing."

—THE NEW YORK TIMES
BOOK REVIEW

ENTER THE WORLD OF D. E. STEVENSON IN THESE DELIGHTFUL ROMANTIC NOVELS:

AMBERWELL
THE BAKER'S DAUGHTER
BEL LAMINGTON
THE BLUE SAPPHIRE
CELIA'S HOUSE
THE ENCHANTED ISLE
FLETCHERS END
GERALD AND ELIZABETH
GREEN MONEY
THE HOUSE ON THE CLIFF
KATE HARDY
LISTENING VALLEY
THE MUSGRAVES
SPRING MAGIC
SUMMERHILLS
THE TALL STRANGER